HOW ABOUT THURSDAY

FRANCES COWIE

BLUE BUTTERFLY PRESS

COPYRIGHT

To Laura
May your advice always keep me on the
straight and not so narrow.

CONTENTS

HOW ABOUT THURSDAY

SPECIAL DELIVERY

Thursday. A nondescript, 'take it or leave it' kind of day. Thursday couldn't hold a candle to the emotion of Monday, the excitement of Friday, or even begin to touch that day of all days, Saturday. And yet, Ally Dobson had arrived in London on a Thursday, found a place to live the following Thursday, and secured a temp job two weeks later on yet another Thursday. Maybe her animosity toward the day was misplaced.

But that Thursday, as she alighted from a cab and stepped into a muddy puddle, splashing her skirt and stockings with drips of dirty rainwater, Ally wondered again why Thursday disliked her so much.

She glanced up at the detached Victorian house in front of her. High fencing, hung with the obligatory *Keep Out* signs and warnings about unauthorized entry, surrounded the street frontage of the renovation. She entered through a side gate, ducked under the scaffolding, and knocked on the open door. Receiving no reply, she stepped inside. The large home looked like it had been savagely attacked by an overzealous developer, and the high-pitched whine of a Skilsaw sent a shiver through her veins. In the distance, a nail gun fired and a radio pumped out 'You Don't Own Me'—the Grace version.

"Yo! What's up?" A young man sauntered toward her, a nasty hickey at the base of his neck and his dreads covered by a hard hat.

"Hi, I'm Ally. Is Jono here? I have a package for him."

His gaze drifted downward, then slowly back up again. "Ally. Pretty name." It'd been ages since a guy had looked at her like a piece of meat, and she struggled to keep her amused mouth shut.

"You know he's married, right?"

"No, I didn't know that. What a shame."

"Anyway, he's not here. But I'm the apprentice." He flashed a cocky grin. "So it's me, or me. If you play your cards right, maybe we could meet for a drink later, and I just might have a package for you. I like a bit of cougar, me."

Cougar? At twenty-three? "Really?"

"Yeah. Really."

"Jack, what are you doing? I'm waiting for a lift." The owner of the booming voice—all black tank, muscles, and tight jeans— grabbed a hard hat from the peg on the wall and plonked it on Ally's head without saying another word. Her hair flattened down around her face, and she could hardly see out from under the rim.

"Sorry, mate. Got talking to Ally here."

Black Tank still didn't look Ally's way. "Okay, well finish up and get back to work." He went to walk away but turned back. "And, miss." He looked at her now with the most beautiful hazel eyes that had ever refused to smile. "Next time you come onto one of our construction sites, grab a hat and wear it."

She tipped the hat slightly to get a better view. And what a view it was! Chiseled planes of hard muscle everywhere she looked, and shoulders that could carry a girl through an entire rock concert. On his left wrist sat a large hammer-proof watch and, just to prove he didn't take himself too seriously, a couple of multicolored woven friendship bracelets.

"So where's yours?"

He paused, his expression one of wry amusement. "My what?"

"Hard hat."

Staring at her with narrowed eyes, he rubbed his fingertips over his lips in a gesture of contemplation, any hint of amusement gone in an instant. "You're wearing it," he said finally.

"Very gallant of you."

Shaking his head, he turned to walk away.

"Excuse me," Ally called after him. "Are you the foreman?"

He didn't turn around. "No."

She pulled the package from her bag. "I'm supposed to give this to Jono."

Looking at the apprentice, Black Tank cocked his head in the direction he'd come from. The young man winked at Ally as he ambled past, pulling up his jeans in the process. "Might see you later, sugar."

Black Tank huffed out a heavy sigh and turned to look at her, his expression softening. "That boy has a Casanova complex."

"So I see."

"Jono had to leave early." He looked her in the eye as he reached for the courier bag. "I'll see he gets it."

"Thank you."

The guy went to walk away once more, still all businesslike and looking like someone had just murdered his grandmother. Ally called after him again. "Excuse me, may I have your name?"

He turned and frowned. "For what?"

"Gina, my boss at Farra."

The frown froze on his face, but oh, what a face. He was what her housemate, Jia, would call a 'bells and whistles' kind of guy. Chiseled jawline, light stubble, and full lips that could kiss away a boring Sunday. And those bells and whistles went very nicely with the rest of the package. This guy was built—and not only built— but also tall, with arms that could easily hold a girl the way she ached to be held. Still, he could stand to lose the arrogance.

"Why didn't she just use a courier?"

His question drew her attention to his voice instead of his body. "She tried. They never turned up, so she asked me to drop it off."

He paused for a moment. "Ryan."

Ally pulled out her phone and opened her contacts. "Sorry, did you say Ryan?"

As if he knew she'd heard him correctly, he didn't bother repeating himself.

"And your number?" she asked.

"You're asking me for my number?"

She glanced up. Although his lips had moved a fraction, it wasn't so much a smile; it was more of a 'cat toying with a mouse' kind of expression. "In case we have to get in touch. The last package went missing. Gina asked me to give this one to Jono and no one else."

"Yes. So you said." He grabbed his phone out of his jeans pocket and unlocked it. "How about you give me your number, and I'll forward my details. Name?"

"Ally." She rattled off her number and a few seconds later, her text alert sounded. Ryan went to walk away, but turned back, grabbed the hard hat off her head and put it on his own. He held up the package. "I'll make sure Jono gets this."

"Great. Thanks."

With a satisfied smile, Ally made her way toward the gate, only to find it locked with a padlock and chain. After plonking on another hard hat from the peg, she wandered back through the building looking for Jack—who seemed a safer bet than the stoic Ryan. But as she walked down the hallway, Ryan stepped out of a room, a question on his brow and his mouth pressed firmly shut.

"Sorry to bother you again," she said. Ryan stared at her—no smile, no warmth. Ally reminded herself that maybe his granny had just fallen off her perch and he had to attend her wake later. "Someone's locked the gate."

His yellow tape measure flicked back into its case as he

dropped his pencil into the leather tool belt slung low on his hips. "Looks like you'll be staying the night then."

Maybe he was expecting some witty response, but Ally was all out of those right now. "Would you mind asking someone to let me out?"

Ryan walked toward the entry as if expecting her to follow. When he reached the gate, he grabbed a set of keys from his tool belt and unlocked the padlock. He stepped back, leaving barely enough room for her to slip past.

"Thanks."

He reached over and removed her hard hat. "No problem, Ally." The words were softly spoken, as if he'd decided to play nice. He smiled, just a touch. "Watch your step."

"I will. Thank you."

As she relaxed in the back of the cab, Ally felt her face flush. She'd never experienced lust at first sight before, but the feeling was unmistakable—and unexpected.

"Putney High Street now?" the driver asked.

"Yes. Thanks for waiting." Opening Ryan's text, she expected to see a business card contact with his name and number, but when she glanced at the screen, there was only one word.

Click.

THE PINK COAT

James 'Ryan' Farrell picked up his phone and opened the dating app. Locating the delete option, he pressed down with a determined finger. Online dating. It wasn't for the fainthearted, but after checking out hundreds of profiles, he hadn't expected to be stood up on his first try. *Shit.* It was like being back in high school. And what pissed him off more than being stood up, was the ribbing he'd receive from his mates when they met for a beer later.

He looked around the hotel room as he slipped on his coat and scarf. The luxurious interior, with its percale sheets and well-stocked minibar, definitely deserved its five-star rating, but he couldn't wait to leave the opulent furnishings, the stuffy air pumped through state-of-the-art air conditioners, and the small, windowless bathroom.

After grabbing his messenger bag and keycard, Ryan caught the elevator to the ground floor. As he crossed the lobby, several staff members greeted him by name. While he appreciated their affability, he certainly wouldn't miss living with his life constantly on display once he'd completed the house renovation.

The morning was crisp yet sunny, and as Ryan waited for his ride, his thoughts shifted to the concept plans for Farra Corporation's latest project, the Precinct. If he had any say in it, the Precinct would be their last major development. The sheer size of the project meant having to rely on a much larger team, and in his experience, large-scale developments equaled large-scale headaches.

He stepped onto the curb and opened the door of the town car.

"Morning, Boss." His driver, Anton, was a cocky lad who knew every shortcut to London's best pubs and nightclubs. He loved to talk as much as he loved cars and had an opinion on everything. "Nice scarf. The office is it?"

"Thought I'd better make an appearance for a change."

"Coffee's in the holder."

"Thanks." Ryan clicked his seat belt into place and sipped his Americano, unable to recall the last time a project had concerned him to this degree. His mother would quote the '*All work and no play*' bullshit speech he'd heard a hundred times before, but Farra's success depended on precisely that. Hard work. After all, it was his father's playing ways that had almost destroyed the company in the first place.

He released his seat belt as Anton pulled into the curb outside the office. "I'll text if anything comes up. Otherwise, I'll see you at sunset."

"Yeah? You planning to get lucky?"

Ryan checked Anton's amused expression in the rearview mirror and grinned. "It's Thursday. I've never had any luck on a Thursday."

"I know a club where the ladies go for guys like you."

"Guys like me?"

"You know, the suave type with plenty of bills in their back pocket. Just say the word, and I'll hook you up."

"I may be over thirty, but I could still teach you a thing or two on how to pick up a woman."

"So, bit of a dry spell, is it?" Anton questioned.

"Didn't your mother ever teach you the importance of diplomacy and discretion?"

"How can I be discreet if there's nothing to be discreet about?"

Ryan chuckled. The kid was right; it had been months since he'd had anything that even vaguely resembled a date. "I'll see you at six. And stop calling me Boss."

"Right you are, Boss." Ryan shot him a dirty look. "Well, you still call me kid."

"But not to your face. See you tonight."

When he stepped into the elevator, he was still smiling. Anton may have a motor mouth, but he never failed to brighten Ryan's day. Several people filed in after him, offering mumbled greetings to one another. Just as the doors were about to close, Courier Girl dashed across the foyer and squeezed inside. With a pink coat draped over one arm and her eyes hidden behind a pair of oversized sunglasses, she stared intently at the floor.

She wore a pencil skirt, heels, and a silk blouse with impossibly small buttons fastened all the way down her spine. He smiled to himself. When was the last time he'd dealt with the buttons of a silk blouse? Months ago. Many months.

The elevator stopped on the third floor, and Ally stepped off into the lobby. The door whooshed shut behind her. She hadn't noticed him. But he'd noticed her, just like the first time they met.

Two floors up, Ryan walked into his office and paused at his PA's desk. "Morning, Tim. What's on the agenda for today?"

Tim's fingers flew over his keyboard. "I'll print out a list. It's pretty full, and Gina wants to see you in her office."

"Shouldn't it be the other way around?"

"Yes, but when the Secretary of State requests an audience..."

"I go without complaint."

Gina, their head of admin, had worked for Farra for twenty years. She knew more about the business than almost anyone on the team.

Ryan pushed through the third-floor stairwell door just as Ally, in her stylish pink coat, walked out of Gina's office. He stood for a moment and watched her enter the elevator. Searching for something in her bag, she didn't look up before the doors closed.

He rapped on the glass partition before entering. "Good morning, Gina. Who was that girl?"

Her eyes narrowed as she looked up at him. "A temp. In London on her 'overseas experience' as she calls it. She comes in three days a week. Her name's Alta Dobson, although she prefers Ally."

Remembering names wasn't one of Ryan's strengths, but he took a mental note of Alta—an unusual name. "How's she getting on?"

"Fine." Gina chuckled. "Once you get used to her antipodean version of the English language. But Patrick should be back soon, all going well with the baby."

Gina's antipodean comment intrigued Ryan. When they talked at the building site, he thought Ally may have been South African. He'd always had a soft spot for girls from 'down under.' Kiwi or Aussie, he wasn't fussed either way, but he'd learned early on—from a rather unfortunate personal experience—that the words *screw*, *crew*, and *boss* definitely didn't go together.

"Anyway, you wanted to see me?"

She picked up a folder and handed it to him. "We've found that file you were looking for. At least, Ally did, and I need to talk to you about my leave."

"Don't tell me you've finally decided to go on that cruise?"

"Only because you and the hubby have pushed me into it."

3

MR. CLICK

The steady stream of people in and out of Munro's Bar and Grill in Putney never seemed to diminish. Ally was used to packed bars, but this was ridiculous. She hesitated just inside the door before pushing her way through the bottleneck toward the bar.

Drink in hand, she searched for her housemate, Jia. With her eclectic style of bright-on-bright colors and a mixture of patterns and fabrics, Jia always stood out, even in Munro's. Tonight, her faux fur jacket moved like a multicolored lion's mane, and her thigh-high suede boots—covered in studs and laces—would have looked right at home in a strip joint. By day, Jia Choi was a violin player of the child-prodigy variety, belonged to a prestigious symphony orchestra and attended the same college as Ally. By night, her alter ego bubbled to the surface.

"Hey, you made it." Jia jumped out of the booth and hugged Ally around the waist. At five foot nothing and a half, she barely made it to Ally's shoulder. She motioned to Ally's drink. "What are you drinking?"

"Lime and soda. I'm holding on tight to my inhibitions tonight."

"How come? Rough day?"

"Just the usual." Ally slid into the booth and leaned forward. "Hey, what does it mean when a guy sends you a text that just says 'Click'?"

"What?" Jia said. "You're joking, right?"

"No." Ally frowned at her, puzzled. She honestly had no idea what the word meant. Maybe his predictive text had run amok. "Click what?"

"Click. You know, you *click*," Jia replied. "He's interested. Wants to get down and dirty between a set of linen sheets."

"What? No way!"

"She's right." Jia's cousin, Jade, joined the conversation. "What's he like, this Mr. Click?"

Ally swirled the ice in her drink with the straw. "Sullen."

"Sounds mysterious," Jia replied. "Where did you meet?"

"On a construction site last week. I had to deliver a package, and he appeared out of the shadows, dressed in a leather tool belt and flaunting an attitude."

"You can't be serious." Jade shook her head. "You dished out your number to some construction worker you'd just met, and you're only telling us now?"

"It was purely for business purposes."

"Really?" Jade smiled and cocked a brow. "Maybe you need to take a night class in street smarts 101."

"No, I don't. It's just, well he didn't seem at all interested. In fact, he was rather prickly."

"I love a good 'lust at first sight' story," Jade continued. "Especially a smoldering one. You gonna text him back?"

"Of course not. I don't even know the guy."

"Text him," Jia said. "See if he wants to meet for a drink."

"What? No way!"

"What's his rating?" Jade asked.

Ally thought for a moment. Ryan was easily a nine looks-wise, but she'd deduct a point or two for his demeanor. "Seven point five, moving to an eight or maybe a nine when he bothered to crack a smile."

"Dark? Ginger?" Jade took another sip of her beer. "Twenties, thirties?"

"Possibly early thirties," Ally replied. "Light brown hair streaked with blond."

"The Aussie surfer type," Jia jumped in. "I like him already. Are we talking the Thor guy and his brother?"

"No, more like—"

"That guy who played Tarzan?" Jade asked.

"Not really. I'm not sure how to describe him."

Jade cocked a brow and smiled. "If he's a construction worker, he must be built."

Jia moved in closer and whispered, "Just because a guy's built, doesn't mean he's good in bed, does it?" They both turned to Jade.

"Why are you looking at me?" Jade flashed a grin. "But I did go out with a ripped guy once. He'd taken so many steroids, he couldn't keep it up."

"Stop it," Ally said with a grin. "I'm not going to date the guy. I was simply window-shopping with no money in my wallet."

Ally glanced around the room. Punters stood two-deep at the bar, waiting to be served—some lost in conversation with their friends, others glued to the screen of their phones. Jia continued talking, something about a guy she'd met for a coffee recently.

Ally missed the detail, because Ally's attention was on the guy *she'd* met recently. The guy standing at the bar looking at her. The usual smile of recognition didn't follow, but his gaze lingered a little longer than one would consider appropriate for strangers. With his hair tousled and gelled, he looked different, but there was no mistaking those eyes. She muttered a series of 'shits' and added an F-bomb under her breath.

Jade followed her line of sight. "Is that him? The tall guy with the bulging biceps and skinny jeans?"

"I think so. Maybe he lives around here."

Jade lifted herself slightly to get a better view. "Very nice. If you're not interested, I'm keen for a click."

"Who are you looking at?" Jia craned her neck as well. "The hottie in the black jacket?"

There were at least five guys in black jackets around the bar, and Ally knew Jia's idea of hot didn't match her own. "That's the one. Anyway, enough about me." She turned her attention to Jia. "Tell us more about this guy. How did the date go?"

"Let's just say, we both swiped right and ended up in a place called Left of Ideal."

Ally laughed as she glanced toward the bar. Mr. Click had turned away.

"Call him over," Jade said.

"No way," Ally replied. "That would be weird."

"Look, you're in London on a big adventure. It's time you got a little slutty. And besides, guys hate mixed messages. If you want to purchase the goods, you have to enter the auction."

"I'm not entering any auction. I don't have the emotional funds or the energy to lift my paddle."

Jia sighed. "I figure if you have a connection with someone, the universe will conspire to bring you together."

Ally didn't share Jia's sentiment, but she loved her black-and-white assessment of the world. "Or not."

As Jia continued to relay her disastrous dating story about the conversationally challenged guy she'd met on Tinder, both Ally and Jade struggled to keep a straight face. Jia was one of those people who was funny without even realizing it.

Every so often, Ally would glance Mr. Click's way. Once, he stared back for a second then looked away. Was he shy like Jia's Tinder guy? Or perhaps he was the moody type. Ally knew to steer clear of temperamental men, but for the first time since breaking up with Angus, she couldn't deny the attraction.

As she slipped out of the booth to use the restroom, Ally

wondered if he had a girlfriend. The more she thought about it, the more the idea of a no-strings 'Click' appealed.

But by the time she returned to the booth, Ryan the construction worker had vanished.

4

BOUNDARIES

Ally Dobson met Angus Chapman at school the year she turned fifteen. She was new in town, and Angus was athletic, charming, and more handsome than any other guy she'd ever met. It had taken a while to warm to him, but by the night of her seventeenth birthday, she knew he was the one.

Now, six years later, she understood life didn't always fall into the tidy scenarios we planned for ourselves. Their parting had been less than amicable, and while time hadn't healed the hurt, it had smoothed over the wound just a little, to the extent where they now emailed each other and even talked occasionally.

However, when Ally first found out about Angus's impending visit to the UK, negative energy had once again coiled in her gut. When he emailed several days later with a plea to meet him at the airport, Ally realized that no matter how much she told herself she'd moved on, saying no to the man she'd invested years of her life in was not so easy.

From East Putney Underground Station, she caught the train via Paddington to Heathrow's Terminal Three, arriving an hour early. Sipping a cup of strong coffee as she flicked through the latest issue of *Hello*, Ally tried to smother her nerves with a slice of coconut cake covered in thick pink frosting. By the time his flight landed, she'd not only eaten the cake, but had also bitten her thumbnail down to the quick, finished another cup of coffee, and had made two trips to the restroom. When Angus finally walked through the Arrivals door, she wanted to turn on her heal and run.

"Hi." Angus stood back to look at her. "You look amazing." He dipped down to kiss her mouth. Trembling slightly, she turned away, and his kiss brushed her cheek. He pulled back. "Don't I get a kiss?"

"Friends have boundaries, remember?"

He frowned. "Yeah, sorry. I'm just... It's so good to see you."

Ally ushered Angus toward the exit without reply. She'd only been to Heathrow once before, the day she arrived in London three months ago, but Jia had given her directions, and like everything Jia did, they were detailed down to the square inch. And if she did get lost, she now had the Citymapper app on her phone.

She'd expected heart palpitations and tummy flutters when she first saw him—the 'Angus Effect' as she'd once called it. One look at his smile and all doubts and fears had typically disappeared. But as they left the terminal, the Angus Effect had still failed to fire. There were no flurries of butterflies or weak knees. Not even that inward smile of contentment he used to inspire. Ally finally understood the meaning of freedom—detachment even. Not the type of freedom one might crave, but the type that grips you by the throat with a hefty dose of reality, leaving you with no option but to embrace it.

"Where are you staying?"

"I hoped you'd let me stay with you for a few days."

Ally stopped mid-stride. "You didn't say anything about that in your email."

"My plans fell through at the last minute."

"Angus!"

"Come on, baby. You won't even notice I'm there."

She pushed through the crowd. "Two or three days, no more. I'll go stay with Liz and AJ."

"Don't you have a sofa?"

"Not one large enough for you."

"It will do. I can sleep anywhere."

Never had a truer word been spoken. Apparently, Angus had slept all over the place.

Ally had wondered how long it would take Angus to break the 'stay on the sofa' rule. To give him credit, he lasted until after midnight. When he entered her room a touch before one, he sat on the edge of her bed and said nothing.

"You okay?" She felt obliged to ask as she switched on the bedside lamp. Sure, he'd hurt her badly, but she hadn't stopped caring.

"I can't sleep." Angus ran his hands through his hair and across the back of his neck. "I guess I'm overtired."

"Jet lag will do that."

"It's not only that. Seeing you again, it's made me realize what a dick I've been."

Ally hadn't often seen this side of Angus. The humble side. She lay on her back, studying the cracks in the plaster ceiling and said nothing. She'd only lived here for a short time, but she already knew every crack by heart.

Angus reached for her hand. She'd once loved resting her hands in his—loved how he squeezed with gentle pressure when he wanted to let her know he cared, and how he'd played with the tips of her fingernails when deep in thought. "Come with me to France."

She pulled her hand away. "Please, don't do this."

He lay down, resting his head on her spare pillow. "Some days, I can't imagine my life without you. I still need you, Ally." He turned to face her. She didn't meet his gaze, but the emotion constricting his throat was unmistakable.

In all the time they'd been together, Ally had only ever seen him cry once, and that was under similar circumstances. He'd arrived on her doorstep less than twelve hours before her flight left for London, begging her to reconsider. At that point in their splintered relationship, she hadn't yet had time to experience the kind of closure distance brings. It was all she could do to get on that plane the next day. If it hadn't been for her sister, Liz leading the way, she'd still be in New Zealand.

This time, the tears of Angus Chapman had an altogether different effect. Ally still felt compassion for him, but now, her sense of survival was stronger. She grabbed a box of tissues from her nightstand and handed them to him. "Here." She waited as he wiped his eyes and blew his nose. "It's going to be okay."

"I'm sorry," he said. "Shit, look at me. I didn't want to do this."

"You'd better go back to the living room and get some sleep."

"Let me sleep here. Please, baby."

***

While Angus slept off his jet lag, spread-eagled across her bed, Ally ate breakfast alone, her mind focused on their conversation from the night before. And as she smothered honey on a second slice of toast, she wondered why he'd suggested she move to France, as if her world still revolved around him.

While walking to the bus stop in the brisk morning air, Ally still couldn't get Angus off her mind. And as she caught the bus and sat through the twenty minute ride, she questioned her character judging ability. How did she get it so wrong?

Stepping off the bus outside campus, she fully intended to go to class, but instead found herself in the library, skimming over a textbook while her mind refused to shut up.

Around midday, she bought a sandwich from a street vendor

and strolled to a nearby park, where she sat on a bench next to a woman with a Hungarian vizsla that looked identical to their family dog, Leka. Ally longed to pat it, to strike up a conversation with the woman, but the vizsla's owner wasn't in the mood for chatting with a stranger.

All around her, people hurried past. Lovers holding hands, children in high-vis vests on a school outing, and office workers showing life's struggles in the slopes of their mouths and shoulders. It seemed everyone had a story—somewhere to go. Rising from the seat, she straightened her back and took a deep breath. *Get a grip.*

It was after five when she walked through the door of her tiny apartment to the sound of the shower running. She dropped her bag on the sideboard, sat at the dining table for two and waited. Her thoughts turned to the many times she'd showered with Angus—when they'd laugh and joke and wash each other's hair. Happy times. Sad memories.

But Angus Chapman, the guy she'd thought was too good to be true, had turned out to be exactly that. All charm and smiles wrapped in a thin layer of cheat's paper, so transparent, yet she'd failed to see through it.

She looked up to see Angus standing in the doorway, the clichéd white towel slung low on his hips barely covering what was underneath. They'd called him The Body in high school—all six foot five, two hundred and fifty pounds of him. He used to shrug it off. Now, Ally realized how different his public and private personas were.

"Hey, baby." He smiled. "How was your day?"

Ally cringed at his use of the endearment. "Good."

"What happened to you last night? When I woke around three, you were gone."

"I took the sofa."

He opened the fridge and poured a drink, making himself at home. Her 'sofa' comment hadn't even registered. "One of the other players has a spare room," he said. "I'm gonna take a look, and then we're heading to the pub."

He sat at the table and slid his hand toward her, his palm upward in an invitation to touch. She looked at his bare chest—the rings in both nipples gleaming in the light from the window—and kept her hands in her lap. Safe. Non-committal.

"You okay?" Angus frowned when she failed to answer. "Come out with us tonight. It'll be fun."

"Sorry, I'm meeting friends."

"So you've made friends?"

Not many. "A few."

"Boyfriends?"

She stared at him and released a heavy sigh. Once, she'd told him all her secrets, her desires, but with everything that had happened lately, she'd learned to hold her words—her business—close to her chest.

"Sorry. I forgot," he said. "Boundaries."

5

SULTRY UNDERTONES

The band at Munro's didn't live up to the hype of their social media posts, and Ryan was pleased when they took a break. He couldn't remember the last time he'd jammed with his friends, but they were still better than the guys now walking off the makeshift stage. He missed playing in a band. Catching the bartender's attention, he squeezed in beside Ally, who stood waiting at the bar. "So, we meet again."

Ally looked his way. "Mr. Click. I didn't think you'd recognize me without the hard hat."

Ryan smiled at her little dig. He had to stop himself from openly staring. With her sleek dark hair, pale skin, and deep blue eyes, she was beautiful to look at—even more so than he remembered. "A nickname already? I'm impressed. May I buy you a drink?"

"Um, I should really get my own."

He loved the sound of her voice. The deep tenor and carefully executed pronunciation of her words as if she didn't quite know whether it was okay to let her accent out. He wondered how that voice, with its sultry undertones, would sound wrapped around the lyrics of a song. "Why's that? It's only a drink."

"Okay, thank you." Ally leaned in a little closer so Ryan could hear. "A single shot of Pimm's, hold the mint."

"That's what my granny drinks."

"I hear it's an English tradition." She flashed a shy smile. "Mr. Pimm was a farmer's son from Kent, wasn't he?"

"I'll have to remember that if it ever comes up in a pub quiz."

"I love pub quizzes."

This didn't surprise Ryan. She looked like the competitive type. "I hate them with a passion."

"See. I knew we'd have nothing in common."

"So you've given it some thought?"

Her smile playful, Ally looked him straight in the eye, pausing for effect. "Only for a split second."

This girl knew how to flirt, and for the third time in as many weeks, Ryan felt the stir of interest. He leaned in again, struggling to make himself heard over the noise of the dimly lit bar. "I'm flattered. It's not every day a beautiful woman gives me a split second of her time."

Ally stepped back, brushing against the girl next to her, and Ryan reached out a steadying hand. He smiled at the flush of her cheeks and was about to say more when the bartender stole his thunder by filling their order. Still, her body language suggested she felt slightly on edge, which was exactly his intention. He wanted her to wonder, to imagine. For her interest to be piqued. He wanted a fling, not a girlfriend, and by the time they parted ways, she'd be long gone from Farra. Still, how would she react if she found out who he was? But Ally didn't need those details right now.

He motioned toward a spare booth. "Would you like to grab a seat?"

"Actually, a friend's just texted me." She checked her watch. "He'll be here any minute."

She removed her coat before sliding onto a bar stool, the tight-fitting dress underneath showcasing her gentle curves. They talked for a while, mainly about the renovation in Battersea.

"I didn't expect to see you here again," she said. "Do you live nearby?"

"Not anymore, but I did live in Putney for a while. Munro's has always been one of my favorite haunts, especially when I'm working in the area." He sipped his beer. "What about you?"

"I share an apartment not far from here."

The way she spoke intrigued him. Not only her accent, but her tone. "So what's that accent? Are you Australian?"

"Same hemisphere. I'm a Kiwi. And it's not me who has an accent; it's you."

"Me?" Ryan chuckled. A beautiful girl with an attitude. Perfect. "How long have you been in London?"

"A few months."

Her relaxed expression quickly disappeared as she looked toward the door. Ryan followed her line of sight to a group entering the bar. The four men looked like they belonged in a rugby scrum, with crooked noses to match. He knew the type, loud-looking guys with even louder mouths. Ally stood before he had the chance to register her movement.

"Sorry, I have to go." She drained her glass in one gulp, and with a smile, grabbed her coat and bag. "Thanks for the drink. It was nice seeing you again."

Ryan stood and watched her walk away, staring as one of the men, a show-pony type with a flashy smile, introduced Ally to his friends. Roughly six four and with thighs that could probably crush boulders, he had to be over two hundred and fifty pounds. But there was something about their interaction that didn't quite gel, and as the guy ushered Ally into a booth like a great hulking bodyguard, Ryan joined his friends at another table.

He cast a brief look as the scene unfolded. She never took her eyes off the men, and within an hour, Ally and her male companions had left.

6

MEET ME

Studio Hudson, a boutique gym directly across the street from Farra, had been a subsidiary of the company for over two years after Farra purchased it to help implement their wellness program. All employees received free membership as part of their employment package, and even Ryan used the facility several times a week. But he hadn't expected to see Ally there.

He spotted her sprinting on the treadmill across the room as soon as he walked in. He hadn't seen her since that night in Munro's but had thought about her more often than he should, wondering if she and the show-pony were an item. She wore a bra top in sherbet green and dark gray gym pants. The outfit highlighted her bare midriff and pale skin, and Ryan had to force himself to look away.

"Hey." Dave, the gym manager, slapped Ryan on the back. "What do you think you're doing?"

Grabbing the only available rowing machine, Ryan glanced at him and smiled.

"You know her?" Dave asked.

"We met a few weeks ago. She dropped something off to the Battersea site."

Dave chuckled and shook his head. "You'd better get started. You can't stand around checking out the clientele all morning. It'll give the place a bad name."

"Thanks for the encouragement. You're all heart."

As he watched Ally slow her pace, her face flushed and gleaming with sweat, Ryan took out his frustration on the machine. She grabbed her water bottle and took a swig, wiped her neck with a small baby-blue towel, and headed to the lockers without once looking his way. Ryan kept a steady pace, mulling over his current dry spell as he rowed to the edge of nowhere and back.

After an hour of half-hearted effort, Ryan crossed the street to Farra's temporary headquarters and took the elevator to the fifth floor. He entered the small bathroom attached to his office, where he showered and changed for the business day ahead. Suits weren't really his thing, but making a good impression went with the job, and if a suit and tie commanded more respect than a hard hat and tool belt, why buck the trend? No matter how much he initially disliked the situation he'd found himself in, he'd learned to play the business game. There had been no other choice.

"Morning, Boss." Tim breezed through the door of Ryan's office.

"Morning. What's on the agenda today?"

Tim flipped open his MacBook with the usual flourish. "You have meetings at ten, two, and four thirty. The design team's emailed the concepts for the Precinct's apartments, and the latest interest rate forecasts have come through from the bank."

"Okay, thanks. I'll take a look."

"Oh, and Britt called. She thinks you must have dropped your phone in the loo again. You haven't been answering her texts."

"My phone's as dry as a bone. If she calls again, tell her I'm unavailable for the next few days. I've already called her three times this week." Tim turned to walk away. The guy was a good PA but loved drama and gossip, and some days, he struggled to handle the pace. Ryan had high expectations of his staff, often to his detriment. "And, Tim?"

"Yes."

"Don't engage her in small talk. You know what she's like."

"Would I do that?"

Ryan chuckled as Tim closed the door behind him. He sat at his desk, pulled his phone from his pocket and unlocked it, hesitating as he searched for the right words. He decided to keep it brief and to the point.

Ryan: We keep bumping into each other. Maybe we should grab another drink sometime?
Ally: Who is this?
Ryan: Seriously? You've already deleted my number?
Ally: Just kidding. Mr. Click. Is this something to do with the package?

Ryan chuckled at her double entendre. Ally had seemed a little on the timid side—a refreshing change—but perhaps she had a spark to her after all.

Ryan: You could say that.
Ally: You'll have to talk to Gina at Farra. Do you want her number?
Ryan: Meet me. No strings, no stories, no expectations.
Ally: Excuse me?
Ryan: How about Thursday?

He rocked back in his chair, waiting for a reply that didn't come. Maybe he'd misjudged her interest—the twisting of her hair underneath the hard hat, the lingering looks at the bar, and the brief conversation they'd shared at Munro's before she'd hightailed it away from him like Cinderella at midnight. Still, he only wanted a fling, and if she wasn't interested, fine.

7

NO EXPECTATIONS

Ally slipped her phone into her purse and grinned. After spending time with Angus over the past few days, she was more than ready to smile at a text from another man. She'd never once thought starting over would be easy. Starting over was tough. But after months of being single, she looked forward to a new chapter.

As agreed, Angus had left after two days, but it seemed every time Ally picked up her phone, he'd blown it up with yet another text. And despite her efforts to do otherwise, she was struggling to disconnect. After all, he'd been a part of her life for a long time, and they'd shared many firsts. Maybe too many.

But Mr. Click wasn't the sort of man she'd intended to break the drought with. Not only was his age a factor, but his standoffish nature also raised a flag. The flag wasn't necessarily red, but it certainly wasn't green either. She decided to put aside the 'How about Thursday?' text for a few days. If they happened to bump into each other on Thursday, maybe he could buy her a drink. If not, she'd happily spend the evening with Jia and Jade.

However, the following Thursday, as Ally stepped onto the crowded street outside Munro's, she felt disappointed Mr. Click hadn't made an appearance at the bar. She walked toward St.

Mary's, glancing up at the blue face of the clock as it struck seven. Someone called out, "Ally," but she ignored it. She hardly knew anyone in London so it couldn't be her name floating above the noise of the evening. The male voice called again. This time she turned back, scanning the crowd. Her gaze met Ryan's, and as he strolled toward her, a flicker of excitement surfaced.

"Mr. Click."

"Are you heading home?"

"Not yet." Her gaze darted around as she slipped her hands into her pockets. "I was in Munro's, but I needed some fresh air. It's so hot in there."

"I'm about to grab a bite to eat. Would you care to join me?"

Ally considered his invitation. She'd rather spend time with Mr. Click than meet Angus, but as she studied his expression, she felt a little apprehensive. "I'm not sure."

"Is everything okay?"

She hesitated. They'd only met a few weeks ago. For a casual acquaintance, the question seemed rather personal and misplaced. "Fine. Why?"

"There's a troubled line across your forehead."

"Oh? I must be thinking too hard." She'd noticed the same line every time she caught sight of herself in a mirror or window. It seemed her default look of late. "I'm meeting someone in an hour, but I'd love something non alcoholic. I feel a tiny bit tipsy now that I'm in the fresh air."

He gave her an amused smile. "Come on."

They settled into a fast-paced stride, neither of them speaking as Ryan led the way. She'd considered his 'Meet me' text many times over the past few days, wondering what it would be like to sleep with someone other than Angus. The thought both excited and scared her. Jade had made a valid point one evening when she said sex could be stressful. It was almost surreal, imagining how another man made love. How he'd react to her inexperience, her body—her inhibitions.

Ryan ushered her down a side street and into a small café. "This place is one of my favorites."

She looked around, taking in the concrete walls, blonde wood tables and low back chairs, and inhaled the rich aroma of coffee, suddenly feeling hungry.

They sat at a quiet spot by the window. Ryan pushed aside the unlit candle in the middle of the table and passed her the brown clipboard holding the menu. "They do great food. Keen for a couple of tasting plates? They only take a few minutes to arrive."

He caught her gaze with those hazel eyes, and for a moment, she could only stare. Handsome men were a dime a dozen in London, and Ally liked to look, but Ryan the construction worker was so much more than handsome. With an almost flawless complexion and neatly trimmed designer stubble, he possessed a beauty she couldn't categorize.

"Okay. Sounds good." She placed the menu back behind the candlestick and looked at him shyly. "You order."

When the server arrived a few seconds later, Ally watched Ryan's interaction with the young man. Her father always said you could tell a lot about a person by the way they treated wait staff. Ryan was pleasant, but not overly friendly. He had a commanding presence. Not so much 'I don't give a damn' but more a quiet confidence that intrigued her.

"So, you're not with your bodyguard tonight?" Ryan said as the server left.

"Bodyguard?"

"The guy from Munro's last week."

Ally pressed her index finger to her lips and smiled. "I thought you didn't want to share stories."

"I don't. But if there's competition, just say the word, and I'll step back."

"You haven't stepped forward yet."

He looked at her without an ounce of humor. "That's why we're here, isn't it? To take that step?"

He smiled, and she immediately raised his hotness rating to a nine point five. "So, if we're not exchanging stories, what shall we talk about?"

Ryan leaned back in his chair. "What are your thoughts on the sustainability of inner-city living?"

Ally burst out laughing. "What? Is that your edgy ice-breaker question of the day?"

"What can I say? I'm passionate about my craft." Ryan shot her another dimpled smile.

She attempted to pull her thoughts out of the erotic space they'd slipped into, but her next words tumbled out before she had a chance to edit them. "I like passionate men." *Oops.* That second wine back at Munro's had been a mistake.

Clearing his throat, Ryan rubbed his fingertips back and forth across his chin. She liked how his stubble was so much darker than his crowning glory. It made him look even sexier. "So, getting back to my question…"

"What was it again?"

Ryan didn't bother covering his amusement as he shook his head.

"Oh, that's right; something about sustainability." She thought for a moment. "In my humble opinion, it's great when developers utilize otherwise empty urban spaces to build sustainable communities. I like the concept of mixed use—blending residential, outdoor living spaces, specialty stores, and offices, all within the same complex. I'm not a fan of unchecked urban sprawl. There's something almost soulless about it, don't you think?"

He raised a brow. "I'm impressed. The Kiwi girl knows her stuff."

Ally finished her mouthful of water with a quick gulp. "What? You think just because I'm from the bottom of the world, I won't have an opinion?" Her words held a hint of tease. "We do have schools and universities in New Zealand you know. We're educated people, *and* good rugby players."

"Don't I know it. The All Blacks are arguably the best rugby team in the world right now. And I didn't think for one minute you were uneducated." Ryan grinned. "I like your answer. I once asked another woman that question on a date. She looked at me like I was insane."

"Okay. I'll let you off. But just this once."

"And how do you like working at Farra?"

"It's okay. I'm not sure how much longer I'll be there. I'm temping while some guy takes parental leave." Ally momentarily forgot his 'no stories' rule. "I'm studying part-time as well."

As the server placed two drinks and four plates in front of them, Ryan nodded his response but didn't ask what she was studying. He served several small portions onto her plate, and Ally hummed a grateful 'yum' as she savored a baby meatball covered in dukkah.

She reached for another. "Do you know the big boss at Farra?"

Ryan leaned forward. He held her gaze. "Yeah, I know him."

"What's he like? I've never met him."

He finished a mouthful of food and took a sip of his beer. Ally couldn't read his expression but registered the hesitation.

"Arrogant, cocky…and private," he said finally.

"A couple of the women in my office have plenty to say about him."

He cut a slice of bruschetta in half and offered her a piece. "Like what?"

Ally smiled as she recalled. "Well, his suits and shoes are a great topic of conversation. My housemate, Jia, would use the term 'oh so expensive,' and apparently, he's tall and well built."

He chuckled.

Ally checked her watch. "Oops, look at the time. I've been talking way too much." She fished in her bag for her phone. "Sorry to be rude, but I need to check my messages."

"Go ahead." Ryan paused as she looked down at the screen. "You obviously didn't receive my last text."

"The 'How about Thursday?' one?"

"And here's me thinking it's still floating around in cyberspace."

Grinning, Ally dropped her phone back into her bag and reached for another slice of bruschetta. "I have to go shortly. Is that what you want to talk to me about? Thursdays?"

"Who's the bodyguard?"

"Are we breaking the rules already?"

Drumming his fingers lightly on the table, he stared at her but said nothing.

"His name's Angus Chapman, a friend from home. He's over here playing rugby."

"Are you together?"

"No."

Ryan kept his gaze squarely on her as she popped a piece of bruschetta in her mouth and chewed.

"Were you ever?"

She leaned on the table and placed her index finger to her lips as she silently stared back. *No stories.*

He finally spoke. "One day a week, no strings, no expectations."

His bluntness took her by surprise, and in the seconds of hesitation that followed, she felt her face burn with an unexpected blush. "Like an orchestrated hookup?"

"For want of a better word."

Ally paused as the server cleared their plates. She picked up her glass with unsteady hands and took a sip. She'd never flirted with anyone apart from Angus, and it felt good—risqué. "What makes you think I'd be interested?"

"What makes you pretend you're not?"

"So confident. Or, if I were to be unkind, arrogantly cocky."

He cleared his throat, leaned closer. "Don't you ever fantasize about being picked up in a bar by a stranger who can't wait to take you to bed?" he whispered.

She narrowed her eyes and felt her face flush even more. *Who was this guy?*

"Or is it something that happens to you all the time?" he continued.

The words *out of your league* screamed in her head. "I'm not what you're looking for."

"Isn't that my decision to make?"

"Of course. But that decision directly affects me, so surely I have some say."

"You have all the say. But if you didn't wonder about me, you wouldn't be here." Ryan gave her a few moments to weigh up the pros and cons. "Look. I lead a busy life, and frankly, I find the whole dating scene a bore. I'd rather express my needs in a way that suits us both. I'm not after a relationship, but maybe we could have a little fun together without getting hung up on blending our worlds."

"So you think it might be fun?"

"There's only one way to find out. What do we have to lose?"

"My dignity."

"That won't happen. You look like the kind of girl who knows what she wants."

Did she? "It's not something I'd usually do."

Ryan's expression held a question. "No?"

Ally had never experienced the chase, but she liked it. Did Ryan like it too—the pursuit of a hesitant girl?

"Think it over," Ryan continued as he reached into his pocket for his wallet. "I'll text you the details next week."

"So, strictly casual?"

"No stories, last names, or questions asked."

"No dinners, movies, or visits to meet the family?" she asked.

"I don't want anyone to know, so this stays between us and no one else."

She gave a nervous giggle. "You're repeating yourself."

He frowned.

"Between us and no one else is a redundancy."

He had a way of smiling that wasn't quite a smile. His eyes gave him away first, followed by the dimple in his left cheek, but there was never a full-on grin or a show of teeth. It was more of an amused glance. "That smart mouth of yours is going to get you into trouble one day."

"I can hardly wait." Ally gazed up at him through her lashes, mentally admonishing herself. She'd never realized she could be such a flirt. "So, why Thursday? That's a whole week away."

"It gives you time to consider, or reconsider, as the case may be. And it's one of my few free days."

"What if we meet and I change my mind?"

"There's no pressure."

"It sounds so…dispassionate."

His only answer was an amused huff. The guy obviously rated himself as a lover, but according to her girlfriends, most men did. "Where would we meet? Do you have a place?"

"I'll sort something out." Ryan signaled for the bill. When Ally offered to pay half, he wouldn't hear of it. "Come on. I'll walk you back to Munro's."

"Actually, I'm heading into Oxford Street." She pulled her phone out of her bag, unlocked it and opened the Uber app. "I'll just order an Uber."

He waited for her to finish. "So you're off to meet my competition?"

She pressed her index finger to her lips again. He'd said no stories, and that suited her perfectly.

They pushed through the door and out onto the street. Ryan turned to face her, so close she could smell the faint woodsy mix of his cologne mingled with the leather of his jacket. He leaned forward, and she stiffened as he kissed her on both cheeks. "So, 'Ally from the land of the long white cloud,' what are your initial thoughts?"

She grinned as her Uber pulled alongside. "Run. Run as fast as I can."

"Do you like to be chased?"

"Depends who's doing the chasing."

Opening the car door, he ushered her inside. She wound down the window. "Goodnight. Thanks again for supper."

He stood on the curb, his hands in his pockets and that half smile flirting on his lips. "My pleasure, Ally."

8

TOMORROW'S THURSDAY

For Ally, being single in a big city brought with it a heady mix of excitement and apprehension. Having Angus around was throwing her off balance even more than she'd expected, but the longer he stayed in London, the more her resolve strengthened. She just wished he'd move on and leave her alone.

As she left the gym the following Wednesday morning, Ally half-expected another 'How about Thursday?' text from Ryan. When it didn't come, she tried to convince herself the disappointment she felt was misplaced. After all, it meant she'd no longer had to compromise her morals by spending the night with a virtual stranger, even if she wanted to do exactly that.

She caught the elevator to Farra's third floor, stopping at the receptionist's desk when he called her over. "Morning, Ally. Gina wants to see you in her office."

Gina Moretti had been the first person to welcome her to the Farra team. Warm, friendly, and with a bright, red-lipped smile, she was the sort of woman you felt you could confide in. One who would give you her honest opinion whether you liked it or not. Gina was standing at the window, her sight on the park below when Ally knocked on her door. She turned, looked Ally up and down, and frowned. "Come in. Don't tell me you've been to that sweaty gym again."

"It's the best way to start the day. You should try it sometime."

"No thank you very much. I'm good." Gina shuddered and sat at her desk. "Have a seat. It looks like Patrick will be away longer than we expected, so I was wondering if you wanted a few extra hours."

"I'm at college two days a week, so I can only work the three days, sorry."

"Of course. What are you studying?"

"Music management. My housemate and I go to the same school. She's studying for her Master of Music, and I'm doing a couple of first year papers."

"And is it as exciting as it sounds?"

"Well, I'm enjoying it. But I majored in PE, then taught for a year, so being a student again is hard work."

"Ah," Gina said with a chuckle. "My heart bleeds for you, missy. Enjoy it while you can. Best days of your life. Will you go back to teaching?"

"At some stage. But I'm not registered yet."

"How come?"

"I only managed to pick up a one year contract. I need to teach for two years before I'm registered." It was time to change the subject. "Hey, there's something I've been meaning to ask. Do you know Ryan? I met him at the Battersea job when I made that delivery."

"What does he look like?"

Ally grinned. "Every woman's dream."

"You mean the tall, buff guy with the pancake-stacked abs and low-slung tool belt?"

"That's the one." Ally stared at Gina's broad smile. "What's so funny?"

"Don't tell me you're crushing on Ryan, because if you are, you'll have to join the queue."

"Is he a nice guy?"

"I've always found him pleasant to deal with. He's got many strings to his bow, does our Ryan." She paused. "Did he hit on you?"

"Why do you say it like that? Guys do occasionally hit on me."

"I have no doubt of that, but just be careful. And don't say I didn't warn you."

"So, he's a player?"

"I didn't say that, and we should get to work. I've been here half an hour already, and I haven't done a thing." Gina handed Ally a spreadsheet printout. "Here, speaking of Battersea, I need a fresh pair of eyes on the creditors' file. Some of the data's been loaded incorrectly."

"I'd love to see the house when it's finished. It's huge."

"The interior looked like Miss Havisham's when we picked it up. The boss has *great expectations*, but it's well behind schedule."

"I loved that book when I was a kid."

"So Kiwis read Dickens too, do they? And you're *still* a kid."

"Of course we do. I read it in school. I thought Farra only did commercial ventures."

"They usually do, but the house is the boss's pet project. He likes getting his hands dirty occasionally."

Ally had never met the 'Big Boss,' as the other staff called him. She'd begun to wonder if he was merely a figment of everyone's imagination. "What's he like, this elusive Mr. Farrell?"

Gina looked up from her keyboard. "Focused, and tough when he needs to be. But Farra's a great company to work for. It's a family business. His mother still holds a share, along with his brother and sister. But they have nothing to do with the day-to-day running of the show." She took a sip from the cup of tea on her desk. "Anyway, how are you finding London?"

"Loving it." This was Ally's stock answer. She didn't want Gina to know that every time she caught the bus from Putney High

Street to work, she wondered what possible reason there could be for the dramatic turnaround in her once-perfect world.

"I love it too. It's a great city. Some days, I wish I was your age again."

"What would you do over?"

Gina thought for a moment. "Ignore fad diets, mean girls, and overly opinionated men. And, I'd party more—maybe even go to the gym." She chuckled. "Now get out of here and get to work."

As she left Gina's office, Ally thought about her 'mean girls' comment. Sure, life was what you made it, but sometimes, other people's choices had a direct impact on yours, and there wasn't a thing you could do about it.

Ally pushed through the double doors of the Farra building just after six, to find Angus leaning on a lamppost—like he'd been lying in wait, ready to pounce. She'd hoped he might forget inviting himself for dinner, but no such luck.

"Hey. How was your day?" Angus asked as soon as she looked his way.

"Good. But I had to work a little late. Why didn't you text me? I thought we were meeting at home."

"I was in the area so decided it made sense to share an Uber. I've picked up some lasagna." He lifted the brown paper bag in his hand. "We just have to heat it."

"Thanks."

"Maybe we could talk about our plans after dinner."

Ally nodded slowly. She understood his intentions—he'd made his feelings clear, but *her* plans no longer included him.

"And, I need a bed for a couple of nights, if that's okay. My housemate's parents are staying, and I said they could have my room."

Ally sighed as she glanced at his full backpack. And as she

pulled out her phone and hit the Uber app, she muttered her annoyance under her breath.

They'd eaten dinner in virtual silence, and afterward, watched some stupid movie on TV that Angus thought was hilarious. Now, they lay on her bed, both on their backs. Despite her room being the smaller of the two, it came with a king-size bed, and even with Angus's bulky frame claiming his unfair share, Ally still managed to keep her distance.

"Okay," Angus said. "You start."

"You know how I feel," Ally replied. "I had questions at the time, but you didn't want to answer them, so…"

"Is there really any point in dragging up the past?"

She considered his words for a moment. Was that what he thought they were doing? Dragging up the past? "I just wanted to know why, Angus. But I don't think you even knew 'why' yourself."

"What does it matter? We're past all that now, baby. You know how I feel about you."

"Yes, well, now's your chance to explain to me what it's like to totally destroy a long-term relationship for the sake of some…what did you call them? Oh yes, for some 'game fucks' in the restroom of a sports bar."

"They didn't mean anything. You know that. I love you, baby. Only you. Always have."

"So you've said. Many times."

Angus stared silently at the ceiling. He'd never been one for detailed explanations—about anything. It seemed nothing had changed. He sighed and rubbed his hands over his face. Ally knew he wasn't lost for words, he simply never voiced them.

She waited. Nothing.

"What was it like," Ally continued, "to pick up a girl after a game and have sex with her, before coming home to me as if nothing had happened?"

He turned to face her, and for once, she hoped for an honest answer. "I need to know," she said softly, "so I can understand."

He hesitated. Ally waited. It seemed a metaphor for their relationship. She was always waiting for Angus Chapman.

"The rush is different." His words struck like a blow. She'd wanted honesty but had never expected it. "It's…forbidden, and that's exciting when you're pumped after a game. It's all part of the culture, you know that. But when the beer wore off, and we were traveling home on the bus the next day, I did feel guilty."

Part of the culture? "So sex with me was boring?"

At least Angus had the decency to pause before replying. "I didn't say that. Look, people have one-night stands all the time. It doesn't mean anything."

"Do they? Not me."

"But you're different."

Ally held her breath, bracing for the next blow.

"You're pure. Chaste. Sex with you was…safe, loving. Like coming home."

Ally mulled over his words, analyzing their meaning. She was second best. That was the crux of it. The person he'd come to when he needed the comfort and familiarity of commitment. Had he joked about her with his friends—called her the missus, or the noose around his neck? The ball and chain? "Maybe I need to have a few one-night stands of my own. Experience that excitement, that rush."

"Baby, don't. You know that's not who you are. We need to start over."

"So, what are you proposing? An open relationship?" The question wasn't confrontational. Ally had left behind the need to confront Angus months ago, but she still wanted answers. "One where I'm free to have a few 'game fucks' of my own?"

"Don't be ridiculous."

Ally bristled at his reply. How dare he think she didn't have the guts to explore her sexuality. "I'm just keeping it real."

41

"What? By making up for lost time? How's that working for you?"

"It's working just fine," she lied. "And what about you? How's it been for you over the past few months?"

"What do you want me to say? You finished with me. Did you expect me to live like a monk while you were swanning around over here with your new friends?"

Ally knew Angus only went to bed alone by choice. The rumor mill had already been in full swing by the time she left New Zealand. But she still sought his confession—longed to hear the truth.

"Marry me, and I'll never stray again," he said. "You have my word."

In all the time they'd been together, Angus had never once mentioned marriage, so this shitty attempt at a proposal took her completely by surprise. "Marry you?"

"You know how I feel about you, baby. But one little slip-up and you take off halfway around the world to punish me. What's that about?"

"I'm not trying to punish you, Angus. Your cheating nearly destroyed me, both physically and mentally."

"I know that, but it wasn't all my fault. I had no idea Brogan would come after you."

Unbelievable. "Now I understand why some of your teammates used to hit on me. They probably thought I was fair game."

"What? Who? Why would you keep that from me?"

"Because I never dreamed of cheating, so it didn't seem important." Ally disliked raising her voice, but she struggled to keep her tone even. "But it was okay for you to hide your indiscretions from me. And do you know what? Now that we're over, I enjoy not being the type of girlfriend who stays home most weekends while her man plays away games…on and off the field."

"I hurt you. I know that, baby. But what we had, you don't find that often. And maybe when we get back together, we could spice things up a bit, eh?"

Being called 'baby' grated on her nerves almost as much as the 'spice things up' comment did. So he *did* think she was boring in bed. "You shouldn't be here."

"Let me stay. Please, baby. We're still friends, right? We'll always be friends. I promise I won't touch you until you're ready."

"Two more nights. That's all you've got. Understand? And I want my bed back."

"What? I can't sleep on that sofa. I can hardly fit my butt on the thing."

"Right, well stay on your side and go to sleep. But the next time you call me baby, you're out, get it?"

9

FUNNY BUSINESS

Ally lay awake until well after midnight. No woman wanted to hear they were useless in bed, and while Angus probably hadn't meant to hurt her, it still triggered her insecurities. Despite having to fake an orgasm sometimes, she'd mostly enjoyed their sex life, but this was the first time Angus had ever mentioned her failings. It seemed she didn't know how to please a man. And he'd waited all this time to tell her.

Rising before six, Ally showered, dressed, and applied her mask of makeup while scarcely registering the routine. When she walked into the kitchen, Jia was already up and making breakfast.

"Good morning," Jia said in her usual cherry manner. "How did you sleep?"

"Not so good. Angus decided he wanted to share—his feelings *and* my bed."

"Well, I hope you know what you're doing, because from where I'm standing, it looks like a whole lot of breakup 'funny business' is going down. Do you get what I'm saying?"

Ally grinned. "Perfectly. Don't worry; there's no breakup 'funny business' going down. Anyway, why are you up so early?"

Jia sipped her smoothie. "I'm too nervous to sleep. Today's a

44

big day. I hate recitals, especially when they count toward my finals."

"I wish I could be there to cheer you on."

"No way!" Jia looked horrified at the thought. "That would make it even worse."

"You don't get stage fright, do you?"

"Sometimes. It all depends on my states."

"States?" Ally asked.

"You know, my state of mind, the state of my love life or lack thereof, the state of my bank balance. All those states."

"Yeah, I know what you mean."

"Right." Jia downed the rest of her smoothie and placed her glass in the sink. "I'll see you later. I'm going in early to practice."

Ally pulled her in for a hug. "You've got this. Break a leg."

"Thanks, Ally Cat. Love you."

As Jia walked out the door, Ally tiptoed back to her room to grab her phone. She looked at Angus, asleep in her big comfortable bed. It reminded her of the last days of their relationship. How he'd fallen asleep before she'd had a chance to express her feelings— her hurt.

Back in the kitchen, Ally popped two slices of bread into the toaster. Her text alert chimed and she glanced down to see the screen light up with Ryan's name.

Ryan: It's Thursday. Are you keen to catch up?

She picked up her phone with unsteady hands. Was she? Keen?

Ally: You'd only be disappointed.
Ryan: I doubt that very much.

Minutes ticked by. Just as she was about to bite into her second slice of toast, another text arrived.

45

Ryan: We could have dinner first. Get to know each other a little more.

Ally: What happened to the no dates, no dinners, no stories?

Ryan: I've decided to try a different approach.

She was about to text back a straight-out 'no' but remembered what Jade had said about sending mixed messages so sat on it for a while. Although she wanted to see him, these nerves were a whole new sensation for her. She'd never been propositioned by a man like him before—older, confident, the kind of guy who knew what he wanted.

By the time she was ready to leave, he'd sent another text with a repeat of the dinner invitation, a time, and a screenshot of a Google map to show where to meet. He said not to text back; that he'd wait at the café for fifteen minutes. If she didn't show, he'd leave. Ally smiled at the sad face emoji on the screen. Ryan expressed more emotion in his messaging than in person.

Walking home from the bus stop that afternoon, Ally decided to heed Gina's warning. Mr. Click's secret affair was a complication she didn't need. If he wasn't prepared to be seen with her in public, he wouldn't see her at all. Although, he had asked her out for dinner. Maybe mixed messages were his thing. But as she unlocked her door, his last text played on her mind.

"I'm meeting some friends in the city for a drink soon," a smiling Angus said before she'd even taken off her coat. "Keen?"

There was that word again. *Keen.* "Not tonight. I want to catch up with Jia. She had an important recital today."

"Oh yeah, she came home to change. Said to tell you she's gone to her parents and she'll text you."

Ally checked her texts. She'd missed the notification.

Jia: Nailed it. Taking tomorrow off so I can stay with the family tonight. Thanks for believing in me. xx

Angus was still talking as Ally slipped her phone into her pocket. "Come on," he said. "Willow's going to be there. We might grab an early dinner."

"Willow? From school?" Ally hadn't realized her old hockey teammate was in London. She and Willow had played together for five seasons in high school. They'd been close for a while, but they'd drifted apart once Ally started university.

"She arrived in London last week. Plans to do her two years if she can find a job."

"How did I not know this?"

"You need to get back online. Make more of an effort."

She stared at him blankly. *Unbelievable!* "I need a minute."

"So, are you coming or not?" Angus called after her as she headed down the hallway. "Ally?"

Resisting the urge to slam the bedroom door behind her, Ally flopped down on the bed and sighed. Angus knew why she wasn't online; how could he be so flippant about it? In some ways, the freedom of no social media had helped her reevaluate her life, but there were many times when she missed it.

She pushed off the bed and flicked through her sparse wardrobe, choosing a black off-the-shoulder dress, sheer black stockings, and a nude-colored leather jacket. Perhaps Angus was right. Maybe she did need to make more of an effort.

Angus stood as she entered the living room. "Wow. Look at you." He stepped into her space and reached for her hands. "I've been thinking about you all day, and I just want to say I'm sorry. What I did was wrong, and I'm an asshole. But it was never about the girls. It was just sex. I don't even remember most of it."

Ally pulled away, swallowing the lump in her throat as she turned to grab her bag from the sideboard. She didn't want to cry in front of him. He would see it as a chance to comfort her, to try to talk her around. "Let's not go there right now."

"So, you understand?"

She thought back to the hours they'd spent studying together when they were younger. Even though he'd struggled with assignments and exams, he wasn't unintelligent. But if Angus thought his attempt at an apology would wipe the memory of what had happened, well, she wondered if the guy had any emotional intelligence at all.

"We'd better get going," was all she could manage.

Ally glanced around the bar. Spying Willow across the room, she weaved her way through the crowd to a long table against the back wall. As she approached, Willow stood to greet her. They exchanged air kisses, chatting for a few minutes before she introduced Ally to the rest of the group—all rugby guys and their partners. The type of tribe she'd once belonged to. But as she sat and waited for Angus to buy her a drink, she realized how different her life was now. She no longer needed to mix with the sporting elite to have a good time. She was perfectly happy watching movies with her friends or eating street food while roaming around the London markets.

An hour later, bored with the small talk, Ally made her way to the restroom. She checked her phone while waiting in line and smiled as Ryan's last text with an eight forty-five meeting time flashed on the screen.

When she came out of the stall, Willow was waiting for her. They chatted while Ally washed and dried her hands and Willow reapplied her lip gloss. Just as they were about to leave, Willow turned and leaned her hip against the counter, picking imaginary fluff from the lapel of her too-tight jacket.

"I'm pleased you came tonight," she said. "Angus hasn't

stopped talking about you since you left. So, are you guys back together?"

"No. But we've agreed to act like civilized adults."

"That's great. Have you done any singing recently?"

"I'm not sure if I'll ever get back into it. But who knows?"

"That's a shame, but I understand." Willow hesitated. "Um. There's something I want you to know..."

Ally waited, wondering what was coming next.

"I'm sorry about what happened," Willow continued. "With the court case and everything. It must have been so scary for you, being attacked like that."

Checking her reflection in the mirror, Ally pulled at the ends of her hair as if to lengthen it. "Yes, I'm glad the whole sorry business is over and done with." It was her default answer, one Ally had repeated many times without conviction.

Willow nodded. "I'm so impressed with how you've handled it. Everyone says you never said a bad word against Angus. Or that bitch Brogan."

Ally rubbed the scar on the back of her neck. The whole town knew what had happened. Gossip spread swiftly in Tulloch Point, clogging people's minds until they had something better to talk about. And even after many sessions of counseling, the memories still haunted her. She met Willow's gaze in the mirror. "Anyway, I'm trying to forget that night."

"Of course. It's just, well..." Willow chewed her lip as Ally waited for her to continue. "I truly thought you guys had an open relationship. That's what everyone said, anyway."

Willow's confession fell at Ally's feet as her stomach tightened in a familiar knot. She shuffled her words carefully before saying, "Well if we did, no one told me."

"It...it didn't mean anything. We all knew he loved you. I was just a sideline. Quite frankly, I understand why you dumped him. He's a lazy lay. I really hope we can still be friends."

Ally pushed through the restroom door without saying another word. She stopped at the table to grab her jacket, and as she stalked toward the doorway, Willow's shrill voice cut across the crowded bar. "Ally? Ally, wait."

Angus grabbed her arm as she reached the exit. He looked puzzled, but then, why wouldn't he? Apparently, Willow had meant nothing to him, nor had any of the others. "Are you leaving already?"

She blinked back her tears. "Didn't I tell you? I have a date. Don't be there when I get home tomorrow."

"Baby, what's the matter?"

He'd called her baby. He couldn't even get that right. "I have to go."

He glanced back at Willow, and as she slipped out the door, Ally heard Willow call his name and Angus snap, "Shit. What the hell did you say to her?"

She raised her arm and ran to grab the cab pulling into the curb. "Where to, miss?" the driver asked as she opened the door.

"Soho."

A HINT OF SCOT

All the way to Soho, Ally worried she'd miss Ryan's deadline, and as she stared out into the mist-shrouded night, she questioned her motives for the umpteenth time. Why was she in this cab traveling toward a man she hardly knew—away from one she had thought she'd known inside and out? Was this a tit-for-tat reaction to Willow's cryptic confession, or was she trying to prove to herself that she could sleep with another man, even have a one-night stand, without the world falling apart around her?

Arriving at the café with only minutes to spare, Ally stepped from the cab and closed the door. She hesitated, turning back with second thoughts, but the cab was already halfway down the street.

A bell rang above the door as she walked inside, and Ryan stood to greet her. He gave her his signature smile, and her shoulders relaxed as he leaned forward to kiss her on the cheek. "You made it."

"Only just."

"Why? Did you have something better to do?" he asked as he helped her out of her jacket. Ally wasn't used to men with such impeccable manners. Not that Angus lacked manners, but the nuance was different. Angus's country charm was no match for Ryan's city sophistication.

"Nothing important." Ally took in the intimate space as Ryan pulled out her chair. She loved places like this—red brick and black iron fused with the aroma of tomato, garlic, and basil wafting from the kitchen. "How do you find these out-of-the-way places?"

"I've lived in London for years. I know the city pretty well."

"But you're Scottish?"

The lopsided smile appeared. "How can you tell?"

"You still have the hint of an accent."

"Aye. It gets worse when I'm drunk, excited, or angry."

"And do you get drunk, excited, or angry often?"

"Drunk, occasionally. Excited"—he looked at her and grinned —"when the opportunity arises. Angry, not normally. Only when I'm around cheats, liars, and assholes." Ryan motioned to one of the waitstaff hovering nearby. "What are you drinking?"

"I'll just have water. I'm practicing for Dry July."

"But it's only May." He paused and looked up as the waiter handed them the menus. "A large bottle of sparkling water, thanks."

"I don't expect you to join me."

"It's fine. I've got a lot on tomorrow, so I could do with a clear head."

"So, there's plenty of work in the construction trade?" She noticed his hesitation.

"Enough to keep me out of trouble."

Ally scanned the menu, suddenly hungry as a waiter waltzed past with two plates of lamb shanks in one hand and a loaf of bread —perched on a board and dripping with butter—in the other. "The food looks delicious."

"The beef cheek ragù with pappardelle is amazing."

She closed the menu. "I'll have that since it comes so highly recommended. I love beef cheeks."

When the waiter returned with their water, Ryan ordered for

them both. Ally had never had a man order dinner for her before, and the traditional part of her quite liked it—a man who took charge of the little things.

They talked for a while, general conversation about London's tourist sites. Ally wanted to ask him if he had siblings or parents in London but realized that would be one of his off-limit topics. He kept the conversation light until he asked a question that took her completely by surprise, "So, what do you want out of life?"

Ally pondered this for a moment. It seemed Ryan's 'no stories' rule wasn't going to plan. If he wasn't careful, she might start to enjoy his intellect and personality, along with his tight muscular butt contained in a pair of form-fitting black jeans. "To have a passion for what I do and confidence in my choices."

"Interesting answer."

"What about you?"

"Contentment. I'm not looking for a Happy Ever After."

"Are you always so forthright?"

His large hand lifted to his chin and he paused. "We're both here for the same reason. There's no point in pretense."

Ally had never experienced such a strong physical reaction to two short sentences before, and for a moment, she was lost for words. "But we're starting with just dinner?"

Holding her gaze, he slid his hand across the table, stopping before it touched hers—an invitation to meet him halfway perhaps. "If that's what you want. But I get the impression you'd be keen for more."

"So you think you have me all figured out, do you?"

"A man would be a fool to admit such a thing to a woman."

"Handsome *and* perceptive. An interesting combination."

Her reply had the desired effect. His brow cocked, quickly followed by that lopsided smile. "You think I'm handsome?"

"You know you are."

Soft laughter filled the void between them. "And you know I

think you're beautiful. I told you the second time we met. But maybe you've forgotten?"

"I haven't."

"That's good. So I don't have to repeat myself?" Ryan's gaze shifted briefly as the waiter placed a small loaf of bread on the table. He inhaled the aroma, then returned his attention to Ally. "Or should I?"

"Sweet talk just rolls off your tongue when you want something."

"Is it a problem, me complimenting you?"

"No." She tapped the saltshaker. "But remind me to take a grain of this home with me."

He laughed again. "I always mean what I say, so you won't be needing that."

"And so do I."

"So you don't mind me telling you how incredible you look in that dress tonight?"

Ally shook her head and smiled, but inside, the tingles swiftly connected with his intended target—a target that hadn't been hit in many months.

"What?" he asked with a cheeky grin.

"Just drink your water. That's all the compliments I can handle for one night."

They sat in the café for over two hours, finishing off their meal with pear tart and coffee. Ryan's praise of the beef was justified; Ally had never eaten a pasta dish like it. Stories were shared, but not ones that conveyed secrets or set out the domestic lives of one another. Instead, they talked of politics, movies, and sports—Ally claiming that she hated rugby; Ryan apparently loved it. Whenever she spoke, his attention was undivided and full of interest. She tried to dismiss the chatter in her head—the comparisons between Angus and Ryan—but the more they talked, the more she realized Mr. Click was like no other man she'd ever met.

Throughout the meal, Ryan never once mentioned spending the

night together or meeting the following Thursday. But when they stepped out into the crisp spring air, he made his intentions clear by ushering her into a cab before she could ask where they were going.

As the cab headed away from the café, Ally tried to remember street names for reference, but they became a blur after the first few. Up one, down the next. Oxford Street she knew, and Dean and Coventry Streets, but by the time they'd stopped outside a hotel, Ally had no idea where they were.

Ryan paid the driver with a fifty-pound note, telling him to keep the change, and held the door open as she slid across the seat. As her heels hit the pavement, she looked up at the four-story Regency building in front of them. The neatly attired doorman, the perfectly shaped potted plants flanking the entrance, and the gold-edged font of the hotel's name—the Heaton—were all clear indications that she couldn't afford to share the cost of this establishment.

"Is this where you're staying?"

"It is. Are you coming up?"

"I'm not sure."

"Come on. I'll order you a non-alcoholic cocktail."

Cocktail? "No pressure?"

"None whatsoever."

11

THE HEATON

Located on the top floor, the suite—with its formal furnishings and mood lighting—was understated but elegant. She inched her way inside and glanced around. The turned-down bed, plush towels, and artisan chocolates on both pillows would have met with Jia's approval. 'Oh so classy,' she would call it.

Ally chewed her thumbnail as she watched Ryan remove his jacket and hang it in the closet, and held her breath when he stood behind her, offering to take hers. "Are you okay?"

She inhaled the stuffy air, the heat of the room intensifying her need for a drink. Ally knew the risks of entering a hotel room with a man she hardly knew but had allowed herself to be swept along in the moment. Now, here she was—feeling vulnerable, unsure, and more than a little gullible. What would Liz say if she ever found out? Or worse, their over-protective brother, Mitch. Ally swallowed hard. "To be honest, I'm not sure I should be here."

She allowed Ryan to remove her jacket anyway and watched as he hung it in the closet next to his.

Opening the bar fridge, he offered her a bottle of sparkling water, his gesture earning him a tight smile. "There's no pressure here, Ally. Remember? If you're uncomfortable in any way, I'll take you home."

"Maybe that would be best."

He sat on the edge of the bed, his expression unreadable. "The guy at the bar last week, the bodyguard, is he the reason you don't want to stay?"

She shook her head. They'd been over this already.

"But you two have a history?"

"I thought our agreement didn't allow such questions."

Ryan nodded, then stood, staring at her for a moment before reaching into the closet for their jackets. "Come on. I'll take you home."

Ally hesitated. Had she expected to be persuaded? Seduced? She had...and hadn't. And could she spend the night with this man and walk away afterward with no regrets? The thought of sleeping with someone else worried her. Someone handsome, and controlled, and older. Someone not Angus.

He frowned, waiting for her to make a move. "Do you want me to beg you to stay?"

She grabbed her bag. "No, of course not."

"Good, because I don't sleep with women who'll regret it in the morning."

His words hurt more than they should have. He'd dismissed her, and so swiftly. "May I use the bathroom first?"

"Sure." His lips curled upward a little, and Ally exhaled. "But give that thumbnail a break. If you keep chewing it, you'll make it bleed."

They stepped out of the elevator in silence, Ryan seemingly comfortable at her side. It was after midnight, and only one receptionist staffed the desk. She glanced up as they passed but lowered her head again without offering a greeting. Ally had never done a walk of shame, but those slow steps across the tiled lobby seemed to take forever, even when she'd done nothing to be ashamed of.

When they reached the cab rank outside, Ryan opened the door of the waiting car and slipped in beside her.

"You don't have to see me home," she said. "I'll be fine."

"Are you sure?"

"It's getting late. I guess you need to be up early tomorrow."

"Okay." Ryan reached into his pocket, peeled off a fifty from a clip and handed it to the cab driver. "Give us a minute would you, mate?"

The driver opened his door and stepped out of the cab. He lit a cigarette, inhaled like it was his last breath, and strolled over to talk to the doorman. Ally turned to Ryan, expecting him to say there would be no more Thursdays. Instead, he sat side-on, one arm resting on the seat in front of him as he smiled at her with those hazel eyes and full lips.

"Please, you don't have to pay."

"Yes, I do."

"I'm sorry, I—"

Ryan placed an index finger to her lips to halt her apology. "Don't ever apologize for doing what you feel is right." Leaning forward, he kissed her cheek and playfully nudged his nose across the bridge of hers before taking her face in his hands. He kissed her gently. Once. Twice. But it wasn't until the third time that he slipped his tongue into her mouth with gradual force, holding her exactly where he wanted her.

Ally pulled back first, shocked by the intensity of the arousal coursing through her veins. Her fists opened from their clench, and she licked her bottom lip as if to catch another taste. Ryan exhaled and dropped his shoulders. He murmured, "Fuck," under his breath, and then, "Good night, Ally," before slipping out of the cab and shutting the door. He stood on the curb with his hands in his pockets and a frown on his brow before turning to the cab driver. "Thanks, mate."

Ally stared back at him as they drove away. "Where to, miss?"

The driver's question drew her attention. She thought for a second. "Oh, um…sorry, Clapham."

Staring at the window, Ally focused on the reflection of her face instead of the street names, buildings, and vehicles they passed. Unsteady fingertips traced her lips with a feathered touch. Trust her to pick a man like Mr. Click to break the drought. She wanted to ask the driver to turn around. Wanted to go back and tell Ryan she'd changed her mind. But instead, she remained silent.

Hopefully, next Thursday would bring a similar text.

When the cab pulled up at Liz and AJ's, Ally reached into her wallet for the fare.

"The gentleman already paid, miss. Don't you remember?"

Gentleman. "Of course, sorry."

Checking her watch, Ally hurried up the front steps. Even at this late hour, lights glowed in the foyer and living room. She rang the bell.

AJ offered a welcoming smile as he opened the door. "What are you doing here at this time of night?"

"I need a bed if that's okay."

"Sure. Come in. Is everything all right?"

"Fine. But my bed's been invaded by a burly rugby player and I need some space."

AJ's frown held a question.

"Angus is here," Ally explained. "At my place."

"Are you guys back together?" AJ's surprised tone made Ally realize how foolish she'd been in allowing Angus to stay with her. She should have said no from the outset, but when it came to Angus, she just didn't have the energy.

"Of course not. But I felt mean making him sleep on the couch. Still, he's found his own place now, so it's all good. He just needed a bed for a couple of nights."

"Right, well I'm gonna hit the sack. Don't keep Liz up too late."

"As if. She's the night owl, not me."

Ally wanted to go straight to bed too but knew Liz would have other ideas. She took a deep breath and entered the kitchen, bracing herself for the inquisition.

"You're out late for a school night." Liz put the kettle on and reached for two mugs. "Don't you have class tomorrow?"

"You sound like Mum. I'm staying the night if that's okay. Sorry, I should have text, but—"

"Let me guess," Liz said. "Angus Chapman?"

Ally pulled out a chair and sat at the large kitchen table. "I thought I could handle it, but I feel overwhelmed. We went for a drink earlier, and Willow was there."

"I heard she was in London."

"Anyway, she followed me into the restroom, and not only told me she'd hooked up with Angus but was also less than flattering about his performance. Called him a lazy lay."

"What? No way."

"I'm beginning to wonder who the hell he hasn't slept with. We had a heart-to-heart and you know what he told me? Sex with me was loving and safe, like coming home, and that maybe we could spice things up a bit when we get back together."

"He still thinks you're getting back together?"

"Apparently. But why would he even want to if I'm so boring in bed? And this from a guy who couldn't last more than a minute unless he'd been drinking. I never thought I'd say this, but I'm totally over him. And he said I need to get back online. Has he always been such a dick?"

"I plead the fifth."

"You can't. We're not American."

Liz quickly changed the subject. "I have leftovers if you're hungry."

"I'm good. I had dinner with a friend."

"Who?" Liz peered at Ally across the kitchen table. "You've met someone?"

Ally suppressed the urge to tell her nosy sister about Mr. Click, not that there was much to tell. "When I do, you'll be the last to know."

Liz pulled a sad face. "You are so mean. Actually, our friend Chris was here tonight. He's in his mid-thirties and a lovely guy. How about I introduce you sometime?"

"I'm looking for a bit of fun, not a Mr. Lovely."

"Tea?"

"Chamomile, thanks. Any cake?"

Liz smiled. "No cake, but I do have some caramel and chocolate brownie."

"Yum. What would I do without you?"

A container of brownies passed between the sisters. "If you don't start spilling your secrets, you might find out."

Half an hour later, tucked up in bed in the guest room, Ally stared into space, still trying to come to grips with Angus's 'safe lover' comment. What if she slept with Ryan and it was a disaster? Tales of disappointing sexual encounters were commonplace among her friends. How would she cope if Ryan was indifferent, or even unkind after the event? Or worse yet, wasn't good in bed. This last thought made her smile. If that kiss was anything to go by, Mr. Click knew a thing or two about sensual pleasures.

In some ways, Angus had done her a favor. She no longer loved him, but his attitude had helped cement that realization. Polygamy may be alive and well in his world, but Ally didn't have to embrace that lifestyle choice. And what about Ryan and his other lovers? The difference between Angus and Ryan was that this time, the rules were clear right from the get-go.

But now, she'd stepped onto the playing field and given herself a yellow card before the game had even begun.

12

THAT KISS!

Back in his hotel room, Ryan couldn't keep still. Although he kept this room for convenience, he preferred the comforts of a proper home—with food in the fridge and his own bed—so he mostly lived with his brother, Chris. He had no idea why some people like staying in hotels. To him, they were a necessity, not an indulgence.

Initially, a no-strings fling with Ally had seemed a good idea. How he'd come to that conclusion, he had no clue. Young and emotionally immature, she seemed the sort of girl who'd say she wasn't looking for a relationship, but within three weeks wanted to cook you dinner, walk your dog, and meet your mother.

Still. That kiss! When had he last kissed someone with the same depth of passion? He certainly hadn't kissed Britt that way, ever. Ryan grabbed his messenger bag and headed for the door. As he stepped out of the elevator into the lobby, the hint of a smile crossed his face. Ally may not be his type, but after that kiss, he couldn't wait to see her again.

Stopping at the front desk, he handed his keycard to the concierge. "I won't be staying after all. Can you let housekeeping know?"

"Certainly, Mr. Farrell. I'll leave them a note."

"Thanks, Janice. How's occupancy?"

"We're fully booked."

"Good. The place looks great. Have a good night."

Unable to sleep, Ryan sat at the breakfast bar in Chris's apartment, a glass of cognac in his right hand and the fingers of his left hovering over his laptop's keyboard. He typed Alta/Ally Dobson into the search engine. Nothing.

Thinking there might be some connection, he tried to remember the bodyguard's name by using the association he'd formed when Ally mentioned him—something about a bull and ChapStick. *Angus Chapman.* Angus rocked the net like a narcissistic movie star, and none of his accounts were private. But when he searched for Ally's name on the guy's friends lists, he drew a blank. It would appear that Ally Dobson had no online presence whatsoever.

As he sat at the piano and played an old Bonnie Raitt song, Thursday sprang to mind. Gina had told him Ally would be gone from the firm in a few weeks—a convenient coincidence. Ryan wanted to meet her again, to experience another kiss, and maybe, take things further, but the fact she worked for Farra at present was a complication he didn't need.

It was still dark when Chris barged into Ryan's room a few hours later, pulling back the drapes with a dramatic flourish. "Ryan, get up. You slept in."

"What the hell? What time is it?"

"Six thirty. I thought we were going for a run."

Ryan pulled the covers over his head. "Piss the hell off. You know I hate running. I only went to bed a few hours ago."

"You canceled on dinner last night."

"I had a meeting," he mumbled.

"I hope she was worth it. You missed a great meal."

Ryan grabbed a pillow and placed it behind his head. He rubbed his eyes. "Believe me, I would've been better off coming to the Tanners with you."

"I still get the feeling Liz wants to hook me up with her sister."

"Was she there? The little sister?"

"No. I haven't had the pleasure yet. Anyway, I'm away too much right now to have a relationship."

"Pity you didn't end up making it over to New Zealand for Liz and AJ's wedding. You and her sister could have been all loved up by now."

"Nah, she's too young anyway. And by the sounds of it, the girl has enough baggage to fill a 747."

"Don't we all?"

"Yeah, but someone who was screwing her boyfriend at the time waged a vendetta against her. Sounds like her *loving boyfriend* couldn't keep it in his pants."

Ryan shook his head. How some people could mistreat their fellow human beings was beyond his comprehension. "Sometimes the world seems like a fucked-up mess."

"Indeed," Chris replied. "That's why I'm off for a run."

It took Ryan another hour to drag his butt into the shower. As he leaned back against the wall and let the water rain down over his head, he was struck with an overwhelming urge to drive to his sister's place in the Scottish Borders. Up there, he could spend the week hiking without having to worry about other people's shit.

Later, as he stood at the window and stared out over the Thames, he sipped strong coffee and thought about Farra. His grandfather had purchased this warehouse complex back in the fifties, buying it for little more than a song. Since its recent conversion, they'd been offered ridiculous money for the two penthouse apartments. But Farra wasn't in the property sales game. They held on to their real estate portfolio, no matter how volatile the market. He mentally toasted his deceased grandfather for his investment-savvy ass while feeling a touch of regret for the way his own father had handled the business.

Back in his room, Ryan stifled a yawn as he chose a suit and grabbed one of his pinstriped shirts. When thoughts of Ally—with her porcelain skin and tantalizing mouth—entered his head as he dressed, he pushed them aside for more practical considerations; like what he'd do if the bank declined his final finance application for the Precinct.

As he left the apartment a while later, his thoughts returned to Ally. Physically, she was definitely his type. Tall and elegant, with dark expressive eyes and tiny facial imperfections that only made her looks more interesting, he'd never met a woman who held his attention so fully.

Except for one…

Ryan had already dealt with several emails by the time Gina appeared at his door. They had an interesting relationship. Gina was only ten years his senior, but she clucked around him like a mother hen, worse than his own mother.

"You wanted to see me?" She took a seat opposite his desk, notepad and pencil in hand. "This better be good to call me all the way up here."

"It's two flights of stairs."

"Yes, and I'm wearing heels. What's up?"

"The temp, Ally. Do you have her CV, or do the agency handle that?"

Gina narrowed her gaze. He almost squirmed in his seat but reminded himself he was in charge, not Gina. "What?"

"I thought something was going on," Gina said.

"What do you mean?"

"She asked about you the other day."

"Did you tell her who I was?"

"It's not my job to connect her dots. She'll find out soon enough. I've decided to take the wait-and-see approach. Anyway, I don't have her full CV. And you do realize she won't be here much longer. I've suggested she apply for a PT job at the gym."

Ryan's brow furrowed. "Is she qualified as a personal trainer?"

"Well, she's a PE teacher."

"Right. Well, email me what you have. Please close the door on your way out."

Gina stayed where she was, her back ramrod straight and her knees tightly pressed together. *Here we go.* Ryan leaned back in his chair and attempted to outstare her. "What?"

"Seriously? You asked me up here to discuss Ally Dobson? I hope you know what you're doing. She's just a kid, and by my observation, a naïve one."

"Point taken."

"Please tell me you haven't slept together."

"What the hell, Gina. I haven't slept with her. And who I *do* sleep with is none of your business." He stood, indicating their meeting was over, but couldn't resist a slight smile.

"Why are you smiling? You think this is funny?"

"No. I just can't believe you asked me if Ally and I had slept together."

"I thought you learned your lesson last time. That's all I'm saying."

"Believe me, I get your point."

Gina walked out of his office without another word.

Back in his chair, Ryan leaned his elbows on the desk, massaging his forehead with his fingertips as he mumbled, "Shit" under his breath. Gina had been in his office less than five minutes, and he already had a painfully tight jaw and a dull headache. And none of it was Gina's fault.

Roll on Thursday.

Several hours later, Gina sent through a copy of Ally's details. He scanned the email, not sure what to expect. She was born in

1994—that made her twenty-three—held a Bachelor of Education in PE and had graduated from high school as *proxime accessit* in 2011.

Ryan studied the screen in front of him. Apart from her name, date of birth, and basic education information, that was it. But Ally was obviously a smart girl. You don't receive runner-up to the top academic prize unless you know your stuff.

So, why was she temping at a property company?

13

SECOND-CHANCE THURSDAY

Ally glanced down at the caller ID and smiled. Hesitating for a moment, she answered on the fifth ring, just before it went to voicemail. "Hello."

"How's this Thursday looking?"

That voice! "I don't know. Last week didn't go so well."

"You know what they say about practice."

Ryan's voice was full of amusement, and the thrill of the chase surged through her. But was she ready for another rendezvous with Mr. Click? "It doesn't always make perfect."

"Maybe, but it can be fun trying." A pause followed. "Meet me. Same place, same time?"

"So, second-chance Thursday?"

"I'll text you the details."

With that, the line went dead. Apparently, Mr. Click didn't believe in long conversations or in giving her the opportunity to say 'no.' Her thoughts drifted to the Heaton. Would he talk during sex? Would it be over in a flash like his phone call, or would he set a more leisurely pace? And when they were done, would he expect her to get dressed and leave straight after, or ask her to stay and hold her for a while?

On Thursday, the anticipation of Ryan's text brought with it more questions. She'd had no experience of casual hook-ups. What was the protocol? Ryan had said he'd text her, but on the bus to Putney after work, her phone didn't chirp once. She cast her mind back to their conversation. He hadn't mentioned food. Should she eat or wait to see if he wanted a late supper?

Ally stopped by the supermarket on the way home, filling a basket with necessities and a spur-of-the-moment packet of chocolate fondants. With the line at the checkout several people long, she dashed back to the freezer for a carton of vanilla ice cream. Who ate chocolate fondant without ice cream?

Although it was pleasant enough, Ally had never really thought of Jia's apartment as home, and a sense of detachment rolled over her as she walked through the door that evening. She'd felt the same way when she and Angus had met at their cottage for the last time. They'd made their home cozy with whatever they could afford or scrounge from their parents. But once their relationship ended and her belongings were gone, she'd had no choice but to move on.

She stood in the middle of Jia's tiny living room and looked around, wondering if she'd ever feel at home—or secure—anywhere again.

Deciding Ryan had forgotten their Thursday arrangement, Ally made herself comfortable in front of the TV, a bowl of left over stir-fry balanced on her lap. *Britain's Got Talent* had just started, and she loved that show. It reminded her of the many talent contests she'd entered in her youth. She'd almost finished the stir-fry when her text alert chirped. She checked the screen.

Ryan: Meet me in the Heaton's bar @ 8:30. No need to confirm.

Placing the phone on the coffee table, Ally slumped down into the sofa and considered his text. The Heaton seemed so far away, and Ryan totally out of her reach. But as she stood at the kitchen sink ten minutes later, devouring a fondant she'd just heated in the microwave, and with every sense on high alert, Ally knew where she'd be within the hour.

High stools covered in sapphire-blue plush velvet lined the intimate bar, and along the side wall, booths and armchairs faced each other under low-hung chandeliers. The room was long and narrow, but tall tree ferns in waist-high pots gave it a sense of spaciousness.

Unable to spot Ryan in a room crowded with well-cut suits and red-soled stilettos, Ally sat at the bar and ordered a lime and soda, which the bartender insisted was on the house. As she sipped her drink, she sensed someone standing behind her.

With no acknowledgment, Ryan slipped onto the stool to her right. All part of their Thursday game. A rush of excitement hit her head on as the bartender placed a drink in front of him before he'd even ordered. No payment was requested or given. Did he come here with other women; have a longstanding tab? Ms. Tuesday, Wednesday, and Friday perhaps?

Ally glanced over at his left hand holding the glass. No wedding ring. No sign of a tan line or indentation of any kind. She turned to look at him. "Is it you I have to thank for the free drink?"

"What sort of man would I be if I left a beautiful woman to buy her own drink in a bar?"

A slight smile lifted her lips. "A smart one."

"Are you meeting someone special?"

His tone held a touch of amusement. Ally liked this game, a game she'd not played before but had found herself fantasizing about over the past few days. "I'm not sure yet. You?"

He swirled the ice around in his glass. "I'm open to it, but it's not easy."

"What's not? Meeting someone?"

"No." Ryan paused, smiled. Sipped his drink. "Meeting someone special."

Ally said nothing. Did Ryan think *she* was special? Surely not. Special wasn't part of the 'casual hookup' deal. She sipped her drink with slight reservation. It wasn't that she felt unsafe around him, perhaps more out of her comfort zone. Although, uncomfortable seemed to have become her new normal.

Ryan reached for her hand. "Come on. Let's go somewhere a little quieter?"

Ally hesitated as the elevator stopped on the fourth floor. Ryan held the door open, a 'you coming?' clear in his expression. She stepped into the hallway, her hands clenched at her sides.

Once in the suite, Ryan lifted her jacket from her shoulders, his breath hot on her neck. She should have brought a scarf, an added layer of comfort. After the attack, she'd worn a scarf every day for months. A security blanket as her therapist called it. Now, she only wore one when necessary—to add a touch of color or protect her from the cold. But tonight, her need for security returned.

The room was once again overheated and stuffy, but Ally shivered under his touch. He moved to the closet and hung her jacket first, then removed his own and placed it on the hanger next to hers —their sleeves barely touching, just like the week before.

Taking a seat on the bed, she watched him unbutton his shirt, each button a slow tease devoid of embarrassment. She thought they might talk first. After all, 'no conversation' wasn't on his list of rules. But it seemed words were optional where Ryan was concerned, and even though he remained silent, there was no misunderstanding his intention. He obviously wanted to start the ball rolling before Ally had the chance to change her mind again. There would be no small talk tonight.

As she waited for his attention, she took note of the room—the velvet drapes hanging floor to ceiling from tracks hidden under pelmets, and the quiet hum of the bar fridge. The formality of the decor didn't really fit with her perception of Ryan, and neither, she imagined, would the bill.

He sat next to her, his shirt undone, and leaned over to remove his shoes and socks. His nails were neatly clipped, and Ally was surprised by how tanned his skin was—the result of a recent vacation perhaps.

Angus passed through her thoughts, and for a moment, she wondered if being here with Ryan was a betrayal of her years with him. But as Willow's words rang in her ears, Ryan drew her closer, away from her irrational misgivings.

"Let me." He motioned for her to turn side-on and placed his left hand on her shoulder, the right grasping the top of her zipper. She inhaled sharply as he guided the dress over one shoulder, exposing her neck to his touch. As his lips caressed her nape, Ally closed her eyes and waited for him to say something about her scar. But the question she'd expected, didn't come.

She turned, her cheeks burning as he reached for her, his hands gently cupping her face. Their first kiss was gentle, more so than her expectation, but there was nothing gentle about the effect as he guided her with his hands, his tongue, his lips.

"You're a beautiful kisser, Courier Girl," he whispered, before pulling back to look at her, his eyes hooded with want and the suggestion of a smile on his lips.

"A nickname, already?"

"Thought I'd better catch up."

"You're not so bad yourself, Mr. Click."

Ryan stood and offered his hands, ready to pull her deeper into their Thursday world. "Stand up." As she did, he stepped back two paces. "Take off the dress."

What the hell?

His gaze never left hers as she shimmied out of the heavy

stretch fabric and draped it over the end of the bed. She bent to remove her stay-ups.

"Leave the rest."

They stood only an arm's length apart, she in vintage-style lingerie, he in pants and an unbuttoned shirt, the definition of his torso on full display for her eyes only. As Ryan slowly unbuckled his belt, his gaze drifted downward, pausing momentarily on her breasts and coming to rest on the light strip of shadow showing through her panties. Her skin tightened as a shiver ran down her spine. His lips curled into a faint smile as he shook his head and muttered, "Fuck," just as he had that night in the cab.

What did his particular brand of 'fuck' mean? Was he pleased at what he saw, or something else? He stepped out of his pants and pulled the comforter off the bed, sending it tumbling to the floor along with her dress. He offered his hand. "Come here."

Ally remained silent, suddenly lost for words. She stepped toward him, knowing it signified consent. "I want to take things slowly," she finally whispered, the words shaky on her breath.

"Slowly. Right." Ryan reached for her hands and held them loosely. He leaned forward and gently kissed her neck, their hands still clasped as she closed her eyes, stretching her head back slightly. "I understand."

"It's just—"

He placed his index finger against her lips. "No need to explain. I'll leave my boxers on. When you're ready, let me know." His slight smile helped her relax. "Otherwise, nothing will happen."

It was the most he'd said since they'd entered the suite. In contrast to his abrupt commands of a few minutes earlier, the words were reassuring and his patience surprised her. She'd thought he might be the eager type. The kind who'd push you against a wall and take you standing, but apparently, Mr. Click knew how to seduce a woman gently.

He pulled her closer still, his touch confident. "Lie down," he whispered.

She sat on the edge of the bed then lay back, one knee bent in an attempt at modesty as she instinctively pulled the sheet across her breasts. Ryan lay beside her and reached over to switch off the bedside lamp, plunging the room into the semi-darkness of the city, where lines were visible but blurred and time falls from the cracks in the curtains. "Roll over."

As he rolled her away from him and onto her side, Ally didn't understand his command. Didn't he want to look at her? The drawer of the nightstand opened, closed.

"Pull your hair off your neck."

She hesitated but did as he asked. She still wasn't used to the touch of the bob and missed the warmth and security of long hair.

"I've waited so long to kiss you here." Ryan brushed his lips from her hairline to her shoulders, one hand guiding her hips into his groin. "That day on the building site, when you pulled your hair off your neck, I wanted to reach out and caress it." The warmth of his breath set off a strong contraction between her legs. "To suck your skin and mark you, so faintly that no one would ever know, except me...and you, when you studied yourself in the mirror, your hands cupping your beautiful breasts as your teeth scraped across your lower lip."

The words washed over her skin like a wave of cool, invigorating surf only to be swept away again on a warmer current. She moved toward the edge of the bed a fraction to escape the intensity of his touch. Ryan released his grip slightly, tangled his leg around hers, and pressed his erection against her butt. Running a hand down her spine, he stopped at her bra to undo the hooks. On reaching the top of her panties, he trailed his way back up, his other hand firmly gripping her hip. He repeated the action, skimming across the skin of her belly and up to cup both breasts with one calloused, oversized palm.

She stiffened.

"Relax," he whispered, before tugging lightly on her earlobe with his teeth. "Breathe with me." Ryan rolled her onto her back and exaggerated the action. "In and out slowly."

She did. In. Out. *Relax?*

"Let go. I promise you're in safe hands."

Liar.

"Come here. You feel like nothing else." He pulled her close, bending down to kiss her lips.

As Ryan deepened the kiss, Ally could scarcely form thoughts let alone words. But it didn't matter. Ryan the construction worker was quite the conversationalist between the sheets. He continued the one-sided tête-à-tête with passionate phrases that carried her along on a tide of desire. The combination of words, his scent, and gentle touch reassured her. And as he sucked her skin, leaving the faint mark he'd mentioned, she felt more sexual than she could ever recall feeling in her life.

Their kisses intensified, and so did his touch as he removed her unhooked bra. The sensation of his palms as they rubbed over her tight nipples and the way he teased his fingertips through the light smattering of newly trimmed pubic hair, had her arching off the bed. And as he drew her breast into his mouth and sucked hard, she could hardly catch herself from falling.

"Take off my boxers," he whispered.

"Is that a command?"

His laughter brought lightness to the encounter. Ally loved the sound—a laugh from deep within his throat, with no nervousness or restraint. "No, it's a plea. Don't make me stop now."

Leaning over to the nightstand, he grabbed a condom. The momentary distraction gave her a few seconds to think. It was time to leave her doubts behind and, not only take, but also give what she wanted.

"Take off my panties first," she whispered back, her lips brushing his earlobe.

"Is that a command?"

"Yes."

Ally had no time to dwell on anything else as Ryan took the lead, moving forward with gentle force, his chest brushing over her tightened nipples. Skin to skin. Heat to heat. And as they danced through the sensual steps, Ryan didn't have to ask Ally if she'd come. He knew she had, but still brought her back to the heights of ecstasy once more, her explosive release pushing him over the edge with her.

Spent, he fell onto the bed, his breath panting from his chest in unison with hers as he stared up at the ceiling while Ally reached for the sheet to cover herself. Almost a minute passed before he rolled his head over to look at her, his eyes smiling more than his lips.

"Do you always come like that?"

What could she say? She had *never* come like that before. "Do you always ask such personal questions?"

Rolling onto his side, Ryan propped himself on one elbow and gazed down at her. "You've just shared your body with me in the most amazing way. I'd say that allows me one personal question."

Ally released a breath and relaxed a little, her performance anxiety eased by Ryan's encouraging words. "No. Not…no."

"Me neither." He kissed her gently. "Wait here. I'll be right back."

She watched him leave the room. What would the next half hour be like? Now that the flush of excitement had faded, leaving only the awkward details. Where had he flung her bra? What about her shoes? Should she order an Uber, or would Ryan walk her across the highly polished lobby like the week before, past the concierge desk and through the double doors to a waiting cab? Would he leave the hotel too, or snuggle down in layers of white percale while she stood on the curb, cold and unsure, waiting for her after-midnight ride?

And who would pay the hotel bill?

The sound of Ryan returning to the room brought her back to

the present. He sat on the edge of the bed and held out a washcloth and a small towel. "Would you like me to…"

"What? No." A hot blush crept up her neck and face as she accepted the towel. "I should get going. I don't want Jia to worry."

Ryan reached for the duvet off the floor and spread it over the bed. The air in the room had cooled and Ally was glad of the weight against her naked body.

"Text her," he said. "Tell her you'll be home in the morning."

"You want me to stay?"

He slipped in beside her and traced his index finger across the seam of her lips. "We're not finished yet."

14

RED LIPSTICK AND KITTEN HEELS

The Heaton's compact bar was busier than usual when Ally arrived the following Thursday. She'd received Mr. Click's text midmorning, and surprisingly, he'd also been in touch once during the week. Other than that, communication had been as per their agreement.

As she walked into the bar, her form-fitting, midnight-blue dress shimmered under the lights, and for the first time in a long while, Ally relished playing dress-ups in her sister's gown, kitten-heeled sling-backs from her other life, and deep red lipstick she'd found on sale that afternoon. Earlier, as she'd stood in front of the mirror, admiring how the cut of the dress showcased her curves, she'd had no doubt as to how this evening would play out. She hadn't felt so desired—so sensual—in a long time. *If ever.*

She slipped into a seat at the end of the bar, and when the bartender took her order, the drink was once again on the house.

Ryan arrived a few minutes later, but he wasn't alone. Two men dressed in business suits held his attention for several minutes before he glanced over at her, seemingly without recognition. His way of telling her not to approach, perhaps. Within seconds, drinks were served to the men, and, once again, there was no sign of payment.

Turning in her stool, Ally watched as the piano player flowed from one easy listening song to another—slow, sensual melodies she'd once loved to sing. And when the man looked at her and smiled, Ally realized she was humming, something that hadn't happened in a long time. But if Ryan was still busy when the guy finished his set, she'd text him good night and leave. Sitting alone in a crowded bar was definitely not her idea of fun.

Ally glanced Ryan's way again. Physically, she liked every-thing about him, and that scared her a little. His dress sense, that half-smile, how his fingers—with their neatly clipped nails—lightly skimmed over her breasts when they kissed, and the touch of his lips on her neck. Since their last meeting, he'd been on her mind constantly, and as the week progressed, Thursday couldn't come soon enough.

And now, here they were. The cat and the mouse.

Ryan ignored her as he strolled from the bar. She'd been waiting over twenty minutes and couldn't face another lime and soda on an empty stomach. Disappointed, Ally made her way to the restroom and stared at her reflection in the mirror. What was she doing in some grand hotel half a world away from home, meeting a man who's only interest in her was sexual? It was time to go.

However, when she returned to the lobby, Ryan sat waiting for her, alone. He stood, his gaze never leaving hers as he murmured, "I'm so sorry about that. Let's go up and order room service." She thought he might suggest another drink at the bar, but he didn't miss a beat as he directed her toward the elevator, his hand on the small of her back, guiding her into his Thursday night world.

She expected to feel a degree of hesitation, but it didn't eventu-ate, and as they caught the half-full elevator to the top floor, Ryan gently brushed his hand over hers and shot her a sideways glance. Just as he'd done the week before. Ally's reaction was immediate and surprising. How could he turn her on with just one look, one touch of his hand?

Once again, the room was hot and stuffy. In the lobby, he'd mentioned ordering room service, but now they were alone, eating had lost its appeal. Ryan unlocked the window and opened it, then moving to the dial on the wall, he turned down the thermostat as though he knew the system.

Of course he did. He worked in construction.

Ally placed her small bag on the coffee table and sat on the end of the bed, passion rising deep within her as she watched him unbutton his shirt. She stared, unable to shift her gaze from the thin strip of hair trailing from his navel to his—

"Sorry about before." Ryan tugged the shirt from his pants and shrugged it off as he strolled across the room. "My bank manager wouldn't take the hint. When I went back to the bar, I thought you'd bailed on me." He opened the small refrigerator and handed her a bottle of water, perfectly relaxed in his semi-naked state.

She unscrewed the lid and took a sip, her gaze exactly where she wanted it to be. She'd always enjoyed the visual of a male with strong arms and shoulders, and Ryan didn't disappoint. "I had."

He flashed a wry smile as he sat next to her. With the water bottle halfway to his lips, he paused. "And yet, here we are. Have you eaten?"

She shook her head, but as she opened her mouth to speak, he leaned in to kiss the side of her neck, before grazing his lips across her collarbone. Her head dropped back in response. And as she closed her eyes, Ryan's sweet, musky scent, the trail of his lips, and the way his hand held hers, almost sent her over the edge.

"Shall we order now...or after?" He gave her no time to answer before kissing her—hot and heady and more demanding than the week before. The word *urgent* sprang to mind before slipping away in favor of *possessive*.

"I'm glad you stayed," he continued to murmur. "I've been looking forward to this all day. All week, to be honest."

Ally struggled to form thoughts let alone speak as a longing, so powerful it almost hurt, washed over her. "Me too."

They slowly undressed one another, until his pants and her dress lay in a heap on the floor. Her lingerie was new, midnight blue to match the dress, and on first seeing it, he pulled back and smiled. "That color, it's beautiful. But not as beautiful as the body wearing it."

All the right words.

Ryan knelt in front of her and removed her shoes, placing them neatly next to the bed. Bending forward, he kissed around her navel. On reaching the lace of her panties, he looked up at her with hooded eyes. "That scent. And those stockings. *Fuck!*"

She'd never had anyone mention her smell before. It made her slightly uncomfortable. "I can go take a shower."

He chuckled. "What? Are you really so innocent? Or do you say these things to turn me on even more?" He pulled her hands to his lips and kissed them—first one, then the other. "No shower. We'll do that later…together."

Ally didn't want to be innocent, not anymore. She liked his smell too, that raw hint of male mixed with the woodsy notes of his cologne. "So you want me to leave the stockings on?" she whispered.

He sat back on his haunches, his expression amused. "What do you think?"

Ryan returned to the bed and leaning back against the headboard, pulled her over to straddle him—hot and hard beneath her.

"Lift up," she said as she slipped her hand underneath the band of his boxers. And as she eased them off, her eyes widened at the sight of him. Taking him in her hand, she pumped gently. He gasped and closed his eyes, his hands clutching the sheet as she found her rhythm—increasing the pace as his arms and neck tensed, and his butt lifted off the bed.

He reached out and grabbed her wrist. "Ally, slow down," he panted. "Fuck. I'm about to lose it."

Slipping off the bed, Ally dropped her panties and bra to the floor as his gaze fixed on hers. Ryan reached out and pulled her back. "Come here." She straddled him again, her modesty slipping away as he entered her in one swift movement. Leaning forward, she trailed her tongue around his nipple, and as she nipped, he held her butt in his large hands, moving her with purpose as he cursed under his breath.

She arched back, a soft murmur leaving her lips, then reached behind her, bringing his hands to her breasts. "Ryan! Please."

"What? Tell me."

"Don't stop. You feel so good. So good."

Later, when they lay together naked, exhausted, and satisfied, Ally finally understood the meaning of total abandonment. They stayed locked in one another's arms, so tightly interwoven, she never wanted him to let go.

Room service arrived just after eleven and they ate at a leisurely pace, feeding each other through gentle smiles and muted laughter. Afterward, they lay naked under the sheets; Ally curled into him while he held her as if she were his.

"Are you okay with this?" Ryan asked.

The same question had been on Ally's mind every day for the past week. *Was she?* "Yes, why?"

"I don't know." He hesitated. "It's hard sometimes, meeting someone new. Feelings quickly come into play, especially when the physical side's so good."

His honesty surprised her. It wasn't part of the deal. "I understand what no ties mean."

He kissed her lightly on the forehead. "I know you do."

She cleared her throat. Went to speak but stopped herself.

"What?" he asked.

"I know our agreement was no stories, but may I ask you one personal question?"

His lack of response spoke volumes. He stayed on his back, staring up at the ceiling. She decided to ask anyway. He didn't have to answer.

"Have you ever been in a long-term relationship?"

With a sigh, Ryan reached for her hand. "I have. But I can't have kids, so that's a game changer right there."

His words echoed in her head. He couldn't have kids? Ally wanted to ask him more, but it was such a personal revelation, she didn't know what else to say. "I'm sorry. I had no idea."

"Don't be. But I'm not the type of guy you should fall for, Ally. It's important you remember that, so we're both clear about what we expect out of this."

"I understand."

But did she? It was one thing to tell herself she was fine with a fling, but quite another to separate lust from the warmth and excitement she felt every time they met. She decided to try to lighten the mood. "Actually, I've rather enjoyed being on my own since arriving in London. It's helped me discover strengths I never knew I had. But obviously, I'd like to settle down one day."

Ryan caught her tone and went with it, the seriousness of their conversation left to flounder in their wake. "I can see it now. You, back in New Zealand with your two point five kids, a fat little pug dog, and a husband who can't keep his hands off you."

She propped herself on one elbow and smiled down at him. "So what will he do, this future husband of mine?"

"Sheep farming, of course. He'll be called Trevor, Trev for short, drive an obscenely large double cab with mud on the tires and several dogs on the back, and he'll call you the missus. Or 'mate' when you're having sex."

Ally burst out laughing. "*Mate?* I've never been called mate by a man in my life."

"Yep, and you'll bake bread and grow kale, which you'll sell at the local farmers' market, and your kids won't know what the internet is until they go to school."

"I never knew you could be so funny. Anyway, I'm keen on marrying an American rock star with long hair and lots of tattoos. We'll go on tour and live on a bus, and he'll call me his muse. We'll have five kids, and they'll be beautiful, feral wee souls."

Ryan nodded, his gaze turning serious. "I can imagine you being someone's muse," he said quietly. "Why an American?"

"I don't know. Guess it's my sense of adventure, and I love the accent."

He leaned over and clasped the back of her head, pulling her in for a kiss. "Well, you looked beautifully adventurous in that dress tonight, with your glossy hair and red lipstick. Any rock star would be lucky to have you."

"Thank you."

"Will you meet me next Thursday?" He cupped her face, such a tender gesture.

She nodded, too emotional to speak.

Ryan cleared his throat. "While we're in the truth booth, there's something else I should probably tell you."

Ally placed a finger to his lips. "Let's go back to no stories. It's easier that way."

15

MS. POLLY

The anticipation of another night at the Heaton helped Ally survive an otherwise boring and predictable week.

Ryan's text arrived early Thursday evening, almost as if he'd decided at the last minute. Her 'sensible self' constantly questioned the wisdom of their hookup sex. But the heady anticipation of their drink at the bar, of the elevator ride—where he would lightly brush his hand against hers as he stared straight ahead—and the nervous fluttering in her stomach as he opened the door to the suite, pushed aside any rational thought.

This was their third night together, fourth if you counted their first unsuccessful attempt. Ryan had been more adventurous this time, and less careful with the condom, but had insisted he was clean. His sterility hadn't been mentioned again, but she had no reason to doubt him. He didn't seem like the reckless type.

Ally woke to Ryan's fingertips tracing the arch of her cupid's bow. Her eyelids fluttered as she adjusted to the muted light of the room and the sight of the naked man beside her. She studied his face—the almost-boyish shadow of his morning growth above his beard line, those mesmerizing hazel eyes, and the way his hair flopped over his forehead—and smiled before adding a husky, "Hi."

He returned the gesture, studying her, his eyes full of want.

"What time is it?" Ally glanced down at his bulge under the sheet.

"Seven fifteen." He pulled her closer, his lips brushing across her neck. "We'll have to be quick."

The sound of his phone drowned out that of the early morning traffic drifting up from the street below. "Hold that thought." He frowned at the caller ID and pulled himself up to lean on the headboard as he answered the call. A series of one-word replies followed before he threw back the covers and moved, stark naked, to the privacy of the bathroom. *Okay. I stayed in town. Yeah, sure. Polly, listen a minute.*

The door closed behind him. Seconds later, water hummed through the pipes. Ally lay in bed, her sight straying to the bathroom door every so often. Uneasy thoughts careened around in her head, and her stomach turned somersaults. Who was Polly? Was he married?

Ten minutes later, Ryan returned to the room, shower fresh and wrapped in a low-slung white towel. *Of course.*

"Something's come up. I have to go."

His preoccupation spoke volumes, and his tone lacked the intimacy she'd come to expect. Momentarily lost for words, she spewed out the first thought that came into her head. "Shall I order breakfast?" *Stupid.*

"Not for me." His manner aloof, he opened the closet and reached for his clothes. "I'll grab something later."

The words *adulterous affair* joined *what the hell have I done?* in her head. She closed her eyes as she lay there, searching for retrospective signs her Mr. Click was a married man. Despite any evidence of a ring, everything else pointed that way. He'd wanted discretion. To keep it a secret. And now, the phone call with a hushed but curt exchange.

Ally watched him dress at a leisurely pace, going through the motions like it was just another day. And to him, it probably was. He slowly buttoned his shirt, and at one stage, stared back at her—his gaze intense but his thoughts obviously elsewhere. Ryan grabbed his wallet off the nightstand and stuffed it into his pants pocket before sitting on the edge of the bed. As he slipped on his shoes, he didn't speak.

"Thanks for last night," he said finally as he bent down to plant a soft kiss on her forehead. "I'll text you."

She smiled up at him, not expecting anything in return, but hoping he'd sense her tenderness. "Okay."

"I'm sorry I have to leave early. Order breakfast and stay as long as you like. I'll have them put it on my tab."

His tab! After the way he'd cuddled her until dawn, Ally expected a small flicker of connection between them, but there was none. "It's fine. I'm not really hungry."

Ryan didn't offer another goodbye kiss before rounding the bed and heading for the door. And before Ally had a chance to say, 'Thanks,' or 'Goodbye,' or even 'Who on earth is Polly?' he was gone.

She flopped back on the pillow—the essence of him tingling between her legs and his branding on both breasts—and muttered, "shit."

Ally had let down her guard. Given herself to a man she knew nothing about without first asking the all-important 'relationship' question. She wasn't familiar with this feeling of post-coital regret. Her friends talked about it sometimes—their contrition after a hookup, but Ally had never experienced it. And as the sun rose above the already bustling city, one thing was clear. She wasn't mature enough to have a purely sexual affair. It already hurt, and they'd only spent a few nights together.

When she left the hotel half an hour later, there was a pre-paid cab waiting for her at the curb.

16

CHARCOAL SUIT

Ryan opened the PDF attachment and ran his eye over the signed loan documents. Although the bank had tentatively approved the finance for the Precinct months ago, a delay with the Historic Places Trust had knocked their schedule sideways. He massaged his temples while reading the email from Andrew, his personal lending advisor. As usual, the guy had promised the world in their early discussions, but as the deadline loomed, it became apparent Andrew was simply another link in a long line of conservative bankers, all wanting to stamp their mark on the transaction. And while the significant financial commitment required for the Precinct was well within their limits, the logistics of the project still played on his mind.

Tim scheduled a meeting for Ryan and the project team, then left work with a headache ten minutes later. By mid-afternoon, all Ryan wanted was to head to a bar for a cold beer, and to text Ally suggesting they meet up. Why wait until Thursday? Five days had been long enough. He needed to come clean.

He picked up the phone and dialed Gina's number. "Hey, are you free to take some minutes? Tim's gone for the afternoon."

"What, again? Sorry, I have a dentist appointment. I'll see who else is around."

"Thanks."

With instructions from Gina to take minutes of a meeting for the head honchos, Ally caught the elevator up to the fifth floor. Although she fought it, her thoughts kept drifting to Ryan. Each Thursday had been more intense than the last, and she already missed his touch—the scrape of his stubble between her breasts and legs—and the way he looked at her like she was the most desirable woman in his world.

And yet, as soon as he'd finished his morning shower, his manner would instantly change. She'd recently read an article about how to spot an emotionally unavailable man, and Ryan checked nearly every box. And then there was Polly.

There would be no more Thursdays at the Heaton.

She entered the empty boardroom, expecting a traditionally furnished space with dark wood paneling and black leather chairs. Instead, natural light flooded the interior from a bank of windows facing the park, and there wasn't a wood panel or leather hide in sight.

Ally sat her pen and notebook on the table—an oversized trestle fashioned from off-white wooden planks resting on black supports—and glanced around the room. Black wishbone chairs with woven reed seats surrounded the table, and mounted blueprints of various buildings lined an internal wall. At one end, a lime-green feature wall yelled a cheery 'Hello,' and at the other, hung an oversized framed print with the words 'Do Epic Shit' scribbled across its width. Ally knew nothing about design, but she knew what she liked, and this was it. She

As she strolled to the window to take in the view, she wondered if the Big Boss, Mr. Farrell would be in attendance. She took a deep breath and hummed a few bars of a song to steady her nerves. Being in the presence of 'the boss' always made her nervous, no matter what the job. How had Ryan described him? Cocky and arrogant. But some of the women in the office swooned over him, especially the older ones. Maybe he was the silver fox type.

The first person to arrive introduced herself as Nava, the firm's on-staff architect. She welcomed Ally warmly and indicated where she should sit. Ally hated taking minutes. She was a teacher, not a PA. But when you're a lowly temp, you do what you're told and smile while you're at it. She was lucky to have a job that allowed time for her studies.

She set her phone on the table, planning to record the meeting as well as take notes, and stilled as at least a dozen other people took their seats. But the chair at the head of the table remained empty. As Ally checked her phone for the second time in as many minutes, two older men entered the room, followed by a younger one.

It only took a moment for her to take a second look, one that slotted the younger man into the place where he belonged. Because the man standing in front of her didn't belong here. Minus his tool belt and hard hat, Ryan the construction worker—her 'How about Thursday?' lover—now stood at the head of the table.

Charcoal suit. Pinstripe shirt. Cufflinks. An expensive-looking watch with a large look-at-me face. With a touch of product in his hair, neatly clipped facial growth, and a silk tie, Ryan had never looked so hot. He removed his jacket and hung it on the back of the only available chair. The chair at the head of the table.

He seemed distracted, but as his gaze drifted over her, a hint of stunned recognition crossed his face. Ally glanced from Ryan to the two older men, wondering which one was Mr. Farrell. Both were graying at the temples and looked roughly the same age as her father, but when Ryan cleared his throat, she frowned. He didn't take a seat like the others but stood in front of a whiteboard covered in building plans.

Her heartbeat raced.

"Okay. Let's get this show on the road," Ryan said as he started the PowerPoint presentation. "Thank you for coming. I'm relieved to say our bankers have finally given us the go-ahead for the Precinct, so it's a positive result all round." Everybody clapped; Ally had no idea why.

He glanced over at her again. "Ally. I'll give you a list of attendees after the meeting. But," he addressed the room again, "it would be helpful if you said your name before speaking so Ally can get a handle on who everyone is."

He looked at her as if expecting a reply. "Thank you," was all she could manage.

As the meeting progressed, Ally sat glued to her seat—clutching a pen in one hand and wishing she held a double gin and tonic in the other—as people called Ryan 'James' left, right, and center.

She managed to avoid eye contact with 'James' for the rest of the meeting, but she couldn't avoid his voice—smooth and authoritative. He spoke articulately with ease and command, his address peppered with words and phrases such as 'sustainability, beneficial percentages, efficient energy management, positive borrowings, monitoring and targeting, and returns compared to occupancy' along with the occasional 'organic growth.'

And, just to make things interesting, Ryan asked everyone for their opinion on the project. Conversationally challenged Ryan was nowhere to be seen. Mr. 'Big Boss' Farrell was in the driver's seat, and while she'd already decided to take a U-turn out of his life after the Polly incident, him being her boss, added extra mud to an already murky puddle.

Ally scribbled down as much as she could under the circumstances, and after more than an hour of discussion among the team, Ryan called the meeting to a close. He stood and slipped into his jacket as the rest of the staff filed out of the room. She moved to leave.

"Ally." He waited for her to return his gaze.

"Yes, Mr. Farrell."

He stared for a moment and cleared his throat, offering no smile. "Please wait in my office next door. I'll be there shortly."

Nerves twisted her stomach. By mixing business with pleasure, she'd crossed one of her own very straight lines, without even realizing she'd plugged in the mixer.

Ally stood waiting in Ryan's office for more than five minutes, shifting from foot to foot as she cursed her one and only pair of office heels. Looking around the large, elegant space—with its matching leather couches, low table spread with architectural magazines, and potted plants in a perfect fern-green—she struggled once again to reconcile the decor with Ryan the construction worker.

Mr. Click entered with one of the older men, who hung his jacket on the stand in the corner. Ryan reached for a file on his desk as the other man pulled out a chair.

"Here's that list of attendees." He thrust a sheet of paper at her, his business card attached by a paper clip to the top right-hand corner. Ally glanced at it. White card printed with an embossed dark blue font in a traditional script. *James Ryan Farrell, Farra Corporation.* His cell phone number and email address were the only other details given.

"Please email the draft minutes to me by noon tomorrow." His expression and tone held not even a hint of warmth. Demanding and forthright about covered it, not to mention, he'd played her for a fool and she'd naïvely allowed it.

"Um…sure," she stammered, fiddling with the page in her hand. "Thank you."

Ryan held the door open for her, and as she swept past, his hand brushed against hers. She walked into the elevator lobby without another word. Mr. Click was her boss—the Big Boss—and she'd slept with him. Well, there hadn't been a whole lot of sleeping, but still. And as she entered the elevator, her shocked face stared back at her from the tinted mirror on the far wall.

Back on the third floor, Gina greeted Ally with a knowing smile. "How did you get on upstairs?"

"You knew?"

"What? That Ryan and the Big Boss are one and the same?"

"You could have warned me."

"And spoil the fun? I can't believe you haven't run into him around here before. But that's what happens when you work down here in the dungeon. I can go for weeks without seeing him."

Ally didn't have the energy to share in Gina's amusement. "Does he make a habit of wearing a tool belt?"

"Only when he needs to blow off some steam or has a project he's passionate about. Which, now that I think about it, is every other week."

Still standing at her desk, Ally gathered her notes and phone, trying to look calm. Underneath the mask, her head throbbed, and she struggled to steady her hands. "Do you mind if I leave a little early and take the minutes home? I feel a headache coming on."

"Sure. It's almost five anyway."

"Thanks. I'll see you tomorrow."

At home, Ally repeatedly listened to the recording, Ryan's smooth voice sending shivers down her spine. Her thoughts were in overdrive. Even though she and Ryan had shared a bed, made love until the small hours, and held each other while they slept, she knew very little about him. *No stories. No last names. No nothing.*

Now, pieces of the puzzle slowly clicked into place. He'd probably read her resume and now knew everything about her. So why the big secret? Was it all just a joke to him? Did Ryan play the Thursday game with other unsuspecting temps who were happily content with no stories? Maybe she was merely one of seven. Or perhaps he had Sundays off, which would make her one of six. Did he have a roster system; was there a way to climb the weekday ladder? Would she be moved to Friday or Saturday if she played her cards right?

She booted up her laptop and got to work, determined to email the minutes well ahead of tomorrow's deadline, so the Big Boss had no excuse to contact her.

Her phone chirped.

Ryan: Ms. Dobson. Are you ok? The look on your face. It was adorable.
Ally: You're my boss!
Ryan: Technically.
Ally: Did you know I worked for you?
Ryan: You told me the day we met, remember?
Ryan: Does it matter?
Ally: Maybe not to you.
Ryan: Meet me? Mr. Farrell sounded so incredibly sexy coming from your beautiful lips.
Ally: It's only Tuesday.

Ally searched her emojis but couldn't find one that expressed sarcasm. She didn't really know how she felt. Angry? Betrayed? Used? *Overwhelmed!*

Ryan: We've already smashed the rules to pieces. Same place, same time?
Ally: I don't think so. And you were right in your self-assessment.
Ryan: ???
Ally: You are demanding. Not to mention stoic, arrogant, and last but not least, cocky. Oh, and deceitful.
Ryan: Meet me. We'll talk about it.
Ally: But you don't do conversation.

Ally lay back on the sofa, wondering how she'd never joined the dots. Since starting at Farra, she'd heard all about James Farrell, the youngest grandson of the original company's founder. The one forced to take over the business when his father passed away after suffering a heart attack while playing golf on a cold London day several years before.

Ryan was the guy who'd left behind his partying lifestyle to turn the company around. According to corporate legend, his grandfather had built up the successful firm from one small green-field lot, but when he died, Ryan's father—a well-meaning nice guy with no professional skills and even less desire for business—nearly destroyed everything his father-in-law had worked so hard to achieve. Following the retirement of several key board members, the company struggled financially. But after his father's sudden death, Ryan, with the help of a new board of directors and advisers, had turned the rebranded Farra Corporation around.

Ryan was a respected CEO with a Ms. Polly waiting for him at home, and Ally was just a temp who'd slept with the boss. And now, the prude she thought she'd left behind in New Zealand was setting up residence in her head, ready to begin her lecture with *OMG, what have you done?*

17

KARMA

The following day, Ally stood in the elevator, her eyes glued to the adorable twin girls standing next to an older woman. She loved kids, always had. A small hand touched her arm. "Excuse me?" Wide eyes set in an expressive face looked up at her.

"Yes, sweetie."

"Your perfume smells really nice."

Ally smiled at the girl's charming comment. "Thank you."

"What's your name?" she asked in her adorable upper-class English accent.

Ally bent down until she was at eye level with the twin, inviting her conversation. "Alta, but everyone calls me Ally."

"Alta? How do you spell it?"

"A.L.T.A. I'm named after a mountain."

"I like that name. Alta the mountain."

"Do you work here?" the other twin asked.

"I do. On the third floor."

"Our dad works here too. He's the boss."

Ally straightened as the elevator doors whooshed opened, her body suddenly stiff. And there stood Ryan, one hand in his suit pants pocket and the other holding his phone.

The twins ran out, followed by the older woman. "Hi, Dad," the girls cried in unison.

Ryan frowned briefly at Ally before smiling warmly at his daughters and hugging them both. "Where's your mother?" he asked as the doors closed on the cozy family scene.

It took only a second for the realization to hit. Ryan Farrell was definitely married. Ally mentally scolded herself. It had never occurred to her to ask before they started their Thursday game, and he certainly hadn't offered any information in that respect. But that's how cheating men operate. *No ties, no stories, no expectations, no darn anything.*

Ally got out on the next floor, where a communal lunchroom overlooked the street below. After taking a seat at an empty table, she unwrapped her sandwich and took a deep breath, determined to practice the art of mindful eating. As she took a bite, her thoughts turned to a university friend who had unwittingly slept with a married man. Ally had wondered at the time, with a touch of smugness, why her friend hadn't asked the question. Now, the karma of judgment had returned to bite her on the backside. And damn, it hurt.

She glanced down, the empty sandwich wrapper taunting her. How many bites did it take to finish two slices of bread spread with pickles and packed with salad and cheese? It seemed she couldn't even master mindful eating, let alone sexual self-control.

Standing in front of the vending machine fifteen minutes later, Ally studied the chocolate bars lined up for her perusal as she slipped a five-pound note through the slot. She knew a headache would follow hot on the heels of the euphoria, but eating chocolate wasn't always about pleasure. Eating chocolate could also be about easing heartache and pain. Add a sad country-and-western song to the mix, and she had all the makings of a pity party.

But by the time she made it back to her desk, the chocolate was gone, and she hadn't listened to a single song about making love in the back of a pickup.

Just after four, her phone buzzed with an internal call.

"This is Tim, Mr. Farrell's assistant. I understand you took the minutes for the last meeting. Thank you for that."

Ally had never spoken to Tim before. For some reason, she'd expected Ryan's PA to speak with a posh English accent, but this guy was as Scottish as they came. "No problem."

"Mr. Farrell has requested you pack up your desk at four thirty. He has a job for you in the boardroom."

"But I've not finished the invoicing."

"Don't be late. He detests tardiness." The line went dead.

So. James Ryan 'Cheating Bad Boy' Farrell wanted to see her.

But it was only Wednesday. And, to top it all off, she had a headache.

Tim, a broad man with an even broader smile, rose from his desk to greet her. "You must be Ally." His high percentage of belly fat and overly ruddy complexion made Ally want to take him under her wing and whip him into shape. An occupational hazard. "Mr. Farrell's expecting you. Please go in."

Ally knocked before opening the door. "Mr. Farrell, you wanted to see me." She kept her tone professional.

Outside, rain pelted the windows, and the sudden change in the weather made her shiver. He looked up, smiled and shook his head a fraction. Ally remembered what he'd said about her calling him Mr. Farrell.

"Ally." He paused as he continued to stare. Was it simply to make her squirm? "I have a meeting in a few minutes and need someone to watch the girls for half an hour." Ryan walked over and removed his jacket from the stand. She wondered who tailored his suits. Whoever was responsible for restraining those biceps beneath the expert cut of worsted wool, did a fine job.

Get a grip.

"I understand it's not part of your job description," he said as he tugged at his shirt cuffs. "But their nanny has had a family emergency. They're doing their homework, so they may need some help."

Unbelievable! When they first met, he'd struggled to say a civil word. Next minute, he was blowing up her phone with his 'Meet me' texts and no-strings 'How about Thursday?' rendezvous requests. And now suddenly it's 'Ally the babysitter'? She had nothing to say except, "Of course."

Ryan opened the door to the boardroom and held it while she followed, whispering, "We need to talk," as she brushed past.

"Isla, Ava, this is Ally. Ally's going to look after you for a bit. I won't be long, okay?"

Two pairs of intense hazel eyes looked her way. "Her name is A.L.T.A. She's named after a mountaintop."

Ryan stood with his hands in his pockets. His eyes sparkled with that look of affection all proud parents bestow upon their children. "How do you know that, Isla?"

"She said so in the elevator, didn't you, Ally?"

Ryan's gaze shifted to Ally.

She ignored his questioning stare. "I'm impressed you remember, Isla."

"They remember everything these two, so be careful what you say. Right, I'd better go. I'll see you soon."

"Okay." The girls answered in unison again, not looking up from their homework.

"Make sure you behave and do what Ally tells you, okay?"

"We will."

He winked at her as he left the boardroom. Smug prick, acting as if they shared a private joke. But this was no joke to Ally. There was no mistaking the twins were his biological children. Ryan Farrell had fathered two mini-mes, and he'd told Ally he couldn't have kids.

Feeling all kinds of stupid, she slumped in the chair between the girls, her mind racing at the memory of their only skin-on-skin encounter in the early hours of last Friday. Her phone chirped and she glanced down, unlocking the screen to read Ryan's message.

Ryan: In case you're wondering, A.L.T.A, I'm not in a relationship with their mother. Other than the fact she's my ex-wife.
Ally: What happened to no sharing?
Ryan: The rules have changed.

Ally left it at that. He was right. The rules *had* changed. They'd changed the minute she realized he'd fathered two children, the hour he'd called on her to babysit, and the day he'd left the hotel to go home to Polly. And who was Polly? Ally wouldn't usually stoop to using innocent children to garner information, but the need to cleanse herself of adulterous guilt was enough to make her compromise her standards.

"Where's your mum today? What's her name again?"

"Polly. She's shopping for the wedding." Ally had no idea which of the twins replied. She'd thought she had it sorted. Isla on her right and Ava on her left. Or was it the other way around? "We're the flower girls," they both said.

"So, your mum's getting married?"

"Yep. To Mr. Marc," the twin on the right replied. They both giggled.

"What's so funny?"

"He's a producer. We call him Mr. Marc the Music Man. Mum told him he has a dad bod, so they might as well get married. We can't wait."

"Your phone keeps chirping. Is someone calling you?"

"Who am I talking to?"

"Ava, silly."

Ally glanced at her phone as the twins giggled again. "No, Ava, it's just my text alert."

"You can check. We won't think you're rude, will we, Isla?"

Forthright, just like their father. "Thank you."

Ryan: Come on, Ally. Give me a break.
Ally: I thought you were in a meeting.
Ryan: It's boring as shit. I'd much rather be meeting with you. Are we still on for Thursday?
Ryan: ???
Ally: Does the phrase 'workplace sexual harassment' mean anything to you?

Ally glared at her text as it popped into a green speech bubble on her screen. *Shit.* She hadn't meant to hit send.

Ally: I'm sorry, I didn't mean that. I'm confused. You should have been honest with me.

Nothing.

When Ryan returned to collect the girls, apart from indicating she could leave, he barely acknowledged Ally's presence.

She hoped to hear from him that evening but didn't. Feeling a little queasy, she went to bed early and lay in the dark, staring at the numbers on the bedside clock until well after midnight. She recalled their text exchange—more specifically, her last text. The comment had been overly harsh and unnecessary, but that was the problem with texting. Words were tossed around without rational thought or depth of emotion. It was almost worse than having an argument. Once you'd hit send, you could never take back your words. They were there forever, waiting to be reread and misconstrued repeatedly.

At work the next day, time dragged from seconds to minutes to hours until, just after four thirty, Ryan appeared on the third floor.

He stopped at Gina's door and spoke to her briefly. Ally still couldn't get used to seeing him in a suit, and when he shot her a sideways glance and walked toward her, she quickly looked away.

"Ally, may I have a word?" His tone was businesslike and formal as he stood in front of her desk. Everyone stared as she followed him into one of the smaller offices. He closed the door behind them and shut the blinds with an efficient tug on the cord. "Take a seat."

His comment about cheats, liars, and assholes sprang to mind. Ryan had told her he was not easily angered, but no other verb more accurately described the emotion he currently displayed. She sat on the chair in front of the desk, her hands linked in her lap and her legs clamped tightly together.

Ryan picked up a pen and played with it end-to-end while he left her to stew.

"I've been mulling over our little text exchange yesterday—"

"I—"

He held up a hand. "To say I'm disappointed would be an understatement. If you're not interested, that's fine. We had an understanding. No strings, no stories. What we do outside work hours is our own business. But I agree, the fact you still work for Farra is a complication."

"That's not—"

He spoke over her. "I enjoyed our little game of pretend while it lasted. However, it's never been my intention to make you feel uncomfortable while you're working at Farra, and if I have, I apologize. But..." He paused, inhaling deeply. "Being accused of sexual harassment is something I won't forget in a hurry." Ryan leaned back in the chair, his gaze drilling into hers, leaving no room for reply. "So, I'm going to treat your 'harassment' text as an error of judgment on your part, and I hope you will do me the same courtesy."

"What do you mean?"

"Well, it was clearly an error of judgment on my part not to introduce myself properly. I never meant to deceive you. In fact, I'd decided to come clean the next time we met. Unfortunately, you came to the meeting and found out sooner than planned."

"But you let me talk about you without revealing who you were. You let me embarrass myself, and—"

"We had a private conversation. I found it amusing at the time. You handled my questions discreetly, but now you seem to have lost your sense of humor around me, which is regrettable." Ryan remained seated. "You may go."

Ally's bottom lip quivered. She would have done anything to take back the text, to explain, but he hadn't given her the chance. She had so many questions, but Ryan wasn't about to let her voice them.

As she returned to her desk, everyone stared—Gina being the main culprit. Ryan was right, Ally had made an error of judgment, but it seemed in Mr. Farrell's world, the concept of 'second chance' didn't apply. Nor did offering an apology for that matter.

On the dot of ten to five, Ally packed up her desk and headed for the restroom, where she washed her hands and splashed her face with cold water. When she looked up, Gina's concerned expression stared back at her from the mirror.

"What was that all about?" Gina asked. "The visit from Ryan?"

Ally choked a heavy sob to the back of her throat. "Nothing much."

Gina frowned as she handed Ally a box of tissues. "Look, I know it's none of my business, but you're too young to be playing with Ryan's kind of fire."

Pressing her lips tightly together, Ally nodded. Gina wasn't stupid; she knew the score. "Do you mind if I leave early?"

"Of course not. But think about what I've said, eh? You're a smart kid, and I know you'll get over it."

The sob burst free.

Gina pulled her in for a one-armed hug. "Hey, come on. It's okay." She paused and pulled back. "You know, I had a crush on a boss once. It was exciting, that whole 'forbidden fruit' thing. I was only nineteen at the time. He was ten years older and recently divorced. When my parents found out about us, they were furious."

Ally wiped her eyes. "What happened?"

"We celebrated our twenty-third wedding anniversary last Easter." Gina smiled like she understood how Ally felt, and maybe she did. "But there's an exception to every rule, and in this case, I'm it. Ryan's a good guy, but don't blur those lines any more than they already have been."

"It's not what you think."

"Isn't it?" Their eyes met in the mirror, and Gina offered a reassuring smile. "Anyway, I'm off home too. My leave officially started yesterday." Gina checked her watch. "I only came in to tidy up a few loose ends and now look at the time." She moved toward the door.

"Gina," Ally called after her. "Thank you."

"No problem, hon. I'll see you in a couple of weeks if you're still here. Otherwise, don't be a stranger, eh?"

"Enjoy your cruise."

Ally stayed in the restroom for another few minutes, feeling clammy and off balance. All she'd wanted was a bit of fun with an interesting guy. To feel in control for once rather than be known as some sports star's girlfriend—a WAG. However, her association with Ryan Farrell was now over. She inhaled sharply as that realization slammed into place.

Before heading home, Ally called into the gift shop across the street to buy a card. After inscribing another apology, she caught the elevator to the fifth floor and asked Tim to put it on Ryan's desk.

"Is everything okay between you and the boss?"

"What do you mean?"

"He's been in a foul mood all day. Next minute, he's storming out of the office, apparently to talk to you. He never deals with the temps. I thought maybe you could shed some light."

Ally shrugged. "I have no light to shed, sorry."

Tim held the card, flicking it across the tips of his fingers. "I'll see that he gets this."

"Thanks, Tim." Ally said nothing more, just turned and walked toward the elevators. The last thing she needed was to confide in the self-appointed head of the office gossip committee. In her experience, people who gossiped to you would also gossip about you.

Ally slept badly that night, struggling to quieten her head trash as she stressed about her failed apology. During their exchange, Ryan's professional facade had conveyed no hint of the intimacy they'd shared. Still, it was better they end it now, before she forgot the rules of their game.

Over the next couple of days, Ally moped through her lectures, keeping one eye on her phone at all times, in case he should happen to message. But there was no sign of a 'Meet me' text. Not even a lousy emoji.

Instead, when Ally arrived home from college on Friday, there in her inbox was an email from the temp agency, terminating her position at Farra. The following Wednesday would be her last day.

18

NEVER JUDGE A BOOK

Jia leaped onto Ally's bed and turned her back, indicating with a pointed finger for Ally to unjam the zipper of her top. Although, to call it a top would stretch anyone's imagination. Between that, white over-the-knee stockings, a tiny tartan skirt, and a bare midriff, Jia looked more like a naughty schoolgirl than anything else.

"What are you doing in your PJs?" Jia asked over her shoulder.

"Thinking. I have nothing to wear."

"Big Thursday night date?"

"Not this week. I'm meeting an old friend at a club in town. You should come."

"Is he a hottie?"

"What makes you think it's a guy?"

Jia shrugged. "Just a hunch. Hot or not?"

Ally thought for a moment. Would she call Hamish hot? "I guess. Shy though, and I mean painfully."

"Shame. Shy boys are hard work. But I'll come for a while." Jia pulled her phone out of her pocket. "I'll just text my friends. What's the name of the club?"

"I can't remember, but I have a map." Chewing her lip, Ally

surveyed her limited outfit options. She flopped down on the bed. "Maybe I should just stay at home."

"You unhappy about losing your job, Ally Cat?" Jia pulled a sad face.

Was she unhappy? "No, I'm fine. Something else will turn up."

"And what happened with Mr. Click?"

"It seems we didn't click after all."

"That's bleak. Care to spill?"

"No spill necessary. I've already mopped up." Ally returned her attention to the closet. "Anyway, what do you wear to a London club?"

It was Jia's turn to chew her lip. "Pity you're so tall. I could lend you something."

"I don't think so!" The thought of wearing anything of Jia's made Ally smile.

"You seriously need to hit your credit card and update your wardrobe." Jia held up an off-the-shoulder LBD. "What about this?"

"It's too short."

"Perfect." She threw the dress on the bed. "Get dressed. I'll bling it up for you."

Ally chuckled. "You will never, ever, touch me with any of your bling. Not even one sparkle!"

Ally scanned the club with unease, wishing she'd stayed at home. As she tugged her dress lower, she hoped the DJ would do the same with the music. Once, she'd happily party until five in the morning, but lately, she struggled to feel comfortable in a crowd.

A strong arm snaked around her waist. Her heart pounded in her chest as she spun, expecting to push away some lecherous guy. "Hamish! Don't do that. You nearly gave me a heart attack."

"Shit, sorry."

Ally had met Hamish Baxter at university where they'd played together in a band. After graduating, he'd returned to Australia and made a name for himself as a DJ around Brisbane before moving to London two months ago. "Sorry I'm late. I'm still finding my way around. I hope you haven't been waiting alone?"

"No, my housemate came with me, but she's just hit the dance floor with her friends."

They talked for a while and ordered drinks, then pushed through the crowd in search of a table.

"I have a favor to ask," Hamish said with a grin as they sat on the high stools. Ally narrowed her eyes, wondering what was coming next. "I'd like to cover one of your songs, and for you to feature on the demo."

Ally cupped her hand to her ear. "Sorry, I can't hear you over this racket."

"Very funny. What do you think?"

"You're welcome to use the song, but I'll pass on the feature."

"Seriously? What if it turns out to be a hit?"

Ally stared at Hamish and laughed. He was an eternal optimist. Very much like Jia. "I've learned not to worry about 'what ifs.'"

"Speaking of which, I saw Angus last week. He said you guys are getting back together."

"What? He's seriously starting to piss me off."

"Thatta girl. He didn't deserve you."

Didn't he? Hamish had never liked Angus. Now she understood why.

"Anyway, what do you reckon? About the demo?"

Ally shook her head. It was too soon to test those waters. "I'm not that person anymore."

"We both know that's not true. But you have to want to do it." He stood and offered his hand. "Come on. Let's go upstairs."

"I'll just let Jia know."

Hamish followed her line of sight. "Jia? The Korean girl? The one who plays the violin? She's your housemate?"

"Do you two know each other?"

Hamish shifted uncomfortably, his expression impossible to read. "I saw her playing at a concert recently. She's good. Exceptional."

At the top of a short staircase, Hamish guided Ally to a roped-off area. Hundreds of small spotlights shone against a charcoal double height wall, and everywhere she looked, beautiful people—dressed to impress—lounged on leather booth seating, sofas, and bar stools.

"Should we be up here?"

He grabbed hold of her hand, pulling her around a cluster of punters posing at the bar, and flashed a cheeky grin. "I know people who know people."

They stopped at a table where several guys were seated. Ally inhaled quietly. She'd never been shy when she dated Angus, but now, she didn't feel confident around strangers. Hamish pulled up a couple of chairs. "Take a seat. What would you like to drink? Another lime and soda?"

"Thanks."

As Hamish left for the bar, a long-haired bad-boy type with an impressive array of tattoos along his forearms pulled Ally into the conversation.

"Hi, I'm Stuart." He offered a hand and a tight grip.

"Ally."

He moved a little closer. "How do you and Hamish know each other?"

"We're old friends."

Stuart leaned back, splaying his legs across the seat like a rock star. He had to be one of the sexiest men in the club, but Ally wouldn't be swayed by the Stuart Effect. He smiled. "Yeah? So, are you into music?"

Ally cleared her throat. She knew Stuart's type—warmed by

alcohol and ready for sex up against a restroom wall while still fully clothed. But that was no reason to be rude to him. "Hamish and I played in a band together briefly, back in the day. Another life, another direction."

He nodded, holding her gaze as if she were the only person in the room. "I used to dream of a career in rock when I was younger, even went on tour with a band once, but my other life got in the way. So now I deal with other people's shit instead."

She thought for a moment. "Are you a plumber?"

Stuart burst out laughing. "Even worse. A lawyer, but I'm a classically trained pianist."

Ally raised a brow. The words 'classically' and 'Stuart' didn't quite gel.

"What?"

"Nothing," she said. "It's just, I can't imagine you playing the classics."

He leaned in close and rested a hand on her knee. "You don't look like the sort of girl who would judge a book by its cover," he murmured. "Come home with me later, and we can play on my Steinway."

Ally felt her face flush. Even if she were in the market for a little harmless fun—and after what happened with Ryan, she wasn't—it wouldn't be with a guy like Stuart; Steinway or no Steinway. She wondered if Ryan played any instrument, other than his own, and smiled at the thought.

Before she could politely decline Stuart's invitation, Hamish appeared at her side. "One lime and soda."

"Thanks." She took a sip and sat back as Hamish and Stuart drifted into a conversation. The distraction gave her time to consider Hamish's proposal. Her therapist had suggested she use singing to unwind—not necessarily in front of people, but during those long, lonely nights of reflection. With everything she'd been through, Hamish had always believed in her. Maybe it was time to return the favor.

As others joined the table, Ally excused herself and headed to the restroom. Sitting in the stall, she checked her phone for texts, but apart from a brief message from her sister, Sydney, her phone was unusually quiet. A dull ache of homesickness stirred in the pit of her stomach. Or maybe the feeling was more to do with Ryan sacking her.

And yet, the thought of never seeing him again saddened her. Although their nights at the Heaton had been fleeting, when she recalled his murmured words of seduction, the way he'd caressed her neck with warm lips, and his fascinated stare, she realized how much those Thursdays had meant to her.

Back in the VIP area, Ally returned to her seat next to Hamish and took a sip of her drink. She wanted to ask the bartender to add a shot of vodka, but she'd had a few too many hangovers since arriving in London, and it was time to go on a health kick.

Hamish looked at her and smiled. He was one of the sweetest guys she'd ever met, but because of his shyness around women he was attracted to, he'd never had a serious girlfriend. "We're heading downstairs. You keen?" he asked.

Ally downed her soda. "Sure, why not."

As soon as they hit the dance floor, Stuart took the lead, placing both hands firmly on her hips and steering her through the crowd. Surrounded by a sea of bodies gyrating to the thumping beat, she scanned the room for Jia, but another familiar face caught her eye. Ryan Farrell stood at the bar, doing shots with a rowdy crowd. She watched him down one, then another, laughing with his friends. It appeared Ryan didn't share Ally's sentiments. Apparently, he couldn't give a damn if they never shared another Thursday.

He lifted his head, but as their eyes met, Stuart and Hamish pulled her deeper into the crowd. She gave a half-hearted protest, but the men failed to hear her over the pounding drum and bass. Stuart swayed behind her, moving her hips in rhythm with his own.

He whispered, "Relax," and she could smell the alcohol on his breath as his hands tightened around her waist.

Her attention returned to Ryan, who'd stopped drinking and now stood watching her with his back to the bar. When someone offered him another shot, he refused with a wave of his hand.

Ally didn't know what she expected from her ex-boss. Maybe some form of acknowledgment, even a slight smile, but Ryan offered no nod of recognition. He simply stared then stared some more. She looked away, losing herself in the music. The next time she glanced over, Ryan had turned his attention to the woman standing next to him.

One, two, three, scull!

Later, when Stuart and Hamish mentioned a party, Ally decided to tag along just to escape Ryan's disapproving stare.

Ally reached for her phone on the nightstand, her heartbeat racing when she read the time. A text alert at three in the morning was always a concern. She unlocked her phone and scanned the text.

Ryan: Seriously?
Ryan: Stuart Harrison?

Throwing the phone down on the bed, Ally got up to use the bathroom. When she returned to her bedroom, she had one missed call, and her text alert sounded twice more.

Ryan: Ally? Where are you?
Ryan: We need to talk.

It seemed Ryan Farrell got a bit keypad trigger-happy when he'd been downing shots.

Another call quickly followed. She considered picking up but stared at the ceiling instead, her mind recalling the cold and impersonal wording of the email: *Farra Corporation no longer requires your services at this point in time, therefore...*

Ryan: Ally? WT actual F. Pick up!
Ryan: Ally!!!

WT actual F indeed. She could almost hear the intensity of his Scottish burr in his words. She wondered if he'd been out with the new Ms. Thursday and couldn't sleep. Whatever the reason for his texts, he'd sacked her. What more could he possibly have to say?

19

SOLD HER SOUL

When Ryan arrived at work the following Thursday morning, rain pelted the streets below, and the office seemed darker than usual. He went through the motions—removing his jacket, switching on his laptop, and plugging the charger into his almost flat phone. A printed file of specifications for the Precinct sat on his desk. He opened it, scanned the first few pages and closed it again, his mind on Ally Dobson.

All of his efforts to contact Ally over the past few days had failed. She hadn't answered a single text, and every time he phoned her, it went straight to voicemail. He didn't have time for games, and he certainly wasn't about to march downstairs and drag her away from her desk again. That had been a big mistake. One he wasn't proud of.

Holding his finger on the intercom, Ryan spoke into the micro-phone. "Tim, can you come in here for a minute."

When Tim walked into the room, he took one look at Ryan and frowned. "What's with the eye bags? Are you sick?"

"No, just tired. Find out where Ally Dobson is and ask her to come to my office, would you?"

"She's not here anymore. Wednesday was her last day."

"What? She just up and left?"

"Patrick's back. You know this already."

"Yeah, right." He sighed. "Okay, thanks."

As Tim left the office, Ryan rocked back in his chair, unable to get the image of Ally in the arms of Stuart Harrison out of his mind. The way Stuart had rubbed against her, simulating sex to the rhythm of the drum and bass beat, made him cringe. He liked Stuart. They'd known each other for many years, but his track record with women sucked and Ryan didn't want him anywhere near Ally.

Now he wasn't sure what annoyed him more—Ally's sexual harassment comment or the sight of her and Stuart leaving the club together.

Unable to reach her over the next few days, Ryan opened his phone settings, blocked his number ID and phoned her again.

"Ally Dobson speaking."

"It's Ryan. Are you at home?"

She hesitated. "Yes, why?"

"I'll be outside your place in twenty minutes. Buzz me in."

"But—"

He hung up.

Ally didn't bother changing out of the oversized hoodie she'd pinched from Angus when they were still together. She may not love him anymore, but she still loved that hoodie, especially when she was feeling unwell, or moody—or both. It reminded her of home and the life she'd once thought was hers. And right now, who cared what she looked like?

She opened the door to see Mr. Click standing there, looking his usual stunning self. He wore his suits well and carried himself with presence, but she'd also seen the arrogant side of him, and that was the memory she chose to recall. Ally used to be the type of girl who did 'sweet' so well, but ever since the attack in that not-so-dark alley on a quiet Thursday night, she'd learned how to play it cool.

He offered no smile as he looked her up and down. "Thanks for seeing me."

She stepped back. Ryan strolled into the open-plan living space and dropped his keys on the hall table as if he'd been in her apartment many times before. He glanced around the sparsely furnished room with its one couch, table and chairs for two, and distinct lack of lighting. What was his home like? A penthouse apartment? A CEO's mansion?

"It's freezing in here."

"The boiler takes a vacation every now and then. We've learned to live with it. Would you like a drink?"

"Thanks. Peppermint tea if you have any." He undid the top button of his shirt and loosened his tie. It reminded her of their nights at the hotel, those surreal moments before he reached for her. "You don't look so good."

"It's just a bit of a cold. Please, take a seat."

A strained silence fell between them.

He cleared his throat. "I'm sorry about the other night. The texts and calls, I mean."

"I didn't see them until the next day, so no harm done," she lied. "Still, you don't seem like the drunk dial type."

"I'm not usually."

Ally moved to the kitchen and flicked on the kettle. "What can I do for you?"

"Did you have a good night...at the club?"

"I did." Ally had no intention of elaborating. Ryan didn't need to know she'd left the party by Uber not long after they'd arrived, leaving Stuart and Hamish behind. But she couldn't resist adding a little footnote. "It's a great club for dancing."

"I didn't realize you knew Stuart."

"Ditto."

Ryan narrowed his eyes. "Anyway, I want to talk to you about a job."

"Really? I thought you'd made your point when you sacked me."

"Temp staff have nothing to do with me. Do you honestly believe I'd fire you just because you pissed me off?"

"It makes sense."

"Hardly my style. And about that. I don't see why you're so annoyed. The flirtation was mutual."

"Don't you? You run a multimillion-dollar company, have two children, probably live in a mansion with a beautiful wife and a large dog, and just happened to be my boss. And silly me, I had no idea."

"Sometimes I like to fly under the radar, but I don't have a beautiful wife *or* a large dog."

"Well, at least I didn't sleep with a married man."

"I don't recall you asking me if I was married. But if I was, I'm not the sort of guy who would cheat on his wife, believe me."

Ally turned her back on his smug attitude as she poured hot water into two mugs. She added a tea bag to his, and a teaspoon of honey and a wedge of lemon to hers, desperate to sooth the knot forming in her throat. He'd shown her this arrogant side before, so why did his tone upset her? Placing the drinks on the table, she took a seat opposite him. Ryan sipped his tea before he spoke.

"I'll get straight to the point," he said. "First of all, I had nothing to do with the cancelation of your contract, and I can't believe you think I did. You're a temp. It wasn't personal." Ryan didn't wait for her to respond. "Second, I need someone to nanny the girls for a three-week stint, and I wondered if you might be interested."

Ally stared at him, speechless. Being an office temp had been a stretch for her, but a nanny? *Seriously?* She sipped her drink, the heat scorching her tongue as she held his gaze. "I don't have any experience working with young children."

"You're a teacher. How hard can it be? They're good kids."

"No doubt, but still, you want me to look after your daughters without knowing anything about me?"

"Gina followed up on your referees and ran a background check."

This day was going from bad to worse. It seemed like only yesterday that she'd met this guy on a building site, a tool belt slung around his hips and a reluctant smile on his face. And now, he thought he knew everything about her. "You contacted my referees for a position I didn't even apply for?" Ally resisted the urge to add *unbelievable*. She didn't have the energy. Taking another sip of her drink, she let the warm hit of honey calm her. "I'm waiting to hear from the agency about another contract, so…"

"Do you want to at least hear the details?"

"Actually, I don't."

Ryan ignored her. "Six hours a day, Monday to Friday, afternoons and early evenings only. You'd start at two and finish around eight. If you could manage to stay Sunday of next week, I'd appreciate it. I have something I can't get out of."

"So it's not a live-in position?"

He smiled that half-smile as if the idea of her living under his roof held some merit. "The usual requirements apply. After-school care, dinner, homework supervision. I'll aim to be home between seven and eight to take over, and I'll also handle breakfast and the morning school run."

"Sorry, but the hours don't suit my schedule. I have commitments on Thursdays and Fridays until two. And anyway, working for you hardly seems appropriate, wouldn't you agree?"

"Anton, my driver can pick you up as close to two as you can manage on those days. I'd like you to be there when he collects the girls from school."

"I can't. I'm sorry."

"Look, I understand your reluctance after what happened, but it's not like we can't stand each other. Besides, this is purely business. Just think about it over the weekend." He stood, holding her gaze with an intensity that forced her to recollect—his touch, his smell, his taste. "Oh, and there's a thousand-pound retainer up for grabs if you let me know in the next twenty-four hours. Otherwise, it's the same rate of pay as Farra, but you'll get the agency fee."

"A thousand pounds extra? For three weeks' work?"

Ally noticed the tight muscle in his jaw smooth out. He thought he had it in the bag. "Just say the word, and it will be in your bank account tomorrow."

"I couldn't accept that kind of money. Why would you pay so much?"

"Because I'll have the girls full time from next Sunday while my ex-wife gets married. Unfortunately, their nanny has had a family emergency. My mother's in South America at the moment, and my sister lives in Scotland. Sure, I could employ a nanny from an agency, but I prefer someone I know and trust, and I'm prepared to pay for it. What happened between us was regrettable, but we can move past it."

"I'm sorry, but I can't," she repeated.

He studied her, his expression serious. "Pity. I was counting on you."

Ally couldn't believe the nerve of this guy. Trying to make her feel guilty because she didn't want to nanny his children. He finished his tea. She took a deep breath. *Here goes.* "I wanted to ask you," she said with hesitation, "about the girls."

"What about them?"

"It's just…we had unprotected sex and I'm not on birth control. You said you couldn't have kids."

"I can't. Not anymore." Ryan looked like he might elaborate, but he didn't. "Call me tomorrow either way. It may seem like a better idea once you've slept on it." He moved toward the door. "And take some vitamin C."

Ally shut the door behind Ryan and his medical advice. At least this time she'd dared to ask about his fertility status, even if his explanation provided no details. Maybe he didn't want more children and he'd had the snip. It made sense. He was over thirty and the girls must be around eight or nine. She relaxed a little at the thought, trying to put his job offer out of her mind. There was no denying a thousand pounds would come in handy. But looking after the girls at Ryan's place? Worst idea ever.

———

Woken by her text alert, Ally coughed her way to the bathroom, took one look at herself in the mirror and went back to bed. Her phone chirped again, and again a few minutes later, but she didn't have the energy to even look at the screen.

Jia appeared at her bedroom door. "You're awake. How are you feeling?"

"Terrible." Ally coughed. "What time is it?"

Jia checked her watch. "Ten past ten."

"What? No!" She flopped back on the pillows and groaned. "I wanted to go to the gym this morning."

Jia opened the curtains. The look on her face indicated she was about to launch into mother mode. "No gym for you today, Ally Cat. How about I make you some breakfast?"

"Thanks. Can I have porridge?"

"Coming right up."

As Jia left the room, Ally checked her texts and sighed heavily.

Ryan: Hope you're feeling better. Call me. I'd like to get this settled.
Ryan: I'm guessing you're not interested? Pity.
Ryan: Please reconsider. I need your help!
Ryan: Ally?

She threw her phone onto the bed. Selfish man. He couldn't even let her sleep in when she was sick.

Still in her pajamas, Ally padded into the kitchen her hairbrush in one hand and a box of tissues in the other. "Will you brush my hair? It's all knotty, and I don't have the energy."

"Sure," Jia said as she opened the microwave. "But eat something first."

"Why aren't you at college?"

"I don't have a lecture until one. Thought I'd go in late for a change." Jia spooned the hot oatmeal into a bowl and sprinkled it with fresh blueberries and brown sugar. She reached into the fridge for yogurt, plopped a dollop on top of the berries and pushed the bowl across the island, watching Ally as she took her first spoonful. "Any word from the agency? Not that you're capable of working right now."

"Yum. This is so good. Thank you." The sweetness and warmth of the porridge helped Ally relax. "And yes, re the agency. They want me to do Thursdays and Fridays. I've already told them I can't."

"I can pay your share of the rent for a while if that helps."

Ally looked up from her breakfast and smiled. Jia was such a kind soul. "That's so sweet, but I can still pay my share."

"Okay, well I'm off." Jia cocked her head toward Ally's bedroom. "Go back to bed. You need to rest."

Struggling to keep her eyes open, Ally didn't argue. But when she reached her bedroom door, she turned back. "Hey, Jia? Thanks for playing Nurse Nightingale."

"No problem. See you tonight."

Ally awoke around mid-afternoon, and while her cold seemed no better, her thoughts were much clearer. She had to accept Ryan's offer. There was no way she could ask Liz for help. She and AJ had come to her rescue too often lately.

She picked up her phone and flicked Ryan a text.

Ally: I'm interested, as long as we keep it strictly professional. I'm available Sunday next week from two. Text me your address.
Ryan: I'll send a car.
Ryan: What made you change your mind?
Ally: Circumstances.

By Tuesday, one thousand pounds sat in Ally's bank account. But as Sunday loomed, she wondered why she'd sold her soul for a quick grand.

OVERLOOKING THE THAMES

All through the week, Ally tried, without success, to disregard the stupidity of accepting Ryan's child-minding gig. Just before two on Sunday, she hauled herself down the stairs and waited under the awning for her pumpkin to arrive, barely registering the gunmetal colored SUV—with shiny mags and a ski rack—pulling alongside the curb. Ally didn't know why she'd expected someone other than Ryan, but there he was. Mr. Click—no suit, no tie, no smile.

Out of the car, he stepped toward her and opened the door. "Ready? Where's your gear?"

Ally held up her small overnight bag.

"That's it?" he asked. "One bag?"

"It's all I need for a night."

Ally couldn't get used to this formal version of the man. In another life, he'd washed her hair in the shower before they'd made love and groaned her name as he came. Now it was all business. Ryan the construction worker had vanished, replaced by the professional executive, and that same hesitation she'd felt last week when he stood in her home offering her one thousand pounds without an ounce of emotion, reminded her of why she shouldn't be here.

They drove in silence across Putney Bridge toward the inner city. Ally had no idea where Ryan lived. She'd assumed he lived at the hotel because they'd always had the same small suite with the same clothes hanging in the closet.

As light rain misted across the windshield, she watched familiar streets become unfamiliar. The farther they traveled from Putney, the tighter her fists clenched in her lap and the louder the alarm bells chimed in her head. When they stopped for a red light, Ryan reached over and covered her hands with his large one as he said, "Relax."

Ally inhaled sharply. "This is a mistake."

Ryan removed his hand as he drove through the intersection. "You'll be fine. We've shared the same bed more than once; surely we can share a few more hours together?"

"That was different."

"You're right about that," he murmured.

"And please don't bring it up again."

Ryan shot her a sideways glance but said nothing.

Fifteen minutes later, they pulled into a gated warehouse development with an underground garage and landscaped grounds. "This is us." There were at least twenty parking spaces in the garage, many filled with expensive-looking cars and SUVs, and several mountain bikes chained to a bar along the wall. "You okay?" he asked.

She nodded.

"Don't look so worried. You'll feel right at home once you see the place."

Ally hadn't felt 'right at home' in a long time, so she doubted today would be any different.

An industrial-looking elevator carried them to the top of the four-story building, where they alighted into a small lobby. Ryan unlocked the door of apartment 4A with a keycard, holding it open for her to step past. Once inside, she stopped. "Wow. Is it yours?"

"No, it's my brother's place. He's away for a few months."

"It's stunning."

"Farra did the conversion five years ago. It was one of our first, although my grandfather bought the property in the fifties. Have a look around and make yourself at home. I just need to make a call."

Ally stepped farther into the apartment—a large open-plan space, infused with light and pleasantly scented with a hint of coffee. Vertical wooden slats defined a reading nook at one end, while a U of three couches—backed by a long sofa table and a pair of tall palms in charcoal planters—defined the other. Textured rugs covered the polished concrete floors inside the seating areas, and large skylights, angled to enhance the mood, flooded the room with natural light. But what caught her eye the most; a gleaming baby grand standing proudly in one corner.

She moved out onto the covered terrace—accessed on three sides from the living area, a media room, and the master bedroom —and looked out over the River Thames as the rain slowed to intermittent drips. She smiled. If she had to spend three awkward weeks working for Mr. Click, this was the place to do it.

"Amazing view isn't it?" he said as he joined her. "We'll go grocery shopping when the girls get here. I usually eat out, but that's not practicable on school nights. Can you cook?"

Toast, spaghetti, chicken salad. "Not very well."

"Really? I thought you'd be right at home in the kitchen."

She frowned at his sexist remark. "I can do the basics, and I make a mean salad."

"I guess that's a good start." Ryan's tone softened. He leaned back against the railing and looked at her. "I'm sorry about the other day at work. I overreacted."

"You don't have to apologize. I overreacted too. With the text, I mean."

"I'm not in the habit of sleeping with my staff. The truth is, I thought you'd only be at Farra for a couple of weeks, so I took advantage of an opportunity I shouldn't have."

She managed a small nod. There was no point dragging up that text again, and his closeness unnerved her. Ally's gaze swept across the river. Did Ryan still see her as an *opportunity*? His interest in her had not only awakened her nonexistent sex life but had also helped her regain control of who she was. And she still wanted that 'opportunity,' no matter how loudly her 'sensible self' protested otherwise. But here and now wasn't the time or the place. And Ryan would not be that man.

"What time are the twins arriving?"

He glanced at his watch. "Polly said around three, but she's usually late. Right, I'll show you around. And, Ally?" He waited until he had her attention. "Relax. I'm not about to seduce you with my children around. And I'd appreciate you not discussing our history with anyone. I prefer to keep my private life private."

"Of course."

With an 'I can do this' expression firmly fixed in place, Ally followed Ryan into the kitchen. He grabbed a six-pack of beer from the counter and put it in the fridge, giving her a chance to peek into the pantry. Apart from a few boxes of cereal, the usual herbs and spices, and staples like rice and pasta, there wasn't even an egg, an apple, or a moldy loaf of bread.

Ryan took a credit card from his pocket and placed it on the island. "Use this for whatever you need. I'll text you the PIN."

"Thank you."

"Come on, Nanny, I'll show you your room."

"Please don't call me that."

He chuckled. "Remember what I said. Relax."

With windows overlooking the road side of the complex, the guest bedroom was compact but comfortable. In one corner sat a low back lounge chair, a floor lamp, and a small side table. A white linen comforter covered the bed, with a chunky cable-knit throw in mid-gray draped over the corner, and instead of a closet, a wooden slat system held baskets, hooks, and hangers.

Ryan placed her overnight bag on the chair. "This okay?"

"Perfect. Thank you."

"I'll let you settle in." He hesitated in the doorway. She wanted him to step back into the room, hold her face in his hands and kiss her hard and urgent as he'd done at the hotel. But instead, he simply said, "The bathroom's second on the left," before heading into his bedroom across the hall.

IRRITATED TONES

The doorbell rang right on the dot of three. So much for Polly's lack of punctuality. Standing in the kitchen, Ally watched as Ryan opened the door and his ex-wife breezed in with the twins in tow. Dressed in figure-hugging black right down to the ankle boots on her feet, and with vivid red lipstick and impossibly high cheekbones, Polly looked every inch the quintessential London model. Ally took a deep breath and stood tall as she stared in awe at the striking woman before her. Standing five eleven in her stockinged feet, she seldom met women taller than her, but Polly must have been at least six one.

The twins broke the ice, pulling Polly toward Ally. "Mum, Mum, this is Ally. She works at Dad's office."

Polly took a swift glance at Ryan and turned back to Ally. "Oh, I assumed you were the nanny." She offered a delicate hand, but their contact didn't really constitute a handshake. "Nice to meet you."

"Ally *is* the nanny," Ryan said.

Polly looked her up and down with a dismissive frown. She stepped back. "Do you have any experience with children?"

"Polly," Ryan warned. "We've been over this."

"I'm a teacher," Ally said, suddenly glad of the qualification attached to her name.

"Are you between jobs?"

"I've taken time off to travel and study."

Polly nodded. "Girls, why don't you show Ally your room while I talk to Dad."

"Come on, Ally," the twins said in unison.

From the bedroom down the hallway, Ally could hear Ryan and Polly talking in low, irritated tones. She couldn't make out their words but could tell Polly did not approve.

The twins chatted away as usual, sharing knock-knock jokes as Ally helped them unpacked their bags. Several minutes later, Polly appeared at their bedroom door.

"Okay, you two munchkins, Mummy has to go now." Ally watched as Polly hugged her daughters. She turned to Ally. "Ryan has my number. I suggest you put it into your phone."

"Of course." Ally forced her thoughts back to the phrase her mother had taught her as a teenager—*You're the only person you need to be good enough for*—and recited this repeatedly in her head.

"Right. I'd better go. I've left a folder of instructions in the kitchen. Please take good care of them."

"I'll do my best."

Ally stayed in the bedroom while the twins said goodbye to their mother. The affirmation hadn't helped. She didn't feel good enough, not by a long shot. Not for Ryan, or the girls, or for her new life where she struggled to find a place to fit in.

She looked up to see Ryan leaning on the doorjamb. "You okay?"

"Where are the twins?"

"Watching TV."

She swallowed hard and blinked back an annoying tear. "I gather she doesn't approve."

"Polly's a mother cat when it comes to her babies. I told her about you last week. She's just marking her territory."

"She has quite the presence."

"She does." He stepped into the room, and as he dipped his head to catch her gaze, he reached for her hand and squeezed it. "Don't worry. You're going to be fine."

Ally broke the contact. She couldn't let this caring side of Ryan get to her. Meeting Polly had reinforced her belief that Ryan was well out of her league. "You mentioned we needed groceries."

He stood in silence, rubbing his hand across the back of his neck. Ally wished she could rewind a week, to a time when she still had the option to say no, and much earlier, to delete his 'Meet me' texts with the swipe of her finger and laugh about it with Jia and Jade afterward.

To a time when she didn't 'Click' with James Ryan Farrell.

"Right," he said finally. "I'll get my keys."

———

Ryan arrived home just before midnight, feeling a little buzzed and a whole lot horny. As he undressed, he took note of the neatly made bed, the clean en suite, and the recently vacuumed carpet. She'd even picked up his clothes from the floor, and for some reason, he found the whole thing amusing. But then, he'd always been a happy drunk.

The sound of Ally leaving the bathroom drew his attention. He'd noticed the shaft of light under her bedroom door when he'd passed but hadn't wanted to disturb her. Now, his curiosity got the better of him, and he stepped across the hallway.

He leaned on her doorjamb, a pair of low-slung sleep pants the only thing covering his otherwise naked frame. "You're still awake."

"I shouldn't be."

He entered her room and sat on the bed, nodding toward her laptop as he gave her a cheeky grin. "What are you watching?"

Ally closed the lid and pulled her duvet up under her chin. "Nothing interesting. Did you have a good night?"

"I had a great night. How were the girls?"

"Perfect. They went to bed with no problems at all. Mind you, I had to read them each an extra chapter of their books."

Ryan studied her, noticing her small frown of concern. He'd seen it before, on those Thursdays at the hotel, just before they'd had sex. "Thanks for tidying my room. Mrs. Jacks usually takes care of the housework. I'll interview some cleaners during the week."

"I don't mind doing a little cleaning while I'm here."

The right side of his mouth kicked up a fraction as he thought about how quickly their relationship had shifted. Here she was, offering to do his cleaning and all he could think about was taking her to bed. "You need to stop this."

"Stop what?"

"This Little Miss Perfect routine."

Ally shifted in the bed, but she didn't break eye contact.

"It's arousing to the point of distraction."

She looked away. "I thought we agreed to keep this professional."

"We did. But hey, it's going to take some getting used to…on my part, anyway."

"Maybe I should go home and come back in the morning," she said.

"No. Stay. It's cold outside."

"Are you drunk?"

"Yeah, a bit. Well, you know…" Ally went to climb out of bed but stopped. Ryan wondered if she had panties on under her nightshirt because she definitely wasn't wearing a bra. "Please, don't go. I'll be good, I promise."

"Okay, well, you need to get to bed."

He leaned forward and whispered, "I know. But I really want to have hot sex with you right now."

As Ryan's lips brushed against hers, Ally closed her eyes. Her sharp intake of breath and irresistible organic scent made him long for her touch. But she pulled back.

"It feels like you're drunk dialing me again," she whispered, "but in person,"

"I don't normally drink and dial." He grinned. "That shit can get you into serious trouble. But damn, you're so beautiful, and I'm—"

"Please don't do this."

"I'm sorry. You're right." He leaned forward again, holding her gaze as he traced his fingertips along her forearm. "But I want you to know something. Every time I look at you over the next three weeks, I'll want you. Each night when I climb into bed, I'll imagine you there, your legs curled around mine. And every time you worry that scar on the back of your neck, I'll want to kiss it and take away whatever the hell is going on inside your head."

Ryan pushed up from the bed. He gazed down at her, her wide look of innocence and the scrape of her teeth against her bottom lip more of a turn on than she would ever know. "Good night, Ally."

"Morning." Ryan padded over to the fridge to grab the orange juice and proceeded to drink it straight from the carton. Feeling Ally's stare, he stopped mid-gulp and reached for a glass and two painkillers.

"Would you like some breakfast?"

"We're having dippy eggs," Ava announced from the table. "You cook them for *exactly* four minutes, so the yolk is just right for soldiers."

He found this domestic scene strangely comforting. It had been a long time since anyone had cooked him breakfast at home, and even longer since he'd had soft-boiled eggs with fingers of buttered toast. "Sounds great. Thanks."

"Dad, can we watch cartoons until it's time to go?" Isla asked.

"As long as you've made your beds and cleaned your teeth."

Ally lowered two eggs into a saucepan of water as the twins hurried down the hallway to their bedroom. "Bit of a headache?"

"More like a hammer pounding against my skull. Maybe I should join you in your Dry July practice."

She shot him a knowing look. "Maybe you should."

"So you're not back on the Pimm's?"

"No, I feel much better when I'm not drinking."

Ryan watched her move around the kitchen. Something about her had changed. She'd never seemed the nervous type, but it was clear she no longer felt comfortable around him. His 'in person' drunk dial episode last night wouldn't have helped. He wondered if he should broach the subject but decided to let it slide.

He scanned the headlines of yesterday's paper as Ally served his eggs. He wanted to reassure her but didn't know what to say that hadn't already been said. "Thank you for staying last night."

"No problem. But I should get going soon. Is there anything you want me to do before I leave?"

He glanced around the tidy kitchen. "I don't think so. Feel free to stay here during the day if you want."

"Thanks, but I have things to do at home."

Ally turned and stood at the sink with her back to him. He recalled their Thursdays. It was the first time he'd been with a younger woman; they'd never interested him before. Although it had been foolish to pursue her, especially while she worked for Farra, there was no denying the chemistry between them. Even now, with her sexuality folded neatly behind a wall of domesticity, he wanted nothing more than to take her to bed, pull the covers over their heads, and remind her why some rules begged to be broken.

"Polly phoned while you were in the shower." She glanced

over her shoulder at him, her hands still in the sink full of soapy water. He had no idea what she was washing until she opened the fridge and started wiping down the interior.

"What did she say?"

"Nothing much. She wanted to talk to the girls. Actually, she was quite pleasant."

"Good." He rose from the table and put his plate in the dishwasher. "Thanks for breakfast, Nanny. It was delicious."

Ally shot him a dirty look and shook her head.

He watched her, amused by her reaction. "You look nice today."

She stared him down.

"Oh come on, I can't even pay you a compliment now?" He smiled as she closed the fridge. "You didn't seem to mind at the Heaton," he said softly.

"That's entirely different."

"Is it though?"

"Can we not discuss this right now? It's totally inappropriate."

Ryan chuckled to himself. What had started as an innocent compliment to the woman he'd slept with several times—the woman who'd lost herself in his arms and ended up in his dreams—had somehow turned into a battle of wits. He enjoyed a bit of friendly banter with a beautiful woman; it made his day seem lighter. How would he manage to keep his distance for the next three weeks?

"Okay. Let's get the girls to school. I'll drop you off after that."

"I can catch the tube."

"No need."

22

JUST THE NANNY

Ryan wasn't one for idle chitchat while driving. Ally decided this intense concentration was all part of his morning persona. However, in stark contrast to their father, the twins never stopped talking, so there was no awkward silence until they drove away from the school gate.

She'd survived her first day on the job, and congratulated herself for the way she'd handled Ryan's advances the night before. But as he maneuvered through the morning traffic, Ally couldn't get their late-night exchange out of her head. Even if it had been the booze talking, he'd said he still wanted her, and the feeling was mutual.

"Do you want me to drop you home?" he asked finally.

"I'll just get out at the office. I'm going to the Tate Modern."

He glanced her way. "Are you meeting friends?"

"Not today."

Ryan pulled into his space in the parking building, and they sat in uncomfortable silence for a moment before he turned to look at her. "I'm not going to break our agreement, Ally. So relax, okay? I was a little drunk last night, and I'm sorry."

An unexpected lump caught in her throat. She had no idea why she'd been so teary lately.

"Just because we've slept together," he continued, "doesn't mean we can't be friends."

"I know, but—" They both glanced sideways as another car parked beside them. Ally hesitated. "I don't want to be *that* girl. The one who sleeps with her boss, and when it's over, feels used and awkward."

Ryan shifted in his seat and stared straight ahead. Ally immediately regretted opening her mouth. She knew the Thursday score. The rules had been clear from the start. *No questions, no expectations, no...*

"So what are you saying?" he asked. "That there's no going back?"

"What? Back to our Thursdays? I'm not sure casual's my thing, so..."

He glanced down at his watch. "Anyway, I'd better go. Anton starts at one. Text him with a pickup place. Try to give him a bit of notice. And he's a cocky little shit, so watch what you say to him."

"Okay. Thanks for the ride."

———

Using the Citymapper app, Ally had easily located the Heaton on her way back to Putney. Not that it was important. She would never return to the hotel. She'd made the decision that morning, in the back of a double-decker bus, less than an hour after Ryan had shut down their conversation with one casual glance at his watch.

Anton arrived right on time. She opened the car door and popped her head in. "Hi. You must be Anton. I'm Ally."

"How's your day been?" Anton asked with his welcoming smile as she climbed inside and fastened her seat belt.

"Great. I met a lovely Australian couple on the bus. Eighty-year-olds who are traveling for the first time. Amazing. We went to the Tate Modern together."

"Have you been to the Elizabeth Tower?"

"Not yet. It's not the same with Big Ben out of action."

"Yeah. I miss its chime. Why they need four years to do the work is beyond me. Still, that's life these days. We all have to sprint to keep up, but cleaning a bell takes forever."

Ally warmed to Anton straight away. Within a few minutes, she almost felt more comfortable with Ryan's driver than with Mr. Click himself. The guy didn't stop talking, and as they drove through the city to the girls' school, it surprised Ally how much he knew about London's landmarks and tourist spots.

"The twins usually come out of this gate," he said as he pulled into the school parking zone. "But we're a little early."

"How long have you worked for Ryan?"

"Almost eighteen months. He's a good guy. There's no bullshit about him." Anton glanced her way and smiled. "But I wouldn't like to cross him."

Ally wanted to ask him to elaborate but remembered Ryan's warning. She knew her place. She was Ryan's employee, not his girlfriend.

Anton craned his neck toward the gate. "Here they come. Get ready for the onslaught."

23

LONELY NIGHTS

Ryan left the office over an hour late, making it home just after nine. When he walked in the door, the apartment was unusually quiet. He glanced around the kitchen; the smell of spaghetti sauce and the small bowl of green salad on the counter made him smile. Ally had worked for him for just over two weeks now, and in that time, he hadn't ordered takeout once.

Despite his best intentions, Ryan rarely made it home in time for dinner with the girls. The Precinct had become an insatiable mistress, and he often worked late. And Ally? Every time he walked in the door after a long day, he wanted nothing more than to reach out and caress the back of her neck—to initiate an intimate exchange and take her to his bed.

It was evident by her shyness around him and the way she raced out the door as soon as her shift had finished, that he had the same effect on her. But the few times he'd asked her to eat with him or stay and watch a movie, she'd politely declined.

Ryan undid the top button of his shirt and loosened his tie as he walked down the hallway. He'd called earlier to say he'd be home late but was surprised by what he found when he entered his bedroom. Ally, asleep on his bed with the twins either side, a pile of books scattered around them. He picked up a paper-back from the floor, and as he placed it on the nightstand, she stirred.

"What time is it?" She whispered as she struggled to sit. She looked tired and pale. Had he been asking too much of her? "I'm so sorry. We were reading. I must have fallen asleep."

He reached over and lifted Isla into his arms. "You stay there. I'll come back for Ava in a minute."

Ryan carried Isla through to her bed and tucked her in.

"Daddy, can I stay in your bed?" she said in a sleepy voice, her arms still clasped around his neck.

"Not tonight, sweetheart. It's late, and you have school tomorrow."

"I miss Mum and Marc. So does Ava."

They were good kids—beautiful little souls—and he loved how close they were to Polly. As for Marc, Ryan couldn't have asked for a nicer guy to co-parent his children with. He kissed her cheek. "How about we FaceTime them in the morning?"

"Okay. Love you."

"Love you, too, Button."

By the time Ryan returned from putting Ava to bed, Ally was stacking the books away in a book bag. "I'll get my things." She clutched the brightly colored bag over her chest. "I've left you dinner."

"Thanks. It smells great." He followed her down the hallway and into the kitchen. "Why don't you stay?" She looked at him and shook her head. As he'd expected. "We could watch a movie. I can text Anton and let him know."

"I can't. I have a class in the morning." Ally pushed past him and picked up her things from the arm of the sofa. He came up behind and helped her into her coat, leaning toward her as he smoothed the back of her collar.

"You promised," she whispered.

"I know." He stepped back. "But I meant what I said. Every

night when I come home, I wish you didn't have to leave…didn't *want* to leave."

"But it's safe, isn't it? To say those words when you know I won't act on them—when you know there's a car waiting downstairs to take me home."

"Is that what you think? That I'm toying with you?"

"Aren't you?"

Ryan reached for her hand. Her fingers were cold and her touch unresponsive.

"You didn't want anything more, remember?" she said. "Just a Thursday-night affair. But there's one thing I don't get. Why take me to a hotel you own if you wanted to be discreet?"

"How do you know I own it?"

"Anton told me."

"So you've discussed our personal life with my driver?" he asked with a frown.

"He just happened to mention it."

Ryan hesitated. Taking Ally to the Heaton hadn't been the smartest move. "I keep a room there for convenience. It seemed the best option at the time."

Ally nodded, frowned. "Anyway, I have to go. Anton must be wondering what's keeping me."

"He isn't paid to wonder. Look, I don't get what went wrong. We had a small disagreement, and suddenly it's over? Surely we're better than that."

Ally shook her head.

"Talk to me. Please?" he said. "Tell me what the problem is."

She took a deep breath. "I thought I'd be okay with just the physical thing, no strings attached, but every time I see you, my stomach ties itself in knots. I don't want to feel that way, about any man. And you're a successful businessman who drives an expensive car and owns a flash hotel. I don't belong in your world, Ryan. Not even on a Thursday. And don't tell me 'it's bullshit,' because that's how I feel."

"I wasn't going to say it's bullshit. I understand. In hindsight, I probably shouldn't have asked you to look after the girls. We've had sex—amazing, mind-blowing sex. And now here you are, doing my laundry, and my housework, and cooking me dinner."

"It's my job, a job I'm grateful for."

He studied her. Dangling a thousand pounds in front of her now seemed more like a bribe than an incentive. "Are you okay, financially?"

She glanced away. "Yes, fine."

"Look, why don't we go out for dinner and a movie next week?"

"And what happens if we run into someone you know? Will you introduce me as the nanny?"

He remained silent.

"Anyway, I have to go. I'm tired. I need a good night's sleep."

Ryan sighed deeply. "Yeah, me too. I'll see you tomorrow." He didn't see her to the door. He knew he wouldn't be able to resist kissing her if he got too close.

After she'd gone, he headed to the kitchen and sat at the breakfast bar, staring at the plate of meatballs and spaghetti he'd removed from the oven and the salad she'd left for him. He glanced around the apartment, the glow of the TV in the media room the only other light apart from the kitchen downlights.

Of course, Ryan knew loneliness. Anyone who'd been through a divorce did. Eating alone night after night, waking up in an empty bed, but he wasn't one for self-pity. Ally was right; he'd promised to keep their interaction professional and had broken that promise.

Lying in bed later, Ryan buried his face in the pillow she'd slept on and inhaled deeply. The smell took him back to the hotel, to those nights when he'd held her while she slept. And as much as he tried to tell himself what they had was just a casual fling, there was little conviction to his words.

24

A TIME AND PLACE

Standing in the girls' closet, Ally ran her hand along the empty hangers on the rail. Earlier, she'd helped them pack, said an emotional goodbye at the door, and tried her hardest to swallow the lump in her throat as Ryan escorted them across the lobby and into the elevator.

With the sheets spinning in the dryer and the rest of the apartment tidy and clean, Ally sat on the terrace with a steaming mug of green tea, and picked at a plate of leftovers. She stared out over the Thames through the steady rain. The trees on the other side of the river were now in bud, their leaves ready to burst, and she reflected on how spring lifted her spirits, but also made her long for home.

Back inside, Ally sat at the piano, her hands poised above the keys. It had been months since she'd played, and while she'd initially vowed not to lift the fallboard, tonight she couldn't resist. She stilled, feeling the seat's cushion beneath her as her bare left foot grazed the cold metal of the soft pedal. A deep breath filled her lungs as tentative fingers found the right chords. Her voice followed. Hesitant yet focused, she was surprised by how easily 'Rust on White Linen,' the last song she'd written, came back to her.

Later, as the evening chill settled in, she lay on the couch, tucking herself under a woolen throw. She switched on the TV and watched the end of a quiz show, wondering if she would ever be brave enough to share her music and words with anyone else—and why she didn't want to go back to Putney.

"Hey, sleepyhead."

Ally woke to Ryan's gentle shake.

"Sorry?" She glanced around the room—the glow from the TV the only source of light—and swallowed against the unpleasant taste in her dry mouth. She rubbed her face. "What time is it?"

He reached down and switched on the lamp next to her. "Getting on for nine."

"I was out to it." Ally stood and stretched before folding the throw and draping it over the back of the sofa.

"I wasn't sure if you'd still be here."

She stepped away, ignoring the heat in his gaze. "I was waiting for the dryer to finish," she lied. "I'll go check."

"Leave it. I'll do it later." Ryan removed his jacket and hung it over a chair before opening the top buttons of his shirt. Through the gap, she could see the form of his pecs and a smattering of chest hairs curling in all directions, and his hair was wet.

"Did you get caught in the rain?"

"I stopped to help one of the neighbors with a flat battery." A silence fell between them. "I'm glad you stayed."

Ally moved behind the breakfast bar and filled a glass of water from the filter in the fridge door. She took a sip. "Have you eaten?"

"Yes, I had something at Polly's."

"Okay, well I'll get out of your hair."

He nodded slowly. "I'll take you home. Just let me have a quick shower first. I'm freezing."

She felt her face and neck flush. The Click Effect, she called it.

While the twins were there, his formal words and detached manner after that first Sunday night had been firmly on show, but there was no mistaking his intention tonight. With the three weeks up, they were back to a level playing field. "It's fine. I'll grab an Uber."

"Why so shy?" He stepped forward, blocking her exit from the kitchen, and stood with his hands in his pockets, his eyes expressing a lazy smile. "I've kissed you in the most intimate of places, washed you in the shower, and slept with my legs wrapped around yours—and suddenly, you can barely look at me."

Ally dropped her gaze for a second as she whispered, "I told you. I don't belong in your world."

He reached out and lifted her chin with his finger, his hazel eyes sincere. "That's because your interpretation of my world is based on the material. I'm just a guy like any other, trying to do my best for the people who depend on me as I plow through the bullshit."

"So, what would you do in my situation? What do you suggest?"

"That you stay. We don't have to answer to anyone but ourselves." Ryan stepped closer. "Three weeks without your touch is twenty-one days too long."

"And on Thursday?"

"We'll text back and forth. You'll play hard to get, and I'll do my best to persuade you. And later, I'll meet you at the hotel—or here if you prefer—with a wide smile on my face. Because I spend my whole week looking forward to seeing you again."

"But what would Polly say if she knew we were sleeping together?"

"Who I sleep with is my business. Besides, she already knows."

"You told her? Why would you do that?"

"I had one too many whiskeys at the wedding. It was after the twins had gone to bed. Marc and his groomsmen had been on the shots and were hammered, so I helped Polly drag him to their room. We had one of those emotional moments that tend to occur as a result of too much alcohol and a touch of regret. So naturally, I spilled my guts all over the flagstone floor."

"She must hate me."

"She's fine with it. Although I prefer to keep my personal life private, Polly is the twins' mother, and for that reason, she deserved to hear it from me before someone else told her."

Ryan and Polly's past relationship intrigued Ally. She wanted to ask what went wrong—who left whom—but sensed he'd already shared all he was willing to.

"But, as I've said before," he continued, "I don't sleep with women who'll regret it in the morning. So I'm off to the shower. If you'd like to join me, please do. If not, I'll drive you home as soon as I've finished."

Ally didn't know what to say. She'd worked through the process of letting him go, had told herself there would be no more 'How about Thursday?' texts and was ready to walk away like she knew she should. And yet, her hedonistic side wanted him to make love to her once again, because when it came to sexual pleasure, Ryan didn't disappoint. "What are we doing here, Ryan?"

Ryan stepped forward and rested his hands on the counter. She stretched her neck to one side as he reached up to brush away a lock of hair and kissed the spot just below her earlobe. "*We* are doing whatever the hell we feel like. There's no need to label it." He kissed her again, the heat of his lips giving her goosebumps, and whispered, "We're adults, we make the rules."

He moved away. She heard the swish of his tie as he pulled it through his shirt collar, the click of the hallway light switch and, moments later, the soft hum of the shower. Ryan was right. There was no point in regret. She knew the score. It was up to her whether she wanted to leave it at nil or try to solicit a draw.

She followed his footsteps. Removing her denim jacket, she draped it over the chair in his room along with her dress and lingerie. As a cloud of steam greeted her at the en suite door, she reached for a towel and wrapped it around her naked body.

A tiled partition obscured the shower so Ryan would have no idea she'd entered the bathroom. There was still time to walk away, leaving him and their Thursdays at the Heaton behind. But right now, the anticipation of his moan as he came and the touch and feel of him was all that mattered. Taking a deep breath, she stepped closer and when she said his name, he smiled and offered his hand. He bent to kiss her, his tongue hot and eager as her towel fell to the floor.

"I thought you'd left."

"I couldn't get the front door open."

As Ryan pulled her under the water, several jets pulsed across the steam-filled space. "What?"

"The lock wouldn't budge."

He threw back his head and laughed. She loved making him laugh. "Remind me to check it out."

His lips traveled across her shoulder as he licked the water from her skin. Ally clasped her arms around his neck and smiled up at him. "You're excited?"

He glanced down at his growing erection, the smile still on his face. "How can you tell?"

"Your accent."

"Aye," he said. "That's because your gorgeous nipples are rubbing against my chest and I can't wait to kiss them."

Ryan leaned forward and kissed her gently. Like their first kiss in the back of the cab. Soft lips, eager tongue. Pulling back, he wrapped his arms around her. "Please don't shut me out again," he murmured. "That shit hurts."

Ally looked up at him and frowned. An admission of hurt was the last thing she'd expected from Ryan Farrell.

"What?" he said. "You think it doesn't hurt when someone I care about rejects me?"

"You care about me?"

Ally held her breath as he cupped her face in his hands. "Of course I do."

"I care about you too."

"Good."

The following morning when Ally awoke to Ryan nuzzling into her neck and rearing to go, she hesitated. After all, there were some disadvantages to early morning sex, the luminosity being one. In the later hours of the evening, anticipation played its part in seduction. Lines became blurred. Add mood lighting and an attentive man who couldn't keep his hands to himself, and everything seemed slightly surreal. But while Ally loved being naked, having her body on display in the morning light always made her a little uncomfortable. And what about her scar? Sometimes, he would kiss it, and other times, gently run a finger over its length. Would today be the day he mentioned it?

"What are you thinking about?" Ryan moved closer, pressing his erection against the cleft of her buttocks. And as if reading her mind, he lifted her hair off her nape and gently kissed it. But as usual, he didn't ask for an explanation. *No stories.*

"Nothing much."

He turned her gently to face him. "Should I be offended that you're thinking 'nothing much' when I'm lying naked beside you?"

She matched his smile. "No, not at all. It's just...I'm going to miss spending time with the twins. I feel kind of sad about it."

"I'm sure they'll miss you too. But you don't have to stop seeing them. We could all go to the movies one weekend."

"I'd like that."

"And, I have a charity dinner in a few weeks. You should come. Polly and Marc will be there, and Stuart and his partner. It's for a Scottish nonprofit we all support."

Ally thought back to meeting Polly—the figure-hugging head-to-toe outfit, the Hermes handbag, and the beautiful symmetry of her face. "What? No, I couldn't possibly. Not if Polly's going to be there."

He rolled onto his back and pulled her over to straddle him, his lopsided smile on display and hair tousled from sleep. "Would you stop worrying about my ex-wife and come and seduce me?"

"Only if you say please." She traced a fingertip around his nipples. "But we can't stay in bed all morning. I'm meeting my sister for lunch."

"What's with the roast?" Liz laughed as she gestured toward Ally's plate. "I haven't seen you eat a roast in ages."

"It's the cold. It makes me ravenous. Besides, I'm building up strength for my exams."

"So, tell me about this guy you've been working for. Is he tall, blond, and handsome?"

Ally didn't want to discuss Ryan with Liz. Not yet, anyway. "No. He's older, balding, and has a bay window for a gut. Happy?"

Liz studied Ally through narrowed eyes. "That's a fib. You've always been a terrible liar."

"And you are a nosy brat."

"Did I mention our friend Chris is single? He's a doctor and such a nice guy."

More than once. "Thanks, but no thanks. I hate the thought of being set up, especially by you."

Liz clutched her hands to her heart. "Ouch. You wound me."

"Imagine being with a doctor. They touch sick people all day and work such long hours."

"He's probably a little old for you, anyway. He does have a younger brother, but he's divorced and has kids. And you don't want to go there."

Didn't she? Ryan was divorced and had kids. And even though she knew it wouldn't last, she still couldn't resist the thrill of a casual affair with a divorced father of two. "Thanks, but I'm perfectly capable of finding my own man."

Liz's expression turned serious, and Ally knew what was coming. The 'Angus Talk.' When it came to Angus, she wished her family would give her a little credit, but they all worried about her, and rightly so.

"I just don't want to see you and Angus back together. That man can be very charming when he puts his mind to it."

"Yes, so you keep saying. But you know what? I just don't see him that way anymore. He's shown his true colors, and those particular hues don't appeal."

"Good."

Ally became pensive. "He did love me though…in his own way."

"Probably still does. But sometimes, love is only on loan until it runs its course."

Ally burst out laughing. "Quick. Take a picture of an ocean sunset. You sound like an inspirational meme."

"Feel free to post it on Instagram."

"I'm not on social media anymore, remember?"

"Yeah, sorry." Liz cleared her throat and picked at the cake in front of her. "Tell me about your new job."

"It's at a gym downtown, Studio Hudson. Split shifts, three days a week and the occasional weekend, so it's perfect. But it's only casual at this stage."

"What's the pay like?"

"Not bad, and I get extra for PT sessions. Right, shall we get going?"

"Before we go, can I give you a piece of advice?"

"Go on then."

"When you do find someone, don't give them mixed messages. I did that to AJ for months. It's a waste of everyone's time."

"But I don't want to scare him off."

Liz pointed a finger at her younger sister and laughed. "See, you have met someone."

Ally had walked straight into that one. Trying not to smile, she stood and grabbed her bag off the floor. "Come on. Let's go and do some credit card damage. I need a new bra and panties."

2 5

A KILT AND TIE

Dressed in a kilt, long socks, and lace-up shoes, Ryan stood in the doorway of Ally's apartment. Of course she'd seen men wearing kilts many times before, usually pipe band members at the local agricultural fair they held every autumn back home. But Mr. Click in a kilt? *Wow.* He grinned at the expression on her face. "What?"

"You look amazing."

"Aye? You like a man in a kilt, Ms. Dobson?" He lifted the tartan and flashed his muscular Scottish thighs.

"Ryan! Do you have boxers on?"

He slapped her playfully on the butt as he followed her inside. "Do you have panties on?"

"You'll have to wait and see."

"Ditto." Bending forward, he pecked her on the lips. "You look pretty amazing yourself. Where did you get that dress?"

Ally pulled back and did a twirl while she tried to convince herself that going on a proper date with Ryan was a good idea. "I borrowed it from my sister."

"Your sister has beautiful taste."

"Thank you. I'll tell her you said so."

"Right. We'd better go. The traffic's crazy."

When Ally and Ryan entered the ballroom over an hour later, no one even glanced their way. The sky didn't fall nor did the earth shake, and as they made their way to the table, Ryan held Ally's hand and stayed close to her side.

Just like a real boyfriend.

He ushered her toward a seat next to Stuart—also dressed in a kilt—who immediately stood and hugged her. Stuart introduced his girlfriend, Jacinta, who smiled tightly through overly plumped lips while staring straight ahead. When Polly and Marc, and Dave and his wife joined them, Polly bent down and kissed Ally on the cheek, before taking a seat. Totally unexpected.

All through the formalities, Ryan kept reaching for Ally's hand. Once or twice, he looked her way and smiled. This was a side of him she'd not seen before, and she wondered why she'd been so nervous.

But as she cut into her steak, Jacinta reminded her why in less than a dozen words.

"So, Ally." Jacinta waited until she had Ally's full attention. "Weren't you the twins' nanny?"

"Well, more of an after-school carer."

Jacinta picked up her wine, her nails almost too long to hold the glass. She had a way of staring that made one feel uncomfortable. "Do you go through an agency? Because if not, I may be able to get you some work."

"Thank you, but I don't have the time these days." Ryan put his hand on her leg under the table and gently rubbed her thigh, not in a sexual way, but rather as a show of support.

"Ally's agreed to help out at the gym for a while," Dave said.

"Really?" Jacinta frowned. "Any other ambitions, Ally?"

Ally didn't miss a beat. "To be content."

Removing his hand from her leg, Ryan cut into his steak.

"No, I mean career-wise." Jacinta stabbed a small mouthful of salmon with her fork, took an uninterested bite and glanced at Polly.

"I'm still trying to figure that out." Ally rarely told people she was—or rather had been—a teacher, who on her arrival in London, had declared a twelve-month holiday from making plans. Before the attack, she had planned everything, from their weekly dinner menu to what days she did the laundry. Looking back, that constant struggle to maintain perfection now seemed suffocating.

Ryan shot Jacinta a questioning look. "So, what are you doing with yourself these days? Still in the movie business?"

"I'm taking a break for a while," Jacinta replied. "Good roles for female actors are rare. Studios don't want to take a risk on raw talent."

"Pity." Ryan sipped his wine. "This steak is delicious by the way."

They maintained their polite conversation throughout the rest of the meal. But things became more heated once the charity auction started. Ally couldn't believe the money being thrown around, with Stuart, Polly, and Ryan right in the thick of it, bidding against each other for expensive wine, trips to Paris, and sought-after West End tickets.

Taking a break for a while, Ally walked through the double doors leading onto the balcony and looked out over the small enclosed lawn. A half-moon peeked from between the clouds, and a light breeze carried the scents of star jasmine and honeysuckle in the air, reminding her of home.

When Ryan appeared at her side, his hand skimming around her waist as he pulled her close, she felt happier than she had in a long time, despite Jacinta.

"You okay?" he asked.

"Yes, fine. I'm just heading to the restroom. I'll be back soon."

He kissed her on the cheek. "Okay, I'll be inside."

Sitting in a stall of one of the most opulent restrooms she'd ever seen, Ally congratulated herself on how well she was doing in front of Ryan's friends and ex-wife. As she was about to finish, the main door whooshed open and Jacinta's voice filled the small room. Ally stilled.

"I can't believe he brought his nanny with him."

"Ally's not his nanny," Polly said.

"Well, whatever he calls her, I wonder if they were at it while she was looking after the girls?"

"Jacinta! Stop it. Ally seems like a nice enough girl."

"Girl is right. How old is she? Sixteen?"

"Granted, they're from different worlds, but so are Marc and I. Ryan's happy, and that's all that matters."

"Please. She's no more than his sideshow entertainment, only good for a dirty weekend. He'll soon get sick of her."

"Maybe, but it's none of our business." Polly lowered her voice to a terse whisper. "Ryan wouldn't have brought Ally here if he didn't care for her. You know that."

"And did you see that dress?"

"It's beautiful," Polly said. "The blue really suits her."

"I bet Ryan paid for it. I know my labels, and that frock's no High Street knockoff. It's been hand-picked off a designer's rack."

"Look, give the girl a break. For Ryan's sake."

"You still have a soft spot for him."

"Yes, because he's the twins' father. If he wants to bring a date, it's fine with me. He deserves to be happy."

"Did you know they were together?"

"He mentioned it. Said it was casual."

"It won't last. Britt will see to that. I saw them having lunch together last week. Very cozy it was."

Ally sat in the stall with her head bowed and listened as Jacinta's deep voice trailed out of the room.

As she washed her hands and stared at her reflection in the mirror, she was overcome by a rush of emotion. She looked up to stop the tears from falling and ruining her mascara, a trick she'd once seen on *Oprah*. It'd been one of her mum's favorite programs when Ally was growing up.

Jacinta's words stung; she'd never been called 'sideshow entertainment' before—well as far as she was aware.

And who on earth was Britt?

2 6

SIDESHOW ENTERTAINMENT

Apart from the occasional word, neither of them said much on the way home, but as they entered the CBD, Ryan reached over and rested his hand on her knee. "You're awfully quiet."

"I'm just enjoying your playlist. I love this song."

"I never thought of you as a music buff. What kind of music do you like?"

Ally shrugged, her attention on the street signs as she found her bearings. "A bit of everything. I'm not fussy."

"Should we go to the hotel? We could sleep late, go out for brunch."

An image of her walking through the Heaton's lobby in her borrowed dress and heels flashed through her mind.

Sideshow entertainment.

"I should go home. I need to study tomorrow."

"Okay." He reached for her hand, entwining his fingers with hers. "I could stay over if that's easier?"

Easier? Would it be the last time they'd have sex? The last time he'd whisper words of seduction across her skin and spoon her while they slept? The last morning she'd watch him dress without conversation as he contemplated the day ahead? "I'd like that."

As Anton stopped for a red light, Ryan leaned over and kissed her on the cheek. "Thanks for coming tonight. It was nice to see you and Polly talking. She means well but can be a bit abrasive at times. But nothing like Jacinta. That woman's coated in steel wool."

"Yes, I got that vibe. How long's she been with Stuart?"

"Five years, on and off." Anton pulled through the intersection and took a left. "They have an open relationship. I can't see it lasting much longer."

"Really? I've never met a couple in an open relationship."

He grinned. "So you wouldn't be keen for a threesome?"

"Are you making fun of me?"

"No, not at all. It's not my thing either." Ryan paused. "But watch Stuart. He can be a very persuasive man."

"What do you mean?"

"Let's just say he's a firm believer in 'all's fair in love and war.' His feet are constantly itching to go elsewhere."

Silence filled the space between them as Ally's thoughts turned to Angus. How long had his feet itched for? Had it been months? Years? "Do you think polygamy's becoming more of a trend?" she asked finally.

He didn't answer straight away. "For some people, maybe."

———

Ryan turned on the bedside lamp and sat on Ally's bed, waiting for her to finish in the bathroom. She'd been quiet since leaving the venue. Had Jacinta, or maybe Polly, upset her in some way? He glanced around the room, expecting to see knickknacks and personal items, but apart from a spiral notebook and a couple of dog-eared paperbacks on the bedside table, the room was devoid of possessions and decoration, and there were scarcely any clothes hanging in the open closet.

Makeup-free but still dressed in her gown, Ally walked into the room and sat on the bed with her back to him. "I might need some help."

As he freed the zipper, he felt a familiar stir in his groin. Inhaling her scent, he bent down to kiss the scar across her nape. He'd often wondered how it came about, but as she'd never offered an explanation, he hadn't wanted to ask. "You looked beautiful tonight. When you were dancing with Stuart, I couldn't take my eyes off you."

"He's a good dancer."

"So are you. You have a certain rhythm about you, the way you move and talk."

Ally glanced over her shoulder at him, a slight smile in her expression. "Thank you, but I must admit, I felt a little out of place around your friends."

"Why? You're an amazing young woman." Ryan peeled the dress over her shoulders, his lips still caressing her neck. "A young woman who isn't wearing a bra."

She turned in his arms, her hands reaching for the buttons of his shirt. "But I do have panties on."

"Show me."

Her dress pooled around her ankles as she stood, those alluring breasts on full display in front of him. He shook his head as he muttered, "Fuck" under his breath. He'd been more than a little jealous when she danced with Stuart. Now, he couldn't wait to lie beside her. To touch her and taste the slight saltiness of her skin. To lose himself in her warmth.

She undressed him until all he had on was his kilt, his growing erection evident under the green and fawn tartan. "Can I look now?"

"Look where?"

"Under the kilt."

"Aye." He released her and leaned back on the bed, propping himself against the pillow with his hands behind his head. "Be my guest."

Slowly lifting the fabric, Ally swallowed hard as she took a peek. "You pranced around the ballroom all night without boxers on?"

"It's the only way to wear a kilt. Feels amazing, and when you're with a beautiful woman, highly sexual." He grabbed her around the waist as she straddled him, then lifted his hands to her breasts. "Have you ever had sex with a guy wearing a kilt before, Miss. Dobson?"

"No, never."

"So you're a kilt virgin?" Ryan lifted the kilt, freeing his erection. "Come here." He pulled on the lace of her thong. "I've been waiting all night to do this."

"Don't rip them."

"Why? Were they expensive? I'll buy you a new pair."

"You are not ripping my thong." As he reluctantly let go, Ally shuffled backward and reached into her nightstand to pull out a condom.

They'd had sex without protection for a few minutes once, in the early hours of the morning, when passion had overridden caution, but he knew it had been a stupid move. For a moment, he was tempted to ask if she'd consider being exclusive, but there was plenty of time for that. Right now, with her straddling him, he had better things to think about.

He stopped her as she pulled at the buckle of his belt. "Don't. Leave it on."

"I thought you were joking."

Ryan laughed at her shocked expression. Ally was shy in the bedroom. She liked the lights dimmed and the bed covers close, and that turned him on more than he ever thought it would. "I'd never joke about having sex while dressed in a kilt."

"So you make a habit of it, do you? Kilt sex?"

He chuckled, and as she entwined her hands behind his neck, his lips captured first one breast and then the other. "I can honestly say"—he pulled her down onto him and watched her almost pained expression as they found their rhythm—"I've never had sex wearing a kilt before."

"I'm not sure I believe you."

"It's true," he assured her. "I'm losing my kilt cherry too. Right here, right now. With you. And…shit!" He tipped his head back and closed his eyes. "It feels so good. So. Damn. Good."

THAT'S BLEAK

It was Sunday morning, and apart from study, Ally had nothing to get up for. In the end, Ryan had left early, so there was no one wanting breakfast. No one to share a shower with.

She left the warmth of her bed and opened the curtains. Storm clouds brewed in the west with the promise of rain, and she stood for a moment, watching the sky darken until the cold drove her back under the covers. She'd nearly drifted off to sleep again when Jia barged through the door and jumped on the bed. "So, he's gone?"

Ally pulled the duvet over her head. "Go away. I'm sleeping."

"Did he stay the night?"

Placing another pillow behind her, Ally nodded and grinned. Jia knew Ryan had stayed but still wanted verification.

"Wow. Way to go, you. Apart from Angus, that's the first guy you've ever brought home. It must be serious."

"It's not. I have a lot going on, and he's busy, so…"

"I thought you two were clicking again."

Ally recalled Jacinta's 'sideshow' comment and Ryan's goodbye kiss when he'd mentioned he wouldn't be available for the next two weeks. "I don't know. We're from different worlds and, to be honest, I felt awkward around his friends. Ryan's ex was there, in all her understated elegant glory. I'm sure her dress was Versace. That Bruno Mars song popped into my head every time I looked at her."

Jia hummed several bars of 'Versace on the Floor,' making Ally laugh. "But you had a good time, right?"

"I did. You should have seen the gowns and all the bling. You would've loved it. And heaps of the men wore kilts."

Jia cocked her head and studied Ally closely. "Are you feeling okay? You look a little green around the gills."

"I feel like I'm hungover but I only drank lime and soda all night. Maybe it was the rich food."

"That's bleak. You need to go for a checkup."

"What I *need* is to take a shower, but I'm kind of naked under here, so…"

Jia jumped up and headed for the door. "Eww. TMI!"

―――

"Ms. Dobson?" Ally stood and followed the doctor down a labyrinth of corridors and into a small office at the back of the medical center. A combination of stuffy heat and the smell of antiseptic had her struggling to breathe, and when the doctor closed the office door, Ally felt a little lightheaded.

"I'm Helen Darcy. Sorry about the wait. Monday's are always busy."

Ally had requested a female doctor but hadn't expected her to be so young. Taking a deep breath, she grasped the back of the chair to steady herself. "It's so hot in here."

"I know what you mean." The doctor indicated for Ally to sit and opened the window a fraction before doing the same. "What can I do for you?"

"I've been feeling a bit off-color lately, so I thought I should have a checkup."

Doctor Darcy's hands hovered over her keyboard. "Symptoms?"

"I'm exhausted. I think I might be low on iron."

The doctor placed the blood pressure cuff on Ally's upper arm and proceeded to squeeze the bulb. "Your blood pressure's slightly elevated." She released the cuff and removed the stethoscope from her ears. "Have you experienced high blood pressure in the past?"

"Not that I know of."

"When was your last period?"

"About three months ago. But that's normal for me. Last year, it stopped all together for a while. I've had some spotting, though."

The doctor focused on the keyboard, typing with her index fingers. "Were you overdoing the dieting?"

"No. I eat like a horse normally. But I had a stressful breakup, and my body went a bit haywire."

"Any weight gain lately?"

"A few pounds maybe. I blame the cold. It always makes me hungry."

"Breast tenderness?"

"A bit. And I've been a little nauseous some days."

The doctor stopped typing and frowned. "Has it occurred to you that you might be pregnant?" Her tone bordered on sensitivity, but Ally couldn't read her expression.

"No. My… The guy I've been seeing is sterile."

"Sterile? Or he's had a vasectomy?"

"I'm not sure. But he definitely can't have kids."

Her hands returned to the keyboard. "And have you engaged in unprotected sex recently?"

"We were less than careful one night."

For one so young, Doctor Darcy was certainly adept at getting her non-verbal point across. Ally squirmed. Surely Ryan wouldn't have put her at risk? He didn't seem the reckless sort.

"Okay, let's get the internal out of the way. Pop behind the curtain and jump up on the bed. There's a gown on the hook if you're modest. Otherwise, the sheet is fine."

Ally lay on the bed and watched the doctor flick her gloves into place. She stared up at the dead moths in the fluorescent light above and inhaled sharply at the first touch of the unfamiliar hand.

"Relax." The doctor glanced upward as she felt for clues. She removed her hand and the gloves came off with a snap. "I'd say you're definitely pregnant, and several weeks along."

A wave of nausea crashed over her. This was ridiculous. How could she be pregnant? "What? I can't be."

"I'd prefer to do a scan right away. Do you want to call your partner for support?"

Support? Would Ryan offer his support? He told her he couldn't have children! "No, he's...um... Don't I have to pee on a stick or something?"

"I think we can safely skip that step."

"I can't be pregnant. There must be something else going on."

She looked at Ally with concern. "Right, well let's take a look, shall we? I'll check with radiography and be back in a minute."

Tears welled in Ally's eyes, but as she tried to convince herself that the doctor was mistaken, she refused to let them fall. What was the medical code for an unplanned pregnancy? *SGKU—Stupid Girl Knocked Up.* She took a deep breath. This wasn't happening. No way. But what if she *was* pregnant?

One minute stretched into two, then three, and then five. The delay offered Ally time to panic, to slot Ryan into a different role. The role of a father, not only to the twins but also to her baby. A baby he maintained he could never conceive.

The door edged open, held in place by a young man pushing the ultrasound cart. Dr. Darcy followed behind. "Okay, Ally. Let's see what's going on."

PURELY HYPOTHETICAL

Chris often worked offshore for months at a time, and with internet coverage patchy at best in the refugee camp, Ryan hadn't spoken to his brother in weeks. So when he received a text from him saying he'd be in Dubai for a few days' R & R, Ryan took the opportunity to schedule a Skype call so he could broach the subject on his mind.

Chris was the no-nonsense type—a studious high achiever and their mother's pride and academic joy when he graduated as a doctor just days before his twenty-seventh birthday. Ryan was the party boy who seemed to dodge bullets left and right. Occasionally, one would hit him dead center, but he'd never got into any serious trouble once he met Polly. Now they were both in their thirties, the brothers seldom exchanged a cross word.

"Hey," Ryan said. "What the hell are they feeding you out there? You look like you're sucking sherbet."

"Yeah. I've had a virus, but I'm on the mend now."

Questions bounced back and forth between them. How were the twins? The weather in Dubai? Inconsequential small talk.

Now the time had come, Ryan didn't know how to raise the

subject so was relieved when Chris asked, "How's Farra's forecast looking? Anywhere near the mark?"

"Not as good as last year. Building costs are on the up, which isn't good news for the Precinct. But I'm not worried. We're still in a great position."

"You're fidgeting," Chris said. "Everything all right on the home front?"

"Fine. But the house reno is giving me a few sleepless nights." Ryan paused. He'd been stressing about this conversation all day, and now they were face-to-face on the screen, he'd forgotten his rehearsed speech. "I have something to ask you. But before I do, I just want to say, I won't be offended if you say no."

Chris leaned in as if expecting bad news. "Sure."

"If I ever wanted to have another kid, would you act as a sperm donor?"

"You've met someone?" Chris grinned from ear to ear.

"I said 'if.' It's purely hypothetical."

"Is it Britt?"

"Hell, no. She's too full on, not to mention her boys are little terrors."

"I thought you'd decided not to go down the IVF road again?"

"I had. But time is a great healer, apparently. What if I meet someone younger who wants kids? Do I just say no outright?"

Chris frowned at Ryan's response. "You *have* met someone. Come on, what's she like? Obviously younger. That's new for you."

"Piss off. More importantly, how's your love life going?"

"Backward."

"So you're not getting any then?"

"Not that it's any of your business, but no. I don't do casual, and we're all transients at the camp. Hardly the environment to establish a relationship."

Ryan thought of Ally and his step into the world of casual

dating. The word *transient* echoed in his head. He'd never asked about her long-term plans, whether she intended to stay in London.

"Anyway, this may be my last overseas stint for a while. It's starting to take its toll," Chris continued. "Maybe I should take Liz up on her suggestion of a blind date with the elusive younger sister when I'm back."

"Doesn't she live in New Zealand?"

"No, apparently she's in London now."

"I haven't seen the Tanners in months. We should grab a beer with AJ when you're home."

"Sounds like a plan. As for the donor thing, I'd be honored."

"Really. That's great. I owe you one."

The brothers talked a while longer, mainly about Farra, but as Ryan went to sign off, Chris came back with a question. "This mystery girl? What's her name?"

Ryan chuckled. "Sorry, you're breaking up. Talk soon."

29

THE SCORE

Ally ran from the bedroom to the bathroom, retching into the toilet several times before sinking to the floor. Leaning back against the wall, she drew her legs to her chest and dropped her forehead to her knees.

The pros, cons, and consequences of her pregnancy competed loudly in her head. But she knew what she had to do. Lift her butt off the floor. Drag herself into the shower. Get dressed. Eat something. Bus stop. College. Work.

A soft knock startled her. "Ally Cat? Are you all right?"

She wiped her nose with the back of her hand. "You can come in."

Jia peered around the door. "What's going on? Are you sick?"

Ally's lips quivered. She looked up, feeling the tears track down her cheeks.

Jia stepped inside and sank down onto her haunches in front of her. "Ally? You're scaring me. You have to go to the doctor."

"I've been to the doctor."

"What did they say?"

She shook her head. Ryan should be the first to know, but she had to tell someone. "I've made a huge mistake." The words that slipped from her mouth were more of a confession than an explanation. "How could I have been so stupid?"

"What do you mean?"

Ally paused before inhaling sharply. "I shouldn't even be telling you before Ryan, but I'm pregnant."

"Ryan? You're pregnant to Mr. Click? Are you sure?"

"Positive. What am I going to do? How will he react, Jia? He said he couldn't have any more kids. And Liz and AJ have been trying for ages. They miscarried six months ago, and here I am, pregnant without so much as a blink. I thought I just had a bug."

"Hey, it's okay. It might seem bleak now, but…"

Bleak. A word Ally seldom used, but as she sat on the cold, tiled floor feeling sorry for herself, the word slotted into her story like it belonged.

"Are you guys a couple now?"

Were they a couple? Did his invitation to the charity event mean he wanted a relationship? He knew almost nothing about her and still hadn't asked for details. She'd never experienced a feeling of inadequacy around a man before. Well, not until she found out about Angus's cheating and later, when he'd called their love-making safe and chaste.

But Ryan Farrell was an entirely different man from Angus Chapman. Older and already a parent, he displayed the maturity of a man who knew the score. The score about life, work, and women.

"I have no idea."

"Didn't you ask?"

"I guess that comes next."

"Right." Jia rose from the floor and offered her hand, helping Ally to her feet. "I'll make breakfast while you have a shower. Then we'd better leave for class." She held Ally's gaze in the bathroom mirror. "Are you up to it?"

"I have to be. I've got an assignment due."

"Okay. Take it one step at a time. Don't rush anything. If you move straight into full speed ahead, you won't be able to breathe."

"Thanks." Ally smiled for the first time in twenty-four hours. "How come you always know the right thing to say?"

"I'm Korean." Jia winked. "Korean women have wise souls. And look, the sun's coming out." Ally glanced over at the window, where a shaft of yellow light glistened across the glass. "Come on." Jia leaned over and turned on the shower. "Let's go and beat the blues out of the day."

───────

Deciding a walk would do her good, Ally got off the bus several blocks from the gym. She needed time to think, to take stock. According to her parents, she'd been an impulsive child, but she'd learned to curb that trait. Telling Ryan about the pregnancy was one thing. Picking the right time and place was something entirely different.

The streets were teeming with people. Up left, down right. Ally moved with the crowd, her focus downward and her sunglasses firmly in place, despite the now-gloomy day. Waiting at an intersection to cross, she absently glanced up and did a double take.

It wasn't the sight of Anton in Ryan's SUV as it idled at the curb that caught her attention, but rather, Ryan as he ushered a woman across the busy street and into the back seat before slipping in beside her. Remaining on the curb as everyone else crossed, Ally watched them pull away. Watched as the woman leaned over and kissed Ryan's cheek, and watched Ryan's face as he spoke to her and laughed at her reply. *Britt?*

Ally scarcely registered the rest of the walk to the gym and paid little attention to Sarah, the receptionist, as she greeted her. Only last month, she'd smugly congratulated herself on how well her new lifestyle suited her; how much she enjoyed the sense of anticipation after Ryan sent his usual 'Meet me' texts, and the heady thrill of his touch.

Now, it was Ally who needed to send the 'Meet me' text.

After seeing him with the twins, she couldn't imagine Ryan walking away. But his possible reaction was an ever-increasing source of anxiety, especially since he hadn't contacted her in over a week, apart from one text on Sunday evening. And, he'd insisted he was sterile. Now, her anxiety turned to dread as the image of the woman in the back seat of his SUV repeatedly played in her head.

———

Ally's trek home from the gym took over an hour. She'd never intended to walk the entire way in the dark after her shift finished, but with Putney Bridge now in her sights, she decided to keep going. It started to spit as she passed St. Mary's, but she pressed on as if heaven's tears—as her sister, Sydney had called rain when they were children—could somehow wash away her apprehension and sense of betrayal.

Rather than going to college the next morning, Ally stayed in bed, focusing her attention on her pregnancy. She pondered various factors repeatedly. Why had she trusted him? How could she have been so stupid? What would her father say? And the rest of the family?

But one thought prevailed above all others. How would Ryan react when she told him?

Ally moped around the apartment all morning, picking at a slice of toast with honey as she checked her phone for texts. After lunch, she went back to bed and drifted in and out of sleep as the rain fell—a drizzle at first, then loud and leaden against the side of the building.

In among her tangled thoughts, one thing was clear. She would never keep Ryan from his child, even if it meant staying in London for the next twenty years. Hamish had grown up without a father and still didn't know if the guy was alive, dead, or indifferent. That separation had caused Hamish much grief over the years, and she didn't want to inflict the same pain on her kid.

But Jacinta was right. Ally was just an employee, and she knew a relationship with the boss rarely lasted, even when there was a child involved.

Ally woke at four thirty in the afternoon to the sound of her text alert. Her heart pounded. Ryan? But when she looked at the screen, it was only Jia, asking if they needed milk.

30

STEP UP

Ally: Could we meet sometime this week?

Ryan leaned back in his chair and smiled. Although he didn't like playing games, he'd purposely waited for her to make contact. After all, if she wasn't interested, there was no point in taking the next step. His fingers flew over the keypad, the now-familiar excitement stirring, an emotion he once thought he'd never feel again.

Ryan: Same time and place?
Ally: How about tonight?
Ryan: Sorry, no can do. It will have to be Thursday.
Ally: Okay. But can we meet at my place? Jia won't be here.
Ryan: Perfect. I'll bring dinner.
Ally: Not this time.

After reading her last message twice, Ryan went to reply, then paused. *Not this time?* What did that mean? Thinking about their situation, he understood an exclusive relationship with Ally wouldn't necessarily be easy. Leaving London wasn't an option for him, so that alone could be a major stumbling block. And although Chris had agreed to be a sperm donor at some time in the future, the chance of Ryan ever taking him up on the offer was probably zero to low.

Still, he wasn't going to leave anything to chance. The younger Ryan had failed to plan for anything, but since taking over the helm at Farra, he'd learned the importance of forethought.

As soon as he stepped into her apartment, Ryan sensed something was wrong. Ally's teeth worried her thumbnail, and she looked like she hadn't slept well in days. "Are you okay? You don't look so good."

She burst into tears.

"Hey, come here." Ryan pulled her into a comforting hug, but her arms tightened around herself instead. He dipped his head and gently tilted her chin, forcing her to meet his gaze. "What's the matter?"

She pulled away, putting a physical distance between them. "I'm sorry. I promised myself I wouldn't cry." Her voice was soft but strained. She wiped her eyes with the back of a hand. "Please. Take a seat."

Ryan waited for Ally to sit before doing the same. She opened her mouth to speak. Hesitated. Her usually expressive hands clenched together as she lowered her gaze, one remaining tear still a trickle down her cheek. Taking the lead, he reached for her hands. "What's going on?"

"I need to tell you something."

Over the years, Ryan had learned to hold back when faced with such a statement from a woman. "Okay."

She stilled, looking down at her hands still clenched in her lap. "I haven't been feeling well lately. I thought I had the flu."

Ryan knew that whatever Ally had to say wasn't good news. He thought, not for the first time, how much she'd come to mean to him over the past couple of months. How their instant sexual attraction had turned into something much more. He leaned forward in his chair, watching her struggle with her thoughts. Moments dragged by as various scenarios played through his mind. "Are you ill?"

"No. Not ill. I'm…pregnant."

Of all the words Ryan had expected to hear, 'pregnant' was not one of them. *Shit!*

"Pregnant?" he repeated. "You're pregnant?"

She nodded. "Almost twelve weeks."

Ryan stood and paced across the room, rubbing the back of his neck. He turned to face her. "You're twelve weeks pregnant, and you didn't think to tell me until now?"

"I've only just found out. As I said, I thought I had the flu."

"But what about your period?"

"My cycle's erratic at the best of times."

He sighed and sat back down, his eyes darting between hers. "You're pregnant? Seriously?"

Ally looked at him, her deep blue eyes filling with fresh tears. Ryan reached for her hand. "I'm sorry. I…shit! I know what we have is casual, but it never occurred to me you were seeing someone else."

"What? I haven't been seeing anyone else!"

"So how are you pregnant? Did it happen before we met?"

Registering the look on her face, Ryan frowned as he caught up. He knew what she was about to say, so decided to shut it down. "You can't be serious. You think it's *my* baby?"

"You told me you couldn't have kids."

Leaning back in his chair, Ryan kept his expression composed, showing nothing of the turmoil chewing him up inside. Ally's baby couldn't possibly be his, and they both knew it. "I can't. I'm sterile, and have been for years."

"Obviously, you can."

"I'm not the father of your baby, Ally." He paused to let his words sink in. "And I think we both know that."

"Why would I lie?"

Ryan thought back to the night he'd seen Ally leave the club with Stuart and some other guy. And then, there was that rugby player who couldn't seem to keep his hands off her. "Come on, Ally, don't do this. Not only can I not have kids, but you've put me at risk."

"What do you mean?"

"We had unprotected sex."

"Yes, which you said would be fine."

"Look, I know it's none of my business who else you've been sleeping with, but I suggest you check your calendar and try to work it out."

"It's your baby. I haven't slept with anyone else—"

"That you remember."

"What the hell? How can you say that? I knew you could be ruthless. But I never thought you'd try to shirk your responsibilities."

Ryan couldn't hide his skepticism. "I may be many things, but ruthless is not one of them. I'm prepared to help you in any way I can, but I'm not the father. And unless you can prove otherwise, I won't be drawn into this. Been there, done that. And believe me, it wasn't pretty when the T-shirt didn't fit."

"What's that supposed to mean?"

He hesitated. What was the point of trying to explain. "It doesn't matter. I have to go."

"So that's it? It's over because you think I'm lying?"

"Check your calendar," he repeated. "Give the guy a chance to step up."

"Fine." Ally stood and walked to the door. She held it open. "Please leave. Thanks for proving you're a bastard, just like every other guy looking for a no-ties screw."

Ryan followed her to the door. Her words made him cringe. How could he have been so stupid? Had she been playing him all along, and he hadn't even realized it? "Let me make myself clear," he said. "This is the last time we will speak of this, understand? Maybe you thought you'd backed a winner when you picked me to be your baby's father, but believe me, you're betting on the wrong guy." He turned to leave but stopped. "Honestly, give the guy a chance. He may surprise you."

"I did give the guy a chance, and he didn't surprise me one bit."

Ryan climbed into his car and slammed the door, muffling the sounds of Putney High Street in the process. He gripped the steering wheel tightly with his left hand and thumped it with his right. Several minutes passed. As much as he wanted to march back through her door and tell Ally how he felt, he knew his only option now was to remove her from his life with a clean break.

He pulled his phone from his pocket, scrolled through the contacts and hit Dave's number.

"Hey, about that beer, can you still make it?"

"You okay? I thought you were tied up."

"Yeah, in goddamn knots. I'll be outside the gym in fifteen."

Ryan pulled out onto Putney High Street. He hated driving right on dusk, when people were either going home or heading out, but right now, he had more to worry about than the London traffic.

Dave stood at the curb as Ryan pulled alongside. He jumped in. "What's up?"

Ally's pregnancy wasn't suitable conversation for the car. "A lot, but I need a stiff drink before I start with the big talk."

"As opposed to small talk?"

"That's the one."

He drove toward Docklands, and stopped at a small bar near Chris's apartment. While Dave ordered, Ryan found a table for two by the side door. By the time Dave returned with their drinks, sweat had begun to trickle down the back of Ryan's neck.

"So, how did it go with Ally?" Dave took a swig of his beer.

"Not well." Ryan fiddled with the coaster in front of him. He knew he shouldn't be discussing Ally's business but trusted Dave implicitly. "She's pregnant."

"Seriously? Who to?"

"I have no idea. She's twelve weeks but reckons she only found out recently. Thought she had the flu." Ryan looked over at Dave and sighed. He shook his head. "She says it's mine."

"No way," Dave said. "Didn't you cover your bases?"

Ryan thought back to the brief skin-on-skin encounter they'd shared and shrugged. Dave raised a brow.

"Don't." Ryan didn't need a lecture on the importance of safe sex.

"The word 'reckless' never left my lips."

"It didn't have to. I know I stuffed up, but I still can't be the father." Ryan took a long draft of his beer. "But it's made me realize something."

"Which is?"

"Things about her don't add up."

"What makes you say that?"

"Just a hunch. Apparently, she has a sister in London, but she's never mentioned her by name. And what twenty-three-year-old has no social media presence? Then there's that rugby player," Ryan continued. "He was hanging around her like a bad smell for a while."

Dave nodded. "Angus? The guy works out at the gym when he's in town. He's a bit of a dick if you ask me, and he's always watching her."

"And now she's pregnant. I don't know what the hell to believe anymore. I wondered why she'd stopped drinking."

"So you think she's been pregnant longer than she's letting on?"

"Maybe."

"I did wonder if her personal training certificate was kosher, but it checked out." Dave swigged his beer. "So, who's your bet for the baby daddy? The rugby player?"

Ryan recalled the night he ran into Ally at the bar. The night she'd left with Angus and three other men. "Damned if I know. But one thing's for sure, it's definitely not mine."

"Are you positive? I know you went through the same thing with Sandy, but—"

"Sally. Her name was Sally. Lying, cheating, cow." Ryan shook his head as he recalled how she'd manipulated him and how gullible he'd been for believing her. "In the seven years Polly and I were together, we never once used protection. It took two years of doctors' visits and test tubes to conceive the twins, and another twelve months of jacking off in some soulless office so I could have my sperm analyzed. The results were always the same. And my count lowered every year until even IVF wasn't possible. That's why we never had more kids, and why I should've steered clear of a younger woman."

"Shit. I had no idea."

"I broke my own rules. Now I'm paying the price. If she'd been honest, told me who the father really was, I might feel differently. Still, maybe I've had a lucky escape."

"Do you feel lucky?"

"No, I'm pissed off. Shit!" Ryan frowned at his friend. "I said some hurtful things. But it was just such a shock."

"You realize her contract's up in another month."

Ryan knew they couldn't let Ally go. Being pregnant, she'd struggle to find another job. "Keep her on. I'll clear it with accounting."

"Why in the hell would you do that?"

"Because I'm a soft-touch."

Dave grinned and raised his beer. "A toast. To cocks and pussies. They sure can get us into a ton of shit. That's what my old man always said, anyway."

Ryan clinked his glass against Dave's. "Wise man, your dad."

EASILY REPLACEABLE

Two weeks after his visit to Ally's apartment, on an unseasonably cold Tuesday, Ryan caught her gaze as he walked from the gym's locker room. Not wanting to acknowledge his presence, she returned her attention to her client, encouraging him to do five more reps as the pain of Ryan's rejection intensified.

Their interactions had been almost nonexistent since she'd told him of her pregnancy. It seemed in Ryan Farrell's world, once he made his mind up about something, he wouldn't back down. He always stared though, running his eyes over her like he still had that right, and even though disappointment had replaced her initial anger, Ally was still struggling to come to terms with his reaction.

Sensing someone behind her, she glanced over her shoulder.

"Can I see you in my office at eleven thirty?" His tone was businesslike and brisk.

Ally excused herself to her client and stepped aside. "Sorry, I have clients all morning," she said. Under the circumstances, she had no interest in spending time with Ryan, especially not at Farra.

Ryan didn't miss a beat. "I've checked with Dave. He said he'd cover for you." He walked off without another word.

Just after midday, Ally crossed the street and took the elevator to Farra's fifth floor. Tim was nowhere in sight, so she crossed the lobby and knocked on Ryan's door. She knew she was late, but too bad. It was her birthday. Her day, her rules.

He looked up from his laptop, his expression guarded. "You're late."

Refusing to give Ryan the satisfaction of seeing her upset, Ally held her head high. He wasn't her boss and could suck lemons covered in chili salt for all she cared. "I told you, I had a client."

Clicking his laptop shut, Ryan motioned to the chair in front of his desk. *The Naughty Girl's Chair.* "Take a seat." He stood and walked over to close the door.

Ally did what she was told, her eyes fixed on the gadgets surrounding him. The office looked like it belonged in an episode of *Suits*, but with signed rugby balls instead of basketballs and without the wraparound windows.

"Do you enjoy your job?" he asked calmly as he returned to his desk.

She looked at him and frowned. "That's nothing to do with you. I no longer work for Farra."

"The gym is a subsidiary of Farra, so technically, you do." He rocked back in his chair and stared. "And quite frankly, speaking as your boss, your attitude toward me stinks. I've greeted you several times over the past two weeks and you've barely offered me a nod."

Attitude? Ally had to stop herself from shaking her head. She would never have expected Ryan to pull out the 'boss card' to make a point. "Are you firing me? I need this job, Ryan. No one wants to hire a pregnant woman."

"Of course I'm not firing you. Why would you even think that? But this pregnancy—"

"Is no longer up for discussion at your request."

He paused. Held her gaze. "I've changed my mind. And let me make myself perfectly clear. I will not tolerate an easily replace-able staff member who seems hell-bent on making me feel uncomfortable, working for one of my companies, understand? I don't care how you treat me outside of work, but when we see each other at the gym, or anywhere during office hours, I expect you to at least be civil."

Ally pulled a tissue from her pocket. Tears were never far away these days and being in Ryan's office didn't help. She was under no illusions about the man. You didn't get ahead in his world without knowing how to manipulate both people and situations, and Ryan Farrell was a tough negotiator.

Leaning forward, Ryan placed his elbows on the desk, resting his chin on clenched knuckles. She braced herself for another blow. "I assume everyone at the gym knows you're pregnant?"

"Not yet. But what do you expect me to do? Wear a corset?"

"What did I just say? Can we please have an adult conversation without all the theatrics?"

She sighed. "I'll make an announcement soon, before the gossip starts. But don't worry, I won't tell anyone who the father is, not even my family."

Ryan stood and grabbed two bottles of water from the bar fridge, offering one to her. She refused with the shake of her head.

"Not even me," he murmured as he unscrewed the lid and took a swig.

Ally didn't have the strength to formulate a response. She'd mulled over Ryan's reaction until she could no longer recall the details of their conversation. She knew he wouldn't see reason until it was staring him in the face, in bold font on a hospital letterhead.

"Do you have any support in London? Where do your family live?"

"All over the place."

His brow furrowed in annoyance. "Specifically?"

It wasn't the time to remind Ryan of his 'no stories' rule. Ally was in his office as a subordinate, not as an ex-lover. "My parents are traveling in Australia. I have a brother and sister in New Zealand and a sister in London."

His expression softened. "Does your family know about the pregnancy?"

"Not yet."

"And when are you going back to New Zealand? Can't you only stay in the UK for two years?"

"My father's English. Those rules don't apply."

"That's convenient."

She chose to ignore his sarcastic tone and play the game. "What's with all the questions? You weren't interested before."

"I'm trying to figure you out. I've no idea what you're up too, but I'm struggling to know what to believe."

"So you're still calling me a liar?"

"Let's just say, I'm calling your bluff."

"Well, in answer to your initial question, I love my job, but if you think so little of me, I'll tender my resignation. You've made it clear I'm on my own, and I accept that. But don't expect me to beg for your help. I never thought of you as apathetic, but I guess that's how men like you roll."

"Men like me? What's that supposed to mean?"

"You told me you were sterile. Is that what you tell all your weekday girls? Are the weekend girls extra special, or is it just some random thing?"

"Sorry, I don't follow."

"I actually thought you cared, just a tiny bit, but you don't usually go for younger women, do you? I was just your *sideshow entertainment* according to Jacinta. Just Ms. Thursday. That's why you kept insisting on no ties, no stories, and no last names."

His fingers steepled in front of him as he stared at her across the desk. She waited. He said nothing. To use tradesmen's language, it seemed she'd hit the nail on the head.

"I saw Ms. Tuesday last week." Ally was on a destructive roll.

"Getting into your car, outside the office. She kissed you in the back seat, the same seat where you once kissed me."

Ryan frowned, obviously thinking back. "Is that what this is all about? You're jealous because I had dinner with a friend?"

Ally couldn't answer. He was wrong. She wasn't jealous. She was nervous, and worried sick, and confused beyond reason as she struggled with her feelings for him. Feelings he didn't reciprocate.

"I want you to take the rest of the day off so you can think about what I've said."

She stilled and took a breath to stop herself from doing more damage with her runaway tongue. "I can't leave yet," she said quietly. "I haven't finished my shift."

"I'll sort it with Dave."

Rising from the chair, Ally clutched the tissue in her fingers and blinked back unshed tears. "May I go now?"

He nodded.

She walked toward the door, but turned back to look at him, biting down on her bottom lip as she struggled for self-control. "In future, I'd prefer to discuss any employment concerns with Dave, not you. Under the circumstances, being in your office is not appropriate."

He crossed his arms over his chest, his expression as cold as the day beyond the windows. "Point taken."

Ally swallowed hard, then spat out her next words. "You're nothing but a bully. And just so you know, I'm not jealous. I'm devastated."

LOOK BACK

Ally left his office before Ryan could reply. *A bully?* And what about the way she'd treated him? The least she could do was offer an apology. But once again, Ryan was left looking like the bad guy. Maybe there was some truth in the saying 'You can't win an argument.' Especially one with Ally Dobson.

His desk phone interrupted his thoughts, and he picked it up, unable to get the sight of her close to tears out of his mind. *Shit!* "Is Ally still there?" Dave asked.

"No. I told her to take the rest of the day off, and she left in a huff after calling me a bully. So now I'm a prick because I've upset her again."

"And were you? A bully?"

"I'll let you know once I've had time to beat myself up about it."

"Okay. I'll flick her a text. An obscenely large bunch of flowers with her name on it has just arrived in reception. Apparently, it's her birthday. She's made us a cake."

"What?" Ryan's face tensed. His exchange with Ally hadn't gone to plan and now this. "Great. Now I feel like a total bastard."

"I would've warned you, but I only just found out. I hope you weren't too tough on her. Remember, she's pregnant and alone."

"Yes, thanks for the reminder." Rubbing the back of his neck, he leaned forward in his chair. "Shit! I need to keep away from her."

It wouldn't be Ally's first horrible birthday. She'd had rotten birthdays before, her twenty-third being the worst, when she'd walked into her cozy cottage back home to the crushing realization that life would never be the same. But today definitely came a close second. And to top it all off, thanks to James Ryan Farrell, she now had to fake a headache.

As soon as Ally entered the gym lobby, Sarah pounced. "You have flowers. The courier just dropped them off."

Ally took one look at the enormous bouquet and figured they were from Liz and AJ. Who else would fork out that kind of money for her?

"Quick, read the card. Are they from your boyfriend?"

Ally liked Sarah, but some days, her dizzy enthusiasm for the lives and loves of others wore a little thin. She smiled. "I'm single, remember?"

"What about that Angus guy?"

"We're just friends."

"Oh. Well, maybe they're from your family. Are you going to open the card?"

Ally pulled the envelope off the paper and peeked inside. They weren't from her sister after all.

Look back. Please!
Angus xx

"Do you think you could find me a vase?" Ally asked as she

slipped the card into her pocket. Angus had been in earlier for a workout. Thank goodness he hadn't delivered them in person. "It seems a shame to take them home when they look so good in reception. How about I leave them here, then we can all enjoy them."

Sarah cradled the bouquet in her arms as if she'd just won a beauty pageant. "Great idea. I love flowers."

"I'm heading off for the rest of the day."

"Are you unwell, sweetie? You've been looking a bit pale lately."

"Just a headache. Thanks for your concern, I'll see you tomorrow."

Back at the apartment, Ally wrapped her feather comforter around her sadness and slept, not waking until the sun's last rays filtered through the gap in the curtain covering her one small bedroom window.

To mark the occasion of her younger sister's birthday, Liz had a low-key family dinner planned, but as Ally crawled out of bed and into the bathroom, she struggled to muster the energy to even turn on the shower. She just wanted to stay home with her crazy hormones and a block of milk chocolate. Because dark chocolate— the bitter, healthy type with seventy percent cocoa solids—simply would not do.

As she showered, thoughts of Ryan 'Bully' Farrell constantly ran through her head. Love and hate. Why did such conflicting emotions cling so tightly together?

While dressing for dinner, Ally composed a gratitude list, which she continued to mumble as she waited at the curbside for AJ to pick her up.

By the time she stood on the Tanner's doorstep, she'd neatly stacked her emotions behind a mask and smoothed them out with a light layer of makeup and muted rose lipstick.

Throughout the meal, Ally tried to figure out how to break her news to her sister and brother-in-law. As it turned out, the subject of her pregnancy never came up because Liz and AJ had an announcement of their own.

"We know it's your birthday and tonight should be all about you." Liz positively glowed as she took AJ's hand. "But we have something to tell you." She pushed out her tummy and patted it. "We're pregnant."

Swallowing hard, Ally reached for Liz and hugged her tight. "Wow, that's fantastic. How many weeks?"

"Only ten, so you can't tell anybody yet. We're so excited."

Ally knew there was only one possible response to their news. Smile, keep her mouth shut, and smile some more. "I'm so happy for you guys."

"As Liz's only family living in London, we wanted you to be the first to know," AJ said. "But you have to keep it a secret until after the twelve-week scan."

"Mum's the word."

"It's a bit of a shock to be honest, falling pregnant so soon after the miscarriage. I still feel like I'm holding my breath." Liz pulled a knife from the block on the counter. "Right, let's have cake."

"Let's," Ally said. "But first, I want to say thanks for the beautiful meal. And the painting is amazing. I now have a genuine Jacobs to hang in pride of place when I get my own home."

She smiled at AJ. Ally had liked him from the minute they'd met. At first, she'd thought Ryan was cut from the same cloth, but she now realized that while AJ was natural linen all the way, Ryan was more polyester, minus the elastane and lined with cheap sacking. "Thanks so much."

"My pleasure," AJ replied.

All the way home, Ally analyzed her reaction to their news, her excitement at becoming an aunt overshadowed by the reality she was about to become a mother. She'd have to tell Liz soon. She was starting to show.

"Hey, you're home," Jia said as Ally walked in the door. "I have a birthday surprise."

"Is it cake? I could do with a helping of unhealthy carbs right now."

"Didn't you get cake at your sister's?"

"I'm not sure I'd call a coconut flour concoction with mushy date-and-chia-seed topping a cake. She's on a health kick again. Poor AJ will be eating it all week."

"That's bleak. Fake cake. What's wrong with people these days?" Jia pulled a face. "So, did you tell them?"

Ally sighed. "No. It turns out I'm not the only pregnant Dobson sister." She pressed her index finger to her closed lips.

"Shut up! She's pregnant too? That happens a lot. Sisters pregnant at the same time."

"You can't tell a soul."

Jia mimed locking her lips shut. "Anyway"—she handed Ally a small white container—"from Jade and me."

The smell of frosting floated from the box as soon as she opened the lid. She picked up a cupcake and inhaled. "Yum. I love you guys. Shall we have one now?"

"It would be rude not to. I'll put the kettle on. Open the card."

Ally picked up the card on the table and opened it, gasping when she saw the pound notes inside. "What's all this money?"

"I'm taking you shopping. It's not much, but you need new clothes because you're going to be as big as a house before you know it. I know this amazing market we can go to."

"But it's three hundred pounds!"

"Yes, but it's from both of us. And you're not to spend it on anything else."

Ally pulled Jia in for a hug. "I don't know what to say. Thank you." She looked into the box, more to dislodge the lump in her throat than anything else. "Can I have two?"

"Of course. One for you, one for baby. And check your phone. You left it behind again, and it's been going off all night."

"Cake first, phone later. I thought I'd lost it."

By the time Ally got around to checking her messages, she had over twenty texts from friends and family, all with the usual 'Happy Birthday, Ally, have a great day!' greeting. However, when she scrolled to the bottom of the screen, Mr. Click's name stood out.

Ryan: Thank you for your time earlier. I'm sorry, I didn't realize it was your birthday. It wasn't my intention to spoil your day. I hope you enjoyed your evening.

Ally stared at the formal message and climbed into bed. Stuffing the pillows behind her head, she grabbed her e-reader off the nightstand in preparation for the long night ahead until her phone rang.

"Hello."

"Hey, happy birthday."

Ally slipped down the bed and pulled the covers around her, her focus on the phone screen as she put Mitch on speaker.

"Ally, are you there?"

"I'm here." She burst into tears. "Mitch…"

"Hey, are you okay? What's going on?"

"I need to tell you something."

33

THE PRESS OF LONELINESS

Ally sat at the table with her laptop open. Every time she logged on to Skype, she prayed her parents would be online. As her status changed to active, she held her breath. Seconds later, the sound of an incoming call rang through the apartment, and her mum's face filled the screen as her dad hovered in the background.

"Hi. Where are you guys?" Seeing her parents' smiling faces as they sat in their RV without a care in the world, reminded her of how her own journey had taken an abrupt turn—straight into impending motherhood.

"We're back in Kununurra now. Just having a cup of tea. You've got to visit the Mitchell Plateau sometime. It's an incredible place. The Kimberly coast is breathtaking—amazing rock formations and such beautiful colors. I feel like it's one of my true spiritual homes."

Ally chuckled. Her mother had always been the excitable one in her parents' relationship. It seemed everywhere she went, she felt she'd found another 'spiritual home.'

"It's been ages since we talked," Frank said with a wink as he came to stand behind Andrea. "Sorry we missed your birthday. How's it going in my old stomping ground?"

"Not too bad."

"I hear Angus turned up," he continued. "I hope he's not making a nuisance of himself. I thought he was heading to France."

"He is, but his Achilles is giving him grief, so he's been working on that. I don't see him much."

"Good. He's a—"

"Dad, don't. I have something I want to say."

"Are you okay?" Andrea's expression reflected the hyper-awareness of a mother.

"Not really." Ally paused for a deep breath and clasped her hands together under her chin. She could do this but needed a minute. "I'm pregnant."

Ally hadn't meant to blurt it out, but there it was, and she couldn't take it back. The word hung in the air. *Pregnant.*

"Pregnant?" Andrea repeated.

And there it was again.

Her mother paused and shot a backward glance at her father, who frowned. "Okay." Andrea drew out the word. "So is it a happy occasion?"

"I'm not quite there yet. Happy, I mean." Through her blur of tears, Ally watched her father pace, one step each way, back and forth across the cramped space of their RV.

"Oh, darling, don't cry," Andrea said. "We're here for you. Remember that."

"Thanks, Mum." Ally pulled a tissue from the box in front of her and dabbed her eyes. "I've made a real mess of things. I'm sorry."

"So you *are* back with him then?" Frank asked.

"Angus isn't the father."

"So, who the hell is?"

"Frank." Andrea looked up at her husband and gave him a warning frown. "Let her talk. You can see how upset she is."

"A guy I kind of dated for a while."

"What happened?" Her mother still wore the frown. "It's not like you to take risks."

"I know. But I can't talk about it right now, Mum."

"So he's an asshole, is he?" Frank never minced his words. "Wait, he's not married?"

"Divorced and uninterested. It makes me sad, but sometimes, that's the way life is. Sad."

"I know, darling. Look, we can change our plans and come over sooner, can't we, Frank?"

"No," Ally replied. "I'm fine. I have good support from Liz and AJ, not that I've told them yet."

Frank sat now, still as a statue and stared into the camera. "Have you thought about coming home? You could live at the orchard."

Ally had weighed up the pros and cons of returning to Tulloch Point until she felt sick to her stomach. As the memory of the attack flashed through her mind, she took a deep breath. "I have, but I need to finish my papers. I may never sing again, but I'd like to get into the production side of the business."

"You'll sing again," Andrea said. "Give yourself time."

"Anyway, I'm okay here until after the baby's born. I have a job at a gym. When that finishes, I'll move in with Liz and AJ for a bit. I'm sure they won't mind."

"Are you okay for money?" Andrea's expression finally relaxed.

"Yes, I'm fine. Don't worry."

"All right," Andrea said. "We're here for you, no matter what. You know that, don't you?"

"Thanks, Mum."

"And this man, the father," Frank added. "Maybe he'll come around."

His words set off another flood of tears. Ally had a lot of respect for her father. Frank Dobson fiercely protected all his children, even Mitch, who wasn't his biological son. In her teenage years, his reaction to her recklessness had scared her, but he'd mellowed over time, and so had she.

"I don't think so. Anyway, I have to go. Love you guys."

"Love you too," Andrea said. "Take care, darling."

"Have you told Mitch and CeCe?" Frank asked.

"Just Mitch. Liz and CeCe are next. I've been putting it off."

"All right, well one piece of advice," Frank said. "Whatever you do, don't burn your bridges. Like it or not, you'll always be tied to this guy through your kid. And who knows, maybe one day things will be different between you. Don't let your pride get in the way of being a decent human. Okay?"

"Okay. But it's not that easy, is it. Especially when the trust has gone. Anyway, love you guys. Talk soon."

Ally ended the call and quickly shut down her laptop. She'd expected to feel relieved, but instead, the weight of loneliness pressed down on her shoulders and she struggled to shrug it off. It was all very well telling her parents she had great support, but from now on, she would always be the single-parent Dobson sister.

Tomorrow she would tell Liz, and by the end of the week, CeCe, their nickname for Sydney, but right now, she needed to go to bed. As she entered her room, she picked up the parcel Jia had left on her nightstand. Wrapped in blue paper and tied with a white ribbon, it was a gift for the baby that Jia's grandmother had knitted. Ally was expecting an old-fashioned dress and booties in some ugly color like her granny used to give women who were pregnant. But inside the parcel was a sherbet-green-and-white striped sweater with a cute little Sherpa hat to match.

Sucking in a breath, she pressed the garment to her chest and snuggled under the covers, clasping the tiny present in her hands as she cried herself to sleep.

34

FAIR AND REASONABLE

Ally sat in the back of an Uber, watching the windshield wipers swish back and forth. Rubbing her hands over her growing baby bump, she tuned out as the hygienically challenged driver offered his views on why England beat Australia in the 2003 Rugby World Cup.

"Did you see the last quarter?"

"No, I missed it. I was just a kid in 2003, and I'm from New Zealand, not Australia."

"Kiwi, Aussie. Same difference."

Ally didn't have the energy to explain the difference between New Zealand and its closest neighbor, Australia. When he pulled up outside the gym, she couldn't get out of the Uber fast enough.

Standing in front of the elevator, Ally knew she should take the stairs, but the doors opened right on cue, and she couldn't be bothered refereeing an argument between her fit and pregnant selves.

Ally made her way to Dave's office and knocked on the open door. "You wanted to see me before I start?"

He looked up, closing the file on his desk. "I did. Have a seat." He waited for Ally to get comfortable—or rather, less uncomfortable. "So, how are you coping with your workload?"

She hesitated.

"Full disclosure. Ryan told me you're pregnant."

"He told you? He had no right."

"Maybe, but it's becoming rather obvious."

"I'm sorry, I was going to tell you this week. But...well it's just—"

"Hey, don't look so worried. With you starting to show, I thought we should have a little off-the-record chat." He leaned back in his chair and paused. "We've decided to put you on the permanent payroll. That way you'll be able to claim maternity benefits when the time comes."

Ally couldn't believe it. "I don't know what to say. Thank you."

"To be honest, it wasn't entirely my decision. I'm acting on Ryan's instructions."

"I see." Ally pushed aside any thoughts of Ryan being fair and reasonable, not wanting to be reminded of his 'great guy' status. She still needed time to work through his reaction, time to heal the hurt.

"He said you've named him as the father of your baby."

She didn't reply. It seemed Ryan no longer felt the need to be discrete where she was concerned. And now, would Dave view her lack of response as an admission Ryan wasn't the father? And did it matter what Dave or anyone else thought?

"I knew something was going on," Dave said. "You two spark off each other like a kid's chemistry set in the wrong hands."

"Maybe once, not now."

"Can I share something with you—confidentially?"

Ally waited in silence for him to continue.

"A few years back, Ryan found himself in a similar situation with a girl called Sally, or Sandy. I can't remember her name. But anyway, she worked for Farra as a draftsperson and they dated for a few months. Long story short, she fell pregnant. Ryan was sure it couldn't be his, but she kept insisting, so they lived together for a while. She left him just before the birth, to move in with her ex. And now he feels like history's repeating itself. So, do you mind if I give you one piece of advice?"

Ally stared at Dave. *Cheats, liars, and assholes.* "Shoot."

"If you aren't telling the truth, step back now. Ryan's a good guy, Ally. And granted, it's not my business, but when my friends are hurting, I reckon filling in the gaps can help everyone understand each other a little better. That's my take on it, anyway."

"Are you suggesting I've hurt him?"

"Haven't you?"

"I'm just playing by his rules. I forgot the terms of our arrangement there for a while—let my heart control my head. But I'm back on track now."

Dave paused. "And what about Angus Chapman? The guy worships you, anyone can see that. I thought maybe…"

"We were in a relationship once. In fact, he was my first boyfriend. All over now, though, and has been for some time."

"No going back?"

"Not in this lifetime."

"Oh to be young again and have lovers falling at your feet," Dave said with a chuckle.

"It's no picnic, believe me. Still, I've plenty to be grateful for. I just need to focus on this baby and get on with my life."

"Ryan does care for you. You know that, don't you?"

Dave sounded more like an agony aunt than a buff gym manager, and Ally was glad he and Ryan were friends. It meant Ryan had support, and sometimes that wasn't the case for guys. Even so, she didn't feel the need to reply. Her father was right with his bridge-burning advice. The less she said about Ryan Farrell, the better.

She stood. "I'd better go. My shift started ten minutes ago. Thanks for the promotion."

TALL STORIES

Waiting for the elevator in the lobby of Studio Hudson's building, Ryan smiled as he listened to the twins chatting about some movie they'd seen recently. After he and Polly separated, assuming the role of part-time father and spending time away from his daughters had been a significant adjustment, but he'd learned to juggle his weekends around them and enjoyed every minute of this precious time.

Ryan pulled his phone from his jeans pocket as it dinged. He glanced at the screen.

Ally: I'm sorry I acted unprofessionally. I gather I have you
to thank for my promotion.

As they entered the elevator and made their way to the gym on the third floor, Ryan reread her text, the words seeming cold and impersonal. But then, what did he expect?

Ava noticed Ally standing behind the reception desk as soon as they pushed through the double doors. "Dad, Ally's here." She clapped her hands with excitement. "Can we go talk to her?"

Slipping his phone back into his pocket, Ryan knew he

couldn't refuse. He didn't want the twins to sense any animosity between them. "Sure, if she's not too busy."

The girls ran to her, and to Ryan's surprise, Ally held her arms wide and hugged them tightly. He followed, not sure what kind of reception he'd receive. The sight of her, with her sleek dark hair now below her shoulders and that tight baby bump on display, made his heart race. "Ally."

"Ryan." She offered a sweet smile, then quickly returned her attention to the girls. Her sincerity was questionable, but at least she'd been civil.

"I'm about to take a lunch break," Ally said without making eye contact. "Is it okay if the twins sit with me so we can catch up on girl talk?"

"Can we, Dad?" Isla asked.

"Of course you can." He waited for Ally to look his way. "Just drop them at the daycare room when you've finished."

"Okay."

She smiled again, and it reminded him of those nights at the Heaton. He pushed the thought aside as he watched them walk away. No matter how messed up the situation was, he still wanted her. Those Thursdays at the hotel had been the most excitement he'd had with a woman in a very long time. And as much as he told himself he didn't want—didn't *need*—her, his inner voice cried 'bullshit' every time that lie surfaced.

Ryan took his time working through his sets, hoping she'd come back on the floor. By the time he'd finished his cool down, the twins were in the daycare room, and Ally was nowhere to be seen. He thanked the attendant as they left and followed the girls to the elevator. Pulling out his phone, he considered a reply to her message.

Ryan: Apology accepted. I appreciate your text.

As he headed for home, Ryan thought back to the three weeks

Ally had spent as his nanny, and how much he loved having her around. While he was perfectly capable of looking after himself and the twins, he missed being in a stable relationship. Although he didn't want to marry again, he hadn't ruled out the possibility of sharing his life with a woman.

Ever since their last conversation in his office, he'd thought about Ally constantly, wondering how she spent her days, and who she spent them with. And every night, when he slipped into bed alone, he admonished himself for not trusting his initial instincts. He'd known it was a risk becoming involved with a younger woman, but he'd always wanted what he shouldn't, or *couldn't*, have.

Even at nineteen, when he'd spotted Polly across a muddy mosh pit at Glastonbury, Ryan couldn't wait to lose his innocence at the hands of an experienced older woman. That she was his best friend's sister hadn't worried him. He'd been determined to have Polly, no matter what.

"Ally's tummy's getting fat." Isla was the first to state the obvious. Ryan glanced in the rearview mirror and smiled.

"That's because she's pregnant," he explained.

"I love babies," Isla said. "And I love Ally. She's cool. She plays hockey, and she snowboards."

"*And* she likes the same songs we do," Ava added. "Her friend plays violin in an orchestra. They go to music college together."

Although Ally had told Ryan she was studying, he hadn't realized it had anything to do with music. "Who told you that?"

"Ally did. And she's been to Africa *and* Australia *and* Fiji," Isla said.

Ryan glanced back at Isla. *Seriously? Africa?*

"Can she bring her baby when she looks after us next time?" Ava asked.

Ryan didn't have the heart to tell Ava that Ally wouldn't be looking after them again. "Maybe."

"I know," Ava said. "She can come to pizza night. After Christmas. When we're in the new house."

What would Ally think if he sent her a 'Meet us for pizza' text on a Thursday night? He pictured the four of them, lounging on the sofa, eating pepperoni pizza out of the box as they drank sparkling water and watched a kids' movie on the big screen in his new media room. Maybe after dinner, she could show them pictures of her African adventures, if they even existed. "We'll see."

36

LOVE SHACK

As they stood waiting to enter the karaoke bar, Ally twisted her fingers tightly together. She looked over at Jia, champing at the bit to get in. Why had she agreed to come? Ryan's visit to the gym that afternoon might have had something to do with it. The mere sight of him—those hazel eyes and almost-perfect facial features—still unsettled her. Reignited the fire she'd worked hard to dampen.

Jia returned her gaze, and Ally forced a smile before tugging at the hem of her dress. She hadn't felt this restless in ages, and they weren't even inside yet.

At her local bar back home, Karaoke Tuesday was a time-honored tradition, and as weeks of eliminations took place, the jackpot would sometimes climb to over a thousand dollars. She'd won it once, the year she turned twenty. Angus had been so proud of her that he'd plastered her picture all over social media along with hashtags and love hearts.

The thrill she felt when singing in front of strangers had always been the draw. It was one thing to perform for people you knew—friends and family who came to your gigs to lend their support—but strangers could be a tough crowd, and Ally had found that surprisingly invigorating.

As she followed Jia across the crowded bar, Ally glanced around at the other patrons. Elegant girls and guys, dressed in slick outfits with hair to match, posed in every corner of the room. Feeling way too drab in her black on black, and suddenly, very pregnant, she wondered yet again what had possessed her to accept Jia's invitation.

On reaching a table at the back of the room, Jia leaped around in her usual excited fashion as she made introductions. And as she sipped her mocktail, Ally clapped and cheered along with everyone else as covers ranging from Sam Smith to Katy Perry and everything in between, streamed from the speakers on the neon-lit stage.

"You okay?" Jia asked as a server set another drink in front of Ally.

"Yes, fine," she lied. "But I can't stay long."

"But you have to sing."

"No way." There'd been times recently when she'd found herself wanting to sing more than she wanted to breathe. But tonight wasn't the right time *or* the right place.

"It's okay," Jia said. "We all get a little nervous, especially when it's packed like tonight. Just imagine everyone naked, and you'll be fine."

Ally chuckled. She'd heard about the naked trick before but had never used it herself. "What have you picked?"

"An oldie but a goodie, 'Love Shack.'"

Ally nodded. Whenever her parents had thrown a party at the orchard, 'Love Shack' had made an appearance, and all their friends would sing along. Like many songs from the eighties and nineties, 'Love Shack' hadn't been one of her favorites growing up, but she'd since learned to love it.

"I'm up next." Jia stood and grabbed Ally's hand. "Come on. I need a backup singer."

Ally shook her head. "You're on your own. Break a leg."

As she left the bar later that night, 'Love Shack' stuck in her head. Jia had done an amazing job. Why hadn't she been brave enough to jump up on stage and join her? Apart from Jia, Ally hadn't known anyone there, so it would've been the perfect time to test the water. Because sometimes, if we don't step up to the plate when given the chance, the opportunity slips away, leaving us disappointed in ourselves for not taking that swing at life.

As the bus made its way toward Putney High Street, Ally stared out at the bright lights of the city. It would soon be Christmas, and for the second Christmas in a row, she faced it with dread. Her first cold Christmas—in more ways than one.

She grabbed her phone out of her bag and clicked on Hamish's last message. She was glad he'd come to London. When she and Angus broke up, he'd flown over from Brisbane just so he could spend two days with her. Maybe it was time to return the favor.

Ally: I've been thinking about missed opportunities.
DJ Mish: Do you mean you want to sing? Are you freakin' serious?
Ally: No. I'm nuts.
Ally: Batshit crazy!!!
DJ Mish: I'll be in the studio tomorrow morning. Can you be there?
Ally: But it's Sunday.
DJ Mish: What else will you be doing? Going to church?
Ally: Send me a map and time. I'll be there.

Located in a tiny basement space below a row of specialty stores in the East End, the studio was cold and poorly lit, downright dingy. The ambiance didn't exactly inspire creativity, but it had all the gear and it suited their needs. Hamish had planned the mix, so all

Ally had to do was listen, get the tempo straight in her head, and polish her pipes.

The first few takes didn't go well. Nerves surfaced and Ally couldn't find her sway. She second-guessed the words, wanting to change a few lines here and there, but Hamish wouldn't budge. He insisted they stick to the original, and deep down she knew he was right.

"Why don't you sit at the keyboard and play how it sounds in your head?" Hamish suggested, his concern evident in his tone. "You have raw talent, Ally. Don't let anyone take that away from you. Because if you do, they'll take more than your music. They'll also rob you of your self-respect. You're overthinking it. Nothing flows through overthought."

"I know. You're right." She rubbed the scar at the back of her neck. Some days it still hurt when she touched it. "Right. Let's have another go."

Ally sat at the keyboard, her fingers cold on the keys. Taking a deep breath, and another, she thought back. Chords followed, harsh and raw. She could almost taste the metallic scent of rust in the air, feel the rough stone of the wall dig into her back as she leaned into it, and hear the commotion as the crowd gathered. Like shouts underwater—out of shape. Distant.

Returning to the mic, Ally opened her mouth. Paused. Started again. And as the words flowed on a breath, she closed her eyes, her hands moving in time to the beat until the last note played.

Hamish removed his headphones. "Wow! What was that?"

"Was it okay?"

"Holy hell, Ally! More than okay. Listen." He played the track back.

"I love the bridge," Hamish said when they'd listened to it one more time. "The way the story weaves through it. I'll have to edit the second verse just a little. You lost strength in a couple of places."

"Okay. And does the bass need to be pulled back a bit?"

"Yeah. My thoughts exactly. Let's go again. Then we'll lay down the backing vocals." He looked at her and smiled.

"What?"

"I love seeing you like this," he replied.

Ally held her hands out in front of her. The tremble had gone. She'd forgotten how good it felt to use her voice. To tell her story and carry herself straighter. "I'm only here because I owe you."

"No, you're not." The words were spoken with kindness, the way Hamish always communicated. "You're here because you don't want her to win. You're here to get on with your life."

She chuckled. "You're such a philosopher, Hamish Baxter."

"You think? Hey, I've been meaning to ask, how's Jia?"

Ally narrowed her eyes. "Jia?"

"Your housemate."

"I know who you mean, but why are you asking? What's going on?"

"Nothing. It's just, I need a violinist for one of my tracks, and she came to mind."

"Do you want me to ask her?"

"No. But can you text me her number?"

37

SPENDING TIME

Ryan looked up from the computer screen on Dave's desk and leaned back in the chair—pen poised in his left hand, right hand covering his lips and chin. Ally hovered in the doorway, unsure of what she should say. He smiled, the kind of smile he'd offered at the Heaton, and she felt her face flush.

"Sorry, I was looking for Dave."

"He just left," Ryan said. "Since I'm here anyway, I said I'd lock up for him."

"Okay. Everyone's out apart from Guy."

His lazy gaze drilled into hers, but he said nothing more. He stood, grabbed his gym bag, and followed her down the stairs toward the lobby.

As Ryan took care of the locks and alarm, Guy approached her. "How are you getting home? Shall we share an Uber?"

Recently divorced and still angry at his wife, Guy, a buffed up personal trainer, had shown a keen interest in all things Ally Dobson from her first day at the gym. But there was something about his curiosity that felt a little creepy.

She glanced at Ryan as he set the alarm. Closing the cover,

Ryan returned the glance, his expression tight. "Thanks, but Ryan's dropping me off."

"Okay, well if you're sure," he said. "I'll call you. Maybe we could grab a coffee or catch a movie over the next few days?"

"I'm pretty busy this weekend. I have an assignment due."

"Sure." His expression bordering on arrogant, Guy watched Ryan walk toward them. "Maybe some other time? I'll see you next week."

Ally and Ryan walked to Fara's parking garage in silence. She didn't look at him, instead focusing on every detail of her surroundings as she waited for the question she knew was coming.

"What was that all about?" he asked as they stopped at his SUV.

"Nothing much, but I appreciate your cooperation."

"That guy's like a lovesick pup around you." He opened the door for her, his concern clearly more than that of a caring boss. "Has he been bothering you?"

"No. But I don't want him getting the wrong idea."

"But you're pregnant."

Ally looked away. Recently, she'd been hit on more often than ever before. "Doesn't seem to matter to some guys. Maybe he thinks I'm available."

It wasn't until they were both in the car with their seat belts fastened that Ryan spoke again. "And are you? Available?"

Ally stared straight ahead. "There's a bus stop around the corner," she said finally. "Would you mind dropping me there?"

"I'll drive you home."

"Please, I'm quite capable of catching the bus. I just didn't want to give Guy the opportunity to insist."

Ryan drove past the bus stop and moved into the left lane, heading toward Putney. "You probably feel the same way about me, but I don't like the idea of you waiting for a bus on your own at this time of night."

She remained silent.

Stopping for a red light, Ryan glanced her way. "Are you still uncomfortable around me?" He waited for a reply, but when she gave none, he continued. "After what we had?"

"Because of what we had."

Rain peppered the windshield, and as they drove the rest of the way in silence, Ally focused on the rhythm of the wipers. Back and forth. Like and dislike. Yes and no.

When they reached Putney Bridge, Ally relaxed a little. She'd soon be home, tucked up in bed with nothing but her thoughts.

Ryan pulled into a parking space outside the apartment building, cut the engine, and unclipped his seat belt.

"Thanks for the lift," Ally said, her words left hanging in the air as he jumped out of the car and walked around to open her door.

"Come on. I'll walk you up."

She wanted to say 'no,' but the pull remained, tilting her in his direction whenever their paths crossed. And as he followed her up the stairs, she couldn't even begin to imagine what he might be thinking. Did he expect her to invite him in? Offer him a drink?

She opened the door and stepped into the apartment.

"Where's Jia?" he asked as he put his keys on the hall table and followed her into the living space.

"At her parents' place. Her mum's sick. Anyway, thanks for the lift."

"Are you throwing me out already? I could murder a coffee." He sat on the sofa, making himself at home. It was as if the words 'I'm not the father of your baby' had never left his lips.

She moved into the kitchen, her senses on high alert as he watched her. He had the sort of presence that commanded respect and for Ally, something that bordered on subservience.

She flicked on the kettle anyway.

"Do you and Guy have a history?"

"We work together, nothing more."

"He was stripping you bare with his eyes, right in front of me."

"Don't be ridiculous. And anyway, it's hardly any of your business."

He stared at her for a few seconds until she had to look away, thankful his request for coffee gave her something to concentrate on. Because at that moment, she desired Ryan Farrell more than anything else she could possibly think of.

Handing him his drink, she joined him on the sofa. They talked about the twins and the gym. Familiar words, but entirely unlike the conversations they'd shared at the Heaton. At least fifteen minutes had passed before she checked her watch.

"It's getting late." She sat forward, ready to stand. "You should probably go."

Ryan moved closer, taking her mug and setting it down next to his on the coffee table. Letting his arm fall along the top of the sofa, he leaned into her neck. "I *probably* should, but..."

Ally touched his chest in a half-hearted attempt to make him back off. She felt the dip of his sternum and the heat of his skin through his shirt as she whispered, "You shouldn't be here."

"I know, but..." His lips skimmed along her neckline and across her collarbone, his hands burying themselves in her hair. "Don't make me leave." His voice held a husky tone, bordering on a whisper, and she loved it when he spoke that way. "Come shower with me."

"Seriously? After everything that's happened, you still want me to wash your back? Why don't you just buy a brush?"

He chuckled. Then turned serious again. "We shouldn't feel guilty about spending time together, because we both know our connection is amazing; there's no denying it."

NO GOODBYES

They stood in the shower, Ally's hands braced against the tiles as Ryan shadowed behind her like a second skin. He lathered body wash between his palms and smoothed the suds across her shoulders, down her full breasts, and over her swollen belly as she stood, wordless but willing.

"I shouldn't want you here," she whispered.

He moved his lips to her neck. "And I shouldn't want to be here. But—"

"Please don't start with all that seductive rubbish. Not tonight."

"I won't say another word."

The blood throbbed into his erection as he watched her face from side-on. Issues of trust and any uncertainty were temporarily pushed aside as his lust for her overtook all common sense.

They stepped from the shower, and Ally stood motionless as Ryan wrapped her in a towel. He wanted to tell her how beautiful she was, how much he'd missed her, and that she'd never left his thoughts. But she'd asked him to keep his mouth shut. So he would, accepting this for what it was—a casual encounter between ex-lovers. Breakup sex, long overdue, no matter how much he wanted it to be more. A night for drowning sorrows in passion rather than alcohol, with no delusions about how they'd both feel in the morning.

They slipped into bed and silently faced each other, their eyes locked in mutual need and desire. Ally cupped his face in her hands and smiled. They kissed, gently at first, but as she opened her mouth under his, fierce desire overtook all thoughts of guilt and remorse.

Staying on their sides, they exchanged tender kisses—touching, reconnecting—until Ally reached into the nightstand for a condom and handed it to him in an unmistakable invitation.

He entered her slowly, watching as her brow creased into a small frown that faded as she relaxed around him. Despite his desperate need to do otherwise, Ryan slowed his pace to match hers. Their gentle back-and-forth rhythm was more sensual than anything he'd ever experienced before. Holding her with uncertain hands, he watched with cautious eyes.

Struggling to control himself, he held their connection until Ally closed her eyes and threw back her head, clenching him tight as she lost herself in her climax.

Afterward, they lay on their backs, connected only by his little finger around hers, making a regretful promise. Ryan turned to stare at her, her face illuminated by the streetlights below. Would this be their last time? The thought saddened him. Left him feeling empty.

He climbed out of bed to use the bathroom, and when he returned, he thought she'd fallen asleep. But when he slid in beside her, she snuggled close, accepting his arms as they wrapped around her. He closed his eyes, and wished with all his heart that Ally was telling the truth. That her baby was indeed his.

Ryan woke around six. Slipping from the bed, he grabbed his discarded clothes from the floor, dressing as Ally stirred. An early start meant he needed to go home to shower and change. To wash away her scent—and his failings.

She opened her eyes, watching him as he bent down to pick up his jacket. And as he sat on the edge of the bed to slip into his shoes, Ally's hands remained still, her eyelids fluttering open and shut as she appeared to doze.

He wanted to reach out and touch her, to talk to her, to tell her so many things, but in the haze of the morning after, he couldn't. Ryan wanted Ally, a lot, but not enough to believe her. Did that make him a selfish bastard? Of course it did.

Leaning over, he planted a soft kiss on her cheek. Her hand moved to touch his, but he couldn't let the connection take hold. Instead, he whispered, "Thanks for last night. I have to go."

Hours before, Ryan had let his desire cloud all sense of what was right and wrong. And now, in the rational morning light, guilt walked him to the door.

Conversation no longer seemed appropriate.

"What's going on?" Jia's gaze followed Ally as she padded toward the coffee machine. She needed to eat, but coffee came first.

"What do you mean?"

"I just saw Ryan. Was he delivering breakfast?"

"More of a late-night snack. Coffee?"

Jia stared at her in confusion. "He stayed the night? Aren't you guys at war? And yes, to the coffee."

"Just because he thinks I'm a liar who's trying to set him up doesn't mean we're at war."

"Well, after that explanation, you should be. You're one crazy Kiwi."

"I know. Or foolish may be a better fit."

Jia was right, of course. Ally had showered as soon as Ryan left, and while the water had washed away any physical evidence of their night together, it had done nothing to cleanse her emotional turmoil. Still, she couldn't change what had happened, and there was little point in crying over spilled milk *or* dubious decisions.

Besides, why should she feel guilty? Sensual seemed to have become her middle name during this second trimester, and their differences aside, Ryan had offered her a chance to explore that sensuality. She had no desire to explore it with any other man. Not during her pregnancy. Or after.

She placed Jia's coffee in front of her. "How's your mum?"

"Much better. Her fever's broken, and she ate breakfast this morning. But my *umma* is not the issue here. Did you, you know?"

"I thought you were too shy to talk about sex unless you'd had a glass of wine first?"

"I'm trying to loosen up. Just because I've never done it, doesn't mean I can't talk about it."

"Okay. Just as a heads-up. Asking someone if they've 'you know,' is not appropriate breakfast conversation." Ally popped two slices of bread into the toaster as she chuckled quietly. "So, what's happening with Mr. Left of Ideal? Are you still texting?"

"It's weird. He hadn't contacted me in ages, and suddenly I get this message out of the blue saying he'd lost my number. We texted back and forth for a few days, but when I suggested another coffee date, he disappeared again."

Jia picked up her drink, warming her hands on the mug. "I just want to know what it's like. None of my friends are still virgins, and I thought Shy Guy might be my chance. We could be shy together, and it would be emotionally beautiful. Like those coming-of-age movies, where it's all peaches, balmy summer days, and bees buzzing in and out of wildflowers."

"Wow, interesting imagery." Ally recalled a similar movie she'd seen recently and chuckled again. "Maybe he's a virgin too and feels awkward around girls."

"Yeah. I'd thought of that. I just don't understand men. What if I never find a boyfriend? *Umma* will want to marry me off to some tech geek who games twenty-four seven and takes his laundry home to Mummy." Jia took a bite of her toast.

"Maybe you should ask him over for dinner."

"Why? He won't even meet me for coffee, so he's hardly gonna agree to dinner. Anyway, you're trying to change the subject. You and Ryan? Yes or no? And don't play coy."

"Yes." Ally didn't need to elaborate; Jia wasn't the judgmental type, but an explanation followed anyway. "It just kind of happened. He gave me a lift home from the gym, and one thing led to another—"

"Yep, I get the picture. And was he...?" Jia cocked a cheeky brow.

"Yes! He's still amazing. Even better than before. Amazing kisser, amazing body, amazing...well, you know." Ally sank her teeth into her toast and chewed while she recalled just how amazing James Ryan Farrell was. "Bleak, isn't it?"

Standing at his office window, Ryan looked out over the park below, with its neat beds of pansies and people walking briskly in the late-autumn air. He'd been at his desk for half an hour and hadn't even picked up a pen. As he'd driven to work, memories of the night before occupied his thoughts. He needed to stay away from Ally before things got a whole lot more complicated. If that was even possible.

Maybe he'd head to the house later, to blow off a little steam with a nail gun, but for now, his thoughts were on the email he'd received from Stuart earlier.

Ryan,

I'd like your opinion on a song (see attached). A guy I know is talking to Marc re a deal and wants me to do the legals. Have a listen and get back to me. But this is strictly between us. Don't share it with anyone.

After playing the song several times, Ryan found the melody stuck in his head. There was something hauntingly familiar about it. Maybe he'd heard a similar mix before, or the vocalist perhaps. But if he had, he couldn't recall when or where.

He searched through his contacts and pressed Stuart's number. As usual, the guy waited several rings before answering.

"Hey, mate. Have you listened to the song?" Stuart asked.

"I have. It's good. Who's the vocalist?"

"I have no idea, but shit, she can sing!"

'Shit' was right. Ryan had played the track over and over, simply to hear her voice.

"So," Stuart continued, "am I right in thinking it's a potential hit, or am I getting soft in my old age?"

"Her voice is amazing. With the right promotion, I think it could make some serious money. But hey, what do I know? I'm just a builder with a love of the keys."

"Just a builder? Is that right?" Stuart chuckled. "But you know good music when you hear it."

"You realize you just paid me a compliment? You *are* getting soft in your old age. Anyway, I better go do some work. I've done nothing but play that song on repeat since I opened your email. Have a good day."

39

CAT

Situated in a dark basement two dozen steps from the gym, Steam Perk Café screamed attitude. Decorated with vintage suitcase-style turntables, and with vinyl records and maps of the Underground tacked to the walls, it desperately needed a thorough spring clean. But Steam Perk had an important claim to fame—they served the best coffee on the block and their food was to die for.

Ally hurried down the steps and pushed her way inside, searching for Stuart as her eyes adjusted to the dim lighting. As she weaved through tables toward him, he stood and pulled out a chair. "Hey, it's nice to see you again." He kissed her on both cheeks. "And looking so radiant."

"Thank you. And thanks for coming."

The server took their order, and they made small talk for a few minutes before Stuart eventually asked, "So, what can I do for you?"

"I need some legal advice if you don't mind. I'm prepared to pay for it, but I wanted to test the waters first."

"Sure. Test away." Stuart glanced over her shoulder, nodding his acknowledgment of someone.

Ally wanted to turn to look, but that would be rude, so instead she waited for him to return his attention to their conversation. "I wrote a song a while back. Hamish wants to record it, but I'm not sure of the legalities. I wondered if you could help. Or, if not, recommend someone who can."

Stuart nodded slowly and leaned back in his chair. "Hamish sent me a song recently. 'Rust on White Linen,' but your name wasn't on the credits."

Ally shifted in her seat, touching the greenstone pendant that hung from a black cord around her neck in an attempt to ground herself. "I don't want anyone to know it's mine. That's why I need someone I can trust to help me navigate the process. I'm reluctant, but his agent's keen. He thinks it could sell a few copies."

Stuart waited for the server to leave their coffees before he spoke. "Who's the female vocalist on the demo? Cat someone?"

Her hands shook as they circled the warm cup in front of her. Just hearing Stuart say her stage name rattled her. Hamish had told Ally he'd made two versions, one with her and the other with a male vocalist. She met Stuart's gaze.

"Thought so," he said. "You do realize it's Marc he's talking to?"

"Marc? Polly's Marc?"

Stuart nodded. "Marc's a good guy. He's preoccupied most of the time, but when it comes to making music, he's up there with the best." A warm smile lit up his face. "Who would have thought you'd have such an amazing tone. Your voice really makes that song come alive. You've got poise and the right amount of control to shade the lyrics. When the guy sings it, it's stiff and lacks emotion."

"Thanks. But I don't want to sing on the final cut."

He leaned forward. She remembered what Ryan had said about Stuart being ruthless, but she didn't share his concern. She felt they had a rapport, and she appreciated that.

"Something happened to you," he said. "Want to share?"

She hesitated as she formulated an answer. "The last time I

sang, I was egged off stage. I know that's no reason to quit, but it was just the tip of a very deep iceberg, one I'd rather not revisit right now."

"That song's yours, Ally. I'll help you any way I can, but don't sell yourself short. Hamish is a talented guy. The raw demo is a credit to him. And to you."

"I've thought about it—long and hard. I can't be on that record, and I definitely don't want Polly to know it's me. Or Ryan." She held out her hands in front of her. "Look, I'm shaking just thinking about it."

Stuart placed a steadying hand on hers. "Some of the best artists I know suffer from anxiety and stage fright. Myself included."

His admission shocked her. Stuart had such a commanding presence, she struggled to see him as anything but confident.

"Do you enjoy singing?" he asked.

"I love it. Have done since I was a little girl. But although I believe in that song, my life's different now, and I have to protect myself where I can. Being pregnant changes things."

"I understand, but let's talk again next week. I'll work out a strategy."

"Thank you. Hamish has always been there for me. I feel, not that I owe him exactly, but I want to support him as much as I can."

Stuart nodded. "Getting back to other mutual friends, how are things going between you and Ryan?"

She'd asked herself the same question, many times, but there was never a satisfactory answer. "They're not."

<hr />

Ally stood at the entrance to the karaoke bar, pulling her coat tightly around her. The sane part of her knew she shouldn't have come, but that slightly crazy side, the side she'd hidden from the world for months, didn't care. The crazy side wanted to sing and wouldn't give up until she held the mic in her hands.

She checked her watch, five forty-five. They didn't officially open until six, but she entered anyway. Apart from staff, the place was deserted.

The bartender gave a slight frown as she approached. "We're not open yet, love. But have a seat. What can I get you?"

"Oh. I was wondering if I could do a number."

He stared at her blankly, narrowing his eyes.

"You know, sing karaoke?" she said.

"We don't usually start karaoke until seven."

Ally struggled to tear her gaze from the tattoo that licked orange flames up his neck. She'd never seen a color like it before. The guy reminded her of Stuart Harrison. Handsome and mysterious. The kind of brooding bad boy sensible women should stay well away from.

"Sorry. I'll come back another time." She turned to leave. What a stupid idea, sneaking into a bar to sing in front of nobody, purely to prove a point.

He reached across the bar and tapped her lightly on the arm. The touch surprised her, and she pulled back. He hesitated, his gaze holding hers. "Do you do requests? I'm sick of the same old songs."

"What do you suggest?"

"You know that Brandi Carlile song, 'Party of One'?"

She knew the song. It was one of her new favorites, but Ally had never sung it before. "You want me to sing that?"

"Yeah." He stared at her for a moment. The kind of heated, intense stare Ryan had offered in his hotel room. She needed to open her coat, so he knew the score. "It's kind of my song at the moment," he continued. "I'll set it up."

Ally removed her coat and placed it over a chair close to the stage. The bartender turned, his amused gaze slowly moving down her frame as he handed her the mic and walked away. Back behind the bar, he leaned his arms on the counter and stared at her, his gaze piercing her soul. She had a story, and he knew it. He had a story too, but it wasn't hers to read.

At the start of the first verse, he straightened, folding his arms over his chest. And as she sang, his attention never faltered. At times, it became too much, and she had to close her eyes momentarily against the heat of his gaze. As she moved through the song, other staff stopped what they were doing to watch.

By the time she'd finished, a small group had gathered at the bar. The bartender started a slow clap, and within seconds, the rest of them followed. As shouts of "encore" filled the room, she took a stiff bow. *She'd done it.* Checked fear number one off her list.

Two more songs followed, each one better than the one before as her voice warmed up. When she'd finished, she walked to the bar and placed a twenty-pound note into the tip jar. "Thank you. I appreciate you allowing me to sing."

"Come back on Friday," the bartender said. "I'll pay you to do a warm-up set. You're talented, but maybe a little out of practice, yes?"

"Thanks, but I'm not sure if I can."

"Who are you?"

She smiled. Did he mean her name, or something else?

"Let me guess," he said. "You're just a girl with broken dreams."

If they'd come from anyone else, the words would have been a cheesy cliché. But the guy behind the bar, with the piercing green eyes and the flaming tattoo, was too beautifully mysterious to be taken any way but seriously. "Something like that. I'm Cat."

"Juan." He offered his hand, and they shook, his grip warm, with just the right amount of pressure. "Nice to meet you. Do you sing professionally, beautiful Cat?"

Who was this guy? "No. I just wanted to test something out."

He nodded. "Stage fright can be an evil beast. I'm on a break at eight. If you hang around, we could grab a coffee, maybe something to eat?"

"Thanks, but…"

Juan motioned to her bump. "You're with someone. I hope the guy realizes how lucky he is."

She smiled. As she turned to walk away, he called out to her. "Cat?"

"Yes."

"Feel the fear. Your voice needs to be heard."

"Thank you, Juan. It's been a pleasure meeting you."

"Likewise."

Ally hurried up the stairs and onto the street, pushing through the evening crowd to the curb. By the time she managed to order an Uber, her face was burning, and her vision blurred with tears.

40

ANTICIPATION

At Studio Hudson eight days later, Ally's bravado after her night of breakup sex with Ryan had all but disappeared. All week, she'd expected to see him working out on the floor, and the anticipation of contact had her nerves on edge. But Ryan hadn't been in.

It wasn't that she regretted the experience, not even when her 'self-righteous' side beat her over the head. But, she knew how those closest to her would judge if they found out she'd had what Liz would refer to as 'Hell, why?' sex with the man who'd rejected her. With this in mind, she'd scribbled down a list of 'Ryan Rules' earlier in the week and stuck it to her bedroom mirror. Her intentions were clear. Her resolve was a different matter.

Alone in the staff office, Ally mentally ran through the next session before making her way to the classroom, their affectionate term for the aerobics room. There had once been a time when standing on a stage in front of strangers hadn't bothered Ally. The adrenaline had worked in her favor, overriding the initial rush of nerves. But those days were gone.

As usual, the room was already half-packed, and as she stood on the small stage and watched the stragglers file in, she scratched the inside of her palms with her fingernails.

"Hi everyone," she said once they all stood in front of her. "Welcome to my class. Are you ready to beat the blues out of the day?" Jia's favorite line perfectly summed up her present state of mind. The group's enthusiastic response helped her relax, and by the time she'd finished the first routine, her mind was fully focused on the next.

The hour flew by, and as Ally guided the class through a series of cool-down stretches, she glanced up to Dave's office on the mezzanine floor, and straight into the eyes of Ryan Farrell. She frowned, expecting him to shut the blinds, but they remained as they were, as did his penetrating stare. Returning her focus to the class, Ally finished off the stretches. The next time she looked up, he was gone.

Once the gym had closed, Ally stripped the sheets and towels from the massage room and bundled them into an overflowing laundry bag before remaking the massage table.

"There you are." Ryan's voice startled her. "Need any help?"

"Why are you still here?"

"Dave had to leave early. One of his kids is sick, so I said I'd lock up for him."

Ally regarded him with suspicion. This was the second time he'd just happened to be locking up for Dave when she was on the late shift. For the CEO of a sizable property company, it seemed a little weird. Still, Farra did own the gym and he and Dave were friends, so maybe it wasn't completely implausible.

"I'm almost done," she said looking away. "Could you carry this bag down to the laundry chute for me?"

Ryan moved forward, his presence filling the room. "Sure."

Ally instinctively stepped back.

"Do you need a ride home?"

She switched off the light and went to push past him without answering, but he blocked her path. She sighed heavily and frowned up at him, his face in partial shadow as the light from the corridor crept into the room. A ride home? *Not likely.* "Thank you, but I'm fine."

"We could grab a coffee."

"I don't drink coffee at night. And I don't like you watching me take a class."

"I was just checking on numbers." His expression remained serious, almost as if he believed his pathetic excuse. "Besides, you usually don't take classes. How was I to know you were the instructor?"

The hairs on her nape prickled and she turned to adjust the same towels she'd straightened only minutes before. "I'd appreciate you keeping the blinds closed in future. I'm nervous enough in front of all those people as it is."

"Maybe you should cut your hours a bit. I'm worried you're overdoing it."

Caring Ryan had appeared once again, but Ally knew what he wanted, and it wasn't to help with the laundry bag. "I don't want to cut back. I need the hours."

Ryan rubbed the back of his neck. He seemed to do this a lot when he was around her, and it only meant one thing. Frustration. "What's with the attitude? I thought we'd sorted out all the bullshit between us the other night."

"You mean when you left after barely saying a word? So you think sex sorts out 'all the bullshit'?"

He stood in silence, just staring at her.

Annoyance flared, and she snapped. "I have to go. We shouldn't be alone together, Ryan. And for a big shot CEO, you're not the sharpest tool in the box."

"Ouch." He took another step into the room. "You're right. I deserved that. I'm sorry." The contrition in his voice sounded sincere.

"Yes, I'm sorry too. But your sorry and my sorry mean entirely different things."

After closing the gap between them, Ryan picked up Ally and

sat her on the edge of the table. He stood directly in front of her, his hands resting lightly around her waist. Although she kept her legs pressed tightly together, just the touch of him, the look and smell of him, made her desire peak. She and Angus had rarely argued, so this love-hate dynamic was a whole new experience, one she couldn't get her head around.

"Let me show you my sorry," he whispered as he leaned forward, inhaling her scent. He kissed her gently—no tongue, just the softest touch. "I've missed you."

She frowned and cast her eyes downward. "Don't say that."

He lifted her chin with his finger. "Why not? It's true."

As he kissed her again, his hands gently stroked her face and neck, and warmth flowed through her, lighting her up inside. She'd become more sexually aware lately, and having him so close, so attentive, pushed her desire to a whole new level.

"Ryan…"

Flicking his tongue into her mouth, Ryan sucked ever so gently in a rhythm of familiarity. When he broke the kiss and looked at her, his thumbs smoothing across her cheekbones, she had to close her eyes against his heated gaze.

"I want you so much," he whispered. "I can't stop thinking about you."

"We can't."

"More like we shouldn't, but…" His breath scorched the skin of her throat. "You hold the power here, Ally. You know that, right?" Pulling her forward so her butt sat on the edge of the table, Ryan used his hips to separate her legs. "But if you want me…"

As his kisses intensified, her body responded of its own accord, betraying any objections as it gave him permission to proceed. Ally knew resistance was the sensible option, but in the moment, that seductive smile and the thought of him inside of her, over-whelmed any reason.

Ryan slipped his hands under her shirt, running them across her tight baby bump and over full breasts, bulging over the lace of her too-small bra. His hands moved around to her back, undoing the hooks and easing it forward as he kissed and sucked gently on her neck and shoulders. Taking a deep breath, he stared down at her in the muted light. "You turn me on so much."

His hands were everywhere as he lightly pinched full nipples, tiptoed his fingers up and down her spine, and murmured words she couldn't quite catch—but there was no mistaking their meaning. And all the while, Jessie Ware's 'Say You Love Me' kept in time with its slapping rhythmic beat as it floated down the hallway from the sound system in reception.

He lifted her shirt, before running a trail of light kisses down her neck and onto tender breasts, first one then the other. Ally leaned forward, tasting the salt on his skin as she inhaled his musky scent. He gazed at her through sex-heavy eyes. "I want this. But you have to want it too." He stopped and gently held her face in both hands so she couldn't look away. "Ask me."

Lost in the moment, Ally's thoughts swayed back and forth as the breath rushed from her lungs. "I'm not asking you."

His lips moved to the shell of her ear. "You want me to stop?" He bent down and pulled her right nipple into his hot mouth before wafting a cooling breath over its peak. He stared up at her. "Do you?"

She looked him straight in the eye. "So you want me to beg?"

"Just so we're clear."

"We're clear," she whispered. "So, so clear."

His lips twisted into that half-smile, and if she hadn't been so turned on, Ally might have found the whole thing amusing or—depending on the day—beyond irritating. Why was it that forbidden fruit tasted the sweetest, but ultimately left such a sour aftertaste? She was pregnant, and he was an arrogant bastard, but she'd never felt so sensual in all her life. Ever since their last encounter, she'd wanted sex more than ever before, but she wasn't prepared to sleep with just anyone. Ryan was the only man fit for the job. She inhaled, a shuddering 'here goes nothing' breath.

Fumbling with the belt on his jeans, Ally undid the buckle, the button, and then his zipper. He reached into his pocket for a condom, ripping it open with his teeth as he wrestled his jeans to the floor. "I've been thinking about this all day. You and me—losing ourselves in each other. You're so damn sexy. So beautiful."

He was aroused to the hilt as he rolled on the condom. It fascinated her how much he enjoyed talking during sex, and as she touched him, the words flowed from his lips as usual. He told her how he wanted her, needed her more than anything else. How he'd missed her. How breathtakingly beautiful she was. Never once letting up—kisses and words of lust tripped off his tongue in hot breaths while his hands commanded her every move.

He gently pulled her forward, bringing them into alignment, then peeled down her leggings and panties. Strong hands clenched behind her lower back as he entered her, and as they moved, her butt rocked back and forth over the edge of the table.

Their gazes locked, never wavering. But moments later, when his eyes closed tight and his head jolted back, Ally couldn't keep up.

Closing her eyes, she rested her forehead on his chest and sighed. Ryan pulled out, one hand holding the condom in place, the other still on her shoulder. "Shit. I'm sorry."

"It's okay."

He lifted her chin. "No, it's not. I knew you were close. But I couldn't hold on. You make me so damn horny." One hand traveled downward. She inhaled sharply as he kissed and sucked the spot just below her ear. It drove her crazy. "But you like coming this way." His hand went to work. "Don't you, Ally?"

"Oh, holy shit! Ryan..." She shuddered, her legs quivering as she grasped the sheet.

"That's it. Let go. Come for me, babe."

Her head jerked back as she clenched the sides of the table. Her release was swift and powerful, and even though the ink of 'Ryan

Rules' had scarcely dried, he'd commanded her with such desire—such lust—she struggled to let go of the fantasy.

Ally let out a ragged breath as she looked down to the jeans pooled at his feet, then up to his unbuttoned shirt. She was no better, with one leg out of her leggings and her T-shirt bunched up around her shoulders.

Ryan reached for her hand and squeezed it. "You okay?"

She nodded her reply.

"Let me use the bathroom, then I'll take you home."

"You don't have to."

"Yes, I do."

Once he'd left the room, Ally cleaned herself up with wet wipes and adjusted her clothes into place. After remaking the table with yet another clean sheet, she buried the evidence of their tryst in the laundry bag, and shoved it out the door. Catching sight of her reflection in the mirror, she winced. Some women glowed when they were pregnant. She wasn't one of them. Tiny splotches of pigmentation marred both cheeks, and she looked tired and pale.

She shut the massage room door and made her way to reception, ordering an Uber on the way. Ryan appeared a few minutes later, dumping the laundry bag into the chute as he passed.

Ally watched as Ryan set the alarm and locked the main door. They caught the elevator in uncomfortable silence as 'Say You Love Me' played in her head.

"So, how's Stuart?" he casually asked as the elevator stopped and he ushered her through to the outside lobby.

She turned. "Stuart?"

"I saw you having coffee in Steam Perk earlier. I didn't think he'd be your type."

A sickening realization slammed into her. "We're just friends."

"Stuart Harrison doesn't have female friends. Don't say I didn't warn you."

"So that's what this was? 'Jealous asshole' sex? A reminder that I still find you irresistible just because you saw me with another man?" Ally's voice rose. "Okay, I've been reminded. Well done! You're sex on a stick. Now I'll have something else to mull over while I beat myself up over how stupid I've been."

Ally hurried through the door and into the back of the waiting Uber.

He ran after her. "Ally, wait. That's not—"

She slammed the door on his words.

As the driver pulled into the flow of traffic, Ally leaned back in the seat and shut her eyes. *Shit, shit, shit!* Her phone vibrated in her bag, and when she finally found it among the keys and makeup and tissues, she glanced down at the message.

Ryan: You think that's why I want you? Because I'm jealous of Stuart?

She reread his words. Answering a text when angry was never a good idea, but she couldn't stop herself.

Ally: I have no idea what goes on in that head of yours.
Ryan: YOU! You're what's in my head. And Stuart Harrison and the rest of your admirers have nothing to do with it.
Ryan: And we need to call a truce. Otherwise we'll destroy what we *do* have. Is that what you want?
Ally: We don't have ANYTHING, and that's the way you wanted it!!!
Ryan: That's bullshit, and you know it.

41

RUST ON WHITE LINEN

A few days later, Ally entered Farra's deserted fifth-floor lobby. Tim's laptop lay open on his desk, and down the hallway, she could hear someone talking on the phone.

"Hey, you." Tim breezed into view. "Are you here to see the boss?"

Ally handed him a large envelope. "No. Dave asked me to deliver this."

"Okay, thanks. It must be my contract and fitness program. Why didn't he email it?"

She had no idea. "You're joining the gym?"

"Well, I'm pretending I am. But hey, who knows? I had a physical last week."

"And? How were the results?"

"Lies, all lies. But, to tell you the truth"—he leaned in closer— "I do feel self-conscious about my body when I'm with someone. I have stretch marks already and I'm only thirty."

Ally could sympathize. She had stretch marks too.

"So, what do you think?" He cocked his head toward Ryan's office and whispered, "Could I ever look like His Lordship? I wouldn't mind a little bit of what he's got going on."

Ally shot him a cheeky grin. "There's only one way to find out. But you have to take that first step. No point in delaying it any longer, or six months from now, you'll still be talking about it."

"But they're all so pretentious, those sweaty gyms. Teaming with steroid-sculptured muscle-men all drinking their protein shakes."

"That's not true. Besides, you've got a great frame. I'm not a fan of steroids, ever."

"That's a relief. Would you be my personal trainer?"

"Really? Are you sure that wouldn't be weird?"

"I'd feel more comfortable with you."

"Okay. I won't be at the gym much longer, but I could start you off. I'm on a late tomorrow. Shall I slot you in for around six?"

"Go on, then."

As she turned to leave, Ryan walked from his office with three other men. Stopping at the sight of her, he told his colleagues to go on ahead, and he'd be down in a few minutes. Once the elevator doors had closed, he turned to her. "Ally. What can I do for you?" His manner was brusque and businesslike.

"I came to drop something off to Tim."

"Right." He indicated to the elevator. "Are you heading down?"

Snippets from their massage table tryst slammed into focus. That first, heady kiss. The song. The rhythm. The fullness. *So much fullness.* "No, not yet."

He paused as if wanting to say more. Ally felt the heat creep up her neck and throat as Tim looked on. The doors swished open and Ryan stepped in, those hazel eyes finding hers and holding them tight as he reached for the down button.

Tim waved his hand back and forth between the elevator and Ally. "Is there something—"

"Not a thing."

"Right. It's just—"

"I might use the bathroom if that's okay," Ally interrupted.

"Go right ahead."

As she pushed through the restroom door, Ally caught sight of her reflection in the mirror, her hand touching the love bite she'd tried to cover with makeup. The night before, she'd gone to bed questioning everything about her massage table romp with Ryan. By the end of the beat-up session, her conclusion hadn't changed. She'd wanted the sex as much as he had. No mixed messages there.

She'd never thought of herself as a sexually forward person but was drawn to Ryan in a way she struggled to comprehend.

Without warning, Ally felt her face flush as her stomach heaved. She needed to go home and make herself something healthy to eat, but home seemed so far away…

When Ryan arrived at the office the following morning, Tim was already at his desk, talking on the phone. Ryan watched as Tim flailed his arms around. The longer he spoke, the more animated he became. On a good day, the guy was hilarious. Other days, not so much.

Ryan left him to it and entered his office. He dropped into his chair and checked his diary, mentally shuffling the day into priorities while his laptop booted into life. At the sound of an incoming text, he picked up his phone.

Stuart: I've found the songbird.
Ryan: Really? Who?
Stuart: Can't say yet. But she doesn't want to feature on the track. You keen for lunch one day soon?
Ryan: Anytime. Just let me know.
Stuart: OK. I'll be in touch.

After placing the phone down in front of him, Ryan sat back

for a few minutes, tapping the bass line of 'Rust on White Linen' on the desk as he hummed the melody in his head. It was a song that stayed with you. One that made you think, made you wonder.

Tim walked in with the mail. "I was just talking to Ally."

Ryan waited for Tim to elaborate. He didn't. "And how is she?" he asked finally.

"Didn't you hear? She had a bad nosebleed and collapsed in the restroom after you left yesterday. The place looked like a crime scene when I found her—blood everywhere. She was unresponsive for a while. We had to call the paramedics. It was drama central. Just as well she hit her head on the door, or I wouldn't have heard anything."

"What? Why didn't someone tell me?"

"Sorry, I thought Dave had."

"Is she all right?" Ryan stood and grabbed his jacket from behind his chair. He hated how they'd left each other after their last time together, and their uncomfortable interaction in the lobby the day before. He disliked playing games—the push and the pull, the truth and the lies—but it seemed there'd been plenty of game playing between the two of them lately.

"Fine, but they kept her in the hospital overnight to monitor the baby."

"Clear my diary for the rest of the morning," Ryan said as he crossed the lobby to the elevator.

Tim called after him, "But you have a meeting with the building inspector soon."

"Reschedule it. Ask Anton to meet me downstairs and give him the address of the hospital."

"Will do."

4 2

LOST IN PRIDE

Ally lay back on the bed and sighed heavily, desperate to go home. Even though the hospital staff were kind and friendly, the night had dragged as her thoughts wandered all over the place and back again. She quietly hummed the melody to 'Rust on White Linen,' closing her eyes as she recalled the words:

> *free of doubts, full of trust,*
> *rust on white linen,*
> *lost in the dust.*
> *truth and lies, words inside,*
> *rust on white linen, lost in pride.*

If she were honest, Ally longed to hear herself on the final take. To stand in a studio, with the headphones to one ear and her mouth to the mic. As she stared out the window, she could almost feel her fingers on the piano keys at home, the curtains floating on the breeze as she lost herself in the music. It had long been her dream to have one of her songs recorded. But why did it have to be this one? The song where she laid her heart bare.

A woman breezed into the room, pushing the ultrasound cart.

"Good morning. I'm Mary, the sonographer. Okay, let's take a look at the wee bundle, shall we?" She motioned to Ally's neck. "Looks like your man needs to learn a little discretion," she teased.

Ally's hands flew to the hickey.

Mary chuckled. "Good to know you're still getting plenty of exercise. Right, let's gel you up."

She spread gel on Ally's baby bump and started the scan. "Okay, Mummy, there's the tiny human. Looks as happy as a bird in a nest full of twigs."

"I'll never get tired of seeing those little fists waving around."

"Look." Mary pointed with her pen. "There's the heart, and here we have his… Whoops, sorry, darlin'. I mean *its* arms and legs." She laughed. "I hope you weren't planning a big gender reveal."

"So it's a boy? They couldn't tell last time because he was facing the wrong way." Ally swallowed the lump in her throat. "That's cool. A boy."

"Everything's looking good. He's all safe and sound in his water world. I'll just take some measurements, and then we're done. You want a pretty picture to take home?"

"Yes, please."

Clutching the printout, Ally leaned back on the pillow and smiled. A boy. How would Ryan react when he found out he was having a son? Thinking about it rationally, she understood why he didn't believe the baby was his, but that didn't make his reaction any less painful.

"Hey."

Ally looked in the direction of the familiar voice. She hadn't heard him walk in, certainly hadn't expected him to come. "Ryan. What are you doing here?"

Placing a large bunch of pink and white roses cradled in olive branches on the nightstand, he leaned down and kissed her on the cheek. The significance of the foliage didn't escape her. *A peace offering?*

"I hear you made a mess of the floor yesterday. How are you feeling now?"

"Okay." The urge to cry surfaced, as it had so many times over the past few months. She'd never been one for tears, but pregnancy had changed that.

Pregnancy had changed many things.

Ryan sat next to the bed looking dejected—almost sad—in his well-cut suit, baby-blue shirt, and striped tie. Ally felt sorry for him. He'd missed seeing his son on the scan. Missed the whoosh of his tiny heartbeat and the wave of his little fists. But she wouldn't pressure him into accepting responsibility for this new life. He had to arrive at that destination on his own.

"The flowers are beautiful. Thank you." Ally wanted to apologize for the way she spoke to him the night at the gym, but she struggled to form the words.

"When are you being discharged?"

"My sister's coming to collect me as soon as the doctor's been, so I'd better go have a shower."

Ryan glanced over at the printout of the scan propped up on the nightstand. Ally held her breath, but nothing was said. He looked at her and smiled. "Is that my cue to leave?"

"It's easier that way. Saves me having to answer any awkward questions. My sister's a shameless busybody." Ally went to say more about Liz's shocked reaction to her pregnancy, but decided Ryan didn't need to hear it.

"Yeah, so is Fiona, my sister." Ryan stood and slid his hands into his pockets as he looked around the room. "Can I get you anything before I go? Juice?"

"No, I'm fine, but thanks for coming."

He nodded. Hesitated. "Anytime."

When Ryan reached over to tuck a lock of hair behind her ear,

Ally placed her hand over the hickey but said nothing. He frowned. "Shit, did I do that? Sorry."

"Nothing a little makeup won't cover."

They stared at each other in uncomfortable silence. "I'm sorry about the other night as well. I should have picked up that laundry bag as soon as you asked and kept walking out that door."

"So why didn't you?"

"You know why." He paused before turning toward the door. "Take care, Ally."

Ally lay back on the bed and closed her eyes. She'd seldom suffered from loneliness, but as Ryan slipped out the door and down the corridor, she let the false bravado slip along with a few wayward tears.

Later, while showering, Ally wondered if her baby would look like his dad. Sandy-haired, with hazel eyes full of mischief and a half-smile on his cheeky little face.

Back in her bed, she closed her eyes and rubbed her hand over her belly. Exhausted and overwhelmed, she drifted off to sleep.

The squeak of shoes on the floor jolted her awake.

"Sorry, I didn't realize you were sleeping," the nurse said as she handed Ally a white shopping bag embossed with gold lettering. "Someone dropped this off."

She frowned. "For me?"

"Yes, for you. Doctor Garret will be here soon. Then you can go home."

"Thank you. You've been very kind."

Ally stared at the large bag. She knew the store, a high-end maternity boutique not far from the gym. Every time she walked by, she would window-shop, coveting the tone-on-tone bedding, cute outfits, and tiny shoes so artistically displayed. But she couldn't afford to shop there.

She checked her watch. Ryan had only been gone just over an hour. Still, when you had the means and a driver, and probably a personal shopper to boot, the world moved quickly on your command.

Reaching into the bag, she pulled out an oversized cotton sweater in cream. It would look great over skinny jeans, and the full cowl neck would hide the hickey. The second top was more formal. Fashioned from cotton lace, also with a high neck, the fabric floated from the bust in true boho style. It was gorgeous, and so was the mustard colored pashmina at the bottom of the bag.

She opened the card, its front painted with tulips, and read the three-word inscription inside.

Sometimes, life sucks.
R. xx

SINGULAR STANDARDS

Slipping into a plush velvet booth, Ryan glanced around the light-filled restaurant as he waited for Stuart. They'd been friends since their last year at high school, and while Stuart could be ruthless, he was also a shrewd businessman who refused to deal out of bounds. Ryan admired that kind of honesty.

Ryan scrolled through his inbox, hoping to find a text from Ally. Images of their encounter in the massage room flicked through his thoughts. What had he been thinking? Putting them both in that situation? But he had, and no amount of regret could change that.

"What's up? You look like you're hungover."

Ryan chuckled as Stuart slipped into the booth. He hadn't slept well the night before, and it obviously showed. "Yeah? I do feel a bit rough, but it's not from booze and debauchery."

"How's everything? Work, the twins, and Polly all okay?"

"Yes, fine."

The men perused the menu, and when the waiter came, both ordered cod on a sweet potato rosti, and a craft beer.

"How are things going with Jacinta?" Ryan asked.

"It's over. It hurt, but it was the right thing to do. I couldn't see us staying together long term. I'm not getting any younger. It's about time I settled down, got married maybe."

Ryan nearly choked on his water. "You? Married?"

"I'm over meaningless relationships with plastic fantastics. That whole twelve-course degustation menu bullshit when all I want is a good old-fashioned hamburger, albeit a gourmet one."

Ryan laughed. He'd never thought of Stuart as the marrying kind. "What the hell's brought this on?"

Stuart turned serious, his brow creasing into a frown. "A good friend's just been diagnosed with terminal cancer. I went to see him last week—and spent days after thinking about it. I want to get married and have kids one day. But I need to meet the right woman. Jacinta isn't interested in marriage. Or children."

"I'm sorry to hear that."

"How's Fiona?"

Ryan paused to formulate his reply. Stuart and his sister had history—complicated history—and it had taken Ryan a long time to forgive Stuart for what he'd put Fiona through all those years ago. "Good. Focused on her business."

"Is she seeing anyone?"

"You want to discuss Fiona? Seriously? You gave up that right, remember?"

"I guess I did." Stuart sighed. "Anyway, have you seen Ally lately?"

"Yesterday." Ryan paused as the waiter placed two half pints of beer on the table. "You two looked pretty cozy in Steam Perk the other day."

"Are you jealous?"

"Piss off." Ryan took a sip of his beer before deciding to cut the bullshit. "Maybe a bit."

"Do you two still meet up?"

"Occasionally."

"Are you sleeping together?"

Ryan lifted his glass and opened his mouth to speak, then

thought better of it. He knew Stuart would draw his own conclusions, but he wasn't about to confirm *or* deny.

"And you call me a ruthless bastard," Stuart continued. "You seriously need to sort your shit out."

"I love it when you give me advice, Stu. It really boosts my ego. Not!"

"Yeah well, someone's got to call you out for being a dick. Who better than me? Been there, done that."

"I never said we were sleeping together."

"You didn't have to."

Conversation stopped while another waiter served their meals. The smell of dill and butter sauce filled the air. Ryan took a bite. "Man, this is good." They ate in silence for a while before he asked, "So what's the deal...with you and Ally?"

"She came to me for advice."

"What? Legal advice? Does she know your hourly rate?"

"There's always a little in the pro bono pot for a pretty woman."

Pretty woman. Ryan let the comment slide. "And was this advice to do with the baby?"

"Piss off." Stuart sipped his beer. "You know I can't discuss her business with you, or anyone else. But I must admit, I did wonder whether you were the father."

"She seems to think so. But I can't be. I shoot blanks."

"You've already had a vasectomy? At your age? How did I not know this?"

"I had a virus when I was twenty. It's not something that comes up in casual conversation. We conceived the twins through IVF. They're my biological children, but we needed help getting them. We weren't able to have any more."

"Shit. That's tough."

"Yeah, so either Ally's jerking me around or she actually believes it's mine."

Stuart sat back in his chair and sighed. "Do you still have feelings for her?"

Now it was Ryan's turn to sigh. He nodded. "Yeah. I haven't felt this way about a woman in years. What the hell was I thinking? She'll probably be back in New Zealand by this time next year."

"Have you told her how you feel?"

"She's pregnant. What's the point?"

"You already have kids, so what's the difference?"

"That's a very liberal way of looking at it."

"Not really. It's just keeping the standards singular. The twins will always be part of your package, so it's not fair to expect her to be a cute little virgin with no ties or responsibilities. Life doesn't work like that. Has it occurred to you she may be telling the truth?"

"Sometimes. But…"

"Maybe she's just dazzled by your big…bank balance."

Ryan chuckled. "No, she's not asked me for a thing."

"Look, for what it's worth, I'm fond of Ally. She seems like a sweet kid with a misty past. Don't burn that bridge, Ryan. Not unless you have all the facts."

He frowned. "What do you mean by a misty past?"

Stuart tapped the side of his nose. Clearly, he wasn't about to elaborate.

44

NOT PERFECT

Dear Ryan,

Thank you for your gift. It was a pleasant surprise and very thoughtful of you. However, I find myself grappling with a range of emotions. It's clear to me, as I'm sure it is to you, that I can't say no where you're concerned. I don't necessarily feel used; I realize I'm responsible for my own actions, but...

I don't want you seeing me as someone you can pick up and drop on a whim. When we're alone, I forget the essence of who I am. Perhaps hormones are playing a part, but ultimately, I have the choice. Lately, I seem incapable of making the right one.

Therefore, I believe it's best if we cut all ties. I need to stay focused and calm, but whenever you stroll back into my life, I'm neither.

Ally.

Standing at the back of the elevator, Ryan popped Ally's card into his breast pocket and exhaled a heavy 'I'm glad today is over' sigh of relief. As he hit the ground floor button, he contemplated her words. The thought of not seeing her again hurt, but she did have a point. And Stuart was right; Ryan had acted like a selfish, arrogant asshole.

When the elevator stopped on the third floor, Ally glanced up as the door opened. Her eyes widened when she noticed him, and she took a step back. He held the *Open* button. "Get in," he snapped. "I won't bite."

"I'll wait for the next one."

"Ally, just get in."

She stepped inside, and he released the button, letting the doors close behind her. Standing stiff and silent, she kept her eyes focused on the floor readout.

"How have you been?" he asked.

"Fine, thank you."

"When do you finish at the gym?"

She turned slightly to look at him. "I'm not sure. It depends on how I'm feeling. I was just discussing it with HR."

The doors opened, and she took off, striding across the lobby and out the front entrance as if her life depended on it. Ryan followed a few steps behind. The night had cooled, and gray rain clouds rumbled above them, about to dump their fury. Ally stopped on the curb, pulled her coat tighter, and pushed the walk button impatiently.

Ryan held her arm as the cross signal turned green. She sighed and stared at the ground, unable to look him in the eye. "It's starting to rain. Let me drive you home."

"Didn't you read my note?"

"I promise I won't try anything. You have my word."

"I'm sorry, but from where I'm standing, your word doesn't carry much weight."

"Look, I have something I want to discuss. Please. It won't take long."

She hesitated, then followed as he walked toward the parking building.

They traveled in silence until they reached a small park on the city side of Putney Bridge where Ryan pulled into a parking space and cut the engine.

She shifted in her seat. Was she getting comfortable, or preparing to bolt? "Why are we stopping?"

"I'm guessing you won't ask me in for coffee, so I thought we could talk here."

Ally tugged at the lapels of her coat, saying nothing as she fiddled with one of the large buttons. Ryan turned to face her, hoping she'd do the same. When she didn't, he continued anyway. "I'd like us to start seeing each other again."

She turned to face him now, her brow furrowed and one hand resting on her baby bump. "What, go back to our Thursdays? You can't be serious."

"I'm deadly serious."

She reached to open the door. "I'll walk from here."

"Please, hear me out." He placed a hand on her arm.

Ryan took a deep breath as he struggled to find his voice. He'd practiced his speech often enough, but now she was in front of him, he didn't know where to start. He cleared his throat. "When we first met, I didn't want to invite you into my world. You seemed so young and carefree, and I was divorced and struggling with my commitments. I didn't want ties, and I thought you felt the same. But your pregnancy changed things. The twins come as part of my package, and soon, you'll have your baby, which will come as part of yours. Although I can't father a child, I could give you and your baby a home and security."

She stared at him, shaking her head.

"Shit," he said. "This is coming out all wrong."

"You think?"

"Look, this attraction between us, it's something I haven't felt in a very long time. And I know you feel the same."

"I had dreams, Ryan. To travel, meet new people, and maybe fall in love with romantic, crazy guys. To drink beer in Germany, eat pizza in Italy, pastries in France, and enjoy my twenties without a care."

He opened his mouth to speak, but she stopped him with a raised palm.

"A baby wasn't part of that plan, but as soon as I saw his little face on the screen and felt him move inside me, my plans changed. The most important thing you can give a child is happy and loving parents, or in my case, parent, so that's my new focus.

"I'd like you to take a paternity test when the baby arrives, not so we can play happy families, but so you can be a part of his life. Ultimately, it's your choice, but I want you to have that opportunity. Until then, I have nothing more to say to you. I can't be with a man who thinks I'm a liar and a cheat."

His? "You're having a boy?"

Staring out the passenger window, Ally sucked in her top lip, obviously struggling to hold her emotions in check. "I have to go." Her voice quivered in an almost whisper. "The walk will do me good."

Ryan activated the central locking from his door and started the engine. "You're not walking home. It's raining. And I'm happy to take the test when the time comes."

They drove across the bridge and down Putney High Street to her apartment building. Ryan cut the engine, and they sat in silence for a few moments. "I don't want to leave you like this," he eventually said.

"Don't stress yourself. Healthy relationships are based on honesty and trust, and it seems we have neither of those virtues between us."

"So is this it?"

"What do you want me to say? That I'm happy to carry on regardless? Happy when you expect me to beg you for sex? And all because you had a point to prove."

"I didn't make you beg. That was simply sexual banter, and you know it."

"And you're an expert in that, aren't you? You know how to make a girl feel desired and special with your 'sexual banter.' Until you get what you want."

"That's bullshit. You wanted me that night just as much as I wanted you."

"Yes, I did. There, I've said it. Happy now?"

"No, I'm not happy. I haven't been happy since you told me you were pregnant. Sometimes, I have no idea what you want."

"I just told you. Trust and respect. That's what I want. I'm not prepared to be your convenient screw. And granted, I'm overly emotional and hormonally messed up right now, but I need to stay focused."

"You're a lot of things to me, but a convenient screw is not one of them."

"Maybe. But I broke the rules and wanted more. How stupid was that? Stupid and naïve."

"You, naïve? I don't think so. You knew the score."

"Yes. How about Thursday for a quickie in a posh hotel? No questions asked, no answers given."

"You can't possibly call what we did a quickie. If I'd only wanted a quick screw, you wouldn't have been calling out my name as you came for the second and third time. And I certainly wouldn't have held you all night as you slept."

"So, all those sweet words you bombarded me with when you're in seduction mode, were they just for me or do you say them to all your girls?"

"There *are* no other girls. Until I met you, I'd never had a casual affair in my life. You're the only woman I've slept with in well over a year. I know you don't believe me, but I do care for you, so much. Some nights, I can't sleep for thinking about you, but that's not enough, is it? What we had wasn't perfect, so you refuse to give us a chance. But real relationships aren't perfect. Real relationships are both dull and exciting, free and restrictive, sensual and mundane." He inhaled sharply. "And sometimes, they're plain hard work."

She went to reply, but it was his turn to stop her with a gesture. He wanted to get everything off his chest while he had the chance. Although he knew anger never solved anything, as the heat crept up his face and neck, Ryan wanted to prove his point. "What do you want, Ally? Because if it's some guy promising you a Happy Ever After, I'm not that man. And as for you being a convenient screw… Well, I could probably get laid any day of the week, no questions asked, but that's not how I want to conduct my life."

"I never said I wanted a Happy Ever After. I just want someone who wants me back. A guy who calls and who asks about my day. One who likes me without the conditions."

"I understand." Looking over at Ally as she cradled her face in her hands, he continued quietly, "And I know I should have been more up-front, but it was a game we played, wasn't it? And to tell you the truth, I loved it. It was reckless and exciting and so damn sexy that I couldn't wait for Thursdays. But now the rules have been shot to hell, haven't they?"

"They have."

"Look, I have the twins and a demanding family business I'm responsible for. What we had was exciting, but it wasn't just some romantic fantasy for me. When we make love—connect in that unique way—and I say you're beautiful, that I want you, and how amazing you are, that's how I truly feel.

"But you're right, we are from different worlds. You're young…precious. I can't offer you more than I already have. I'll take the paternity test when the time comes, but in the meantime, maybe we *should* keep away from each other."

Ally remained in her seat and leaned her head on the passenger window. They sat there in silence. No rebuttals. No excuses.

"You make me sad," she whispered.

"Ditto."

They both released their seat belts at the same time. Not waiting for him to open her door, Ally climbed from the car. She stood on the curbside in the cold wind, staring straight ahead—her hands seeking warmth in her pockets as tears threatened.

Joining her on the curb, Ryan activated the lock function on his key fob. He placed his hand to the small of her back, guiding her toward the apartment lobby. "Where are your keys?"

Ally handed him her bag without making eye contact. "They're in the side pocket."

The apartment was in darkness when Ryan opened the door. She stood motionless and silent as he flicked on the light. He removed her coat and hung it on the hook.

"Maybe you should call your sister? Ask her to come over for a bit."

As Ally pulled out her phone to text Liz, Jia opened the front door. She looked back and forth between Ally and Ryan. "Is everything all right?" She dropped her bag and took Ally's hand, leading her to the sofa. Ally kept shaking her head. Jia turned to Ryan. "What's going on?"

"Ally's upset. Can you keep her company? I have to go."

"But—"

He held up his hand and walked toward the door. Dropping Ally's keys on the hall table as he passed, he left without looking back.

Ryan sat in his car, his fists clenched tight and his gut tighter. He didn't want to go home without Ally and hadn't expected he'd have to. As he started the engine and pulled out onto Putney High Street, it dawned on him how stupid he'd been. *Not the sharpest tool in the toolbox.*

Back at Chris's apartment, he lay on his bed in the dark, his breath sitting heavy in his lungs. With good friends, the twins, and a busy professional life, Ryan seldom experienced loneliness. But tonight was different. It had never occurred to him that she would react so negatively, or how her reaction would sadden him.

He drifted in and out of semi-sleep until a quarter after midnight when his phone lit up with a text. He glanced at the screen and mumbled a frustrated profanity under his breath.

Ally: I'm sorry for some of the things I said.

His fingers began typing a reply before he had time to think about it.

Ryan: Yeah, me too.

Ryan waited for a return text that never arrived. He dropped his phone onto the bed before his fingers had a chance to send another message. Although he wanted to suggest calling a truce again, what was the point?

Now wide awake, he headed to the living room and grabbed a half-empty bottle of Scotch from the liquor cabinet. As he took a swig, and then another, he knew he'd pay for it in the morning. But as he stepped onto the terrace and stared out over the Thames, he didn't give a damn how bad the headache would be.

4 5

TIM TAMS

As she packed the last of her belongings into a cardboard box, Ally looked over at the door. Jia had been out all night, and even though she'd texted Ally to let her know she was okay, the click of the lock still reassured her.

"Sorry, I'm a bit late." Jia rushed into the living room wearing above-the-knee-boots and a tiny skirt, her lion's mane jacket draped over her arm. "I wanted to help you pack."

"A bit late." Ally smiled. "It's after one."

"Yes, I know, but"—Jia held up a packet and shook it—"I have Tim Tams. Want some tea?"

"Where on earth did you get them? I love Tim Tams."

"From my date." Jia smiled coyly.

"Wait, you had a date? I thought you were at your parents. And why would your date have Tim Tams? Is he an Aussie?"

Jia chewed on her lower lip as she moved to the kitchen and flicked on the kettle. Leaning her hip on the counter, she looked at Ally.

Ally's eyes narrowed. "What are you up to?"

"That guy, you know, Mr. Left of Ideal? Well, he invited me to watch a movie at his place, and I decided to risk it, because if I don't lose my cherry soon, I may as well join the convent."

"You went? Jia, you don't even really know this guy!"

"I kinda do. I had coffee with him once and we have mutual friends, so it wasn't like I spent the night with some stranger I met on a construction site." She wagged her finger at Ally and grinned.

"No, you met on Tinder."

She shrugged. "Anyway, his housemates were home."

"And?"

"He was really lovely. Not that he talked much. He'd made a platter of cheese and crackers, and a huge bowl of popcorn. I ate the whole lot while he just stared at me and nodded at everything I said. I always overeat when I'm nervous."

"Go on."

"Well, we watched this movie, right, and he didn't even hold my hand." Jia's shoulders sagged. "How bleak is that? When he asked me to stay, I thought I might at least get a cuddle. But no! He spent the whole time curled in a ball with his back to me, sleeping while I stayed awake for most of the night."

"So why didn't you sneak out and come home?"

"Because it was raining and cold and I didn't want to leave his comfortable bed. Plus, he may be shy and awkward, but he's also hot in a geeky kinda way. And self-contained. And softly spoken—"

"When he speaks."

"Yes. Anyway, I woke up around dawn, busting to pee. There was no tissue left on the roll, so I checked the cabinet. Nothing. Talk about embarrassing. I ended up using those makeup-remover pads. What if I've clogged their system and they have to call a plumber?"

Ally couldn't keep from laughing as she pictured Jia searching through some stranger's bathroom cabinets. "I'm sure it'll be fine."

"It's not funny."

"Oh, but it is. So where did the Tim Tams come from?"

"His nightstand drawer. I thought maybe he was reaching for a condom, but it was full of Aussie treats. Turns out his mum still sends him care packages. So cute." Jia reached into her bag and pulled out an assortment of chocolate bars and another packet of Tim Tams. "He insisted I bring these home. Told me to share them with you."

"Yum. Can I have one now?"

"Have as many as you like."

Ally grabbed a Picnic bar from the pile of loot and tore off it's distinctive red wrapper. "So he knows you have a housemate? Who is this guy?"

Jia screwed up her face and whispered, "His name's Hamish. And he's a DJ."

The penny dropped. "No way! Not Hamish Baxter?"

"Please don't hate me. I didn't realize you were friends until last night."

"Hamish is Mr. Left of Ideal? That's hilarious. Now I know why he hasn't kissed you."

Jade flopped down on the sofa. "It's me, isn't it? Guys just don't find me attractive."

"That's not true. But Hamish is painfully shy around women he's attracted to."

"You think he's attracted to me?"

"Of course. Otherwise, he wouldn't have asked you over." Ally took another bite, savoring the chocolate and caramel as it danced in her mouth. "And I wouldn't be sitting here eating chocolate for lunch."

"So how do I get him to open up?"

"Make the first move. Kiss him like you mean it. Maybe ask him about his music."

"Do you think he's a virgin too?"

Hamish and Ally had discussed his unsuccessful quest to lose his virginity one night over too many wines, but she wasn't about to spill his secrets. "There's only one way to find out. Ask him."

Ally grabbed her phone off the table when it chirped, smiling when she saw 'DJ Mish' at the top of the screen.

"Are you crazy? I am not asking him that." Jia replied. "Anyway, I need to go take a shower."

As Jia left the room, Ally read his text.

DJ Mish: We need to talk. ASAP.

She smiled. This was the best news she'd had in weeks. Hamish and Jia, a match made in musical heaven. Who would have thought?

Ally: About the song?
DJ Mish: No, something else. Can we meet for coffee?
Ally: It's moving day, but I'll call you later. When I've finished the Tim Tams you kindly sent over.
DJ Mish: SHIT. YOU KNOW? What did she say?
Ally: Nothing much. Just girl talk. And don't SHOUT.
DJ Mish: Do you think she likes me?
Ally: What are you, 15?
Ally: Sorry, that was mean. Yes. She likes you.
DJ Mish: She's so beautiful that I clammed up. What should I do? I hardly spoke to her all night. And this morning, I had no clue what to say. So I gave her chocolate. She must think I'm so lame. SHIT!!! (and I'm not shouting, I'm exclaiming - loudly).
Ally: Mish, take a breath. Don't overthink it. And on your next date, ask her about her music.

AJ opened the back door of his Range Rover and placed Ally's two bags and three boxes inside. "How is it you travel so light when your sister has dresses galore?"

Ally clicked her seat belt into place as AJ climbed into the driver's seat. She'd once loved having plenty of clothes, but filling her wardrobe no longer seemed a priority. "I don't like to be weighed down."

He looked her way. "Feeling okay about moving in with us for a while?"

"Of course. But it's not me I'm worried about. I don't like to impose. Especially at Christmas."

"You're not imposing. We keep telling you that."

As AJ pulled out onto Putney High Street, Ally looked back at the apartment building. She watched as it faded from view, a lump forming in her throat at the thought of leaving Jia—her colorful, quick-witted friend. Sure, they'd still see each other, but it would be different once the baby arrived.

"It's really kind of your mum and dad to invite me to Cambridge for Christmas and New Year's."

"Wait until you get there. It's crazy with all of us at home, but we have heaps of fun."

Ally thought back to the summer Christmas days they had at home, where they'd eat salads and ham and play softball on the beach at sunset. She'd always wanted to experience a white Christmas with traditional British fare, but as the day drew closer, her homesickness intensified.

"I keep meaning to ask," AJ said, breaking into her thoughts. "Have you ever bumped into Ryan Farrell at the gym?"

Ally tensed, her heart crashing against her ribs. AJ knew Ryan? How? And what should she say? Because, even though this was a complication she didn't need, there was no point in lying about it. "You know Ryan?"

"His brother and I went to uni together," AJ said as he turned into Northcote Road. "Ryan was always in the background—annoying the crap out of us, wanting us to buy booze for him and his mates. But I haven't seen him in months. He's been busy with some major project."

"Actually, I did some babysitting for him a while back, but he's not at the gym much when I'm there."

"How did that go? I hear the twins are a bit of a handful. Chris says they're like Ryan was as a kid. Constantly asking questions."

"Hold on a minute. Do you mean Chris the doctor? The guy Liz wants to hook me up with? *He's* Ryan's brother?" This conversation was going from bad to worse. She needed another Picnic bar.

"Yep. But for the record, Chris is all wrong for you. He's hardly ever in the country, and when he is, he works ridiculous hours."

Thank goodness. "That's fine. I'm over men anyway."

AJ shot her a sideways glance. "No, you're not. Someone's gonna come along and rock your world one day. Give it time."

Ally thought of Ryan and how he'd done exactly that. Rocked her world, before turning it upside down with a hefty jolt. "You've been around Liz for too long. You sound just like her."

AJ chuckled as he pulled into the curb and cut the engine. "Speaking of Liz, I need a favor. I want you to sing at her birthday. But it's a surprise, so you can't tell her."

She stiffened in her seat and looked straight ahead. "I can't."

"Please. You know I'm a hopeless singer, and we have a special song. Your voice would do it perfect justice. I'll be right there beside you."

"Perfect justice? Is that even a thing?" She relaxed a little at the impish pleading look on his face. "How many people are coming?"

"I don't know. Fifty to sixty? But we have plenty of time to practice."

Her heart sank. "No way. Not in a million years."

THE LIGHTS

Most days, Ally avoided her sister's pregnancy questions. Every time they had a private conversation, Liz would turn it around to the subject of the baby and his father. It wouldn't be long before she'd have to come clean, after all, Liz and AJ knew Ryan, but why spoil Christmas? Because once the truth surfaced, Ally knew there would be fallout.

She'd been home all morning, waiting for Liz to finish work so they could do their last-minute Christmas shopping. This seemed to be her life now—constantly waiting. For the holiday season and the baby to engage, for the birth and the paternity test. Waiting for Ryan's reaction.

Moving around the kitchen, she hummed along to the Michael Bublé Christmas songs streaming from the Bluetooth speaker on the counter. But no matter how many carols she listened to, it still didn't feel like Christmas. Not this year. But at least she wasn't on her own. Moving in with AJ and Liz had been a godsend, one she didn't take for granted.

Ally gazed out over the wintry garden, barren apart from the camellias and a holly red with berries. She'd hoped to have her first ever white Christmas, but the forecast for the next two weeks didn't include snow. In the morning, they were driving up to Cambridge to spend the week with AJ's family. The thought filled her with a mixture of joy and dread. Part of her wished she could just stay home alone and lie on the sofa, watching reruns of *Love Actually* and *The Polar Express* while eating mac and cheese and gorging on chocolate truffles.

Standing at the dining table, she glanced around the room, looking for her phone. She and Jia hadn't spoken in days and Ally wanted to call her before they left. Finding it under the morning paper, she picked it up and searched through her contacts for Jia's number.

"Ally Cat! Where have you been? I tried calling you yesterday."

"Sorry, it's been an interesting few days."

"I hope you haven't been sitting around brooding over a certain someone all week. It's Christmas."

"Not even for a second," she lied. "I went to see the Oxford Street Christmas lights with Liz and AJ a few nights ago. It was exciting, but freezing cold and teaming with people."

"When are you going to Cambridge?"

"First thing in the morning."

"Aww, bleak. My sister has a spare ticket to the carols at the Royal Albert Hall tomorrow night. I thought you might want to come. I'll ask Hamish."

"So things are okay between you two?"

"Yes, good. He's coming for Christmas dinner and I'm nervous as anything. I hope he joins in the conversation. My family likes to talk."

"He's great at family things; it's just you he's scared of."

Jia giggled. "Not anymore."

"What? You haven't! We need to meet for coffee."

"It will have to be in the new year, but don't expect any details."

Ally looked up when Liz entered the room. "Hey. I've got to go. Liz has just arrived home. We're going to hit the High Street."

"Okay. Love you. Keep smiling, and Happy Christmas."

"You too. And give Hamish a hug from me."

Liz walked straight to the coffee machine and turned it on. "Who was that?"

"Jia. She and Hamish are officially a couple."

"What? Jia and Hamish are dating? How did I not know this? Coffee?"

"No, I'm good. They met on Tinder months ago. Isn't that weird? But waiting for their courtship ritual to unfold has been like watching paint dry."

"That's so cute. Speaking of couples, have you seen the baby's father lately?"

Here we go. "No."

"Is that all I'm going to get?"

Ally didn't know what Liz expected her to say—that she and the baby's father were all loved up and ready to make a commitment. But she decided a little disclosure might shut her sister up for a while. "You know what it's like when you meet someone and feel that instant attraction, almost like you know them from somewhere? That's how I felt about him. But we're from different sides of the planet, and not just geographically."

"Do you want to see him?"

"I guess. But we kept traveling to nowhere and back again, so I had to shut it down. Dad said not to burn my bridges, but it's hard, you know, holding my head up high while I pretend I'm strong enough to do this on my own."

"Yeah, I know." Liz sipped her coffee. "You're doing great though. And a few days away will do you good."

"Yes, I'm looking forward to it." And in a way, she was.

"Anyway," Liz continued, placing a protective arm around Ally's shoulder. "Once the baby's born, you can request a paternity test through the courts."

"I won't have to do that. He'll take the test."

"Will he offer financial support as well?"

"Can we discuss this some other time? It's Christmas." Ally didn't want to think about how she'd manage financially if she stayed in London. She could tell Liz wanted to say more, but for once her sister let it go.

"Right, give me ten minutes to get changed. But be warned, it will be crazy out there."

"I can't wait."

Ally checked her phone as Liz left the room, frowning at the name on the top of the screen.

Ryan: What are you up to for Christmas?

She stared at the message for several seconds, wondering what on earth was going on in the man's head.

Ally: Visiting friends for a few days.
Ryan: The twins and I are going to Winterville at Clapham Common tonight. They want to go ice skating. Would you like to join us? We could pick you up.

What? Did he honestly expect her to rock on down to the common and play pretend friends while the girls hit the ice rink?

Ally: Thank you, but I have plans.
Ryan: I guess you do. Maybe some other time. Happy Christmas.
Ally: You too. Please say hi to the twins from me.

Ally slipped her phone into her bag before she was tempted to continue the thread. Although part of her wanted to accept his offer, she'd learned by now, trading whimsical want for respect was never a good idea.

47

ANYTHING'S POSSIBLE

Ryan sat on a too-low leather sofa opposite the medical center's reception desk and surveyed the room. The neutral decor. The mandatory stack of uninspiring magazines on the coffee table. The clinical smell. They brought it all flooding back. He closed his eyes, feeling all kinds of mixed up over Ally Dobson, and wearier than he'd felt in years. By the time Chris appeared, he'd almost dozed off.

"Come on in."

Ryan followed him into his office and took the chair opposite Chris's desk. He looked around the room and smiled. His brother kept his apartment immaculate, but his workspace was anything but.

Chris leaned back in his chair. "Okay, what's going on?"

"I'd like a sperm test."

He raised an eyebrow and frowned. "Rather than a donor?"

"Someone I slept with is pregnant. She's adamant it's mine. Is there a chance?"

"Anything's possible in medical science, but it's highly unlikely in your case. Didn't you suit up for the occasion?"

Ryan let his expression answer the embarrassing question. If he'd been more careful with the condom in the searing heat of the moment, he wouldn't be here.

"Seriously?" Chris grabbed a specimen jar from a shelf above his desk. "When did you last ejaculate?"

Ryan thought back to that last night with Ally, in the massage room at the gym. The night he couldn't forget. The sex had been great, but the regret even greater. "Weeks ago."

"Really? Not even a quick jerk off in the shower?"

"You're enjoying this, aren't you?"

"It's the festive season. I just assumed you'd be getting plenty." Ryan scoffed. "As if."

"In that case…" A knowing smile lit up Chris's face as he chucked Ryan the jar. "You know I can't treat my own family, but I'm happy to send away a sample. Do you have any stimulating photos on that fancy new iPhone of yours?"

"You mean I have to jerk off now, in your office?"

"No, there's a room down the hall with a few old magazines. I'm sure you remember the drill."

"I do, but I thought I was done with this shit years ago."

The space couldn't really be called a room, more of a cleaning closet with an unforgiving fluorescent light overhead. Ryan held the jar in his hand and sighed. He sat and flicked open a magazine, took one look at the centerfold with her huge fake breasts and plastered-on eye makeup, and closed it again. What was he thinking?

He stood to leave, ready to tell Chris that he'd made a mistake. But as his thoughts turned to Ally, he knew he had to do this. Taking a deep breath he squeezed the cold lube onto his palm.

Chris was on the phone when Ryan returned to his office. He sat the jar on the desk and waited in the adjoining room until Chris called him.

His brother lifted the jar. "Looks like a healthy brew."

"Piss off."

"No need to be embarrassed. I am a doctor."

Ryan chuckled. "Whatever."

"Okay. We'll send the sample to the lab. The results take a bit longer at this time of year, so let's put a drop on a slide and have a quick peek."

As he slipped the glass slide into place, Chris watched the screen of his monitor spring to life. "Hmm. Interesting." He turned the monitor toward Ryan and pointed with a pencil. "Here, take a look. While there are a few rapidly progressive swimmers among the immotile and the non-progressive, you definitely have a high degree of poor sperm motility."

"What the hell does that even mean?"

"By the looks of this, your healthy swimmers are *almost* nonexistent, but not entirely. Let's have the experts take a proper look." Chris labeled the jar and printed off the form. "You know, it is possible for your sperm count to improve over time."

"How?"

"Healthy diet, less booze, exercise. Making those changes alone can increase your chances. After all, it only takes two to tango. And if that's the case, one episode of unprotected sex coupled with a ripe uterus and a determined tadpole, and you're on your way to pushing a baby buggy around Battersea Park. Do you trust this girl?"

"To be honest, I'm really not sure."

"Okay. Let's take some bloods while you're here. Roll up your sleeve."

Ryan did as he was told. "What's the blood for?"

Chris tightened a tourniquet into place. "To check your little friend hasn't left you with any nasty surprises."

Ryan flinched as the needle pricked his skin.

"Where did you meet her?" Chris asked as he filled another vial.

"At work. She was a temp and helped look after the girls when Polly and Marc got married."

"You screwed the hired help?" Chris shook his head as he held a cotton ball over the needle entry and secured it with tape. "Are you going through some sort of midlife crisis or something?"

"More like a 'What the hell was I thinking?' phase. The thing was, she was three months pregnant before she even realized."

Chris washed his hands, his expression doubtful. "Unlikely, but possible."

"I must admit, I've been skeptical ever since I found out."

"Who is she? Anyone I know?"

"No. She's from New Zealand. I'm not even sure how much longer she'll be in London." Ryan stood and rolled down his shirt sleeve.

"Speaking of Kiwis, are you coming to Liz's birthday party next month?"

"Wouldn't miss it. I've been so busy at work lately, I haven't seen the Tanners in ages."

48

THE TANNER CONNECTION

Cars lined the street when Ryan pulled into a park several blocks from the Tanners' house. He checked his watch. Arriving late to parties had become a habit—a way to blend in without being noticed. He climbed from his car and hesitated as he pushed the lock function on his key fob. The house would be full of couples, and for once, he'd feel like an outsider.

He didn't bother with the doorbell. They knew each other well enough for Ryan to let himself in. Chris met him in the hallway and pulled Ryan aside. "We need to talk."

"Can I grab a beer first?"

"You'd better make it a brandy."

"Why? What's happened now?"

"I've just met Liz's little sister, and she's not so little."

He frowned. "Meaning?"

"She's pregnant. And her name's Ally. Ring any bells?"

Conflicting thoughts flooded Ryan's mind. Ally and Liz couldn't be sisters. *Could they?* "What? Piss off."

"What was Liz's maiden name?"

"You know what I'm like with names. I hardly knew Liz before

267

she married AJ. Hobson? Robinson?" Ryan thought for a moment. "Shit. *Dobson!*"

"Ally's in the kitchen. Maybe you two need to have a little chat."

Ryan's mind went momentarily blank. Ally and Liz were sisters? No way. He hurried into the downstairs bathroom and shut the door, trying to shuffle his thoughts into some semblance of order as he splashed his face with cold water. "Shit. Shit. Shit."

Minutes later, Ryan paused in the sunroom doorway. Dressed in a full-length flowing gown that showed off her baby bump beautifully, Ally moved around the kitchen, refilling platters and stacking the dishwasher. If she and Liz were sisters, surely she must know he and the Tanners were friends? And there was little doubt they were sisters because, when he looked at her objectively, Ally Dobson was a taller, straighter-haired version of Liz Tanner.

Ally turned to place a tray of clean glasses on the table. When she noticed him, there was no reaction to his presence—no look of surprise. "Ryan. How are you?"

"Are you working here?"

"Just helping for a few hours." She smiled. A smile he remembered well from those Thursdays at the Heaton.

"How do you know Liz and AJ?" he asked.

Before Ally could answer, Liz breezed into the kitchen carrying an empty platter, and placed it on the island. "Ryan, I'm so glad you made it." She stepped in for a hug. "It's been way too long."

"It has. I think I'm the last person in London to hear your exciting news. Congratulations. It suits you."

"Thanks." Liz looked at Ally. "So you've met my baby sister?"

He glanced at Ally as an awkward silence fell between them and swallowed hard. *Shit, shit, shit* was right. "Ally and I have already met. She did some babysitting for me when Polly and Marc got married."

Ally picked up a platter, that sweet smile frozen on her face. "I'd better take this sushi around. Nice to see you again, Ryan."

"What?" Liz laughed. "You're the guy with a paunch like a bay window?"

Ryan didn't know whether to smile or frown as Ally disappeared down the hallway, acting as if this day were just like any other.

"That's crazy," Liz continued. "How did I not know this?"

"It was only for three weeks," he mumbled.

"What are you guys up to in here?" AJ asked as he set a twelve-pack of beer on the counter. "You're not trying to chat up my beautiful wife, are you? I've told you before, she's out of your league."

"Hey, mate." Ryan slapped AJ on the back. "Congratulations."

"Thanks. It took some practice, but we finally hit the target."

"Ryan and Ally know each other," Liz said. "She looked after the twins when Polly and Marc got married."

"Yes, she mentioned that the other day. I was going to ask you if you'd run into each other at the gym, but we haven't seen you in ages."

"Yeah," Ryan said, his thoughts racing. "Work's been crazy."

After a few minutes of small talk, Ryan headed toward the living room to catch his breath. Slipping off his coat, he draped it over a chair in the hallway as he went. Making a beeline for Chris, he noticed Ally standing across the room. She laughed at someone's joke, so stunningly beautiful, it almost hurt to watch. Despite everything that had happened, Ryan's feelings for Ally were still complicated. The physical attraction had always been strong, right from that first day at the building site, but the more he looked at her, the more he wondered what the hell was going on.

Judging by her reaction in the kitchen, Ally had known he and the Tanners were friends. Had she been playing him all along? If so, she'd done it well. And now, she was all smiles and innocence.

Chris pulled him aside. "Well? Is it her?"

"Do you even have to ask? It's her, in all her glory. Screw me up a fucking pole. And she knew I was friends with Liz and AJ. I could tell by her reaction in the kitchen."

"Have you ever thought she might be telling the truth? Miracles do happen."

Ryan felt like punching something. Or throwing up. Or possibly both. "There will be no talk of miracles happening until I see the results of that paternity test. I was played for a sucker once, and I'm sure as hell not letting it happen again."

"So what? You think she's set you up?"

"I haven't a clue. But nothing adds up. At least her sister exists. But come to think of it, she never once mentioned her by name. Shit. How did I not figure it out?"

"So, what's your next move?"

Ryan had no idea, but one thing was clear. He and Ally needed to talk, and soon. If Liz and AJ found out Ally had named him as the father, it could destroy his relationship with them. "I have no freakin' idea."

"You need to talk to her. In fact, you need to talk to all of them."

49

SONGBIRD

As she tidied up in the kitchen, Ally heard an amazing version of 'Handbags and Glad Rags' drifting through from the music room, but gave little thought to who the vocalist was. Their mother loved that song. She'd played it so often when they were younger, the girls had grown to love it too.

Ally crept to the music room door and peeked inside, astounded to see Ryan at the piano, singing with the intense passion she'd only ever witnessed when they'd had sex. She'd never heard him sing before, not even in the car, and as he played the last note, she struggled to contain her emotion.

When Ryan stood to loud applause and glanced her way, she turned and fled, making a beeline for the bathroom. She splashed her face with cool water, then took a deep breath. Things were about to get real, and she wished she had the courage to get on a plane and fly home before it became too late to travel.

As she pushed through the bathroom door and headed back into the music room, AJ was sharing a story in his usual amusing style.

"I played this next song on the drive to Cambridge when I took Liz home to meet my family," he said warmly. "At that stage, we were no more than housemates. She had no idea I spent my nights lusting after her as she slept in the bedroom next door."

"What?" Liz protested as their guests' laughter filled the room. "AJ!"

He looked at Liz and smiled. "But that's another story. For those of you who've heard me sing, you'll know why I've roped Ally in to doing the vocals on this one." AJ looked toward the doorway. "Ally, come up here."

She hesitated. Why couldn't they just sing 'Happy Birthday' like at other birthday parties?

"Can everyone make some noise for Ally? She hasn't sung in public for a while. Oh, and no pictures or videos please. We don't want to see ourselves on YouTube in the morning."

Ally weaved her way through the people sitting on the floor. She didn't want to sing, especially not in front of Ryan, or any of Liz and AJ's friends. Some of them knew her story, but no one except Jia knew who the father of her baby was. AJ was right, apart from that afternoon at the karaoke bar, she hadn't sung in public for well over a year. Why she'd agreed to sing tonight, Ally would never know. But then, she'd not exactly agreed.

Ryan leaned against the back wall by the door, his arms folded across his chest. She glanced his way once, and that was enough. Ally had never suffered from stage fright as a teenager, probably because her ego wouldn't allow it, but his gaze tipped her up with a heave. She missed him, missed their physical intimacy, but his unyielding stance on the pregnancy made her question why she hadn't walked away when she'd had the chance. Returned home with her tail firmly placed between her legs.

She craved a glass of wine, something to calm her nerves, but instead, sipped on lemon water as she stood next to her brother-in-law. In her previous life, Ally would have loved standing in front of this group of people with AJ and his guitar. But that was then.

This 'now' was different.

"Here's Opshop's 'One Day,'" AJ said as Ally leaned her butt on the high stool in front of the mic. She went to kick off her ballet flats, but recalled Ryan's words of how much her feet in sheer stockings turned him on. The ballet flats stayed put.

When AJ started the intro, she froze, forgetting the first line like an amateur. AJ reached over and squeezed her hand. Sucking in a shuddering breath, she glanced up to center herself and catch the lyrics.

She'd sung this song many times before, and once the adrenaline kicked in, the words flowed on a voice she no longer recognized. A voice shaky and slightly off-kilter. A voice tinged with regret.

As they finished, Ally looked at Liz for the first time. Her sister held her hands clasped to her heart, her eyes wet with unshed tears. That one gesture made all the nerves and uncertainty—and suffering the stare of Ryan Farrell—worth it. Liz had always been there for her, and Ryan had nothing to do with that part of her life. As she watched their friends, unmoving and silent before her, she froze. When they roared into life with a standing ovation, she stepped forward and took an unsteady bow.

At the back of the room, Ryan stood and stared, as he'd done many times before. Ally walked past him without a glance and returned to the kitchen to finish tidying up. But as she listened to the guys playing songs she loved, the expression on Ryan's face kept popping into her head. She'd never seen him look so sad.

Later, with the kitchen tidy and people starting to leave, Ally slipped into her room and headed to the shower. Afterward, she stood in front of the mirror in her bathrobe, rubbing coconut oil into her baby bump as she examined the face staring back at her. The pigmentation across her cheeks had darkened. She hoped it would fade once she gave birth. She hoped a lot of things would fade after the birth. Emotions, fears, uncertainties.

The downstairs guest room, a large private space that had once been used as a library, was separated from the rest of the house by a short hallway. There was no need to close the en suite door, but when she turned to see Ryan sitting on the blanket box at the end of the bed, she almost jumped out of her skin. "What are you doing here?"

"You're Liz's sister? Why didn't you tell me?"

Ally walked into the bedroom and switched on her bedside lamp before climbing onto the bed. She draped a throw around her shoulders and propped a couple of pillows behind her head, searching for a degree of comfort. "Until recently, I had no idea you guys knew each other."

He swiveled to look at her. "What do you mean, recently? When did you find out?"

"Just before Christmas. AJ asked if we'd run into each other at the gym."

"And you didn't think to give me a heads-up?"

"I didn't realize you'd be here tonight."

"So you haven't told them about us?"

She shook her head.

"Why not? I would've thought you'd jump at the chance to discredit me. We've known each other for months, and you've never talked about your family."

"You didn't want stories, remember? Anyway, I told you I had a sister here." Ally fought to keep her cool, while inside, she could hardly think straight. "London's a big place. How was I to know you and AJ were friends?"

He let out a heavy sigh. "When are you going to tell them— that I'm the chosen one?"

"Chosen one?"

"Isn't that what this is all about? You saw Liz all loved up and happily married and decided you didn't want to miss out."

"Is that really what you think? That I set you up? Screw you. You're a self-centered bastard. You need to leave."

"You have no idea who the father is, do you? I guess I should be flattered I'm the best candidate. It could have been the rugby player, but I'm guessing something happened there, so maybe not.

Or any one of those guys you left the bar with that night. Or Guy from the gym, or some other punter you met in a club while you were pretending to be all innocent and naïve. So why me? Why did I draw the short straw labeled 'Daddy'?"

Ally jumped off the bed and held the door open. "Get the hell out of my room. Come back when you've grown a pair. Until then, stay away from me."

"So that's it? That's all you have to say?"

"I had plenty to say in the past, but you wouldn't listen."

"Yeah, well, try telling the truth, and maybe I will."

As Ryan left Ally's room, he tried to keep his expression neutral. He didn't want AJ to suspect his relationship with Ally was anything other than professional. Not yet anyway. He could hear people leaving. The front door opening and closing as goodbyes were offered back and forth. He needed to go home as well. To get some sleep and calm the hell down.

"You're still here, mate," AJ said as Ryan entered the living room. "I thought you'd snuck out the back way."

"I've been catching up with Ally. She was asking after the girls. I thought she might have headed back to New Zealand by now."

"I'm not sure she can face going back for a while. She had a messy breakup with her ex. A bunch of shit went down."

"Is he the baby's father?"

"Who, Angus? I hope not, for her sake." Ryan followed AJ into the kitchen, wondering about the 'shit' he'd referred to.

"Would you like a coffee?" Liz asked as she stacked plates and glasses into the dishwasher. "There's still cake left."

"Thanks, but I'd better make tracks. I have the girls tomorrow."

"Don't be a stranger," AJ said as they walked Ryan to the door. "It's been way too long."

"I won't." Ryan turned to Liz. "Enjoy the rest of your birthday."

"She will," AJ said with a grin.

As he walked to his car, Ryan couldn't get the sound of Ally's incredible voice out of his mind. Why had she never told him she could sing? And AJ's remark about her performing in public? Had she been a singer in another life? He pulled out his phone. It was well after midnight, but he knew Stuart would still be up.

Ryan: You prick!
Stuart: What have I done now?
Ryan: I've found the songbird, and she sounds even better in person.
Stuart: Can't say I've had the pleasure.
Ryan: Why didn't you tell me?
Stuart: Because our search for the truth is one journey we need to take alone.

Despite his mood, Ryan couldn't help but chuckle as he opened his car door. Stuart loved to philosophize, but not in a pompous way. And he was right about the journey for truth. At least someone was talking sense.

50

TEAR-STAINED NOTES

After a dreadful night's sleep, Ally waited until AJ and Liz had left for the office before dragging herself out of bed. She'd packed her bags as soon as Ryan had left, written tear-stained notes to both Liz and Jia, and purchased her ticket to New Zealand online. At thirty-four weeks, Ally would still be okay to fly, but if she left it any longer, the airline wouldn't let her on the plane.

She called the medical center, who reluctantly agreed to supply verification of her dates and a medical clearance, and left the house as soon as their email came through. Her flight via LA didn't leave until late afternoon, but she didn't want to wait at home. She hadn't told Mitch or CeCe of her plans; neither of them could be trusted to keep a secret. But she'd deal with that once she arrived in Auckland.

Heathrow was packed, as usual, and the check-in lines were never-ending. Feeling hungry and a little faint, she grabbed a Rescue Remedy pastille out of her bag and popped it into her mouth. Over twenty minutes ticked by as she waited in the queue. It gave her time to think. To deliberate over Ryan's 'short straw' comment. Everything about their exchange from the night before hurt. She needed to go home. Away from the arguments and accusations. Away from Ryan.

Check-in went smoothly enough, but as she moved through to the customs checkpoint—sandwiched between a mother and her brat of a teenage son, and a giant of a man reeking of cigar smoke —Ally broke out into a cold sweat.

She dumped her bag in one tray, pulled out her laptop and placed it in another, and walked through the metal detector.

"Ma'am, are you all right?" someone asked.

"Ma'am?"

Unforgiving bright lights blazed from overhead. Ally looked around the room; her hand luggage rested on a seat to her right, and a soft blanket covered her hips and legs. She went to scratch the back of her hand, where a butterfly stuck to her skin, and dry heaved when she noticed the puncture point.

"How are you feeling?" The voice belonged to a jolly looking woman wearing a nurse's uniform and black crocs. "You caused quite a scene when you collapsed. How many weeks are you?"

Ally swallowed uncomfortably, and the nurse offered her a sip of water. "Thank you." She lay her head back on the thin pillow covered with an overly starched pillowcase. "Thirty-four. What time is it? I need to catch my flight."

"No more flying for you, young lady. Not until you deliver that precious cargo, anyway. Your blood pressure's sky high, and when did you last eat?"

"But I have to get on that flight. It's an emergency."

"Sorry, love. I don't make the rules. I just glue them back together when they're broken." The nurse checked the IV. "We need to keep this drip in for another ten minutes. I'll get you a sandwich and a cup of tea, and then you'd better contact your nearest and dearest."

"But I need to go home." Ally hated crying in front of people, but the tears came anyway. "Please. I have a medical clearance."

"Hey come on, don't cry. You got someone you can call?"

She nodded. Sniffed back the tears.

"Okay. You relax for a few minutes. I'll be back soon."

Ally sank into the pillow. She'd always believed in fate, and it seemed fate had other plans for her that day. It certainly had no intention of helping her fly back to New Zealand.

———

Ryan climbed the steps to Liz and AJ's front door and pushed the bell. Until yesterday, he hadn't seen them in months. Now, here he stood for the second time in as many days. His excuse, the coat he'd left over the chair. His reason, Ally Dobson. Because, as he'd stared into darkness last night, unable to sleep, with the words *what the hell?* pounding in his head, Ally had looked less of a liar than she had hours before, and he'd looked more of an egotistical asshole. The bully she'd accused him of being.

When no one answered, he pushed the bell again, and was about to leave when the door swung open.

"Ryan, hi." Liz looked tired and drawn and, judging by the mascara smeared through the fine crow's feet at the side of her eyes, she'd been crying. "Come in. I thought you might be Ally."

He followed Liz down the hallway and into the large family room that overlooked the garden. "Why would Ally ring the bell? Doesn't she live here?"

Liz looked up, blinking to stop the tears. "She's gone."

"What do you mean?" Ryan fought the rising panic with a deep breath and clenched fists.

"She flew back to New Zealand today without telling us. We don't know what flight she's on, her layover details, nothing. She seemed fine last week. I just don't get it."

"So how do you know she's gone?"

"She wrote me a note. Waited until we left for work and walked out."

"But isn't it too late for her to fly?"

"Almost. I think it's up to thirty-six weeks if you have a medical clearance. Anyway"—Liz looked around the room, her expression dazed—"you didn't come here for me to cry on your shoulder. We have your coat."

"Yeah. I was at the house, so I thought I'd call in."

"How's the build going?"

Sweating under his collar, Ryan kept up the small talk. "I move in a couple of weeks."

"And—"

"Liz. It's okay. I know you're worried. We don't have to talk about me."

"This is all my fault. She suggested going home, but I wanted her to stay in London—to finish her course. But what does it matter now?" Liz stood in the middle of the living room, turning in circles as she searched for Ryan's coat.

"And this is what I do," she continued. "I do it all the time, try to mother my siblings, when our mum does a perfectly good job without me sticking my nose in. I remember when Ally went on a school hockey trip to South Africa once. I practically held my breath the whole time she was away. And then there's all that stuff with her ex. He put her through so much, and now he's here in London, trying to stir everything up. I keep telling her to stay away from him. But does she listen?"

Ryan mentally checked off the trip to Africa. And while Ally had never told him what happened between her and Angus, there was obviously a story. "Do your parents know Ally's pregnant?"

"Of course." Liz stared at Ryan as if to say 'why wouldn't they?'

"It's just, she said she couldn't get hold of them when she first found out."

"Yeah. They were traveling around Western Australia and only had patchy internet coverage. But we soon tracked them down. They're coming over next month. I just don't get it. Why would Ally leave without talking to us first? Without giving us the chance to say goodbye."

Ryan looked around. "Where's AJ?"

"He's gone to see that detective friend of yours. See if he can do anything."

"Mike, or Finn?"

"Finn. And we're meant to be going out tonight." Liz rubbed her hands over her face. When she looked up again, her runaway mascara was everywhere. "A gallery opening for one of AJ's friends. He doesn't want to miss it. I need to shower and change."

"Go. I'll stay here in case your phone rings."

"Are you sure?" Liz smeared a fingertip under each eye. "I must look a mess."

"More than sure. And you look fine."

"Thanks. I won't be long. Help yourself to a drink."

Once Liz had left the room, Ryan picked up a family photo from the sideboard. The Dobson clan—all dressed in their ski gear and laughing for the camera. The older brother, the little sister, their parents, and Ally and Liz, both holding snowboards. He'd seen that photo several times, but he'd never taken much notice. There had been no reason for him to connect the younger Ally— with her waist-length hair and a smiling, snow-tanned face—with the pretty temp in the pink coat, the lover lounging naked in his bed at the Heaton, and the woman she'd become over the past few months.

He opened the liquor cabinet, poured himself a brandy and took a large gulp. Flopping down in a chair by the window, he grabbed a magazine and flicked through a few pages, glancing over the headlines without registering a single word.

He was about to pick up a photo book when he heard the key in the lock, and AJ entered with Ally following two steps behind. Her eyes welled with tears when she noticed Ryan. She walked down the hallway without a word. A few seconds later, the guest room door shut firmly behind her.

"Where was she?"

"At the airport." AJ put his keys on the counter. "She collapsed going through the metal detector, and they wouldn't let her on the flight."

"Is she okay?"

"Yep. I think so. Where's Liz?"

"In the shower." Ryan struggled to keep his voice level. "She said you guys had something on later."

AJ scrubbed his hands over his face. "Yeah. Shit. What a mess."

"Look, you go and get ready. I'll stay with Ally."

"Are you sure?"

"Of course."

Once the Tanners had left, Ryan sat in silence, staring at the photo book in his hands. It was all in there. The trip to Africa, Ally as captain of the school hockey team, endless snaps of her and her band at various gigs, her and her brother standing under a sign saying, *Lime Tree Hill*. It seemed Ally had plenty of stories, but Ryan had insisted he wasn't interested in hearing them, so she'd kept them to herself. Anything he did know about her, he'd found out second hand.

He'd been a selfish bastard—telling himself it was to protect her, that she was too young—not so much in maturity, but more in her choice of lifestyle. But that hadn't stopped him from inviting her to Thursdays at the Heaton, or from thinking about her every day since. Nor had it stopped him from wanting to have sex with her whenever they were alone.

The doorbell rang and he went to answer it.

"I have luggage for Dobson."

"That's us."

The courier driver handed Ryan his POD screen to sign. He lifted her suitcase inside, surprised at how light it was, and trundled it down the hallway. She opened the door a crack when he knocked.

"What are you doing here?"

"I came to see you." He motioned to her case. "And a courier just dropped off your luggage."

"Please, just go."

Ryan had expected her to be confrontational, but her attitude seemed defeatist rather than hostile.

"I don't need a sitter," she continued. "It's not like I can go anywhere."

"May I come in?"

Ally turned her back and walked over to sit on the bed, leaving the door open for Ryan to enter. "Whatever it is you want to say, just say it, and go."

"I don't want to say anything, apart from I'm sorry," he said, as he sat the case by the closet door.

"That's right. You're the strong, silent type, aren't you? You keep your thoughts to yourself until you're between the sheets. Then you have plenty to say. So why are you here?"

"To listen."

"Well, I'm all out of stories right now." She grabbed the throw from the end of the bed and wrapped it around herself. "I don't have the energy."

He sat in the chair by the window. "Why did you do it? Leave, I mean."

Ally shrugged and pulled her lips in tight.

"Help me understand why," he said gently, "if I am the father of your baby, you decided to pack your bags and leave the country on a whim."

Dropping her head, Ally shielded her eyes with one hand as she massaged her forehead with shaking fingertips. "After you left last night, I couldn't face it anymore. I hate feeling sorry for myself. With my privileged life and a family that loves me, I don't have that right. And it might be easier if Liz wasn't pregnant, and Mum and Dad weren't coming for her birth, and you weren't AJ's friend, and if Angus would leave me the hell alone." She stopped for a breath. "But all those things combined make it so much harder, impossible even."

"So you decided the best option was to crawl under a rock and hide?"

"But I couldn't even do that right. I figured it was better to leave than to stay and be called a liar by the man I care about, when all I've ever been is truthful. I despise cheats and liars too." Ally rose from the bed and unpacked her suitcase, hanging each item neatly in the closet.

"I don't get it. Why were you so secretive?"

"You didn't want my stories, remember? But that didn't keep you from making up your own."

"I know. I'm…" *Shit.* Ryan watched her unpack, momentarily lost for words. "It's just, so many things about you don't seem to add up." He motioned to her suitcase. "Like the clothes."

She turned to him and frowned. "What do you mean?"

"You dress beautifully but you seem to have hardly any clothes. What's that about?"

"My sister's wardrobe's full of designer outfits she loves to share."

"You wear Liz's clothes?"

"I lost all my stuff a while back, so I had to reevaluate. But that's a different story." She looked at him sadly. "I've learned to travel light."

Ryan considered her reply. Had she lost her luggage in transit on the way to London? He decided to let it go. "And what are you studying?"

She huffed a frustrated sigh. "Music management."

"I had no idea you even liked music until recently. Or that you could sing." He expected a reply, but she gave none. "And another thing, you seem to have absolutely no social media presence. Why's that?"

When she glanced his way, he noticed a softening of her lips, not quite a smile, but almost. "Should it creep me out that you've been stalking me on the net?"

"I didn't find anything. Not even a photo."

"And you won't. And before you ask me why, I have my reasons, but that doesn't mean they're lies."

Ryan offered his hand. "Please. Tell me your stories."

Ally shook her head and sat back down on the bed. "It's not that I want to be mysterious. I'm just so tired right now. I can hardly think."

He buried his face in his hands. "How the hell did things get so bad between us?"

"I think we both know the answer to that."

He moved to sit next to her. When he reached out to tuck a lock of hair behind her ear, she closed her eyes for a second. "Can I get you something to eat?"

"Seriously?" she whispered. "Sweet Ryan's back?"

"He lost his way there for a while. But for what it's worth, I believe you, and I'd like to be involved with the birth if you'll let me."

Ally fell silent. He wasn't sure if she was formulating a reply, or so annoyed at him that she refused to answer.

"And I'd like to be involved with you as well," he continued. "Could we do that?"

She studied him for a few seconds. "I don't want to get lost in our shadows, Ryan."

"Meaning?"

"The past hurt, the words we've said in anger."

He nodded his understanding.

"And I'd like you to leave now, not because I'm indifferent to your suggestion, but I need time to think."

51

BECAUSE IT WAS A THURSDAY

Ryan left the bedroom without another word. Ally had no idea when they'd see each other again. His admission that he now believed her felt like a hollow victory in a battle she'd never meant to wage.

She picked up her e-reader from the nightstand, desperate to lose herself in a make-believe world, and for a while, try not to think about him. She'd already spent far too many hours mentally consolidating the ifs and buts of Ryan Farrell.

Liz popped her head around the bedroom door. Her sister looked as tired as Ally felt, her usual healthy glow dimmed by the discomfort of late pregnancy. "You're home early."

"My feet were killing me after an hour. I left your brother-in-law with his mates and a full bottle of tequila. He promised he'd be home soon, meaning sometime around dawn. He hasn't had a night out in a while." Liz sat on the bed and rested her hand on Ally's. "You okay?"

"I feel all kinds of stupid, but I'll get over it."

"Why did you do it?"

The question didn't come as a surprise, and now that she was tucked up in bed safe, if not sound, Ally had been asking herself the same thing. "Because it was a Thursday."

"A Thursday?"

Ally swallowed back a tear. "It's a long story." For once, Liz didn't fill the pause. "I'm sorry. All I seem to do is cause you and AJ grief."

"That's not true."

"I appreciate your support, but I need to find my own place soon."

"There's plenty of time for that. Mum and Dad plan to look for an apartment. Maybe you could move in with them for a while."

Ally pulled a face, smiling at the thought of living with her parents again, especially with a baby. But it was an option, and she was thankful for it.

"Did you talk to Ryan?"

Ally shrugged. "A bit."

"I still can't believe you worked for him. He's such a nice guy. AJ say's he can be a bit hot-headed, but I haven't seen that side of him."

Ally's thoughts banked up and tumbled over each other. This was the perfect time to come clean; she simply had to muster the courage and spit it out. "Yes…about that."

Liz's eyes narrowed. She opened her mouth to speak, but hesitated.

"Yep."

"You can't be serious." Liz's expression was that of a mother scolding her daughter. "You and Ryan?"

Ally nodded slowly.

"Ryan? No way." She paused. "And?"

"You want details?"

"You bet I want details. Why did you never mention him before?"

Ally shrugged. "We met a few months after I arrived in

London. I didn't find out he was the CEO of the company I temped for until weeks later."

"You worked for Farra? Where were AJ and I when all this was going on?"

"I did tell you I had a temp job at a property company. Anyway, we met a few times—"

"Like on dates?"

"Not so much. It was more…you know. Those last few months with Angus were horrible. I just wanted to have some fun."

"You had a fling? With Ryan?" As usual, Liz's tone rose an octave at the end of each sentence. "I thought the guy was a serial monogamist."

"Who told you that?"

"It's well known among our friends. Ryan's either in a long-term relationship or single."

Ally wasn't convinced. She'd always seen him as a discreet player. "That's not the Ryan I know."

"Does he know what happened between you and Angus?"

"No. I thought about telling him, but we had an agreement. No stories, no last names, no Happy Ever Afters."

"Ally! Ryan just used you for sex. Don't you get that?"

"It was mutually consenting."

Another long pause followed. "So what did he say when you told him you were pregnant?"

"That it couldn't possibly be his."

"Hold on a minute! *Ryan's* the father? Are you sure?"

Nothing about her story was funny, but the expression on Liz's face almost made Ally burst out laughing. She grabbed her water bottle and took a sip. "Other than Angus, Ryan's the only man I've ever had sex with."

Liz raised a questioning brow.

"What?" Ally asked. "You think I had breakup sex with Angus? Don't be ridiculous."

"I thought maybe you and Hamish…"

"Hamish? The poor guy would be mortified if he knew we were even talking about him in that way. We're just good friends, you know that."

"Anyway, getting back to Ryan. AJ said he and Polly struggled to have more kids."

"That's the problem. He was adamant the baby couldn't be his, that he was sterile. It's an unholy mess. That's why I've kept quiet about who the father is."

"So what's going to happen now?"

"I have no idea."

52

JEALOUS GUY

Seated at a table for four by the window in the same Soho restaurant where he and Ally had eaten months before, Ryan watched Britt as she surveyed their surroundings. He'd once thought their relationship might lead to something permanent. But when the full force of her needy personality surfaced, and her sons both took an instant dislike to the twins, he'd soon realized they would be a match made in domestic hell. He found it amusing that they'd managed to remain friends.

As Dave pulled out a chair for his wife, Veronica, Ryan glanced around the room, his eyes coming to rest on the tall pregnant woman walking through the door. He felt the familiar rush, and for a split second, Ally's gaze held his. She quickly looked away, returning her focus to her dinner date—the infamous Angus Chapman—who was dressed in tight pants and a form-fitting shirt that barely contained his well-defined torso.

All through his meal, Ryan watched them discreetly as Angus controlled both the conversation and her attention. Ally nodded politely, frowned occasionally, smiled rarely, and whenever she opened her mouth to speak, Angus talked over her. At one point, he reached out to cup her cheek in his large hand. His touch appeared to make her uncomfortable, and Ryan knew the feeling.

Despite Ryan's best intentions, the conversation around the table failed to engage him. Britt's sons, Dave's new mountain bike, and Veronica's foray into the world of online fashion retailing paled in comparison to the discussion going on in his head. By contrast, Ally's attention never once strayed from her date.

The couple didn't stay for dessert, and as Angus ushered Ally past Ryan's table, she stared straight ahead, ignoring him and his friends.

"Ally?" Dave called out.

She turned and smiled politely. "Dave. Nice to see you." Her gaze shifted briefly to Ryan. "Hello."

"Ally." Ryan leaned back in his chair, his eyes taking everything in. He loved seeing her beautifully pregnant. Dressed in an elegant style that covered her figure while accentuating everything at the same time, she was positively glowing.

"You remember Veronica?" Dave asked.

"Of course she remembers me," Veronica said. "You're looking well. Pregnancy clearly suits you." She turned to Britt. "And this is Britt Christie."

Ally said hello and introduced Angus, who eyed Ryan with suspicion as he towered over her, his hand on her back the whole time. Ryan had never seen himself as a jealous guy, but right now, with Angus puffing out his chest in front of him, he struggled to unclench his jaw.

"Dave was saying only yesterday, it's not the same at the gym without you," Veronica said.

"So, when's the baby due?" Britt asked, barely able to peel her eyes from Angus and his sturdy rugby thighs.

"Four weeks, so not long now," Ally replied.

"Do you know what you're having?"

"A boy."

"Lovely. I have two sons," Britt gushed, her expression full of warmth. "And with parents like you two, he's sure to be gorgeous."

Ally shifted uncomfortably from foot to foot, glancing up at Angus as he cleared his throat. "Angus isn't my partner. We're just old friends."

"Sorry. Me and my big mouth," Britt said, smiling brightly at Angus. "All the best anyway."

"Thanks," Ally said. "Enjoy the rest of your meal."

As Ally and Angus left the restaurant, Britt said, "Do you think he's single? I'd have sworn they were a couple. Tell you what, I wouldn't mind those strapping thighs wrapped around me on a cold winter's night."

"It's nice to know you're totally over me, Britt," Ryan said with a wry grin. "But isn't he a bit young for you?"

"I'm happy with the cougar label. And I've been over you for a long time, Ryan." She gave him a friendly dig in the ribs. "Besides, you don't deserve a girl like me. You're too quiet."

Ryan mentally gave thanks to the man upstairs.

"Younger men go for women like me," Britt continued. "They're attracted to a woman with experience."

Dave chuckled. "Is that why you dated Ryan? To teach him how it's done?"

"Would you two stop it?" Ryan said, still grinning. "You're putting me off my tiramisu."

"So, who's her partner?" Veronica asked. "Anyone we know?"

Dave shot Ryan a sideways glance. "Ryan knows more about it than I do, don't you, mate? He and Ally were an item for a while."

Veronica and Britt both stared at Ryan as he shot daggers at Dave.

"You guys dated?" Britt asked, looking more suspicious than curious. "When?"

Ryan reached for his wine and took a sip. Then another. "It was after we split," he said to Britt.

"You dated an employee?" Veronica asked. "Naughty boy."

What could he say without adding fuel to the fire? "What is this? Twenty questions?"

"But she's pregnant." Britt won the medal for stating the obvious.

"Yes. I've noticed," Ryan replied.

Later, at Chris's apartment, Ryan stood in the shower, unable to get the image of Ally with Angus out of his mind. *Old friends.* She'd told him that she and Angus were over, and while he believed her initially, he now found himself questioning, not only that, but every other judgment he'd ever made about her.

Back in the bedroom, he grabbed his phone from the nightstand and checked for messages. Although he'd been dying to text her since she left the restaurant, he still couldn't work out what to say. He decided to wing it.

Ryan: We keep bumping into each other.
Ally: Weird, isn't it. Turns out London's not so big after all.
Ryan: Are you alone?
Ally: No. Mr. Puss is kneading his paws into my back.
Ryan: Lucky cat.
Ryan: You looked amazing tonight. That dress is stunning.
Ally: You need to stop staring.
Ryan: I can't. You're too beautiful.

Shit. Ryan immediately regretted his last text. What gave him the right to tell her she was beautiful? Even if he hadn't been able to take his eyes off her all evening. If they'd been talking in person, she would have accused him of toying with her.

She didn't reply.

Ryan stared at his phone screen. Should he continue? Why not! It wasn't as if he could make things worse.

Ryan: What were you doing with Angus?

Ally: Having dinner.

Ryan: The guy couldn't keep his hands off you.

Ally: It's not what you think.

Ryan: I just don't want to see you get hurt.

Ally: I appreciate your concern, but it's a little late for that.

Ryan: I'm sorry I hurt you. And I truly mean that.

Ally: I wasn't talking about you.

Ryan pondered her words. Did she mean Angus? But if he'd hurt her so much, why would she spend time with the guy? He sat on the bed, formulating his response. He wanted to go to her; to lose himself in her arms and make everything right. Despite all that had happened, he couldn't shake the feeling that they belonged together. The trouble was, her pride and self-respect might mean she wouldn't back down.

Not yet, anyway.

Ryan: BTW, your voice is amazing.

Ally: Thank you. So is yours.

Ryan: May I come over?

Ally: Goodnight, Ryan. Sweet dreams.

Ally: I'm sorry. I've made such a mess of things.

Ryan: You have nothing to be sorry for. I'm the one who should apologize.

53

HUMBLE PIE

AJ: You have time for a beer?
Ryan: Sounds good. I'm over at the house. Free in half an hour.
AJ: How about Munro's? For old times' sake.
Ryan: Okay.

As Ryan walked through the door of Munro's, he felt a strange sense of calm. After seeing Chris the day before and receiving the 'medical miracle' speech again, he'd stayed up late into the night, trying to get his head around it all. Did AJ know what was going on? Surely Ally had confided in Liz by now.

He walked up to AJ, who stood at the bar talking to the bartender. The place was half-empty for once, not unexpected at four in the afternoon.

"What are you having?" AJ asked.

"Corona, thanks. Let's get a booth."

After taking their drinks to the table, they sat and chatted for a while—with AJ telling him about his latest exhibition and Ryan talking about the house in Battersea. Ryan enjoyed AJ's company, but he suspected AJ still saw him as Chris's brat of a little brother.

He could tell AJ was keen for information, so he started the ball rolling. "So, what's on your mind?"

"You and Ally," AJ said. "What's going on?"

"Maybe more than I realized." He took a swig of his beer. "I went to see Chris yesterday."

"And?"

Ryan rubbed his fingertips across the furrows on his brow. He wasn't big on man-to-man talks, even with close friends. Shit happened, and after it did, he preferred to just get on with it. "Let's just say, he keeps throwing the words 'medical miracle' around."

"So it's true? You could be the father?"

"Apparently. What's Ally said?"

"Nothing to me, but she had a long heart-to-heart with Liz. She's adamant the baby's yours."

Ryan leaned back against the booth and nodded slowly.

"What are you going to do?" AJ asked.

"No idea. Wait it out I guess and try to make amends. Dish up a large helping of humble pie and choke on it."

"Are you still seeing each other?"

"Not recently."

"Was it just about the sex?"

Ryan frowned. "Shit! Do we have to discuss this?"

AJ shrugged. "It never occurred to you that Liz and Ally were sisters?"

"Never crossed my mind. When Chris asked me, I couldn't even remember Liz's maiden name at first. I can see it now though —the similarities."

"I guess."

"I thought it might be the rugby player's baby. They seemed to be together a lot when I first met her."

"Yeah, me too, but she says it's not. I just wish he'd piss off over to France. He's a manipulative bastard. Ally's a good kid. She's had to deal with a lot of crap lately, but she still puts everyone else first. And she's no liar."

Ryan took another swig of his beer. He appreciated AJ's input. There was no bullshit with the guy. "What if I get my hopes up and it turns out he isn't mine?"

"Valid point. But according to Liz, you're the only contender."

"I thought I had it all sorted a few days ago, even told her I believed her. But when I think about it rationally, about what Polly and I went through with IVF, I can't help but have a niggle of doubt. What do you reckon?"

"Stuffed if I know. But surely the question you need to ask yourself is, do you want to be with her?"

"I do, but it's not that simple, is it? What if she wants to go back to New Zealand with the baby? I can't leave London and the twins. You know that. And she's only twenty-four."

"People move for love all the time. Look at Liz. And she was only twenty-three when we met."

"But Liz had a life here before you got together."

"That doesn't mean Ally can't make a life here too. She loves London. Her father was born here, so it's in her blood."

"But she tried to leave."

"She did." AJ paused as several people walked in and the bartender cranked up the music. "Maybe you had more to do with that than you want to admit."

"Yep." AJ was right. Ally had left because of what Ryan had said to her the night of Liz's party. The night of raw nerves and unfounded accusations, when he'd stuck his foot into his mouth and left it there. "What do you suggest I do?"

"Be there for her. Support her. Make a positive difference."

54

THE ALTA PRECINCT

Ryan: I have a joke for you.
Ally: Really? You, a joke?
Ryan: Are you home?
Ally: Yes, but I'm planning on having an early night.
Ryan: It's not even mid-afternoon. I'll be there soon.

Ryan stepped back from the door as Ally opened it. With dark circles smudged under her eyes and a slight puffiness to her face, she looked like she hadn't slept in days. He reached for her hand and kissed her lightly on each cheek. At her sharp intake of breath, he pulled back. "A hippopotamus thundered into a bar full of rhinos and ordered a shot of tequila."

Ally cocked a brow as she waited. "And?"

"Let's go get a coffee. I'll tell you the rest on the way. It's kind of long."

She managed a small smile. "And inappropriate?"

He grinned. "That too."

"No one's here, and I'm not really in the mood for going out, so if you want to come in?"

Ryan followed her inside and down the hallway to the kitchen. He'd always loved this house, with its sweeping staircase, the vintage-style sunroom full of books, and a long stretch of lawn flanked by flowering shrubs and ornamental trees. He couldn't wait to move into his own place. The Battersea renovation seemed to have dragged on forever. A labor of love and, if he were honest, an exercise in utter frustration.

He sat at the breakfast bar and watched her sort out the coffee machine. "You look tired."

"It's par for the course at this stage. Getting any sleep is a challenge."

"We could go to bed instead of having a coffee if you'd prefer." He flashed her a cheeky grin, wondering what kind of response he'd get.

She searched his gaze for a moment, chewing her bottom lip as she considered his invitation. "Okay, let's."

"Really?"

"No. That's my contribution to the joke."

He laughed. Ally turned to watch the coffee drip into a cup. "I'm sure Britt could help you out with that though."

Ryan took a moment to respond. The line between casual banter and serious conversation had been crossed. "We don't have that kind of relationship."

"Did you ever?"

"Is this how it's going to be between us now? Spilling our secrets all over the floor?" Their eyes met, but she said nothing, and her silence made him realize the time had come for complete honesty. "Yes. For a while."

"And you still see each other?"

"Occasionally. Just like you and Angus."

"It was his birthday last week. That's why we had dinner."

Ryan took a deep breath. "Are you still in love with him?"

"No. But I loved him once. The kind of young, immature love that makes you anxious when you're apart and leaves you wondering how you'd ever survive if they left you."

Her lack of hesitation and direct denial helped Ryan relax. "So, who left whom?"

"I left him in the end. He still thinks we'll get back together."

"What, even though you're pregnant?"

"He says he already loves us both. Maybe he does, but…"

"That's not what you want?"

She shook her head, the movement so slight, he almost missed it. Angus must love her a lot if he was willing to take on another man's child. So what had gone wrong?

"Are you still in love with Britt?" Ally asked.

"I never was. Not the kind of love that tips you over, anyway."

A strained silence fell as she handed him his coffee. He took a sip. Its strength just about blew his head off, and he welcomed the hit. "But I have loved, and deeply."

She lowered her gaze, her head following. Ryan watched from the other side of the breakfast bar as she grabbed a tissue from a box on the counter.

"Are you okay?"

"I'm sorry I tried to go home, but some days, all I want to do is run away and hide."

Ryan stood and moved to cuddle her from behind. Closing his eyes, he inhaled deeply; her scent and the unexpected coolness of her skin making him nervous and excited at the same time. "I know the feeling. But please, don't give up on us, Ally."

She leaned back into his embrace. Released a heavy sigh.

"Come on." Ryan turned her around to face him, selfishly wishing her response to his suggestion they go to bed hadn't been a joke. He wanted to shut her bedroom door and get lost in her warmth. Instead, he said, "Let's get you out of the house for a while. I want to show you something." He reached out and cupped her face. "I don't mean to make you sad. I hope you know that."

She looked up and nodded but pulled away before he could get lost in her stormy blues. "I'll go get changed."

Ally returned in less than ten minutes, with freshly applied makeup, and her hair pulled back into a messy knot. He couldn't believe how much it had grown since that day on the building site. She'd changed into boots and leggings and had the pink coat from months ago draped over one arm. He helped her slip into it.

"I haven't seen you wear this in ages."

"What, the coat? It's Liz's. I haven't worn it before."

"You wore it one day at Farra."

Ally thought back. "Did I? How do you know that?"

"I saw you. In the elevator, and later when you came out of Gina's office."

"What? And you remembered my coat?"

Ryan leaned forward and whispered in her ear. "I remember a lot more than the coat."

When he pulled back, Ally blessed him with one of the most beautiful smiles she'd ever given him.

As they approached an area southeast of the city, Ryan pulled into a narrow side street, coming to a stop outside a row of brick warehouses. Many of the lower windows were boarded up, and along the street, a dumpster held offcuts of construction materials. Ryan jumped out and helped Ally down. She looked at the building and hesitated.

"You okay?" he asked.

She nodded but took a step back. His concern seemed out of place, almost over-protective.

"Those hormones are playing havoc with you at the moment, aren't they?" he said with a grin. "Come on. Let's look inside."

Ryan took a key from the pocket of his jeans and opened the main door. Placing his hands on her hips, he guided her forward into the interior, where natural light streamed through a row of windows on the south side. The air felt close, almost dense, and dust lay thick on the floor. Along one wall, timber and bales of insulation sat waiting to be used. Ally strolled to the windows and looked out over the street.

"What do you think?"

She turned. "It's huge. Is it yours?"

"We bought it two years ago and received planning permission for a development a few months back."

"This is the area you were referring to the day I took the minutes."

"I'm impressed you remember. We're calling it the Alta Precinct."

She stared at him in disbelief and couldn't help but laugh. "You're not serious?"

"Finally, the lady laughs. I told you getting out of the house would do you good. I decided on the name after we talked about urban sprawl that day. We've had to climb through a mountain of red tape to get to this stage, so I thought the name was apt. You are named after a mountain, aren't you?"

"How would you even remember that?"

"I told you. I remember more than the pink coat and that silk blouse with the tiny buttons running down the length of your spine."

"What!"

"The second time I saw you, I was standing in the back of the elevator when you rushed across the lobby and squeezed inside. You were dressed in a pencil skirt, heels, and a cream silk blouse. That was the second time I imagined kissing you—and undoing those buttons."

Ally burst out laughing. "You're kidding? You were in the elevator? Dressed in your CEO gear?"

"I was." He flashed her a cheeky smile. "And you didn't look back once."

"That's crazy." Ally strolled around the space with Ryan following a step behind. "Imagine what would have happened if I'd noticed you."

"Yeah, I think about that sometimes. Would you have agreed to our Thursdays if you'd known who my alter ego was?"

"Probably not...maybe." Scraping her top teeth along her bottom lip, she gazed up at him through her lashes. "But I tend to go for guys who work with their hands rather than the business types."

"Are you flirting with me?"

"Would I do that?" She pressed a dramatic hand to her chest. "So, tell me about your project."

"I'd much rather flirt," he said as he stepped away. He cleared his throat. "It's a mix of energy-efficient apartments, specialty boutiques, a café, green space, and offices. I'm moving Farra's headquarters here when we're finished. The rent where we are now is outrageous. I hate filling other property owners' pockets. It was meant to be just a short-term thing, but best-laid plans and all that."

He reached for her hand and cocked his head toward a vintage birdcage elevator, complete with concertina door. "Want to take a shaky ride?"

She frowned. "Is that some sort of metaphor for our relationship?"

"Not an intentional one."

"Does it even work?"

"Of course. It's safe, I promise." They stepped inside. "We could christen it if you want."

Ally glanced around the interior. "You never change, do you? I'm eight months pregnant and look like I've eaten way too many donuts washed down with copious amounts of beer, but you're still laying on the innuendo."

Ryan stepped into her space, looking down at her with that

half-smile she loved. "It's not just innuendo. I want you, so what's the point in pretending otherwise? I love the way you look right now, with that full belly and silky hair." He laughed at her disbelieving expression. "And I can't deny, I love the way you look at me." His words echoed around the interior of the elevator as he pushed the button for the third floor.

She cocked her head a little, and grinned. "I don't know what you mean."

"You know exactly what I mean, and it's the best feeling in the world. So"—he moved closer and kissed her lightly on the mouth —"I suggest we cut the bullshit and work on developing our game plan." He studied her, as though waiting for a sarcastic reply, but she remained silent.

When they reached the third floor, Ryan pulled back the door and motioned her through.

"This is Farra's main floor. As you can see, we're making good progress."

She looked around, taking everything in as she followed him through the maze of framed-out offices.

"I'll bring you back when it's finished. The apartments and café are on the other street frontage. Are you game to get back into the elevator?"

She felt herself blush and realized that, despite her efforts to do otherwise, she was well on her way to falling in love with Ryan Farrell. "As long as you promise to behave."

"I promise. Sex standing up is my least favorite position, anyway."

"Really?" she murmured as they stepped inside. "So the thought of us both facing the wall, your face buried in my neck, your breath hitching in your lungs and those big, strong arms holding me tight so I won't fall as you—"

"Stop! Are you deliberately punishing me?"

"I'm just cutting the bullshit. But you're more of a missionary man, aren't you? You like to be in control."

He laughed. "I never feel in control when we're together. Never."

"That makes two of us."

"So, what's the next best thing to sex?" he asked as they reached the ground floor.

"Ice cream and hot fudge sauce."

55

REGRETS

They drove back to Liz and AJ's in silence, the energy between them more reflective than anything else. And even though Ryan thought their afternoon had gone well, her reluctance had never been far away. He pulled into the drive and cut the engine, leaving the radio on. Ally sat for a few moments, humming along to 'Dancing with a Stranger,' before saying, "Thanks for the ice cream."

Ryan waited for her to invite him in, but the invitation never came. He turned her face toward him and kissed her gently on both cheeks, her earthy scent reminding him of better times. Those care-free Thursdays at the Heaton, lying in bed after they'd had sex, his face buried in her neck and their legs entangled. "Will you be okay on your own?"

"Sure. I'm used to it."

"I know, but you don't have long to go now. It can't be easy."

"I have plenty of support."

Did Ally count Angus as one of her support crew? She said they were over, but Ryan didn't know their story. Every time he attempted to piece the fragments together, he came up with more

questions than answers. He reached over and turned off the radio.
"Why did you and Angus break up?"

She paused. "Our values didn't coincide."

"Is that all I'm going to get?"

"I don't mean to be distant or evasive, but right now, I don't
have the energy to talk about it. Like you said, my hormones are
all over the place. If I'm not laughing, I'm a blubbering mess." She
reached for the door handle. "Anyway, thanks for coming over.
And thanks for showing me your project, it's impressive. Don't
bother getting out," she said, turning the tables as she took control.
"I'll call you."

Three days later, Ryan received that call. They hadn't talked since
their ice cream date, but he'd texted her several times, and each
time she'd replied—generic, meaningless words in bland little
speech bubbles popping up on his screen.

In between her texts, the empty space seemed more and his
contentment less.

He answered the phone, putting her on speaker. "Hi. Is everything okay?"

"I guess." Her sigh worried him. "AJ and Liz have gone to
Cambridge for a few days. If you're free later, could you come
over?"

"I have to go to a school thing with the twins soon. Is around
nine too late?"

"No, that's fine."

"Okay, I'll see you in a few hours."

By the time Ryan pulled into the Tanners' drive, the drizzle
from earlier in the evening had turned to heavy rain. Ally opened
the door on the second ring of the bell, dressed in black leggings
and the oversized sweater he'd bought for her. Apart from a touch

of mascara, her face was makeup-free. Ryan loved this look on her. Fresh. Natural. *Breathtaking.*

"Hi, come on in. Sorry, I was in the kitchen. It takes me longer to get around these days."

He followed her down the hallway and into the family room. "The sweater looks good on you. I couldn't decide between the cream or the navy."

"*You* couldn't decide? Didn't you get your personal shopper to buy it?"

"No, I picked it out myself, and the other one. And the scarf. Do I look like the kind of guy who has a personal shopper?"

She looked him up and down. "You do actually, with your stylish coats and preppy scarves."

"Preppy? I was going for the rugged look; you might have to take me shopping one day soon." He kissed her on the cheek. "Anyway, this is a surprise. Are you sure everything's okay?"

As she inhaled sharply, her gaze darted around the room. "To tell you the truth, I'm a little anxious." She frowned. "I was wondering if you could stay over."

Ryan took a step back. He knew this could go one of two ways and had to make sure he was reading the situation correctly. "I'd love to. It's not every day a beautiful woman asks me to spend the night with her."

"Are you sure?"

"Ally, relax." Ryan reached for her hands. "Why don't you go and have a warm bath? What's the midwife said? Are you likely to go into early labor?"

"I'm on track for a due date delivery, but I feel like he's moving down. Actually, a bath sounds like a good idea. I'm freezing."

While Ally took her bath, Ryan flicked through what seemed like a hundred TV channels. But no matter how hard he tried, he couldn't stop thinking about her, naked in the tub upstairs.

By the time she reappeared an hour later, he'd had a couple of short catnaps and was heading for a third. Swinging his feet to the floor, he rubbed his eyes. "Do you want me to get you anything? Warm milk?"

"You sound like my mum. She thinks warm milk and honey cures everything. I might go to bed. Do you feel okay about sleeping over?"

She looked so cute asking him that Ryan couldn't help but laugh. "Seriously? Do I feel okay?" He stood and offered his hand. "Come on, if you play your cards right, I might even give you a back rub."

"You look like you need a massage more than I do."

Ryan grinned. "Oh, believe me, I do," he murmured.

"I didn't mean it like that."

"Course you did."

They woke at dawn. Ryan hadn't slept well. He'd forgotten what it was like to sleep in the same bed as Ally and had struggled to relax. His boner wasn't helping either, but although he wanted to have sex, he'd only do so at her invitation.

He reached out and gently stroked her back and shoulders. "Did you get any sleep?"

"A bit. Thanks for staying, and for the massage last night. You forget sometimes, that need for touch. Apart from the midwife and the occasional hug from Liz, it's been a while since anyone's touched me."

"Anytime." She rolled over to face him and he tenderly brushed a lock of hair across her forehead. "What do you think about, when you're awake through the night?"

"Home, mostly. From my bedroom window at the orchard, I could see all the way to the coast and back to the hills. I loved those moody gray days when a mist moved over the ocean and sheets of rain drove across the sky with a blatant disregard for what we humans had planned for our day."

Ryan smiled at the imagery. He loved to travel, but lately, he'd hardly left London. "Liz mentioned your mum and dad are traveling at the moment. They've been in Australia, right?"

Ally nodded. "In the Kimberly. They'll be in London soon. Not in time for the birth, though."

Their hands were no more than an inch apart. Ryan felt the energy—the heat between them. He ached to touch her. To entwine his fingers with hers as they'd done on Thursdays at the hotel. Seconds turned into minutes.

"Ryan?" She paused. "Will you do something for me?"

"Sure, anything."

She shared her smile, the one with the playful dimples. "But you don't know what it is yet."

He narrowed his eyes, wondering what might come next. "I don't care."

Ally inhaled deeply and puffed out a short exhale, almost a 'here goes' breath. "Have sex with me. No strings, no stories, no commitment."

What the...?

"What? Now?"

"Or later. Sometime. I've felt really...sexual since I've been pregnant," she whispered, as if someone other than Ryan might hear. Propping his head in one hand, he waited for her explanation —her justification—as she verbalized her argument. "I don't want to send mixed messages, but..."

She sat up and swung her feet to the floor, turning her back to him. "I'm sorry. It's a bad idea, isn't it?"

"No, it's a good idea. A great idea in fact." He reached out and rubbed her back again. "I'm a little surprised that's all."

"I just thought, well...I wanted to remember the feeling." She glanced over her shoulder, her eyes wide and innocent with an expression that spoke of her sadness more than any words could. Standing, she headed into the bathroom before he could reply.

Ryan flopped back on the bed. "Shit!" He'd ruined the

moment. He heard the shower running, and afterward, the water turning on and off as she brushed her teeth.

Dawn's light crept through the gap under the curtains as he waited for her to return. Ryan had to mentally tie himself to the bed to keep from barging into the bathroom and taking her against the wall the way she'd described on Sunday.

She returned to the bedroom, dressed in a printed cotton robe that barely covered her belly, and sat on the edge of the bed, rubbing cream into her hands. "I might read for a while. You go back to sleep."

"I can't go back to sleep now."

"Why not? It's not even five thirty."

Ryan knelt behind her, his hand lifting the hair off her neck as he gently kissed her nape. "Because," he whispered, "a beautiful woman just asked me to have sex with her, and what sort of man would I be if I didn't oblige?"

"You don't have too."

"Oh, but I do. But I won't let you just use me for sex." His tone was playful.

"Would I do that?" She lifted her chin, opening her mouth in a tiny O, then pressed her lips together while she breathed through the effect of his touch.

"We've already been down that road." Ryan twisted her hair in his hand as he caressed along the curve from her neck to her shoulder. "It was the wrong direction for both of us."

She sighed, and when Ryan nipped her earlobe and ran his tongue over the hollow at the top of her jaw, her shoulders tightened with a shudder. "Oh...you're amazing. So, so good."

"You think I'm a good lover?"

"I don't *think* you are. I know you are."

"So you remember? From before?"

"Every touch."

"Lie back."

She lay on the bed, facing away from him. He slid one arm

under her pillow, the other around her, pulling her closer and rubbing his palm across her full baby bump. Stretching her head back, they kissed gently, their tongues slowly dancing in sync, and at that moment, he couldn't have loved her more.

"You do realize if we do this, there are strings." One hand cupped her breast; the other stayed twined in her hair. "And stories. And commitment. Turn around."

She turned to face him. He tugged at the robe, kissing her neck and throat again. "Can I take this off?"

"I might get under the covers first," she whispered, her words barely a breath against his neck. *So shy.*

"Don't. I want to see you. You don't know how many times I've imagined this moment."

She let him untie her robe and he gazed at her with longing. Her full breasts and flawless porcelain skin, and those expressive lips, turned up slightly into a smile. "So beautiful. So perfectly complete."

Ally took his face in both hands and kissed him. "How are we going to do this?" she whispered.

"Roll onto your other side again."

He slipped in behind her.

"I'm a little tense, are you?" she said.

"Wound up like a freakin' spring. And I want to say one more thing."

"What's that?"

"There will be no more 'no-strings' sex for us, Ally. If we do this, there's no turning back."

"Ryan…" She tipped her head to the side, inviting his caress where she loved it most, just under her earlobe.

"Move in with me. I don't like the thought of you here alone when you're so close to your due date."

His hand slipped between her legs.

"I'm fine. So…fine."

"You can have your own room. You don't have to sleep with me if you don't want to."

"Oh…but I do. I want to sleep with you. So much."

Ryan couldn't hold his chuckle as she rocked against him. "Are you just using me for sex?"

"No. Maybe. Yes. Yes!"

THE STORY

With Liz and AJ still away, Ryan returned for the next two nights. Their routine was the same each time—they ate dinner, watched a movie, bathed together, and had sex before falling asleep in each other's arms.

Ally imagined this was what it would be like if they lived together. There was no need for constant meaningless chitchat. When she'd lived with Angus, he was always talking and asking irrelevant questions. Ryan was more of a thinker; his questions were never irrelevant.

On the third night, Ryan arrived at the usual time. They prepared a simple meal of pasta and salad, and ate at the table with the TV playing quietly in the background. Later, they lounged on the sofa and listened to music, Ryan sipping a brandy, Ally a chamomile tea.

Ryan pulled her closer, tracing the line of her scar with his finger. "That scar on your neck, was it malignant?"

"It wasn't a mole. Not the usual kind, anyway."

"What was it?"

"It's a story," Ally said, leaning back on his chest. "A rather long one."

"I'd like to hear it."

Ally hesitated. She'd been waiting for this day to come, the day when Ryan would ask the most important question so far. The one when she would tell her story and do so willingly. She took a deep breath.

"When I was fifteen," she started, "we moved to the Bay of Plenty, to a town called Tulloch Point."

Ryan shifted to the chair opposite, so she didn't have to turn to look at him. His face already held a frown as if he understood the significance of what he was about to be told.

Once she began, the words flowed more smoothly than she'd expected. Of course she'd explained the events before—to her parents, siblings, and close friends—but each time, part of the story had become lost in the telling.

Her father had always wanted to own an orchard, Ally explained. So when a long-lost uncle died, leaving him part of his estate, Frank had invested the money in a run-down property covered in kiwifruit vines and avocado trees.

Moving to a new high school hadn't been easy, but Ally was a good hockey player, and the school had a strong team, which had helped her fit in.

She'd noticed Angus the first week of school. He was your typical rugby boy with girls flocking after him, and Ally had thought him conceited and arrogant. But when their parents became friends, and Angus asked her to help him with his studies, she saw another side of him. The first time he kissed her, she believed she'd found her soul mate. They were the quintessential high school sweethearts. The perfect pair. Until they weren't.

"Did he mistreat you?"

"What? No. He was a dream boyfriend. Never pretended to be anything else, even in front of his mates."

Ryan leaned forward and reached for her hand, the contact grounding her. "Angus and I did everything together, and when we were alone, he called us soul mates. I thought nothing would ever come between us, and when it did, I was devastated."

"So what went wrong? You must have been together for a while."

"One night, we went out for a friend's birthday. It was a Thursday in early spring. I usually had yoga on Thursdays, but I skipped it that night." Ally stopped, looking up to catch the words, then continued.

She'd been in her first year as a PE teacher at the local high school and hadn't wanted a late night, so she'd told Angus to stay, that she'd catch a cab home. The bar was down a lane, flanked by a pizza place on one side and the back of the Post Office on the other. To the right of the lane, an alleyway led to the cab rank.

Only a dozen or so steps separated her from the cab rank when three girls approached her, asking about the bar. Earlier, she'd pulled her long hair into a low, over the shoulder braid and one of the trio reached out to touch it. As she stepped back, the girl behind her grabbed the braid, and as the other girls held her down, tried to cut it off.

Ryan's frown deepened as the story unfolded, but he remained silent as Ally continued.

In the ensuing struggle, the craft knife sliced the back of her neck. Realizing what they'd done, the girls took off, dropping the knife on the ground in front of her. Her white linen top now soaked in blood, Ally clutched the back of her neck, screaming for help as she collapsed against the wall of the pizza place. A bouncer appeared a few seconds later, and Angus arrived next, yelling for someone to help. Soon, a large crowd had gathered around her.

"Shit. So that's what the song's about? 'Rust on White Linen'?"

Ally nodded, then rose from the couch to grab a box of tissues and blew her nose before sitting again. "There was blood every-where. The warmth and stickiness of it seeping through my fingers —and that smell of rust—is something I'll never forget. Angus wouldn't shut up; he kept asking questions I couldn't answer. The ambulance ride seemed to take forever although the medical center was only a few blocks away."

She stopped. Inhaled.

"When we arrived, my braid was hanging by a blood-stained thread, so the nurse finished the job and disposed of it. It was the first time I'd had short hair since I was a kid, and I don't know why, but that almost upset me more than the injury. With everything that happened that night, my ruined top and the cold feeling around my neck were all I could focus on at first. But that soon changed when the shock wore off."

"Did they ever find the girls?"

"Eventually."

At first, the police had put it down to a random attack, but one of the bouncers wasn't convinced. He visited Ally one day, wanting to know what her attackers looked like, but she honestly couldn't remember.

"Exactly two weeks later, I came out of school to an envelope tucked under my wiper blade. The writing on the front was almost illegible, and it smelled faintly of cigarette smoke and spicy perfume, so I thought it was from one of my students."

She recalled the day. It had been the Thursday before a long weekend—what they call a bank holiday weekend in the UK—and cold and cloudy, unusual for spring. Although there was no reason for her to be uneasy about the contents of the envelope, something didn't feel right. It sat unopened on the front passenger seat of her car all the way home, and for a while, on the kitchen table as she made a cup of tea and put on a load of laundry.

"Looking back, maybe I should have waited until Angus came home from practice before opening it, but you know what they say about curiosity."

Using her late grandfather's letter opener, Ally had carefully sliced through the flap and removed the folded sheets of lined notepaper.

Dear Bitchface…

"The writer claimed she and Angus were in a relationship, and rambled on for three pages, about where they'd been and how he'd slept with groupies on every rugby trip. Everyone knew about it, she said, except for me. While some words were illegible, the rest cut deep. Her final line hurt the most. Apparently, Angus had called me a needy bitch…a nagging weight around his neck, and he'd told her he was worried about what I'd do if he left me."

"Did you have any idea he'd been cheating?"

"Not a clue, and it gets worse. The letter was almost the kindest part."

After a sip of her tea, Ally continued her story. Angus had finally arrived home from practice just after eleven, and when he'd walked in, he could tell Ally was upset. By that stage, she'd cried herself dry as she'd walked around their tiny cottage in a daze, trying to decide what she should take if, or rather *when*, she moved out.

"I showed him the letter, and of course, he denied everything. Told me girls came on to him all the time and flirting was just part of their PR."

Ally explained how they'd bandied words back and forth, getting nowhere, as is often the case in an argument. In the end, Angus admitted he knew who the letter writer may be. There was a girl, Brogan, who lived in a nearby town where the team played and practiced sometimes.

"He told me she wouldn't leave him alone. Apparently, he'd tried to make her see reason, but she'd been stalking him."

Ally had spent that night lying awake while Angus snored beside her as if all were well in their world. The following morning, he got up early to make breakfast before she went to school. She'd forced it down along with more of his empty words—*ridiculous gossip, vicious rumors, so in love with you it hurts.*

After work, she'd arrived home to a spotless house. Angus had already left for an away game. It was the first time he'd ever cleaned the cottage, or left flowers for her on the dining table, or a card saying how much he loved her. And when she opened her laptop, he'd plastered the same message all over her social media.

Ally glanced up, recalling the words she now knew off by heart, "You are my sunshine, my warmth, my light in the darkness."

"His sunshine? Seriously?"

"Yep. He knew how much I disliked PDAs, but he did it anyway."

"Guilt can make you say and do stupid things."

Ally went on to explain how she'd sat in their living room and cried, mourning the loss of their perfectly ordered home and their seemingly ideal life. Grief-stricken and confused, she'd packed a few clothes and had driven to Clifton Falls to see Mitch.

"Your brother?"

"Yes."

That weekend, she and Mitch had talked like they never had before. Maybe he'd finally realized she'd matured and was worthy of engaging in serious conversation. They'd always got on well, but Mitch took his role as a big brother seriously, and he'd never warmed to Angus.

When Ally returned on Monday, Angus wasn't home. His texts over the weekend had been more frequent than usual. And more intense. In hindsight, Ally realized he'd never once said he hadn't cheated, but the excuses had come thick and fast. It appeared she had been playing the co-lead in the glitziest show in town—*the Angus and Ally Show*. All the parties, ball games, and charity events they'd attended together had all been part of the act.

As soon as she'd walked into their cottage, Ally had felt a shift in energy. The blinds were drawn, and a few little things were missing from the sideboard. On the dining table, the vase sat empty apart from the slightly murky water; and the muted TV flickered in the background. Feeling uneasy, she crept down the hallway to their bedroom. The duvet had been stripped from the bed, and there were only two pillows instead of the usual four.

She opened the closet. All her clothes were gone—together with her jewelry, shoes, and bags. And when she entered the bathroom, her side of the vanity counter was bare. Even her electric toothbrush was missing.

"He'd moved you out?"

"That's what I thought. I tried calling him to ask what was going on. But the calls went straight to voicemail."

Ally had driven to the orchard, tears streaming down her face the whole way. Pulling up outside the garage, she'd expected to see a stack of boxes with her name scribbled in Sharpie across the tops, but apart from the usual tools, bikes, and surfboards, the garage was empty.

"When Angus came home he was furious. He arrived at the orchard soon after and stormed into the kitchen, demanding answers. He thought I'd left him, and I thought he'd chucked me out."

"So what the hell had happened?"

Ally reached for her tea and took another sip, then continued. Angus had phoned the police to report what they assumed was a random burglary, and while they were waiting for further instructions, CeCe had called Ally into her bedroom. One look at Ally's social media pages and it became apparent what was going on. Someone was out to get her.

Ryan sighed deeply and shook his head. "So that's why you're not online anymore?"

"Yes. It took a while for the police to piece it all together, but long story short, Brogan had not only removed all of my belongings from our cottage and sold most of them at a community yard sale, she was also responsible for the assault in the alley *and* the social media attacks. She even listed my phone number on a 'Sex for Singles' website. I was terrified, especially when someone slashed my car tires."

"Why didn't the police do anything?"

Ally had asked herself that same question. Repeatedly. Had they done enough? Once they had sufficient evidence, they arrested Brogan. But by then, the damage had been well and truly done. Ally had lost everything, apart from what she'd taken to Clifton Falls that weekend, which luckily, included the pearl earrings her grandmother had given her, and the greenstone carving from her grandfather she'd worn around her neck.

Fiddling with her necklace, Ally swallowed hard. "Brogan swore she never meant to cut me, and maybe she didn't. Apparently, it had been her friend's idea to slice off my braid. Anyway, weeks later, we were summoned to a restorative justice meeting. What a joke. Not only did Brogan walk in wearing one of my jackets and my most-loved pair of leather boots, but she also used it as an opportunity to level all kinds of accusations at me. Her parents started first. Asked me how I could live with myself, and why I wouldn't set Angus free so he and Brogan could be together. I remember thinking, who the hell are these people? Did they think I had Angus chained to the gate?"

Ryan reached for her hands. "I'm sorry you had to go through that."

She nodded. "Me too. Anyway, it turned out Brogan was more than what Angus referred to as a 'game fuck.' She had become well and truly ensconced in his life. When he'd tried to break it off weeks before, it hadn't gone down well. I was tempted to tell her she was welcome to him, that I'd already walked away. But in the end, I refused to give her the satisfaction."

"So you bore the brunt of her scorn?"

"I did. But at least Angus had the decency to put a stop to the meeting. When it was his turn to speak, he admitted they'd had an affair but said it was over, and he never wanted to see her again. He also said he'd support me through the assault case. But his parting shot caused me the most concern. He told Brogan her actions had ruined his relationship with the only woman he'd ever loved. That she'd destroyed not only his present but his future as well."

"So he never accepted any responsibility?"

"And he didn't even realize it."

"What happened to her?"

"House arrest and a pathetic fine. Apparently, she's paying it off at ten dollars a week. It's going straight to a shelter for battered women. Of course, she had the bracelet off after a couple of months."

"What about your clothes? Did you ever get any of them back?"

Ally shook her head. She'd once loved shopping, but somehow, owning heaps of clothes no longer seemed so important. As for Angus, in some ways, Ally had almost felt sorry for him in the end. He'd been a mess. Calling all the time, swearing on his grandmother's grave that he still loved her. But when Mitch made some discreet inquiries, he discovered Angus had been a very busy boy.

"I wish I'd known all of this."

Ally smiled sadly. "No stories, remember?"

"Yes, but this isn't just a story. It's a tragedy."

"And there were certainly signs something was up, but I naïvely missed all the clues. One night I was performing with Hamish and his band at a club. The place was pumping, everyone having a good time. Halfway through the set, I was egged by someone in the audience. The security guard threw her out, but not before she'd screamed obscenities at me. Months later, when the whole sorry business was behind me, I'd lost my trust in people, not to mention my confidence."

"You can't beat yourself up for trusting someone you loved, Ally. Imagine how miserable our lives would be if we constantly doubted people."

"A few days after he arrived in London, Angus asked me to marry him. He said if I did, he'd never stray again."

"Shit, seriously?" Ryan returned to the sofa and sat by her side.

She snuggled into him. "Thank you for sharing that with me," he whispered, his lips in her hair. "I know it took a lot of guts, but I'm glad you've told me."

"It did, but it was time."

Ryan stood and offered his hand. "Come on, let's go to bed."

It was already late. Ryan had a quick shower while Ally locked up. When she thought about it, Ally knew it hadn't all been Angus's fault. Maybe she had been a weight around his neck. He'd taken care of her—paid their bills, invested their savings, even filled her car every Sunday. And in return, she'd played the loyal girlfriend, one who stayed at home and washed and ironed his shirts while he partied with his teammates.

Of course, her friends had all envied their relationship at first, and she'd smugly reveled in it. But when the fairytale blew up in her face, the humiliation had been swift and severe.

When Ryan came to bed, their discussion continued, and as they lay in each other's arms, Ally asked him something she'd wanted to know for a while. "Why didn't you want to have a relationship with me?"

"Actually, I did after a while," Ryan replied. "I prefer the stability of a relationship, that connection on a deeper emotional level. But your age and the fact I couldn't father any more kids were the main reasons. I was worried you'd wake up one day and decide you didn't want to be with me because you longed to be a mother. I've been there, more than once, and I wasn't prepared to go through it again."

Ally understood. Being a mother was important to her.

"And why didn't you want a relationship with me?" he asked.

"Because Angus had been my first and only boyfriend, so the idea of a casual affair intrigued me. I wanted to explore my boundaries a little."

"Makes sense. All the same, you must have been scared out of your wits when I took you to the Heaton that first time."

"It was pretty nerve-racking. But after that kiss in the back of the cab, I was desperate to hear from you again."

"Yeah?" He kissed her gently. "And I couldn't stop thinking about you. But your pregnancy threw me right off balance. My head and heart were at war there for a while."

"I felt so hopeless when you didn't believe me."

He lay on his back and turned to look at her. "I can imagine. And I'm sorry, but, as I said, I felt like it was history repeating itself."

Ally waited for him to say more. She knew some of the story from Dave, but it was important that Ryan told her his side.

"About a year after Polly and I separated, I fell into a relationship with a woman from work," he continued. "When she told me she was pregnant, I wanted to believe I was the baby's father so badly, that I listened to her lies instead of my gut instinct. I'd always wanted another child. Polly and I both did.

"Anyway, despite the niggling doubts and constant instability in the relationship, I supported her through the entire pregnancy. Two weeks before her due date, her ex arrived at the office, unannounced. He insisted the baby was his. That night, after plenty of tears on her part, she admitted he was telling the truth and that they were getting back together. She just didn't have the heart to tell me."

"Did you ever get the test."

"Her ex did. The baby was his, just like he'd said. Looking back, I went through a destructive grieving process after that. Immersed myself into work and drank too much." He cleared his throat. "It wasn't a good time. But we wouldn't have lasted anyway."

"What makes you say that?"

He wrapped her in his arms and kissed her gently. "Because I wasn't in love with her."

57

ALLY'S CHOICE

As Ryan lifted his finger to the bell, the Tanner's front door opened. Angus stood in the doorway, puffing out his chest. Under different circumstances, Ryan would have offered his hand, but as it was, it didn't seem appropriate.

"Is Ally here?"

Angus attempted to stare Ryan down. "I knew it was you. That night in the restaurant, you couldn't keep your eyes off her. It's your baby, isn't it?"

"I'm not interested in having this conversation. Is Ally here or not?"

"She's in the kitchen." Angus leaned in until his face was mere inches from Ryan's. He may have only been a little taller, but his bulk certainly made an impression, and while being confronted by a cocky male was nothing new to Ryan, it was the first time in his life he'd felt puny.

"But let's get one thing straight while we have the chance," Angus continued. "It will never be over between Ally and me, so I suggest you get used to it, mate."

"Is that so?" Ryan kept his anger in check, for Ally's sake. He'd tried to curb his hot-headed tendencies of late, but at that moment, he wanted nothing more than to punch Angus Chapman right in the middle of his smug face. "Shouldn't you be discussing that with Ally?"

"What do you think we've been doing for the past hour? Playing poker?"

"I've no idea, and quite frankly, it's none of my business." Ryan stepped forward, his hand on the door. "Now, if you'll excuse me."

"So you don't care that we're getting back together? What sort of cold bastard are you?"

"Oh, I care. But in the end, it's Ally's choice. And she certainly doesn't need us pissing around her like a couple of tomcats."

"Just don't get too comfortable, mate. That's all I'm saying."

Ryan watched as Angus bounded down the steps and into an Uber. Dusk had settled, and a heavy fog quietened the streetscape. He didn't bother ringing the bell, just walked down the hallway, the dinner he'd picked up from the Japanese place down the road still clenched in his hand.

Reaching the kitchen doorway, he found Ally deep in thought, staring out over the garden as she sipped a glass of water. He stood watching her for a moment, mulling over the rugby player's words.

He stepped forward and placed the bag of takeout on the counter. "Hey. Are you okay?" he asked, his voice soft.

She turned with a gasp, her wide eyes red with tears. He'd seen her cry before, but he'd never seen her look so devastated. They stared at each other in silence. Was this it? The end? The moment she'd tell him she was still in love with Angus?

She took another sip of her drink, then placed the glass in the sink. "Did you see Angus?"

"Yeah, I saw him. He let me in on his way out."

"What did he say? Did he tell you we're getting back together?"

Knowing Ally didn't need a blow-by-blow account of his conversation, or rather, altercation, with her ex, Ryan kept his reaction neutral. "Something like that." He hesitated. Took a deep breath. "Are you?"

Much to his surprise, she smiled—her face still blotchy with tears, but so beautiful all the same—and slipped her arms around his waist. "That would hardly be appropriate under the circumstances, don't you agree?" She pecked him on the lips.

Ryan couldn't recall the last time he'd felt so relieved. "I do agree. Do you want to talk about it?"

She let go. "Not right now. We should eat. I'm struggling to even think straight."

He opened the brown paper bag, the delicious aroma of Japanese food permeating the room. "Good, because I've come prepared." He stepped closer. The scent of her perfume mingling with the damp smell of his jacket as he lifted her chin with his finger and kissed her gently. "I'll get some plates."

"Thanks. I'm so glad you're here."

Cupping her face, he kissed her again. "And I'm pleased to be here."

Leaning into him, Ally rested her head on his chest. "Will you hold me for a while?"

"I'll hold you for as long as you want." He wrapped his arms around her, losing himself in her warmth. "Is that better?"

She looked up and kissed him. "Much better, thank you."

They ate with minimal conversation, watching the news on the small television above the kitchen table as they sat side-by-side, sharing forkfuls of food and silent looks. And for the first time ever, Ryan felt secure in their relationship.

Sitting in the bathtub with his back against the porcelain, Ryan watched Ally undress in the candlelight.

Turning her back to him, she dropped her clothes to the floor. "Close your eyes."

He shook his head, amused by her modesty. Although he'd

seen her naked many times, as she stepped into the tub, he realized his attraction for her was no longer purely physical. And it hadn't been for quite some time. His love for Alta Dobson was the kind of love he'd only experienced with one other woman —Polly.

As she nestled between his legs, he pulled her back against his chest. "Are we okay?"

"We're good." She glanced back. "But life's complicated."

"Why was Angus here?"

"We have a contract on our cottage. He's finally realized I'll never go back there."

Ryan knew her history with Angus would always follow her, much like his with Polly did him, but he had to ask, "Do you still have feelings for him?"

Ally didn't hesitate. "Not romantic ones. But I did find it difficult when we first broke up. My foolish heart sometimes forgot I wasn't supposed to love him anymore. Coming to London gave me the distance I needed. Time to undo the ties."

"So you had that heart-stopping connection?"

"We did, but it wasn't the same…"

"As?"

She looked over her shoulder, her expression playful. "As my connection with you."

"Is that a subtle way of saying you can't get enough of me?"

"Maybe."

He wrapped his arms around her. "I feel it too, that connection. It's something I've only ever felt once before."

"You mean with Polly? How did you guys meet? She's kind of scary."

Ryan laughed. "She can be. We met in a mosh pit at Glastonbury. Her younger brother and I were good friends at high school, but she'd been traveling for ten years, so we'd never crossed paths. I was barely nineteen and still a virgin. Polly was a thirty-year-old model with a substantial trust fund, who couldn't get a job. She wanted kids but hadn't had a steady boyfriend in years. We eloped six weeks after we met."

"Wow. You were a virgin at nineteen?"

"Not by choice. I never had any luck in that department until I hit the gym and lost my puppy fat. I was smitten with her from day one and loved the idea of being with an older woman."

"What did your parents say?"

"Mum just about disowned me. She still blames Polly for leading me astray. Dad was cool with it, much like everything else in his life. His philosophy was always 'go with the flow.' But I was too young and immature at the time. Drank way too much and partied hard. I remember coming home just before dawn one morning, and all my clothes had been dumped at the front gate."

"Who left whom?"

"Polly left me. We'd drifted apart in the end. Everything that happened with the pregnancy and the sleepless nights that followed didn't help. She met Marc about four years ago, at a record launch. Things were over between us by then, so she moved out and took the twins with her. It was one of the hardest days of my life."

"So you loved her very much?"

"I did. But ultimately, it wasn't enough. Looking back, breaking up was the right decision for both of us."

"Are you still friends with her brother?"

Ryan paused as he thought back to the day he received the sad news about his brother-in-law. "I like to think we would have been. Sadly, he was killed in a car crash the year the twins were born. He never got to meet them."

She reached for his hand, pulled it to her lips and kissed it. "I'm sorry. That's so sad."

"Anyway, enough of that." He rose from the tub and grabbed a towel off the rail to wrap around his waist. "When do you want to move your stuff to Battersea? The grounds aren't anywhere near finished yet, but the house is good to go."

"When did we decide this?"

"Last night. Remember?" He bent down to kiss her.

"Um…" She giggled. "I was kind of preoccupied at the time."

"Really? I never noticed." They shared a smile. "Anyway, it makes sense. Otherwise, I'll end up sleeping here every night, and I'm not sure Liz and AJ would like that. Besides, you need time to settle in before the baby comes. If we're going to do it, we should do it soon."

She chewed her bottom lip and frowned.

"You're still not sure?" he asked.

"I don't want to be a financial burden."

"Hey, I understand, but I want to provide for our baby. If we do this, we do it together. Okay?"

She nodded.

"And, I'm more than capable of supporting you, surely you know that by now."

"I do. It's just…"

"You don't want to be with a rich guy?" he teased. "Rich guys make great lovers."

She huffed. "I wouldn't know about that. Well, apart from you, of course."

"Anyway, once you and Hamish release that song, you'll be rolling in cash." He handed her a towel as she stood. "People will be calling me Mr. Dobson."

"Don't be silly."

"It's true. That song's got hit written all over it."

"I'm not sure I'm ready for that."

"You'll have a great team around you, so don't worry. And some people will love your music and some people won't. But no matter what happens, the way you handle it will be what sets you apart *and* sets you free."

"You're quite the philosopher."

"I've been called many things over the years, but never that."

Ally tugged the hair tie from her ponytail and shook it free. She looked at Ryan as he pulled on a pair of sleep pants and tied the cord way below his navel. She could feel him watching as her sight drifted downward. He was a handsome man, no doubt about it, but he was also a good man—honest and reliable—and she wanted to offer him the same virtues as he was offering her.

"Is it true you've never been with a younger woman?" Her gaze shifted to his face, and he flashed that half smile.

"Not until I met you."

"And will that be a problem if we move in together?"

"If?" He wrapped his arms around her. "You mean when. And no, it's not a problem. Is it a problem that I'm only the second man you've slept with?"

"I'm not one to be constantly looking for something better when I know I have the best. Contentment is important to me, and despite our rocky start, I feel that with you. Content."

He frowned. "Shit, we sound like an old married couple already. We'd better go shopping for an RV after the baby's born so we can go traveling. I can't wait to show you Scotland. But if you think I'm going to work on an American accent and pretend to be a rock star to fulfill your long held fantasy, forget it."

"I like your accent. In fact"—she leaned forward, cupped his face in her hands and kissed him—"I like a lot of things about you."

His lips glided downward as he cupped both breasts. "I'm flying to Edinburgh on Friday for that wedding, remember. But I'll be back Monday morning. Shall we move your stuff on Monday afternoon?"

"Okay, but only if you're good."

58

UNEXPECTED DELIVERY

Back in his suite after the wedding reception, Ryan picked up his phone to check the time—a quarter after two on a freezing Edinburgh morning. He'd missed a call from Ally around midnight. Resisting the urge to call her back, he rang his voicemail and listened to her message instead.

"Hi, it's me. I just called to say goodnight. It's been a bit of a strange day. I'm tired, so we'll talk when you get back. I hope you enjoyed the wedding. I have a surprise for you, but I'll tell you about it later. Sweet dreams."

Ryan smiled as he played her message a second time. He loved this side of Ally—the sweet, caring side. As he'd sat in church that afternoon, Ryan's mood had turned pensive. Although he'd always insisted he'd never marry again, as he watched the couple exchange their vows, he couldn't get Ally off his mind. He was constantly surprised by her ability to make him feel things he'd never expected to feel again.

Once in bed, he tossed and turned. Sleeping in hotel rooms was never easy, especially after rich food and one too many brandies. The noise of the city softened as the dark hours after midnight moved toward dawn, and as he lay there listening to the faint hum of the bar fridge, his thoughts once again turned to Ally and the baby.

When his phone vibrated and woke him with a start, he realized he must have dosed off. Glancing at the caller ID, he hit *Answer*. "Anton! What the hell are you playing at? It's the middle of the night. Is this a drunk dial?"

"No, Boss. I'm at the birthing unit with Ally, and it's almost dawn." Anton's voice quivered with barely suppressed panic as he blurted out, "She's in labor."

"What?" Ryan threw back the covers and placed his feet on the floor. "But she's not due for another two weeks. And why are you there?"

"She called me an hour ago because no one else picked up. I had to drive her here."

Ryan stood, immediately regretting that last brandy as his head reminded him with a throb. "Shit. Okay. There's a flight just after six. Can you stay with her? I'll call Chris. He'll meet you there and round up the family. Have they said how long it might be?"

"The midwife said it would be a while. But how long is a while? What if I have to hold her hand? And see stuff I never want to see? This isn't part of the JD."

JD? Ryan had to think for a moment—*job description*. "Calm down. You won't have to see anything. That's what the midwife's for. Where's Ally now? Can I talk to her?"

"In the tub thing. There's no way I'm going in there. She's probably stark naked."

"Okay. And, Anton?"

"Yeah?"

"Thanks, mate. I owe you. My phone's about to die so give Ally my love and tell her I'm on my way. I'll see you soon."

Ryan entered the birthing unit several hours later and made his way down the corridor. As he approached reception, he noticed a good-looking guy sitting next to AJ. Ryan increased his pace as AJ came forward to greet him.

"What's happening? Is Ally okay? I got here as fast as I could. The traffic from Gatwick was crazy and I forgot to charge my phone."

"Ryan. Slow down, mate. Ally's about to have shower, and she's fine. Liz has just gone home to get her some things. Heads-up though. Andrea and Frank are in there with her."

Andrea and Frank? "Who? Her parents?" Obviously, that was her surprise.

"They arrived yesterday morning. And Big Mitch flew in a few hours ago." AJ slapped Ryan on the back. "Best of luck, mate. Go see your girl. Oh, and about Frank. He's a great guy, once you get to know him."

"You're loving this, aren't you?"

AJ grinned widely. "Who? Me? Come on, I'll introduce you to the brother-in-law on the way in."

Ryan recognized Mitchel Harrington from the family photo on the Tanners' sideboard. Tall and broad, and with a face that would make many women drool, the guy had a commanding presence. He stepped forward, his hand outstretched. "Hi, I'm Mitch. Ally's brother."

"Ryan. It's good to finally meet you." As they shook, Ryan tried to recall what Ally had told him about Mitch. Something about growing organic limes. But the well-dressed guy in front of him didn't seem to fit the mold of an orchardist.

"You too. Ally's told me a lot about you."

Ryan couldn't help but wonder how those conversations had played out. Was Mitch the person she confided in the most? He doubted it. Liz would be the one who knew every detail, which meant AJ would as well. *Shit.*

"I'm heading back to Liz and AJ's to get some sleep," Mitch continued. "Good luck. I'll see you on the other side."

"Thanks. I'd better go see what's happening."

Frank and Andrea looked up from their magazines when Ryan entered the room, but the bed was empty. He took a deep breath and offered his hand to the man in front of him. "Hi, I'm Ryan, Ally's partner."

Frank looked Ryan up and down but remained seated. "Her partner? You mean the baby's father."

Andrea stood, taking Ryan's hand and shaking it warmly. With soft curls framing her face, friendly features, and slight build, she reminded him of Liz. "Hello, Ryan, I'm Andrea. It's lovely to meet you. Ally's just in the shower. She'll be out in a minute."

"How's she doing?"

"There have been a few tears," Andrea replied. "But she's a tough wee thing. She'll be happy to see you. She's talked about you all morning."

"Maybe we shouldn't have surprised her by turning up when we did." Frank's butt was still glued to his seat. "Still, we couldn't let her go through this on her own."

On her own? Right! This wasn't the time to challenge Frank, so instead, Ryan opted for the affable approach. "It's great you made it in time for the birth. I bet Ally was excited to see you. If you need anything at all, please let me know."

"We're good." Frank finally stood and shook Ryan's hand, his grip overly firm. Given Ally's height, Ryan was surprised to discover how short her father was. "Don't let my little girl down."

"Frank. Stop it. You'll give Ryan the wrong impression." Andrea turned to Ryan, offering a warm smile and a private wink. He liked her already. "You'd better go and see how she's getting on. We'll be outside if you need us." She looked at Frank and cocked her head toward the door. "Come on, you. Let's give them some privacy."

As Ryan knocked on the bathroom door, he could hear the

shower running—and something else. Singing. As he pushed the door open slowly, he listened for a moment, trying to make out the song, and smiled when he recognized Hozier's 'Nina Cried Power.'

Pulling back the curtain a little, he watched her—her head down and eyes closed as she belted out the song through gritted teeth, the water running in rivulets down her spine. He grabbed the towel off the hook behind the door and waited.

Seconds later, when she realized she had an audience, Ally stopped mid-verse and burst into tears. "You're here."

He stepped forward, cut the water flow, and wrapped the towel around her. "Of course I'm here. I came as soon as Anton called me, but then my phone died and I almost missed the flight."

They stood for a moment, lost in each other. Ryan didn't care that his shirt and jeans were now damp; he just needed to hold her. And as she sobbed against his chest, he realized how much he'd missed her over the past two days.

She pulled back and tightened the towel around her belly. "He's such a lovely guy, Anton. And Mum and Dad are here. I nearly had a heart attack when I saw them."

"Yes. I just met them."

"How was Dad?"

"Fatherly." Ryan grinned. Frank would take a bit of getting used to. Maybe they'd have an easy-going relationship one day, but he wouldn't hold his breath. "Your mother's lovely. She looks like an older version of Liz. Oh, and I met Mitch outside. He's gone back to Liz and AJ's to get some sleep."

"I got all emotional when they arrived." The tears started again. "They came just for me."

"Hey, come on. Don't cry. I'm pleased they came. We're going to need all the support we can get over the next few weeks."

"So you don't mind them being here?"

"Of course not." Ryan watched as she slipped into a loose-fitting gown and tried in vain to brush her hair. He leaned forward to rub her back as a contraction hit, and another few verses of 'Nina Cried Power' left her lips before she relaxed again. Once it had passed, he helped her onto the bed and climbed up beside her.

"Dad keeps calling me his little girl and holding my hand. I think this whole 'Grandfather' thing is freaking him out."

"That's understandable. Anyway, how are we tracking?"

"I have a while to go yet. The midwife's gone to get a coffee. She said to keep singing. Can you tell the family to head home in the meantime? I kinda just want it to be us."

He lifted her hand to his lips and kissed it several times. "Yes, me too. And I've been thinking."

She waited.

"We don't need to do the paternity test. I know he's mine, and I don't need a test to prove it."

Ally closed her eyes. At first he thought she was going to cry again, but instead, she slipped off the bed and stood as a contraction hit. He expected another few bars of 'Nina,' but she obviously didn't feel like singing through this one.

She looked up briefly. "That's too bad. Because *we* are getting that test." She stopped for a breath. "Got it?"

"But I—"

"Right at this moment, Ryan, I don't need your bullshit." She straightened and looked at him. "I don't want you to wonder. Ever. And if we're going to do this, I get to have my say. Make my own decisions. And right now, Ryan, I need to feel in control. You got that?"

Whoa! "Absolutely."

She stared at him, her brow furrowed. He thought she'd start singing again, but instead, she put her arms around his neck and rested her head on his shoulder. "Thank you."

THE CHALLENGE

Ally woke from her nap to see Mitch tiptoeing into her room, a pretty bunch of cottage garden flowers tied with string in one hand and a gift in the other. The snapdragons, cosmos, stock, and rosebuds reminded Ally of her mother's garden at home. Coupled with a lack of sleep and the emotions of giving birth, she had to swallow back a tear.

He peeked into the crib, smiling down at Sam as he slept peacefully. "Wow," he whispered. "Look at all that hair! Congratulations. How heavy was he?"

"Nine pounds exactly. He's so alert. Ryan's convinced he can see properly already."

"Where is Ryan?"

"He went home to shower. His mother and sister are arriving soon, and I'm so nervous. I hope they're not those snobby socialite types. What if they don't like me?"

"Of course they'll like you. What's not to like?" Mitch laid the flowers on the nightstand and sat on the chair next to her bed.

Ryan had said the same thing—repeatedly—but that still hadn't eased Ally's apprehension. "Anyway, Mitchel Harrington, why and how are you even here?"

"I couldn't miss the birth of my first nephew, could I? And I figured it was about time I came to see what you and Liz were up too. I thought I'd have at least two weeks before I had to play uncle, though."

"I told myself I'd be fine without Mum and Dad here, but when they walked through the door, I lost it."

He reached into the crib and stroked Sam's head. "So, Ryan? AJ tells me he's a good guy. And you two seem to have sorted things out. Are you happy?"

"I am. Isn't it funny how fate throws someone into your path? I feel safe with him, such a sense of belonging, which is crazy after our shaky start. Does that make sense?"

"Perfect sense. You're in love with him."

Although they hadn't said those words to each other, Ally didn't mind admitting it. "Yes, I guess I am. But with everything that's happened, it's taken me a while to accept it. He's a good man, and a wonderful dad to the twins. They're going to be so excited when they meet Sam." Sam stirred, gurgling in his sleep. "Babies make so much noise when they're sleeping. I keep wanting to wake him up for cuddles."

"When are you going home?"

Home. In all honesty, moving in with Ryan scared her, and more than just a little. Since Angus, her inability to maintain independence when in a relationship had become one of her deepest fears. However, Ryan's invitation had been given and accepted with grace. Now, she would make the best of it.

"Tomorrow morning. Ryan invited Mum and Dad to stay with us for a couple of weeks, but they've decided to stay with Liz and AJ until they find a place."

Their decision had pleased Ally. Honestly, the thought of her father and Ryan living under the same roof worried her.

"So, what's happening with you?" she asked. "Any girlfriends on the scene, or is it too soon after Prue?"

"Liz asked me the same thing." He grinned.

"And?"

"I may have my eye on someone. But she isn't returning the gesture."

"Seriously? Out of all the eligible women in Clifton Falls, you've managed to fall for someone who dislikes you?"

"Yep. That about sums it up. Still, you know me, always up for a challenge."

Ally laughed. Her brother usually had women lining up for his attention. "Keep me updated, won't you? You know what a hopeless romantic I am."

"There will be no updates. You just concentrate on this little guy and don't worry about me."

As Ryan hurried along the corridor with his mother and sister in tow, he wondered if he should have warned Ally about Annabelle. But what would he have said? In a way, he was curious to see Ally's reaction to their son's paternal grandmother.

He turned to glance back at his mother. Her long hair, streaked with silver threads and the occasional bright pink strand, sat loosely bound in a bun on the top of her head, and gold bangles and woven friendship bracelets graced each wrist. Dressed in black skinny jeans, knee-high tan suede boots, and a floaty top, she looked like she was on her way to a rock concert.

By contrast, Fiona looked positively ordinary—albeit striking—in her flat pumps, jeans, and a blazer, with her shiny bob sitting neatly in place and her makeup flawless.

Ryan stopped at Ally's door. "Okay," he murmured. "This is us. And, Mum." He waited for her to look at him. "Try not to get overexcited. And perhaps tone down the stories."

"Of course, darling." She grinned. "I'll be on my best behavior. And stop calling me Mum. I do have a name."

Ryan and Fiona exchanged an amused look. Their mother was

easy to love, despite her alternative ways and carefree attitude to life, or perhaps, because of them. He was sure Ally would soon grow to love her too.

Entering the room, Ryan marveled at the sight of his beautiful partner, her eyes closed as Sam lay sleeping in her arms. As he bent down to kiss her, a wave of emotion washed over him, catching him off guard.

She slowly opened her eyes and smiled up at him. "Hi."

Annabelle stepped forward, her arms outstretched. "Hello, Ally. I'm Annabelle. Ryan's mother." She kissed Ally on both cheeks. "I know, I know, I don't look old enough, but you're only as old as you feel, and I still feel like a teenager. And look at you! You're positively delicious." She leaned over and bundled Sam in for a hug. "Hello, my little darling. Oh my, I'm going to cry." She glanced up at Ryan, tears spilling down her cheeks as she cradled Sam. "He looks just like you did as a baby. And to be born in the year of the Pig, and a Pisces to boot! He'll be blessed with good fortune and a wise soul, won't you, baby Sam?"

Ryan shot Ally a wry smile. If this was his mother on her best behavior, how would she be once she warmed up?

"Ally, this is obviously my mother, Annabelle, and my sister, Fiona."

"Pleased to meet you, Ally," Fiona stepped forward, offering her hand and a gift as Annabelle cooed over Sam. "Congratulations."

Ryan watched as Ally exchanged pleasantries with his mother and sister. Introducing Annabelle to anyone was always a challenge, but at least the worst part was over. He was thankful they'd decided to stay with Chris instead of him, *and* that Annabelle wasn't wearing her full motorbike leathers.

"Where are the twins?" Fiona asked.

Ryan checked his watch. "Polly said they'd be here around two."

"Oh look, he's had a little dribble," Annabelle said. She held out her hand to Ryan. "Hand me a towel would you, darling?"

"I'm so sorry." Ally said. "He's been unsettled since his last feed. Now it's all over your beautiful top."

"Don't worry about this old thing." Annabelle dabbed her top. "I've had it for years—wore it to the Live Aid concert back in the eighties. What a buzz that was. I went to see Bohemian Rhapsody recently, you know, the movie. I cried all the way through the second half. They don't make music like that anymore. Mind you, we were all stoned for most of the concert. Ah, fun times."

Ryan cleared his throat as Ally stared wide-eyed at the three of them. "Annabelle," he warned as Fiona hid a smile behind her hand.

"What, darling? Ally knows the score, don't you, dear? I rarely let my hair down back then. Chris had just turned two, and I'd weaned him the week before. My parents had him for the weekend, so I thought, why not? Haven't touched it since though."

Ryan wanted to crawl under the bed and hide.

"Wasn't the movie amazing?" Ally said, not missing a beat. "So you saw Queen live?"

"Oh yes, and the rest. When I got home, I was so hoarse from singing, I hardly spoke for a week. Anyway, enough about me. How are your boobs holding up?"

Ally hesitated. "So far so good."

Ryan caught her blush. He knew what was coming next.

"I fed Ryan until he was almost three and cried the day he finally refused me. Two months later, I was pregnant with Fiona."

"Mum!" Ryan shook his head. His mother told that story to everyone. It felt like most of the UK knew how long he'd been breastfed for. "I'm sure Ally's not interested in my feeding habits from thirty years ago."

He studied Ally's stunned expression. When she grinned a few seconds later, he realized how much fun she was having at his expense.

"Of course I'm interested. Wow, that's impressive. Almost three. So, that's why you're so big and strong, Ryan," she teased.

"And apparently," Fiona grinned as she joined the conversation, "I refused the breast at fourteen months."

"She's been an independent little miss ever since," Annabelle said. "Never seems to need her mother."

Fiona laughed. "Our roles were reversed a long time ago, don't you think, Annabelle?"

"I have no idea what you mean, darling," Annabelle replied.

The sound of Ryan's phone interrupted the conversation. He glanced at the caller ID. "Sorry, I have to take this." He slipped out into the corridor. "Hi. What's up?"

"He's mine," Chris said.

"What do you mean, *he's yours?* Who are you talking about?"

"Sam. According to the paternity test, you're definitely the baby daddy so that makes me his uncle."

"Shit. I'd almost forgotten about that." Ryan let out a relieved breath. "Thanks, mate. I told her I didn't want the test, but it means a lot to Ally, so…"

"Yeah. It keeps everyone honest. And Ryan?"

"Yes."

"Congratulations, I'm thrilled for you. Even if you did steal Liz's little sister from under my nose."

"Thanks, but you're not her type, old man. You know that, don't you?"

"Obviously."

Ryan looked up when the doors from the lobby flew open. "Hey, I have to go. Polly and the twins are here, and Annabelle's in with Ally."

"What! You left Mum and Ally alone? Are you crazy?"

"Fiona's there to control her. See you soon."

Isla and Ava broke into a run when they spotted him. "Dad. Can we see Sam? Where is he? We brought him a present. We made it ourselves. It's a knitted hippo. And we made Ally a friend-ship bracelet. Is Nanna Anna here? And Aunty Fiona?"

With both girls talking at once, and hardly any sleep over the past twenty-four hours, Ryan could only stand there, staring blankly at Polly. When she opened her arms, he accepted her hug without reservation. It was the first time they'd hugged properly in years, and as he relaxed into it, a tear escaped and tracked down his cheek.

"Well done," Polly whispered. "I'm so happy for you, you crazy man."

"Thanks." Ryan couldn't restrain himself as he wiped his hands over his face and blurted out, "Chris just phoned. Sam's really mine."

Polly pulled back and nodded slightly. She was tearing up too.

"Come on," Ryan said to the girls. "Let's go meet your new baby brother."

BABY BLUE

The day was cool for spring, and as they walked from Ryan's SUV to the front door, Ally stopped and looked around. The last time she'd stood on the threshold of Ryan's home was the day she'd stepped in a muddy puddle and wondered why Thursday disliked her so much. The same day a hard hat and the delivery of a package had changed her life forever. The day Ryan had looked at her with his gorgeous hazel eyes and gone 'Click.'

"Are you okay, babe?"

Babe? She smiled. He'd only ever called her babe once before, and she kind of liked it. "I'm great. It's wonderful to be home."

"Do you realize how good that word sounds coming from your lips? Home."

"So it's okay if I call your house my home?"

"Of course. It's *our* home. If this little guy hadn't arrived two weeks early, you'd already be living here by now. Come on." He unlocked the door, pushing it open with his foot as he carried Sam in his baby car seat. "Let's get you both inside. I can't believe how cold it is."

She stopped in the foyer, taking in the white interior with its black and gray accents, the sweeping staircase, and the huge mirror above a recycled hall table. "Wow. This looks amazing. It's hard to believe it's the same house."

After placing Sam's car seat gently on the floor, Ryan slipped his arms around her from behind and kissed her cheek. "I'm sorry we didn't get together sooner. You could have helped pick the furnishings."

She chuckled as she glanced back at him. "You can't be serious. I wouldn't know where to start. It looks incredible. Did you do it yourself?"

"No, Fiona did. I'm lucky she's an interior designer. But now she feels bad because you didn't have an input."

"Seriously? She won't feel that way when she finds out how useless I am at choosing colors."

"Anyway, how about we put Sam to bed, and I'll show you the rest."

Ally followed Ryan down the hallway to the back of the house and into a bright and spacious bedroom with French doors leading out to the garden. "This is our room. The nursery's through here." He opened the door. In contrast to what she'd seen so far, the room beyond was devoid of any color or decoration. And apart from a winged-backed rocking chair and the crib she'd bought from Ikea two weeks ago, the only other piece of furniture was a changing table. "We left this room, so you could decorate it to your taste. But he'll be fine in here in the meantime. Liz can't wait to take you shopping when you're up to it."

Ally's thoughts turned to her Pinterest board labeled 'Baby Blue.' Interior design wasn't her thing, but when it came to the nursery, she had plenty of ideas. "Thank you. And we can always wheel him in with us if he doesn't settle."

As Ryan lifted Sam out of his car seat, Ally pulled back the bedding of his crib. He laid him down gently and tucked him in like a pro. They stood gazing down at him, and when she looked up at Ryan, she'd would have sworn he was holding back a tear. He cleared his throat. "Come on. He'll be awake again soon."

Back in the bedroom, Ally circled the space, admiring the neatly made bed, the floaty net curtains, and how Fiona had infused the room with color using cushions, lamps, and even a lime-green sofa; something Ally never would have thought of. But with the garden so close, its evergreen shrubs and Robinia Mop Tops on full display, the color worked beautifully. "It's lovely. And I like that we're sleeping downstairs."

"Me too. There's nothing like being able to walk from your bedroom into the garden, especially in summer. There are two more bedrooms upstairs and a small living room and bathroom for the twins when they're older. In the meantime, they can sleep down here in the room next to Sam's."

"How many bedrooms are there?"

"Six including the guest room." Ryan unlocked the door, and they stepped outside. He pointed across the lawn. "That's it over there. It's accessed through the conservatory. Mum and Myles, her partner, usually stay at Chris's when they're in London, but Fiona likes to mix it up."

"So your family's close?"

"We are now. Chris and I used to have some unholy rows when we were younger. Dad was always stepping in to sort it out with his 'Make love not war' speeches. And Fiona put us all through a heap of crap in her teens, but our relationships have mellowed in recent years. What about your family?"

"Same drama, different names. Although, it was Mitch who constantly played peacekeeper for us girls. He still does sometimes."

They strolled across the lawn. As was typical of the area, the garden was long and narrow, and with its lush appearance, it reminded Ally of Liz and AJ's. Along the back boundary, a stone wall divided it from the neighboring properties. An outdoor sitting space was shaded by a huge umbrella and flanked on each side by tall camellias in large granite pots. There was even a small pond full of goldfish. "How on earth did you finish this in time?"

"I had a good team. I'm really pleased with the result. Come on, let's go see the kitchen." He grinned at her. "I know how you love to cook."

"Excuse me. I enjoy cooking. I just happen to be useless at it."

STUDIO FARRA

THREE MONTHS LATER

Resting back against the headboard with his headphones on and eyes closed, Ryan didn't hear Ally calling him. She spoke his name again, louder this time, and he looked her way, holding out his hand.

"Come here," he said, his gentle voice wrapping around her insecurity, his gaze soft and understanding as she stepped into the room.

Ryan reached over and pulled her gently onto the bed, and as she lay away from him, one strong arm tugged her closer. "You okay?" he asked.

"I'm just tired. My emotions are all over the place."

"It's par for the course. It will get better."

"It's just...sometimes I feel like I'm holding my breath, waiting for you to change your mind about me."

"That will never happen. But our relationship is still new. We need time to adjust, time to be together, time to be parents. And I love you, Ally. I wouldn't say so if I didn't."

Turning in his arms, Ally gave him a soft smile. "Thank you. I need to be reminded sometimes."

Ryan reached for the water bottle on his nightstand and took a sip. He resumed his position at her side, sliding his arm back into place around her. His lips brushed across hers in the softest of touches. "I want to tell you something," he murmured.

"Okay."

"The week before you told me you were pregnant, I'd already decided I wanted you, wanted us. I'd tried to tell myself that what we had was casual, but deep down, I knew otherwise. And even though you're young and had a busy life, and probably no time for an older guy like me, I couldn't shake the feeling that we belonged together. I had it all planned out. You and me, shacked up in unwedded bliss. But before I could say anything, you told me you were pregnant, and it knocked the wind right out of my sails."

"Did it ever occur to you that I was telling the truth?"

"Many times, especially when I was alone and moody. But I had a virus when I was younger. It affected my semen. We had the twins through IVF after a lot of medical intervention. After that, every time we tried to do another round of IVF, my live sperm count was nonexistent."

"I'm so sorry. Why have you never told me this?"

Ryan shrugged. "I did, the day you told me you were pregnant. But I should've explained more at the time. I was in shock, scared it was a repeat of what happened with Sally, so I pulled back. It took me a long time to get over that messy breakup." Ryan drew her closer. "But you're safe with me. I promise."

"Sometimes, I feel like you're out of my league, and you have all the control. I'm scared I'm not enough for you, that we're not equals, especially financially."

"Babe." Ryan kissed the side of her neck, and she shivered. "Don't ever feel that way. I know you want to be the perfect partner and mother but trying to be perfect all day long has never made anyone happy. Relax a little and ride with it, not against it, because I'm not going anywhere."

Ally snuggled in closer. "Okay."

"I know you won't have the chance to experience some of the

things you wanted to, like falling in love with crazy guys. But you could fall in love with me, and the three of us can go traveling together."

"I've already fallen in love with you." She kissed him on the lips. "And you do realize the twins will want to come traveling too, so there might be five of us. Eight, if you count Liz and AJ and baby Etta."

"Sounds perfect. You hungry?"

She grinned up at him. "Not for food."

As the elevator door whooshed shut behind her, Ally stood in the lobby of Farra's new headquarters and checked the time. It was just on seven, and apart from a cleaner, the place was empty.

Earlier in the day, she'd spent time in the East End studio, working with Hamish on the new album. Marc had agreed to produce, and with Stuart's legal help, DJ Mish was tracking along nicely for an end of year release.

Ally still wasn't sure how she felt about providing the vocals, not only for 'Rust on White Linen,' but for two other tracks as well. Initially, the thought of putting herself out there had scared her to the point of panic. But the support she'd received from everyone involved had helped make the decision seem like a natural progression, rather than swimming upstream.

Hearing Ryan on the phone, Ally took a seat in the lobby and picked up a magazine. The office suite was the only finished part of the complex, but the way they'd staged the renovation, it was hard to tell.

A few minutes later, a cleaner approached, pulling her earbuds out of her ears. "We're not open for business yet. Can I help you with something?" She eyed Ally with suspicion.

"I'm waiting for Mr. Farrell. I'm—"

"You're lucky he's still in. He's usually home with his family by now."

The woman didn't wait for a reply, and as she pushed through the double doors to Ryan's office without knocking, Ally suppressed a smile.

The cleaner returned within a minute. "You Ally?"

Ally stood. "Yes. I'm—"

"Okay. Mr. Farrell will see you now." The woman's expression still didn't change as Ally walked toward Ryan's door. "And, Ally?" she called after her. "Congratulations on that beautiful little boy." With that, she winked and walked away.

Ryan glanced down at his watch as Ally entered the office. He looked up at her. The sight of those hazel eyes, the clipped beard, and the way he spiked his hair slightly when he worked at the office, almost took her breath away. She loved him like this—all neat and conforming in a shirt and tie—just as much as his construction worker look. "You're on time. I'm impressed."

"I told you I'd be here at seven. Anyway, what's with the new PA? Does Tim know you've replaced him with one of the cleaning staff?"

"Roberta's been with me for years. She's a little on the nosy side but loyal as they come. I can't believe you two have never met."

"I'm sure she thought I was up to no good."

"And is she right?"

Ally smiled coyly. "You'll have to wait and see."

He held her gaze, that half-smile making an appearance. "Speaking of Tim, you've replaced him already, haven't you? Who *is* that buff guy sitting at reception every day?"

"He's still the same man inside."

Ryan stood and rounded the desk, grabbing his jacket off the hanger as he passed. "Yes, but now all he talks about is how much he can bench press. Did Sam settle okay?"

"No, but when I left, he was snuggled into Mum's shoulder. She loves it when he's awake."

"Maybe he knew you had a hot date." Ryan slid his arms around her waist and kissed her gently. "Hi."

"Hi, yourself, my hot date." Ally straightened his tie and smiled. "How's the new office."

"Great." They kissed again. "So, Ms. Thursday, shall we stop at a little tapas bar and have a bite to eat."

"No Heaton?"

"I'd rather make love in our own bed, wouldn't you? Especially in this heat." He played with the top button of her dress. "Or we could—"

She slapped his hand away and whispered, "No we could not. Roberta is still doing her thing in the boardroom."

Ryan chuckled as he grabbed a set of keys off his desk. "I have something to show you on the way out. It won't take long."

Ally followed him into a service elevator at the end of a short hallway. "Where are we going?"

He smiled. "Don't look so worried. You'll see."

The elevator doors opened into a dark corridor, but as Ryan ushered her forward, automatic lighting flicked on overhead. She shivered as they stopped in front of a set of double doors that looked suspiciously like the entrance to a large chiller. Despite the warm evening outside, down here it was cool and deathly quiet. She stepped back, an uneasy feeling washing over her. "What is this place? It looks like a high-tech dungeon."

His hazel eyes twinkled. "You're not scared, are you?"

She wrapped her arms across her chest. "It's spooky down here…and cold."

He reached for her hand, giving it a gentle squeeze. "Sorry, the ventilation's not connected yet. Shall we go in?"

Ryan unlocked the door, stepping into the darkness as Ally stayed in the corridor. He pulled her forward, and the door shut behind them.

"Ryan? What are you doing? This isn't funny."

"Hold on. I can't find the light. Here, give me your hand." She slipped her hand into his, and with the aid of the light on his phone, he guided her forward until she stood at what appeared to be a window. "Are you ready?"

"I need to get out of here." The panic rose in Ally's chest. "You're scaring me. I hate dark spaces."

He flicked a switch, flooding the area beyond the window with temporary light. She looked down to the floor below.

"What? No way." She flattened her palms against the glass. "A recording studio! You're building a recording studio in the basement?"

"We are. It was Marc's idea. What do you think?"

"It's amazing. But please don't scare me like that again."

"Sorry. I wanted to surprise you, but I guess I went about it the wrong way."

Ryan guided her down a short flight of stairs into the studio. "We have all the latest gear, including state-of-the-art absorption panels." He banged his fist on the wall. "And as you can see, the place is built like a spaceship."

Ally's eyes widened as she took everything in. "It's huge."

"Well, not quite, but I wanted it to have a 'live lounge' feel about it so we can book bands and small orchestras. The electricians should be finished in a few weeks. Then, once we're up and running, we want you and Hamish to christen it."

"What! Are you serious?"

"Of course. I believe in you. And no matter what, I'll always be there to support you and your dreams."

"Thank you. Hamish will be so excited. I can't wait to tell him." Ally leaned into Ryan's back, resting her head on his shoulder blades as she cuddled him from behind. There were days when she had to pinch herself.

He turned and kissed her. "Actually, he already knows. He helped with the design."

"I knew he was up to something. He's been acting weird for weeks."

"Right, come on. Let's go get dinner."

It was just after ten by the time they arrived home, and apart from the sound of the TV in the media room, the house was silent.

After saying goodbye to Ally's parents and checking on Sam, they headed out to the garden, where they sat in comfortable silence as the small fountain in the goldfish pond trickled its tune into the water below. Snuggling on the outdoor sofa and making out like teenagers before going to bed, seemed to have become their thing.

"How are you feeling?" Ryan asked as he poured her a half glass of wine from the bottle in front of them. "About releasing 'Rust on White Linen'?"

"Okay. I was thinking about it on pizza night, when the twins were discussing what they wanted to be when they grew up. I asked myself what I wanted to be."

"And you want a music career?"

"Yes, definitely. Especially now that I've seen your studio. And I'm working on a new song. Not that I've grown up yet," Ally teased as she took a sip of her wine, "so there's still plenty of time. What about you? What do you want to be when you grow up?"

"I'm over growing up. There's only one thing I want to be in the future."

"Really? What's that?"

"A good husband." He shot her a lazy smile. "I'd like that role."

"A good husband?" She frowned with uncertainty as she mentally questioned his words. "You mean partner. And you're already a wonderful partner."

Ryan reached into the pocket of his sleep pants and pulled out a small black box tied with a silver ribbon. Ally's heart raced as he opened it and a pear-shaped diamond sparkled back at her. She didn't say anything, just stared at his smiling face and back to the ring. All the times he'd said he couldn't be her Happy Ever After, that he wasn't interested in getting married again. All the times she'd watched him at the gym and the office, feeling his rejection. She now recalled those times.

"No, I said *husband*, and that's what I meant."

Taking the ring from the cushion, he dropped to one knee and simply said, "Can I? Be your husband?"

"But you said—"

He pressed his finger to her lips. "Marry me!" Ryan lifted her left hand and, closing his eyes, he kissed it. He placed the ring on the tip of her finger. "May I?"

"Yes."

After sliding the ring into place, he took her face in his hands and kissed her gently. "I love you. I never want you to doubt that," he whispered.

She looked at her left hand and smiled. "It's just beautiful. Wait, have you asked Dad?"

"Of course. Well, it was more of a beg."

"What did he say?"

Ryan raised his eyebrows. "He asked about my financial status. When I said I could not only afford to support Sam quite comfortably, but also the twins and a wife, he gave me his blessing—after checking with Andrea first."

"No way. That's so embarrassing." Ryan stayed on his knees until Ally pulled him up beside her. "I love you, Ryan Farrell. So much."

"I'm very pleased to hear that because I feel exactly the same way about you. And before you ask, I didn't pick the ring on my own. Liz and Jia helped. They weren't keen on the one I liked. Jia kept insisting on 'understated elegance' and bossing me around."

Ally grinned as she imagined the scene. Jia could be incredibly bossy at times. She'd been rather secretive lately, and now Ally knew why.

"We should do it soon," Ryan said. "Get married, I mean. While your parents are still in London."

"Can we have a small wedding? I don't want a lot of fuss."

"Why don't we invite all our friends and family to a party, and have the ceremony in the middle of it, here in the garden?"

"Sounds perfect. So, you think we still click?" she asked playfully.

"Loud and clear."

The End

WE COMPROMISE

© WORDS AND MUSIC BY A. CATALINA
DOBSON

do I belong in your world
the corporate train
the concrete stain
tailored men
girls constrained
all vying to be the same

and everyday we compromise
we turn up sharp
with smiley eyes
we fill our screens
behind lonely scenes
searching
for the acclaim

do I belong in your world
the airbrushed age
the fake accolades
slick charities
dress devotees

why do we
seek this fame

and everyday we compromise
we turn up sharp
with smiley eyes
we fill our screens
behind lonely scenes
knowing
it can't be tamed

do I belong in your world
the swipe dismay
the easy lay
we spin our dye
we falsify
why do we
have no shame

and everyday we compromise
we turn up sharp
with smiley eyes
we fill our screens
behind lonely scenes
conditioned
to be the same

Thank you for spending time with Ally and Ryan in London. There's more to come from the Imagined Kiss series, but in the meantime, if you fancy a trip to Clifton Falls to meet Ally's brother, Mitch, then download *Lime Tree Hill* today.

He needs a wife.
She needs a safe haven.
What could possibly go right?

...great characters with a great chemistry. 5 Stars - Goodreads reviewer.

Download *Lime Tree Hill* today.
Book one in the Reluctant Kiss Series.
Available at Amazon stores worldwide.

THE CAST

Team Dobson

Ally Dobson - Kiwi girl living in London
Jia Choi - Ally's housemate
Liz Tanner - Ally's sister
AJ Tanner - Liz's husband
Andrea and Frank Dobson - Ally's parents
Mitchel 'Mitch' Harrington - Ally's half brother
Hamish Baxter - DJ Mish, Ally's friend
Angus Chapman - Ally's ex-boyfriend

Team Farrell

James 'Ryan' Farrell - CEO of Farra Corporation
Isla and Ava Farrell - Ryan's twin daughters
Chris Farrell - Ryan's brother
Annabelle Farrell - Ryan's mother
Fiona Farrell - Ryan's sister
Stuart Harrison - Ryan's friend
Dave - Manager, Studio Hudson

Extras

Tim - Ryan's PA
Anton - Ryan's driver
Polly - Ryan's ex-wife
Marc - Polly's husband
Britt - Ryan's ex-girlfriend
Jacinta - Stuart's girlfriend
Gina - admin manager, Farra
Jade - Jia's cousin
Sarah - Receptionist, Studio Hudson
Guy - Ally's coworker
Willow Parkinson - Ally's school friend

THANK YOU.

Hi there,

Many thanks for taking time to read the tale of Ryan and Ally.

If you enjoyed *How About Thursday*, please consider leaving a review on Amazon or Goodreads. Long or short, reviews help other readers find my work.

To leave an Amazon review:

- Search the book's page on Amazon
- Click on the reviews
- Scroll down to the Write a Review box
- Write away

Best,
Frances

ALSO BY FRANCES COWIE

AVAILABLE AT AMAZON STORES WORLDWIDE.

THE LIST MAKER

Book One in the Imagined Kiss series.

AJ Tanner. He wears a beard, tames his locks in a man bun, and a tribal type tattoo flirts across his upper arm and chest. Some days, wearing a suit and tie is a requirement, but paint splatted jeans and a seen better days t-shirt are more his style.

Liz Dobson. All curls and determination. Savvy, focused, and yet when it comes to men, newly insecure. She meets the mysterious AJ in a moody London bar. He checks every box on her 'Hell No' list, and yet...

Un Beso Imaginado. Strokes on canvas of an imagined kiss. Painted by Jacobs, owned by Tanner, coveted by Dobson. Will Liz ever get her hands on the work she admires so much, or will AJ continue to deny her the opportunity?

Sometimes steamy, often funny, and with tension that leaps off the page, *The List Maker* is a standalone contemporary romance where the worlds of business and art collide.

An artist - A dreamer - An imagined kiss.

"Overall a light-hearted love story and I enjoyed it immensely!"

"I know I've enjoyed a book when I pick it up on a cold Sunday morning and by the end of the day I've only moved to replenish my cup of tea and add another log onto the fire."

"I very much enjoyed AJ & Liz's story. I highly recommend this book."

BUY NOW

THE WATERSHED
A Clifton Falls Novel

Do you believe love can last more than one lifetime? Spanning four decades and three generations of women, *The Watershed* is a tale of love lost and forever searched for.

"The Watershed is well written with complex and believable characters, and full of the intricate web of internal emotions that come with life, death, love and loss."

"The paranormal aspects of this book are unique leaving the reader with a sense of peace and hope in their hearts that more people can find their soulmate even after a tragic loss if they only open their hearts to that possibility."

BUY NOW

FIELD of the WHITE SNOW
A Clifton Falls Companion Novel

Lose yourself in this richly written tale of Vanessa Blinkly, and her love for a crazy black horse and a man who couldn't stay to make a difference. *Field of the White Snow*—so much more than a coming of age story.

> *"I could imagine myself in the kitchen, the smells, and the unfriendly bedroom. Whisper and the visions were worked nicely into the story and I loved the gifts accumulated from over the years, a beautiful touch to the story."*

> *"I love the way Frances Cowie creates complex characters and delves deep into the twists and turns of life's issues and complications."*

> *"I felt their heartaches and joys as though they were dear friends."*

BUY NOW

LIME TREE HILL
Book One in the Reluctant Kiss Series

If you fancy a trip to Clifton Falls, New Zealand to meet Ally's brother, Mitch, then download *Lime Tree Hill* today.

He needs a wife.
She needs a safe haven.
What could possibly go right?

ABOUT THE AUTHOR

Frances Cowie's journey to writing romantic fiction began after waking one morning with the story of an old pump house and three characters—Rose, William, and Jessa—floating around in her head. That story, *The Watershed,* was her first novel.

A country girl at heart, Frances resides with her husband in a small town in New Zealand's Southern Lakes area and has two adult children. For more information, including sneak peeks at upcoming projects, visit Frances online:

www.francescowie.com

ACKNOWLEDGMENTS

Ryan Farrell started talking to me halfway through writing *The List Maker*. I knew he had a story to tell, but it took me a while to listen.

As always, there are many people to thank. Firstly, Laura. I know my manuscript is in safe hands with you as you slash your pencil through my overly flowery and sometimes outdated words. And that's even before my editor does her thing.

Thank you to Jane, for giving me many hours of your time. Kate and Marjorie for your encouragement and for keeping me focused. To Carole B and Samantha B for your never-ending support. Abby-Lee, for your London research and enthusiasm. Louise, Hilly, Sharlene, Phil, Yvonne, Penny, Rachel H, Gemma, and Sarah R, I'm so blessed to have you in my tribe.

Steven Novak, from Novak Illustration for the cover completion. To Liz Dempsey from The Error Eliminator for your attention to detail as you edit my words, so they make sense.

To the members of the Otago chapter of RWNZ, you guys are a great support. I'm privileged and humbled to have you in my writing life.

To Kevin. Thanks for happily watching the Turbo channel alone while I write in the evenings. I know you do it just for me.

Lastly, to my readers. My heartfelt thanks for taking time out of your busy lives to read my books. If you enjoyed *How About Thursday,* please consider leaving a review on your book retailer's site, and sharing the title with your romance-reading friends— either in person or through social media. 'Like' my Facebook page for a chance to win a copy of my next effort, the third book in the Imagined Kiss series.

Happy reading,

Frances

www.ingramcontent.com/pod-product-compliance
Lightning Source LLC
Chambersburg PA
CBHW020819180626
46814CB00001B/22